In the Wild Light

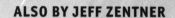

In the Wild Light

JEFF ZENTNER

CROWN

NEW YORK

Text copyright © 2021 by Jeff Zentner
Jacket art copyright © 2021 by Connie Gabbert

All rights reserved. Published in the United States by
Crown Books for Young Readers, an imprint of
Random House Children's Books,
a division of Penguin Random House LLC, New York.

Crown and the colophon are registered trademarks of
Penguin Random House LLC.

Visit us on the Web! GetUnderlined.com

Educators and librarians, for a variety of teaching tools,
visit us at RHTeachersLibrarians.com

Library of Congress Cataloging-in-Publication Data
Names: Zentner, Jeff, author.
Title: In the wild light / Jeff Zentner.
Description: First edition. | New York : Crown, 2021. | Audience: Ages 14 &
up. | Audience: Grades 10–12. | Summary: Attending an elite prep school in
Connecticut on scholarship with his best friend (and secret love) science genius
Delaney Doyle, sixteen-year-old Cash Pruitt, from a small town in
East Tennessee, deals with emotional pain and loss by writing poetry.
Identifiers: LCCN 2020038100 (print) | LCCN 2020038101 (ebook) |
ISBN 978-1-5247-2024-7 (hardcover) | ISBN 978-1-5247-2025-4 (library binding) |
ISBN 978-1-5247-2026-1 (ebook)
Subjects: CYAC: Best friends—Fiction. | Friendship—Fiction. |
Grief—Fiction. | Loss (Psychology)—Fiction. | Boarding schools—
Fiction. | Schools—Fiction.
Classification: LCC PZ7.1.Z46 In 2021 (print) | LCC PZ7.1.Z46 (ebook) |
DDC [Fic]—dc23

The text of this book is set in 11.5-point Dante MT Pro.
Interior design by Andrea Lau

Printed in the United States of America
10 9 8 7 6 5 4 3 2 1
First Edition

For my mom and dad

For Nellie Zentner (1921–2019), who showed me that someone could love me so much she would cry every time I would leave

SUMMER

Chapter 1

The human eye can discern more shades of green than of any other color. My friend Delaney told me that. She said it's an adaptation from when ancient humans lived in forests. Our eyes evolved that way as a survival mechanism to spot predators hiding in the vegetation.

There are as many tinges of understanding as there are hues of green in a forest.

Some things are easy to understand. There's a natural logic, a clear cause and effect. Like how an engine works. When I was eleven, my papaw pulled the engine out of his Chevy pickup and took it apart, letting me help him rebuild it. He laid the pieces out—reeking of dark oil and scorched steel—on a torn and greasy sheet, like the bones of an unearthed dinosaur. As we worked, he explained the function of each piece and what it contributed to make the engine run. It made sense, how he said it.

He wasn't sick then. Later, when he was, I understood that when he used to say *Don't nobody live forever* when accepting another piece of his sister Betsy's chess pie, that wasn't just a phrase he used. That was when he still had an appetite.

Now his appetite has moved to his lungs, which are always starved for air. His breathing has the keening note of the wind blowing over something sharp. It's always there, which means he has something sharp inside him. People can't live long with sharp things in them. I understand this.

Some things I understand without understanding them. Like how the Pigeon River moves and pulses like a living creature, never the same twice when I'm on it, which is as often as I can be. Or how sometimes you can stand in a quiet parking lot on a hot afternoon and perfectly envision what it would have looked like there before humankind existed. I do this often. It brings me comfort but I don't understand why.

Other things I don't understand at all.

How Delaney Doyle's mind works, for example. Trying to comprehend it is like trying to form a coherent thought in a dream. Every time you think you're there, it blurs.

You'll be talking with her and she'll abruptly disappear into herself. She'll go to that place where the world makes sense to her. Where she sees fractals in the growth of honeysuckle bushes and elegant patterns in the seemingly aimless drift of clouds and the meandering fall of snowflakes. Substance in the dark part of flames. Equations in the dust from moths' wings. The logic of winds. Signs and symbols. An invisible order to the world. Complex things make sense to her and simple things don't.

She's tried to explain how her mind functions, without success. How do you tell someone what salt tastes like? Sometimes you just know the things you know. It's not her fault we don't get it. People still treat her like she's to blame.

Some aren't okay with not understanding everything. But I'm not afraid of a world filled with mystery. It's why I can be best friends with Delaney Doyle.

Chapter 2

A carload of girls from my high school is trying to exit out the entrance of the Dairy Queen. I pause to let them. Then I pull in, my lawn mower rattling in the back of my pickup—the same truck whose engine my papaw and I rebuilt.

The early evening July sun blazes like bonfirelight on the hills behind the Dairy Queen. They're a soft green, as if painted in watercolor. Gleaming soapsud clouds tower behind them. Delaney told me once that the mountains of East Tennessee are among the oldest in the world, but time has beaten them down. Sounds about right.

Delaney stands outside, her shadow long and spindly against the side of the building. She's wearing her work uniform—a blue baseball cap, blue polo shirt, and black pants—and holds a cup with a spoon sticking out of it. With her other hand, she twists her auburn ponytail and presses her thumb on the end, tufted like the tip of a paintbrush. It's one of her many nervous tics.

The expression on her face is one she often has—her eyes appear ancient and able to see all things at once, unbound through time and space. It's what I imagine God's face looked like before summoning the world out of the ether.

If God were wearing a Dairy Queen baseball cap, I guess.

I'm in no hurry, so I wait, out of curiosity. It takes longer than you'd think for her to notice I'm there.

"It's fine. I had no plans for my Saturday night but waiting in the DQ parking lot," I say out my open window as she finally approaches. I try to play it straight-faced, but I never manage with her.

She gets in, giving me the cup to hold while she buckles up. "You're late."

"By like two minutes." I go to hand her back the cup.

She refuses it. "That's for you. Started melting because you were late. Your punishment."

"Based on how close you were watching for me, you were obviously deeply concerned. Oreo Blizzard?"

"Your favorite."

"Nice." I take a bite and study her face for a moment. "How was work?"

"You smell like gasoline and cut grass. Did you know the scent of mown grass is a distress signal?"

"For real?"

"It's from green leaf volatiles. They help the plant form new cells to heal faster and stop infection. Scientists think it's a type of chemical language between plants. So you're covered in the liquid screams of grass you've massacred."

"I could've showered off all this grass blood before picking you up, but then I'd've been even more late."

"Didn't say I minded," she murmurs, not making eye contact. "Plant screams smell nice."

"You reek like french fries," I say, leaning toward her and taking an exaggerated whiff. "The smell of french fries? Potatoes shrieking for their babies."

"I'll slaughter some potatoes. I don't care."

"You just gonna pretend I didn't ask how work was?" I put my truck in gear and back out.

She twists the end of her ponytail. "The Phantom Shitter struck again."

"The Phantom Shitter?"

"Some dude who comes in once a week or so and absolutely wrecks the men's room. No one ever sees him come or go. We've even checked security tapes. It's a pooping ghost."

"Imagine dying and haunting the Earth and making it your mission to befoul the Sawyer Dairy Queen."

"Befoul. Where'd you get that word?"

"Dunno. Besides the Phantom Shitter, how was work?"

"Got in trouble."

"Why?"

"Did an interview with NPR on my break and it went long."

"Damn, Red, getting even more famous."

"You too," Delaney says with an impish smile.

"What?" I ask around a spoonful of Blizzard.

"I mentioned you."

"Hell you did." I look at her, aghast.

She smiles again.

I shake my head. " 'I couldn't have made this discovery without Cash Pruitt.' That what you said? 'No one else on planet Earth could have paddled me out to a secret cave along the Pigeon River so I could find some bacteria—' "

"Mold."

"Whatever."

"Big difference biologically."

"Fine. 'Mold that kills the nastiest bacteria.' "

"Don't forget driving me to Nashville to show my results to Dr. Srinavasan. Said that."

"Oh, right. No one else could've done that."

"No one else *did* do that. Anyway, yeah, that's about what I said."

I wipe my hand down my face. "Lord above."

"Stop being dramatic."

I raise my index finger. "What's the one thing you know about me?"

"I know you asked me once if peanuts are a type of wood. No, they aren't."

"That I like to *earn* what I get."

"Right. Cash Pruitt: famously a lover of earning."

"So you're out there telling people I did something without me earning it."

"If it makes you happy, I still took credit for running the experiments and figuring out the mold's antibiotic properties."

I lower the visor against the sinking sun. A ray catches a crack in the windshield and illuminates it, a tiny comet. I've always loved when the light finds the broken spots in the world and makes them beautiful.

I glance over at Delaney. She's turned inward, squinting her honey-colored eyes against the orange glare splashed across her pale skin, on the freckles that dot her nose and cheekbones like an atlas of stars. She brushes a stray piece of hair from her face.

"Seems like you could get a better job than DQ now that you're in the news and doing interviews on the radio," I say.

"It requires no mental energy, so I can think about other stuff and get paid for it."

"Your life. Wanna ride around some, then go watch *Longmire* with Pep?"

"Can't. Babysitting Braxton and Noah later," Delaney says.

"He'll be bummed."

"Tell him I'm sorry and next time I come I'll tell him about gympie gympie."

"The hell is that?"

She always looks happiest right before she's about to deliver some horrifying factoid about the natural world. She radiates pure joy now. "Australian shrub. Read about it last night. The leaves are covered in these little silica-tipped bristles—silica's the stuff they make glass out of—and then these bristles deliver a neurotoxin that causes horrible pain for days, months, and even years. So if you brush up against it, the whiskers dig into your skin and the pain'll be so intense it'll make you puke."

"Good *Lord*. That sounds like it came from outer space."

"As long as the hairs stay in your skin, the pain continues. It feels like being burned alive. They're hard to remove, too. Your whole lymphatic system swells up. Armpits. Throat. Groin. It's a nightmare."

"*Why* are you telling me about this?"

"You're constantly waging war against the plant world. Thought you might like to know they have a revenge weapon."

I point back over my shoulder at the lawn mower in my truck bed. "I mow lawns and trim shrubs. They grow the hell back. That's like saying barbers are waging war on heads."

"There's an apocryphal story about someone wiping their ass with gympie gympie leaves and . . . it didn't end well. Get it? End."

9

"Please tell me *apocryphal* means 'completely and entirely false.'"

She cackles. "The gympie gympie's gonna find you," she says in a singsong voice.

"Won't."

"It's gonna crawl up your ass. Give you gympie butt."

"I'll sleep with my lawn mower in my bed. If it tries, I'll fire that up and mow the shit out of it. Be like, 'Who's in pain now, gympie gympie? Warn your friends.'"

"I wanna be the one to tell Pep about it. Don't spoil it," Delaney says.

"You think his life will improve knowing about this plant?"

"He loves my facts."

"Don't know why. You got time for me to stop for gas?"

"I don't have to be to Noah and Braxton's for a while."

I pull into the RiteQuik, park, and start filling up my truck. Cicadas thrum like a thought that won't leave your mind. The turpentine scent of sun-warm pine tar and distant grill smoke hangs thick in the air, mixing with the smell of gas and oil leaking on hot engines. In front of the store, two girls in neon bikini tops and Daisy Dukes sit in the back of a Jeep with the top removed, talking and laughing raucously, primping and taking selfies. The radio blares Florida Georgia Line.

The night has started to breathe its first cool breaths. They feel like river water on my face. The summer days here end like a kid who's been running as fast as he can, then comes inside and falls asleep in front of a fan.

I go inside to pay. When I come out, the pulsing bass from a car stereo rattles my lungs and diaphragm. A purple Dodge

Challenger with ornate rims is parked behind me. It's an unwelcome sight. Jason Cloud. I loathe his kind—a dealer of weed, meth, heroin, fentanyl, Oxys, Lortabs, Valium, gabapentin, and whatever else people will buy to wake themselves up or put themselves to sleep. He's not the one who sold my mama the shit that killed her. But it was someone like him. Someone who will end lives for a purple Dodge Challenger with rims.

Cloud stands at the passenger window of my truck, talking with Delaney, pausing every couple of seconds to send a plume of vape smoke skyward. He's wearing an oversized white T-shirt, a thick gold chain, huge black shorts that go past his knees, and Nike sandals with socks pulled up almost to his knees. His bleached-blond hair is in cornrows, and his mouth glitters with a gold grille.

He only has a few years on me, but looks far older. His eyes are the shade of weapon gray that someone would pick out for themselves if God didn't have rattlesnake yellow in stock. No compassion or intelligence in them. Only cunning—and sizing you up for cracks. Underneath each eye is a crude teardrop tattoo the color of wash-faded denim. I've heard those mean you've killed someone.

I walk faster, anger scuttling up my throat from my chest.

"What don't you know, girl?" Cloud says to Delaney as I enter earshot of their conversation. "Ain't nothing *to* know."

Delaney stares forward, then turns and catches my eye. She looks afraid and relieved. *Help me,* her eyes say.

Cloud sees me approach and gives me a curt backward nod. "'Sup, mane."

I return the terse nod. "Everything good?"

Cloud pulls a drag off his dragon vape pen. The cords of his neck ripple underneath a tattoo of the face of Jared Leto's Joker character from *Suicide Squad*. He releases a gout of white, cherry-scented vapor in my direction. "We real good. Just having a private conversation."

"We gotta go," Delaney says, her voice taut.

"Won't take but a minute," Cloud drawls. His mouth smirks. His eyes don't follow.

"We're already late," I say in a low voice.

Cloud sidles toward me and spits. I can smell him as he nears—expensive cologne, weed, cherry vape smoke, and something stale and sour. "We're talking now."

I try to slip past him to get in my truck. He steps to cut me off, and I almost run smack into him. "Scuse me," I mutter. "I gotta—"

"You her daddy?" His tone is equal parts mocking and menace.

"No."

"Hmm? Boyfriend? Y'all smashin'?" He gives me a death's-head grin with his grille and humps the air a couple of times.

"Man, I don't want no trouble."

"Naw?" Cloud gets in my face, staring me down. "What's your name, mane?" He's near enough I can feel the sweat evaporating from his skin.

"Cash," I say, avoiding his eyes.

Cloud snickers. It sounds like a call from a buzzard to come feast on a carcass. "Cash. Sheeeit." He lifts his heavy gold chain with both thumbs and lets it drop back down on his chest with a muted thud. "It's me should be named Cash. Look like the only cash you got is your name, bitch."

I look him dead in the eyes. I know the peril, but I do it anyway. "My name's my name. Ain't ashamed."

I'm not afraid to fight him. I grew up having to fight, and it wouldn't be the first time I've fought on Delaney's behalf. But it would probably be the last. I would take him if I knew it would be just him and me, skin on skin. That we'd each take our hits and shake hands afterward. But there'd be tactical knives pulled out of pockets or Glocks pulled out of waistbands. And if I survived that, I'd have to *always* watch my back in this town, until he finally got himself killed or sent to prison.

I lower my gaze in surrender.

Cloud takes a long drag on his vape pen and spews vapor in my face, long and slow. "Cash Money. Better get to your girl." Then he draws in close, until his lips tickle my ear. Intimate, but in the way of a wolf lapping blood from a deer's throat. "You lean on her to say no to me, you'll deadass regret it, mane. On God."

With one last glower, he swaggers away, drops into the driver's seat of his thumping, rattling car, and peels out of the parking lot in a haze of acrid, rubbery black smoke, the back end of his car fishtailing.

I'm shaking and nauseated by the time I'm back behind the wheel of my truck. I take a second to breathe down my sizzling adrenaline.

Delaney murmurs something. I don't hear her at first.

"Hey." Her voice finally reaches through my maelstrom of thoughts.

"What?"

"Thank you."

"Why's he hassling you?"

Delaney sighs and sags into her seat. "Something about *going into business* together. Real vague. Like if you thought cops were listening. He's been on me ever since everything hit the news."

A few seconds of tense silence tick past.

I shake my head. "What's he think? After you save humanity from antibiotic-resistant bacteria, you'll help him cook better meth and make fentanyl out of dish soap?"

"Said he'd make me rich. Piece of shit."

I chuckle bitterly. "Oh, I *bet*. Guess we got this to look forward to next year."

"Maybe not," Delaney murmurs, studying the side of her left thumb, then lifting it to her mouth.

I reach over and put my hand on hers and gently pull it toward me. The side of her thumb is bleeding and ragged. Delaney diagnosed herself a while back with a "body-focused repetitive behavior." She picks and chews at the skin around her thumbnails until it bleeds. It happens when she's stressed or anxious. She can't afford help for it, so my catching her is the best she's got.

"Red," I say quietly.

She quickly pulls her hand back and goes for her thumb.

I grab her hand again and lower it to her lap. "Delaney."

She sighs and sits on her hand. "Happy?"

"Hate seeing you hurt yourself."

"Can't help it."

"Do your breathing exercises." She researched coping mechanisms. My job's to remind her. "What's going on? Cloud?"

"Not just him."

"Well?"

"I said a second ago maybe we don't have to deal with him next year?"

14

"You're not gonna poison him, are you? Not that I'm opposed, necessarily."

"Just replace his weed stash with gympie gympie."

We both laugh.

"I wish," I say. "But for real."

"I got an offer to go to a boarding school up north."

My heart plummets. With all the press she's been getting, I knew this day would come.

I swallow, then nod for her to continue. "Oh wow." The unease in my voice is obvious to my own ears even as the words leave my lips.

"Middleford Academy. In New Canaan, Connecticut."

"Sounds fancy." My head swims.

"It's one of the top five prep schools in America. This lady from Alabama named Adriana Vu, who made hundreds of millions in biotech, went to Middleford. She donated a shitload of money to the school to fund this amazing lab and STEM program. She contacted me and said she'd talked to Middleford and she'd pay for me to go there."

We let ourselves forget the inevitability of things. I guess it makes us feel in control over our lives. And I'd let myself forget that no one with a mind like Delaney Doyle's stays in one place forever. Much less a place like Sawyer, Tennessee. The only thing worse than her leaving would be her staying.

She starts to put the side of her thumb to her mouth. Stops. Squeezes her eyes shut and sits on her hand again. "I told her I wouldn't accept unless she could make it happen for you too. Said we're a package deal. So she said okay, and so did Middleford."

My brain replays her words, like when you're watching

15

TV half-asleep and you're not sure you heard something right. *"What?"*

"I told her I wouldn't go unless you could come with me. Said it would be too hard to go alone to a new boarding school junior year, where everyone's got their friends already. So she came through. Full scholarship. Just like mine. Middleford said okay too. You can come with me."

I scrutinize her face for some hint of a joke. But neither the timing nor the nature of the joke is her normal sense of humor. "Come on."

"I wanted to pick a better time to tell you, but."

"Is this for real?"

Delaney looks away, out her window. Watching the people milling around in front of the store. "Yep."

"You're gonna go, right?"

"I don't want to go alone. That was true when I told her that."

"You saying that if I don't go, you won't?"

"I said I don't *want* to." Delaney toys with the end of her ponytail.

"That's what you meant when you said we might not have to worry about Cloud."

"Yeah."

I stare out the window for what feels like a long time. "You know my papaw's not good."

"Yeah," Delaney says quietly. "That would still be a thing if you stayed."

Silence falls between us like an axe sinking into wood.

"I didn't earn this," I murmur.

"Whatever," Delaney replies. "Without you I never could

have found that mold. You were as important as the microscope I looked through."

"Is this even a thing? People who deserve scholarships getting them for friends who don't?"

"Athletes do it. This hot-shit basketball player named DeMar DeRozan told USC he wouldn't accept a scholarship unless they gave one to his best friend. So they did. It's not like you don't deserve to be there. You've gotten good grades."

"At *Sawyer High*."

"Still."

"This was never *remotely* part of my plan."

"You had a plan?"

"I mean . . . no."

After our laughing subsides, I say, "Know what the farthest north I've ever been is? Bristol damn Virginia. Papaw took me to a NASCAR race when I was little."

Delaney giggles. "Johnson City for me."

A convoy of three black Dodge Sprinter vans pulls into the gas station. In the weeks since Delaney's discovery was announced, Sawyer's been crawling with rented vans full of men and women laden with caving gear. Can't exactly patent something that grows in a cave, Delaney explained, so they're all coming for their piece: The universities. The pharmaceutical companies. The Gates Foundation. Delaney told me the other day that she served a team of French biologists at DQ. They had no idea who she was.

"Don't tell me you're only going to do this if I do it. Don't be telling me that," I say.

Delaney eyes the people getting out of the vans. "They

should try boiled peanuts while they're here. Bet they don't have boiled peanuts wherever they're from."

"Red."

"Don't know what I'll do."

"Mr. Hotchkiss is a good science teacher, and he does his best, but you need more than a key to a high school lab where the teacher has to buy microscopes with his own money. You *need* to do this."

"So do you. There's a big world outside East Tennessee. You don't like it? You can always come back. Everything'll still be here. You know that."

"I'm happy here."

Sometimes Delaney looks at me like my skull is transparent and she can see the thoughts forming on my brain's surface. "There are ghosts here," she says quietly.

There are indeed.

I'm dazed, like I just woke up from one of those long Sunday afternoon naps, when it's a moment or two before you can remember where you are or even your own name. The light is waning. I glance at the time on my phone. "We better get you to Noah and Braxton's." I start my truck and jam it into gear. I pull out of the parking lot.

"You're pissed," Delaney murmurs. She starts to lift her thumb to her mouth, but we lock eyes and she grabs the end of her ponytail instead.

"Just don't know what to think."

"You still haven't thanked me," Delaney says after we drive for a while without talking.

I shake my head, defeated. "Thanks. I think." None of this has quite sunk in yet. I know this because I'm feeling numb, rather than completely panicking at the thought of possibly losing her.

Delaney stares forward with an unreadable expression.

I've always thought she had a strangely elegant beauty. Of something being pulled in each direction toward perfect and broken. I once saw a bird that had been run down in the road. It lay there, pulverized. But the wind caught two of its feathers and lifted them free of the destroyed body, breathing life back into them. I watched those feathers dancing in the wind for a long time, such unexpected grace amid ruin.

Delaney reminds me of that. Couldn't say why.

Chapter 3

We met at a Narateen meeting a few years ago. It wasn't the first time I'd ever seen her. We both went to Sawyer Middle School. She was considered a weirdo and a loner. No friends. Everyone vaguely understood that she was uncommonly intelligent. She wasn't known for getting amazing grades, but when she showed up for class, she would perform so well on tests that—as she later told me—teachers accused her of cheating. She certainly wasn't famous for her social skills or really much else, except spending a lot of time surfing the internet in the school library and hanging around the science lab. Rumor was she had a photographic memory (true). In another time, she'd probably have been called a witch (hell, maybe now too).

There were dark whispers that her mama was a user, and a bad one. Delaney's generally haphazard state of dress and put-togetherness and spotty school attendance gave us no reason to doubt. She had that old-beyond-her-years way of someone who's had to parent a parent. I recognized it from looking in the mirror. It made me not much more popular than her. None of the school's best-liked kids had to survive like we did, and they all avoided the stain of associating with us.

The basement at the First Baptist Church in downtown Sawyer smelled like a mix of the faintly medicinal, woody tang of

Pine-Sol and the cool, mildewed scent of old concrete, which can't keep out the hardest rains. I was glad to see that there was only one other kid there, seated in the semicircle of metal folding chairs. It was Delaney. This was as anonymous as a Narateen meeting in Sawyer would get. Me and a girl who never talked to anyone at school. I sat a few spaces away. Our eyes met briefly and we wince-smiled awkwardly.

We talked for the first time over stale Food Lion cookies and watery orange punch served from milk jugs. I told her my grandparents brought me. She'd come on her own. She pummeled me with facts about the science of drug addiction, talking like her mind was running from something. We found out our mamas were working Narcotics Anonymous together. My mama would later lose the battle. Her mama hasn't lost yet, but things don't look promising.

The next meeting, we sat beside each other. That week at school, we sat together at lunch.

Ever since I first became aware that the world contains mysteries and incomprehensible wonders, I've tried to live as a witness to them. As we came to know each other, I began to see something in Delaney that I'd never seen in another person. I can't name that thing. Maybe it has no name, the way fire has no shape. It was something ferocious and consuming, like fire.

And I wanted to be close to it, the way people want to stand near a fire.

Chapter 4

We pull up to Delaney's half brothers' dad's house. Their scarred gray pit bull, Duke, strains at the swing-set chain binding him to a sickly oak tree in the overgrown lawn, giving us a terse series of hostile barks. A rusting washing machine and dryer mold on the sagging front porch. An algae-scabbed aboveground pool slouches in a corner of the yard. It looks as fun to swim in as an unflushed toilet.

We both start talking at once.

"You go," Delaney says.

"Thank you," I say. "My hesitation isn't ingratitude."

"Okay."

"I'm not saying no yet."

"You're not saying yes yet."

"It's a lot to think about."

"You're smart. Start thinking," Delaney says.

We sit for a second, listening to the drone of the insect menagerie surrounding the house in the tall weeds. Pale neon-yellow fireflies dance their luminous evening waltz. Delaney explained to me once how they make light. I've forgotten. Occasionally, my mind lets me hold on to a fragile bit of magic in spite of practical explanations.

"Thanks again for the Blizzard," I say.

Delaney opens her door. "Thanks for the ride. Bye, gympie ass."

"You can't just impose a new nickname on me. That's not a thing. I reject it."

"Watch me." She starts to step down.

"Hey, Red?"

"What?" Delaney stops getting out and sits back in her seat.

"I always knew."

"What?"

"You'd do something important."

She looks happy. "Yeah?"

"You deserve all this. Your life is going to change so much."

"Not the part about us being friends."

"I'm not worried about that. But." I didn't know where I was going with what I was saying. It just felt like a thing that needed to be said.

"I mean," she says, "it'll be easier to stay in touch if we're at the same school."

I reach over and yank the bill of her Dairy Queen hat down over her eyes. "Go babysit."

She pulls off her hat and smooths the wisps of her hair. Once more she makes to leave.

"Red?"

Again she pulls herself back into my truck.

I don't know why I'm having such a hard time letting her go tonight. "How'd you know that mold would be in that cave?"

"You've never asked that before."

"Been curious for a long time."

"How'd I know?" She looks at me and then into the chirping, humming half-light, then back at me. "Because for every way the world tries to kill us, it gives us a way to survive. You just gotta find it."

Chapter 5

I take the long way home to try to slow the orbit of my thoughts. It's almost full dark by the time I pull up our driveway, the gravel popping under my tires.

Most everyone calls Papaw "Pep"—short for Phillip Earl Pruitt. He's taking in the falling light on the porch, in one of the ramshackle hundred-year-old rocking chairs he restored. His wheeled oxygen tank is at his side. Our redbone, Punkin, sits by him.

Papaw gets lonely. Our house is on a hill overlooking the road, woods all around. He sits out on our front porch hoping someone driving by will stop in to shoot the breeze for a while. It happens rarely now, for a few reasons.

His politics didn't always used to be much of an obstacle to friendships. He and his fishing buddies could sit for hours at McDonald's, nursing cups of coffee, bullshitting, and having mostly good-natured political arguments that ended with everyone saying, *But I'm just an old hillbilly. What the hell do I know, anyhow?*

Things took a nasty turn, though, when Lamont Gardner, a black pastor and lawyer from Nashville, became governor of Tennessee. Papaw's buddies' hatred of Governor Gardner went beyond amiable differences into an uglier place. The racist cartoons of Governor Gardner his buddies emailed around didn't sit well with Papaw, and he wasn't afraid to say it.

Andre Blount was the final straw. He was governor after Governor Gardner. He was from New York and got rich after moving to Nashville and starting a private prison company with money his dad had given him after a string of business failures. He promised to bring high-paying manufacturing jobs back to East Tennessee. But mostly he was concerned about being on TV and crudely insulting rivals on Twitter. Papaw considered him a snake oil salesman, born with a silver spoon in his mouth, who hadn't worked an honest day in his life, full of hot air, braggadocio, vain promises, and venom for everyone different from him. He saw the betrayal of all he knew to be right. That didn't sit well at all with him. And Papaw spoke his mind.

One by one, his friends stopped coming around.

He was popular at church—always with a story or joke ready. With his huge frame and bushy white beard, he was perfect to play Santa Claus at the annual Christmas potluck, a role he performed with gusto, telling kids he was going to bring them a hickory switch or a lump of coal instead of a "video-game doodad." So for a while he still had the church crowd on his side.

But that didn't last either. He'd always taken a live-and-let-live and God-made-us-all attitude toward gay people, not much different from his general policy of nonjudgment and kindness toward others. This put him at odds with his fellow churchgoers, but not irreconcilably so.

Then his sister Betsy's grandson, Blake—his grandnephew—died in a car accident in Nashville. Aunt Betsy later learned from one of Blake's friends that Blake was gay. And that changed everything for Papaw. Not three weeks after Papaw found out, the preacher started going off on how homosexuality is destroying America and how gay people are to blame for school shootings and terrorist attacks, because America's acceptance of them has called God's wrath down upon us.

I was sitting next to him. I could feel his sides pumping like a bellows as he breathed harder and harder. His face reddened. The anger radiated from him, a perilous warmth a few inches from his skin. If he could have jumped up, he would have. Instead, he pulled himself laboriously to his feet, knees cracking, easing up as fast as a back stiffened from a life of hard work would allow. And he walked out. Mamaw and I followed.

Papaw didn't hardly speak on the drive home. Finally said, "I been going to Bible study my whole life. Jesus talked about casting the first stone, not about who people loved." He was silent for a few minutes before he shook his head and murmured, "Blake never hurt nobody. Didn't do nothing but make this world a better place." We've never been back. People from church don't bring by casseroles when you leave like that.

Still, he sits and waits for someone to talk to.

I get out of my truck, and Papaw hails me with a lazy wave. The sort resulting from a constant state of exhaustion. Punkin bays in excitement and tries to lunge off the porch. Papaw catches him with his free hand.

"Lemme square away the mower," I call up to him. Lawn care equipment left out tends to disappear and get sold for pills where we live.

"I ain't going nowhere. Punkin, shush." The vocal exertion sends him into a red-faced coughing fit.

I lock up the mower in the shed and pass the chain-saw sculpture of a black bear Papaw carved out of a tree stump. Every time I pass it, I can't help but think about how his disease has sawn away at him, lessened him, transformed him. I ascend the porch steps to where he sits.

Papaw gives me a look.

"What?"

"You forget something?"

"Did I?"

"Where's my Tess at? No *Longmire* tonight?" Tess is short for Tesla, which is what he started calling Delaney after she told him that Nikola Tesla was her favorite scientist. Before that, he called her Einstein.

"Tending her half brothers."

"Y'all are like to have ruint my Saturday night."

"I'll watch with you." I sit in one of the rockers. Its weathered wood is worn so smooth it feels like touching someone's arm. I lean over to scratch Punkin.

Papaw reaches over with a rough hand, his nail beds blue from oxygen deprivation, and grabs my upper arm. "Get over here, Mickey Mouse." He pulls me out of the chair to him. He was always affectionate, but he never misses a chance anymore to hug me. Delaney studied up on emphysema, said it wasn't a terminal diagnosis. Papaw's doctor said the same. Papaw doesn't act so sure.

His former strength is faded, but he still finds enough to give me a powerful embrace, kissing the top of my head. He smells medicinal, like salves rubbed on aching muscles, with the sharp menthol whine of Vicks VapoRub to open constricted breathing passages. Beneath it is the dense aroma of pine oil and the vague spice of unsmoked tobacco, even though he hasn't been able to work with wood for some time and hasn't smoked in years. His plastic oxygen tube is artificial and cold against my cheek. I hear his wheezing, the deep rattle in his lungs.

"How was mowing?" he asks.

I sit down and push my ball cap back on my head. "Hot. But fine. Mamaw working?"

"Yep."

Mamaw manages the Little Caesars. She usually works Saturday nights to allow as many as possible of her mostly teenage staff to be young and free.

We sit quietly for a while. Our chairs creak and chirp as we rock gently. There's the periodic puff of Papaw's oxygen tank, the idling diesel-engine rumble of his breathing, and Punkin's own snuffly breathing as he dozes at Papaw's feet.

I've spent much of my life feeling unsafe, unsteady, and insecure. Sitting on Papaw's porch with him was always my fortress against the world.

Three deer step out of the woods onto our lawn, nibbling at the ground. We keep stone-still and watch until they move on.

"Speaking of Delaney," I say finally, my voice hushed as if the deer were still there. "She told me something interesting today."

"Girl's a damn encyclopedia." Whenever Delaney comes over to watch *Longmire* with him—one of their traditions—Papaw says, *Tess! Tell me something I don't know!* And she always does.

"This was different. She got into this fancy prep school up north with this millionaire gonna pay her way."

Papaw takes in the news and chuckles softly. "Tell you what. That girl wasn't long for this town. Always knew."

"Yeah."

"She gonna go? She best."

"Looks like." I rock for a couple of seconds, then say, "But that ain't the funniest part."

"What is?"

I squirm. I'm losing my nerve to tell him.

"Go on," he presses.

I sigh, raise my hands, and drop them in my lap. "Apparently she told this millionaire lady that she'd only accept if *I* got a scholarship too." I laugh to myself.

Papaw doesn't laugh. He leans toward me and shakes his head like he's trying to get water out of his ears. "Do *what,* now?" he asks softly.

"And the lady and the school both said yes."

Papaw squints. "The *two* of you have a scholarship offer to—"

"Middle-something. Middleton? Middleford Academy? Can't remember. It's in Connecticut."

Papaw sits slowly back, with a mixed expression of wonder and surprise. He whistles softly.

"It's ridiculous, right? I don't belong—"

Papaw raises his hand to halt me, his brow furrowed. "Just . . ."

"It's nuts," I murmur.

"*Full* scholarship?" He sounds optimistically skeptical.

"Sounded like."

"Good school?"

"Apparently one of the best in America. That's why I'm saying—"

"Hush, now." He says it firmly but not unkindly, like he's trying to tally something and I'm making him lose count.

After a safe amount of time, I say, "Obviously, I'm not gonna—"

"This ain't the sort of opportunity that comes along ever' day."

"I know, but—"

"Sure ain't the kind me and your mamaw could give you. Much as we'd've liked."

"Never bothered me."

"Well? What do you think about all this?"

I draw a deep breath. "Don't know. I heard about it maybe two hours ago."

A long pause. "Now, mind you, I ain't got all the information. But I think you might oughtta do it." His eyes are intense. Like how Moses would look after coming down from the mountain, having spoken with God. He nods to himself. "I think you might ought to," he says softly, as if the opportunity is something he's afraid to startle, like the deer.

I thought he'd laugh with me. *Who knows what goes on in Tess's head?* he was supposed to say. *Tell her that that's mighty kind of her but you're needed at home.* He'd be the stalwart, sane balance to the erratic, staccato electricity of Delaney's thinking, which causes her to do something as bewildering as what she did. Panic rises into my chest, into the back of my throat.

"I'm happy here," I say unsteadily.

"I kindly believe you are. But ever' so often, God opens a door."

"I can't go to a school like that."

"Seems they beg to differ."

"No, I mean I'm not like the kids who go there."

"Now you listen. You're pret' near one of the smartest young men I ever knew."

"Everyone's papaw thinks that about them."

Papaw coughs for a while and then continues. "You get good marks. Way you use words? Remember that essay you wrote for your English class about your mamaw? Made her cry. You started your own lawn business. Your best friend is the damn town genius. You think she'd run with you if you wasn't bright?"

"I don't know how she thinks."

Papaw's getting short of breath and wheezing. All this impassioned talk. He hacks and pauses to let a coughing fit subside. "That Tess is something special," Papaw says, chewing on one of the homemade cinnamon toothpicks he's started carrying around to help him quit smoking. He pulls it from his mouth and points at me with it. "I ever tell you she reminds me of your mama?" He returns it to his mouth.

"How?"

"Always asking questions. Trying to figure out how the world works."

"Mama didn't seem like that to me."

"By then, the dope stole a lot of her. When she was a little girl, though? Shoot. Never without a book."

"Where'd they go?"

Papaw shakes his head and looks down. "She sold them." He rubs at a spot on the porch with his foot, like he's buffing out a burr. "Ever' last one. They wasn't fancy books, and they wasn't in great shape from being read so much. I don't guess they fetched much."

"I wish I could have known her before."

"Me too," he murmurs. He gazes off, his eyes clouding and

forlorn. He coughs. "You got your mama's quick mind. It's why you and Tess are Butch and Sundance."

It breaks my heart how extraordinary he thinks I am. It's worse than *being* ordinary. I flash to a vision of myself wearing my soiled, sweat-sodden lawn-mowing T-shirt and grass-stained jeans and boots, standing in a huge library. All around me are kids my age, dressed like celebrities, polished and gleaming. Their hands are uncallused, their eyes clear, their minds unburdened with worry. They stand in small groups, chatting breezily about lavish vacations—summer homes and beach homes and ski homes—their backs to me.

Their life stories have no chapters on mothers chasing that Cadillac high and succumbing to an overdose of heroin, fentanyl, and Valium mixed together. No fathers who ran off to work on an oil rig shortly before they were born. No slowly dying grandfathers on disability and exhausted grandmothers who work too hard at Little Caesars, to try to maintain some dignity and quality of life in aging and rebuild the nest egg that their addicted daughter decimated. No lawn mowers—used to make those grandparents' lives easier—in the back of pickups that need to make it another year, always another year. No humiliating encounters with drug dealers in RiteQuik parking lots. None of it. They have lived free.

Life has given me little reason to feel large, but I see no need to make myself feel smaller.

A rising glow appears at the edge of our property, and a pair of headlights illuminate the driveway. Mamaw's blue Chevy Malibu creeps up in a crunching of gravel.

"How about that timing," Papaw says. "Let's see what she thinks."

I'm already heading down the steps to help Mamaw in with her things.

"Hello, lovin'," she says, rising slowly from the car, trying to balance a large pizza box.

"That everything?" I take the box and hug her and kiss her cheek. Her short gray hair smells like warm pizza crust and artificial roses. She's wearing a black polo shirt, similar to Delaney's, and khakis.

"Thank you, sweetie. I believe so. Y'all in the mood for pizza?"

I smile at her joke, like always. "Might could be."

She presses on her knees as she climbs the porch steps. She shuffles over to Papaw, bends down, and they give each other a peck on the lips.

"Pull up a chair, Donna Bird," Papaw says.

I grab a rocker from the other side of the porch and slide it over.

Mamaw sags into the rocker with an exhale, leaning her head back and closing her eyes. "Mmmmm, tell you what," she says, trailing off. That's how you know she's really tired. When she's only moderately tired, she finishes the sentence—*Tell you what. I am tuckered out.*

I hold the pizza box in my lap. After a couple of moments, her eyes snap back open with a start as if awakening from a dream. "Y'all eat. Pizza's getting cold."

She offers some to Papaw, but he waves her off. I hope he's eaten something tonight. His once-prodigious appetite is now a ghost of itself.

"What y'all been talking about?" Mamaw asks, like she's not expecting much. And she shouldn't, normally.

Papaw nods at me. "You wanna tell her, Mickey Mouse, or I will?"

"One of you," Mamaw says.

I inhale deeply. It feels gluttonous to do that around Papaw. "Delaney got a scholarship offer from a prep school up north. And she got them to give me one too."

Mamaw searches Papaw's face for some hint of a joke, some glint in his eyes. He has no poker face with her, so he'd be caught quickly. He raises his eyebrows as if to say, *I know, but not this time.* He slaps at a mosquito.

Mamaw turns back to me. I tell her everything I told Papaw.

She sits quietly for a long time, Papaw's oxygen tank punctuating the silence with whispering puffs. Finally, she asks, "So. What do you think?"

I shrug.

"Tell you what I told him," Papaw says. "Said he ought to go."

Mamaw sits still, staring at Papaw. She nods slightly. "I'm with you. I think he ought to."

I start to speak, but Mamaw cuts me off. "Now, hang on and let me say my piece. We've tried to give you everything we could, and it hadn't always been much. Now along comes a chance for you to have something that we could never give you. Falls right in your lap."

"That's the problem. I don't deserve this."

Mamaw sits forward in her chair, energized. The exhaustion has melted from her. "*No,* you didn't deserve to lose your mama. Plenty's fallen in your lap you didn't deserve. This isn't one of those things. Let the Lord bless you with one good thing to make up for all the rest."

"What about y'all?" I ask.

"We'll get by. Wasn't you planning on college in a couple years anyhow?" Mamaw asks.

"East Tennessee State maybe."

"There you go."

"But ETSU is close. I love it here. I love the river. I love y'all."

Papaw coughs and spits off the edge of the porch. "And you can still love all that while you see more of the world. If I'da had the chance? I would've. Donna Bird, wouldn't you?"

"I would indeed." Mamaw drums her fingers on her armrest for emphasis. "You know Aunt Betsy's grandbaby, Blake? She moved him to Nashville so's he could go to a good performing school."

"That didn't turn out well."

Papaw says, "How about Tess? We ain't talked about her yet."

"Didn't you say Delaney got you the scholarship offer?" Mamaw asks.

"That's right."

"I imagine she's scared stiff to go to that school alone."

"What if she don't go because you don't? Or she goes and can't concentrate on her studies because she's too lonely?" Papaw says. He takes a couple of moments to catch his breath. "That girl'll cure cancer someday, she gets the chance. But that there's the key." He pauses to cough. "The *chance*. Sounds like she thinks she needs your support. Else she wouldn't have wheeled and dealed for you."

"Wouldn't you miss her?" Mamaw asks.

"Absolutely."

"You got an opportunity to do something great for yourself and your best friend," Papaw says.

"I know," I murmur. I stare off into the darkness.

"I can always tell when you're thinking about something without saying it," Papaw says after a long while.

"What about your situation?" I ask quietly.

He wheezes, coughs, and spits off the porch. "Something the matter with me?"

We laugh. But our laughter quickly subsides. "I need to be here," I say.

"'Cause I'll live forever if you stay?"

"I owe you."

He snorts. "For what?"

"Everything."

"Tell you something, son." He pauses to take a few shallow breaths. His voice is sober. "I love you. But I'll be damned if I'm why you let a chance like this go." Pause to breathe. Wheeze. Cough. "Death's all around us. We live our whole lives in its shadow. It'll do what it will. So we need to do what *we* will while we can."

With that, our conversation dwindles.

I rock and feel on my face the caress of the cool evening air, scented by the damp green of broken vines and cut grass. Beside me, Mamaw and Papaw hold hands but don't speak.

Above us is an immaculate chaos of white stars and drifting moonlit-silver clouds. I remember how I would sit under the sanctuary of the night sky, into the late hours, waiting for my mama to get home. Or to escape her dopesick moaning and thrashing. Or to avoid the red-rimmed, whiskey-fogged glare of a new boyfriend. Or because I needed to feel like there was something beautiful in this world that could never be taken from me.

Papaw coughs and coughs. Eventually, he collects himself.

I listen to his shallow, uneven respiration. *Ask me to number the breaths I wish for you. One more. Ask me a thousand times. The answer will always be one more.*

For a while it seems like Papaw's about to say something, but he doesn't. Finally, he says, "Welp," and leans forward.

I help him out of his rocker and into bed.

Chapter 6

I didn't even know she was there.

She came and went at such unpredictable times. I had gotten home from school and watched a couple of hours of TV, waiting for her to get back from wherever she was. We didn't always have a TV. It would disappear mysteriously and be replaced some time later with something worse than what we had. Also, we had just gotten our electricity turned back on, and I had to take advantage.

It was only when I got up to pee that I discovered her. She had collapsed in the cramped and squalid bathroom of our cramped and squalid trailer and fallen with her body wedged against the locked door. I knocked, and when no answer came, I pounded and screamed, yelling "Mama" and also her name. I was afraid to call 911 because I didn't want her to go to jail, the evidence of her drug use so plainly on display. I was afraid of going into foster care.

When I jimmied the lock and tried to enter, I encountered the organic weight of a lifeless human body. She wasn't large, but I didn't know her condition and I was afraid of hurting her more, so it took me some time to open the door. The feral stench of shit and imminent decay pummeled my nose upon entry. It was the only thing alive in that room.

I spent two hours in a tomb with my mama.

I tried to call her from death to open a bathroom door.

So now I dream sometimes of an endless hallway of identical doors. I try to open them for some reason. Behind each is that awful slack weight of death. I try to scream in frustration but manage only a hoarse dreamcroak. I awake from that nightmare, cold with sweat, warm tears drying on my face, my jaw muscles sore from grinding my teeth.

I glance at my phone: 3:36 a.m. There won't be any more sleep for a while. Not until my brain has temporarily purged itself of whatever poison causes this particular nightmare.

I put on a T-shirt and some pants and creep past my grandparents' bedroom. Papaw's CPAP machine hums behind his door. Punkin patters behind me. I sit in one of the rockers. Punkin curls up beside me, nose to tail, and immediately dozes off. The moonlight is so radiant it looks like daylight's ghost. The cool and damp air is asleep, with no breeze, and smells like dew and the faint musk of skunk. It's one of my favorite smell combinations. Delaney thinks if you could dilute down the smell of skunk by about a million, it would be the best-selling perfume on the planet. She thinks humans are secretly attracted to everything that repulses us.

I would miss her if she left. Terribly.

I would miss Mamaw and Papaw if I left. Terribly.

After I found my mama, the next memory I have is the police bringing me here, nearly catatonic. Papaw held me on his lap. I was too big for it but I fit somehow. He wept into my hair and I sobbed into his chest.

This porch, with them, is the only place in my life I've ever felt truly safe.

I try to envision not having this. My life is small and simple, but it's a better one than I ever thought I'd have. I have what I love: my grandparents, the satisfaction of working with my hands to bring a lawn into perfect order, the rhythm of paddling my canoe. I'm not keen to trade it in for some vague promise of the unknown.

Then I envision Delaney, dressed in a plaid skirt and a white blouse, walking timidly up to the imposing wrought-iron gates of an ivy-covered school. Her thumbs are ragged and bleeding. The end of her ponytail is frayed like a busted rope from her worrying at it. No one tries to befriend her. They resent what comes so easily to her, what their family's money couldn't buy them.

She folds in on herself, looking for some refuge. Maybe she surrenders and returns, goes back to work at Dairy Queen. Doesn't realize the potential of her great mind, at best. At worst, she follows her mama's path and looks for things to numb the pain of seeing the world in a way no one else understands.

I think about the time Jaydon Barnett started a rumor that Delaney's mama was pimping her out for drug money and he knew because his cousin had banged her. I found him in the school parking lot. Told him to apologize. He told me to stick it up my ass. Something in me flashed and went dark, the way a light bulb sometimes blows out in a bright burst when you turn it on.

I swung on Jaydon reflexively, as someone flinches from a flame. Caught him hard on the side of the head and dazed him, sending him staggering sideways. Before he could mount any punch-drunk counterassault, and before a crowd could even form, I'd thrown him down and rained blows on his face, blacking his eyes and bloodying his nose.

I was a good fighter. I was strong from working, and I had honed my skills in elementary school, where I took a lot of shit. I often showed up for school unbathed, in filthy clothes or clothes washed haphazardly in a sink with whatever we had at hand—dish soap sometimes. I had bad home haircuts with clippers. Strange bruises. I would fall asleep in class. I learned to take only the beatings I couldn't prevent.

The principal told me I could avoid a longer suspension if I apologized. I refused. Jaydon was popular and I wasn't, even before our fight. My social standing sank even lower as a result.

I couldn't say exactly when Delaney became the sort of friend for whom I'd go to battle. It just happened.

Inside, I hear Papaw hacking and struggling for breath. If I leave, what will be left of him when I get back? Every inhalation of his is like the tick of a clock counting down. That I got to experience a seminormal childhood for the last few years, with something like parents, seems like enough good fortune for one lifetime. It feels greedy to desire more.

I thought the predawn tranquility would help me find some peace. But the quiet is just another clamor in my head, calling me in every direction I can't choose between.

Chapter 7

Lydia Blankenship: You're listening to *Morning Edition* from NPR, National Public Radio. I'm Lydia Blankenship, special youth and culture correspondent to *Morning Edition* and, for today . . . special small-town Tennessee correspondent.

Earlier this week, Vanderbilt University microbiologist Dr. Bidisha Srinavasan announced the results of her six-month-long study into the antibiotic properties of a new strain of penicillin mold discovered in a cave outside of Sawyer, Tennessee. Her findings are astounding. It kills every known antibiotic-resistant "superbug," and does so with a ferocity that makes it almost impossible for the bacteria to evolve to withstand it, at least for now. It's a momentous discovery in the war against antibiotic-resistant bacteria, which scientists are calling as important as the original discovery of penicillin.

But Dr. Srinavasan, whom we heard from yesterday, had help discovering the mold and its properties: a high school sophomore named Delaney Doyle from Sawyer, Tennessee. We have her on the line with us. Good morning, Delaney.

Delaney Doyle: Hi.

Lydia Blankenship: Now, many of our listeners might not have heard of Sawyer, Tennessee. Can you tell us where it is?

Delaney Doyle: Um. Yeah. It's just east of Knoxville. Near the Smoky Mountains.

Lydia Blankenship: Let's talk about this discovery. How did you come to find this mold?

Delaney Doyle: Well. Um. Sorry, I'm super nervous.

Lydia Blankenship: You're doing great.

Delaney Doyle: So my friend Cash Pruitt and I like to go canoeing on the Pigeon River. And there are all these caves along the river, and I asked Cash if he could take me inside them, because I figured that one of the only natural threats to mold in a cave would be bacteria, so I thought it's probably evolved to meet that threat. Cash's grandfather used to be a volunteer firefighter and would rescue people from caves, and he had some gear that we used to explore. I guess Cash's grandfather taught him a lot about caves and stuff. So we found the mold in one of the caves, growing on the wall. This was summer between ninth and tenth grade.

Lydia Blankenship: So you two went in this cave and came out with a sample of the mold?

Delaney Doyle: Bunch of different samples, yeah. To test. See which worked.

Lydia Blankenship: Talk about that.

Delaney Doyle: I'm, um, sorry. So I used to hang around in the science lab at my school, and my science teacher, Mr. Hotchkiss, would let me come in and use the lab. Our school doesn't have much money, so he used his own money to buy a good microscope.

Lydia Blankenship: I went to public school in a town of five thousand in Tennessee, and that sounds familiar.

Delaney Doyle: Yeah. It sucks. So Mr. Hotchkiss got me some petri dishes and helped me get some bacteria samples. I started testing the mold on bacteria, and I saw that the mold was killing every bacterium it came into contact with. I even tested it on some MRSA, and it worked.

Lydia Blankenship: For our listeners who may not know, MRSA is a dangerous antibiotic-resistant bacteria. How did you get a sample of MRSA?

Delaney Doyle: I probably shouldn't tell. I don't want anyone to get in trouble.

Lydia Blankenship: We'll move on. Now, how did Dr. Srinavasan enter the picture?

Delaney Doyle: I googled scientists who study antibiotic-resistant bacteria and emailed them. Dr. Srinavasan was the only one who responded. She's at Vanderbilt, which is only a few hours away. Good luck, I guess. So Cash drove me and my samples and the records I made to meet with her. A few days later, she sent a couple of grad students to Sawyer to collect more samples and bring them back . . . Sorry, hang on a sec . . . Okay, thanks. Sorry, I'm at work.

Lydia Blankenship: Where is work?

Delaney Doyle: Dairy Queen.

Lydia Blankenship: Does Dairy Queen have any idea that one of their employees made one of the major scientific finds of the decade?

Delaney Doyle: I think so, because when I clock in, I'm the only one they make wash my hands twice.

Lydia Blankenship: [Laughter] We'll let you get back to work, but one more question: Dr. Srinavasan told us the name she gave this miraculous new mold, but we'd like to hear it from you too.

Delaney Doyle: *Penicillium delanum.*

Lydia Blankenship: I can hear you smiling even over the phone.

Delaney Doyle: [Laughter] I am.

Lydia Blankenship: Delaney, on behalf of young women everywhere, and especially young women from small towns in Tennessee, thank you and keep up the great work.

Delaney Doyle: Thanks, I will.

Chapter 8

It's a lie that water is odorless. Water smells like water. The way wind smells like wind and dirt smells like dirt.

The mossy, metallic fragrance of the river wafts around us in the syrupy humidity, mixing with the flinty scent of wet stone and the yeasty tang of mud. The sun bakes the river water into our clothes, making them stiff, and onto our skin, leaving a taut film that feels like dried tears.

Delaney reclines gingerly on the fallen log where we sit. She shields her eyes against the late afternoon brightness. "I don't think a dog qualifies as a critter."

"Course it does," I say. "When'd you put on sunscreen last?"

"Doesn't. And I forget."

I toss her the bottle. "You'll burn. Why doesn't it?"

"Because a domesticated animal can't be a *critter*." She shakes the bottle of Dollar General brand sunscreen and blats out the last few dregs into her palm, then slops it on her face, neck, and arms.

"Says who? Any animal can be a critter. Come here," I say. She scoots closer and I rub the sunscreen in where she missed.

"Would you call a cow a critter?" she asks.

"Maybe."

"Bullshit. Is a whale a critter? Say the sentence 'A whale is a critter' out loud. See how dumb you sound."

I smile, knowing I've walked right into Delaney's trap. She always wins our debates.

She props herself up on her elbows and pushes at my thigh with a muddy toe. "Huh? I see your guilty little grin." Few people see this teasing, playful side of Delaney.

I grab for her toe but she jerks it away. "Whales aren't domesticated," I say.

"Still not critters."

"Let's look up the definition in the dictionary."

"Waste of time, because either it'll agree with me or it'll be wrong."

"Then you define *critter.*"

She lies back down, resting her forearm over her eyes, dangling one foot off the edge of the log. "A critter is a nondomesticated animal that weighs under twenty-five pounds." She says it with finality and certainty. Another piece of the natural world understood and catalogued—her never-ending quest.

I pull one knee up to my chest and hug it. "So that's it, then."

"That's it. Possums and raccoons are critters. House cats aren't."

She's right. It makes perfect sense. And I would definitely rather be wrestling over this than the topic we could be debating but haven't broached yet today.

Delaney pulls out her phone, kept securely in a sandwich bag, and starts typing as if texting. I know it's more likely she's recording some observation or writing down a question to research later. We let minutes drip past and listen to the burble of the river. Insects dance just above the surface of the water, catching the sunlight like tiny flecks of gold. We're on a small island in the river, where it flows through Sawyer. Not far from us is a bridge to downtown. Cars hum by occasionally.

I lie back on the sun-warm log. There are days when your heart is so filled with this world's beauty, it feels like holding too much of something in your hand. Days that taste like wild honey. This is one of them.

When you grow up with ugliness and corruption, you surrender to beauty whenever and wherever you find it. You let it save you, if only for the time it takes for a snowflake to melt on your tongue or for the sun to sink below the horizon in a wildfire of clouds. No matter what else might be troubling your mind. You recognize it for something that can't be taken from you. Something that can't die with its back against a door, shutting you out in its final act.

This is all I ever need. Nothing more.

But in this reverie, there's space for the Unwanted Conversation to slip in. I fill the silence with a diversion, taking a page from Papaw's book. "Tell me something I don't know."

"Lemme think," Delaney says. A few beats pass. "Oh, got a good one."

"Shoot."

"There's a theory that humans descended from aquatic apes. Like dolphins but apes."

"For real?"

"This lady named Elaine Morgan is big on the theory. I watched her TED talk. She points out all these adaptations humans have that aquatic animals have."

"Like?"

50

"We're hairless, like whales and hippos. Every naturally hairless land mammal except for the Somalian mole rat has an aquatic ancestor. We have a layer of fat under our skin like aquatic animals. We can speak because we can control our breath. The only creatures with the conscious breath control needed for speech are diving animals."

"Dang."

"The scientific community thinks it's horseshit."

"Why?"

"Because they'd rather believe we descended from hunter-gatherer primates. The aquatic ape theory is too gentle. Not manly enough for science."

"I think it sounds good. You and I like being around the water." The only time I ever see Delaney seem completely at peace is when we're on the river together.

"But it's probably horseshit."

"You like the theory?"

"Yeah, but not because I think it's probably true."

"Then why?"

"Because it's heretical. That's how science advances and takes humanity with it. People have to be brave enough to look stupid in a field where looking stupid is the worst thing you can do." She pauses for a second. "Speaking of being afraid of looking stupid."

"What?"

"Been five days."

"Since what?"

"You know. Middleford needs an answer."

"How soon?"

"Like yesterday. They're holding spots."

I release my breath in a pained rush. "I talked it over with Papaw and Mamaw."

"And?"

"They think I should."

"So?"

"So I'm not sure," I say.

"You want to stay."

"Not even a matter of want."

"Then what?"

"My papaw is the only dad I've ever had, and he's in rough shape, so."

Her voice is taut. "I can't stay here anymore, Cash. My mama's using again. Guaran-damn-tee."

"How do you know?"

"Found a prescription pad in the lining of her purse. She's gone all the time and weird about where she's been. This new sketchy dude named Bo has been hanging around. She's been wearing long-sleeve shirts in ninety-degree weather. I can't anymore." She leaves a weighted pause. "Plus, there's Cloud."

I coil like a spring. "He up in your business?"

"Came to my work the other day, looking for me. They wouldn't tell him when I was on next." Then she adds, "Don't do anything stupid. He's dangerous."

I've come to expect a certain lack of permanence in all things. But I feel a sickly torquing inside my lower abdomen at the sudden realization that I'm losing Delaney. Pretty much my only friend. "Does your mama have to sign off or whatever for you to go?"

Delaney sits up. "Told her I'd been studying the law and if she didn't sign off, I'd go file emancipation papers, which would automatically trigger a Child Protective Services investigation."

"That true?"

She snorts. "Hell if I know. She bought it." Delaney bends down, picks up a smooth stone, and tries to skip it. It enters the water with a single *plip*.

I crouch, grab a stone, and wing it at the river. It skips four times.

Delaney picks up another rock.

"Watch me," I say. I make exaggerated motions, showing her how much lower you need to throw from. Papaw taught me. He's a master of stone skipping.

She tries again. It doesn't skip. "I want you to come, Cash."

I avoid her eyes and scan the ground for more smooth, flat stones. "I want to." This is more lie than truth.

"Then do it."

"I don't know." I get a nice angle and skip a stone seven times. "You see that?"

"I'm scared. Being so far from here. Being at a new school." She hurls a stone into the water. No attempt to skip it. "Being far from you," she murmurs.

"Tonight, listen to how Papaw sounds when he breathes."

"And yet he thinks you should go." Delaney hovers her hand just above her thigh, then strikes with a loud smack, obliterating a mosquito in a crimson smear. "Since when does Pep say shit he doesn't mean?"

"This might be different."

Delaney steps back to the log and sits. "So that's a no, sounds like." Her voice teeters, like it's walking a tightrope over tears. "Guess I should tell the school thanks but no thanks."

I sit down beside her and put my arm around her freckled and bony shoulders. She smells like river and dust, clean sweat and the ersatz coconut of Dollar General sunscreen on sun-touched skin. "Hey."

She won't meet my gaze.

"Hey," I repeat, shaking her shoulder gently.

She looks at me, hurt in her eyes. "We made this discovery together. We're a team."

I look away.

"Who knows what we could do if we stay a team?" She quickly studies her gnawed-on thumb and starts to raise it to her mouth. It looks worse than normal. She's been troubled.

I intercept her hand. "You'll catch some river bug and get the scoots."

She shakes free from my grasp and grabs her ponytail, rubbing the ball of her chewed-up thumb on the tufted end.

"Red."

Her eyes brim with beseeching. "You're my best friend," she murmurs, her voice trailing off. "When I go, my mama will probably die. Without me there with the Narcan next time she OD's? I don't want to be alone when that happens."

I almost say, *Maybe you shouldn't go either,* but I think better of it. It's one thing for me to forgo such an opportunity. It's another thing to be what prevents her from going. I sense she almost hopes I'll ask her to stay so she has an excuse not to go. I won't give it to her.

We're silent for a long time before she says, "Please don't say no yet."

"Okay."

"Even if the answer is no. Even if you know it in your heart already. Just let me have a couple more days to envision us there together."

"All right."

Her face goes distant and dreamy. "I've imagined us hanging out at school, wearing goofy-ass private-school uniforms. We have this group of friends who don't know anything about our lives before. They understand us like no one here does. We visit New York City together some weekend and go to museums."

"That sounds great," I say, and I'm not lying.

"What are you gonna do with your life?"

"I don't know."

"You even thought about it?"

I fidget uncomfortably. I haven't, much. That's what happens when your life is constantly shifting beneath your feet. You never have a firm enough footing to gaze into the distance. "I don't know. Work hard. Meet someone. Have a family. Start my own landscaping business."

"Sounds normal," Delaney says.

"Yeah."

"You're not normal. You're not ordinary."

"Well, thanks, but I've had an unordinary life and I'd have given anything for an ordinary life."

"Shitty life and ordinary life aren't the only two choices."

I slap a mosquito on my forearm. "Going to some rich-kid-ass school up north or having an ordinary life aren't the only two choices."

"Didn't say they were."

"Then why are you on my case?" I walk to the river to wash the blood off my arm.

"On your *case?*" Delaney's face wrinkles in disgust. "Don't be stupid." We both know she's smarter than me, so she saves this one for when she either doesn't care that it will sting or wants it to.

"I try not to be."

"All I've *ever* thought is that this could be the sort of opportunity that neither of us has had many of."

"Fine." I splash water on my arm and scrub off the blood and mosquito guts.

"Ain't saying you won't have a good life if you don't come. I'm saying you won't have the *same* life if you don't."

"Fine. Let's change the subject." I walk back to Delaney.

Her face is defiant. "What do I tell the school?" She starts to put her thumb to her mouth.

I catch her hand. "I'm serious about you getting diarrhea from the river water. Don't. And tell them I'm still thinking."

"Okay."

There's another long silence.

"Promise me you won't replace me with a new best friend," I say.

"Only if I meet someone better at mowing lawns."

"It'll never happen."

"Some of those kids will've trained at the most elite lawn-mowing academies. They've come up working on their daddies' golf courses."

I snort. "They got servants and shit."

Delaney gives me an impish grin. "Gonna write you a letter. *Dear Cash. I regret to inform you that I have filled the position of best friend with Mr.—*What's a good rich kid name?"

"Um . . . Remington."

"Like the shotgun?"

"Okay . . . Chauncey?"

"I have filled the position of best friend with Mr. Chauncey T. Ikea."

"Ikea! Like the store?"

"Yes. *With Mr. Chauncey T. Ikea, scion to the Ikea fortune—"*

"Have you ever even been to an Ikea?"

"Stop interrupting with your irrelevant questions. *With Mr. Chauncey T. Ikea, scion to the Ikea fortune and graduate of the Wellington Academy of the Lawn-Mowing Arts and Sciences."*

"Dear Delaney. I regret to inform you that I am the lawn-mowing king and that I am forced to throw you in the Pigeon River." I roar and dart toward her, arms outstretched, like I'm chasing a little kid.

She shrieks, giggles, and bounds backward a couple steps. "I just got dry, you piece of shit!" She raises her tiny fists like a boxer and bounces on the balls of her feet. "I'll whup your ass."

I pretend to spit on my palms and raise my fists, like an old-timey prizefighter, moving them in circles, bobbing and weaving. "All right. Come on. Let's go. Come on."

She feints and breaks for the water, reaching down, grabbing some in both hands, and throwing it at me, cackling. She reaches down again and splashes me.

I duck and move toward the river myself, hurling water at her. She kicks water at me. We go on until we're both as soaked as if we'd thrown each other in the river, laughing until we're breathless and hiccuping.

"Okay, truce," I say, extending my hand.

"Truce." She takes my hand.

"Let's show you how to skip a rock properly. You suck. Seems like you would have figured out all the angles and trajectories and shit."

"Because studying rock skipping is the thing that most intrigues me."

We're quiet for a few minutes while Delaney works on her technique. Then she says, "I wanna go to the zoo this summer."

"You've never even been to the Knoxville zoo?"

"Nope. I want to see meerkats. And a sloth."

"We'll go."

A few more minutes of skipping rocks (or at least attempting to).

"You ever imagined going somewhere where we don't live in the shadows of our mamas' sickness?" Delaney asks quietly.

The question hits me like a stepped-on rake. "I mean. It'd be nice." I nod for a few seconds as the idea gains traction inside me. "Yeah," I murmur.

We skip rocks for a while longer, talking about nothing in particular, until it's time to leave. Delaney takes her position in the front of the canoe and I wade into the cool of the river to launch it.

For a heartbeat or two, I only stare at Delaney's hunched back as she gazes off into the distance, lost but to herself and whatever great question gnaws at the hems of her thoughts. She rests her elbows on her knees, her chin in one hand, playing with the end of her ponytail with the other hand. She already looks like a memory in the gilded, hazy summer light.

As if she can feel my gaze weighing heavy on her, she glances over her shoulder. "We going or not?"

It takes me a second to realize she's talking about leaving right then, and not about the school. "We are."

The river twines insistently around my calves, gently tugging me, as though into an embrace. I look down at the swirling eddies of my river and then back at her.

I don't know how to say goodbye to either of you. I recite it in my mind like a prayer to any God who ever cared enough to listen to me—a petition not for something I want, but to know what I want.

Chapter 9

"You ever think about what the murder rate in Long-mire's county must be like, relative to the population?" Delaney asks, as the end credits roll. She sits cross-legged on the couch between Papaw and me.

Papaw chuckles and wheezes.

Delaney continues. "A tiny rural county in Wyoming, and yet every episode has at *least* one murder. Walt Longmire's actually maybe the worst law enforcement officer in the world."

Papaw coughs with laughter. He points at me. "This here's what I mean by her insights."

"She's ruining the show," I say incredulously.

"She ain't either."

"You cried when the horse died at the end of the episode," Delaney says. She loves to tease him. He adores her teasing.

"And what's it to you, Tess?" Papaw clears his throat and coughs. "That horse gave a fine performance. He ought to win a horse Oscar."

"I think it's sweet," Delaney says.

"Listen, now, before you leave for your babysitting, I been meaning to tell you how proud I am of you, getting into that school."

"Aw, Pep." Delaney lays her head on his shoulder and hugs him sideways.

"You go off to that fancy school, see if you can't come up with something to beat this tickle in my throat I got, okay?" Papaw says it like a joke, but a stripe of seriousness runs through it.

"I will. I promise," she says quietly, no jest in her voice whatsoever—only the unshakable resolve of someone sworn to ride out and meet Death in battle.

There's no one I'd trust more to fight him.

We go out on the porch and sit for a while, chatting aimlessly. Blushing, Delaney asks to use our shower before she goes. Her hot water heater is broken and she's afraid to shower at her half brothers' house. She doesn't feel safe around their dad or his friends.

She rejoins us, her russet hair damp on her shoulders like autumn leaves stuck to a window after rain, smelling like fake Granny Smith apples and Ivory soap. She tells Papaw about gympie gympie. He's duly horrified and she's unduly delighted. Her ride arrives and she leaves to babysit.

It begins sprinkling, the muted notes sounding like someone trying to slowly and secretly open a plastic bag in a room full of sleeping people. The air grows dense with the shimmering perfume of rain, dewy honeysuckle, and mown grass.

Papaw coughs, wheezes, spits off the porch. There's a faint peal of thunder, a bright flicker of lightning, and the rain thickens.

Mamaw drives up, her headlights illuminating the falling drops. I sense something wrong the moment she exits the car. Maybe people emit a distress chemical, like cut grass does.

I run to her. I'm useless against the falling rain, but at least I'm another set of hands if she needs them.

"I've got everything," she murmurs, almost inaudibly. She's empty-handed but for her purse—no usual pizza box.

I stay by her elbow until we clomp to the porch and out of the rain.

"You're early," Papaw says. "Come set with us."

Mamaw sighs and looks away. "I might could use a moment or two alone, collect myself." Her voice is faint and fragile.

Papaw looks alarmed. He pulls himself to his feet and takes a couple of steps in our direction.

"Set, Pep. I'll be fine."

"What happened?" I ask.

"Bad night's all. Full moon maybe." Her voice has a slight hitch. She won't look at either of us.

"Donna Bird?" Papaw says.

I study her face. I notice a bright-pink blotch just to the side of her left eye. She has a couple of drops of what looks like dried tomato sauce on the same side of her glasses. I reach out to touch, and she gently catches my hand and lowers it.

"I'm sorry I forgot the pizza," she mumbles, and starts again for the door. "I'll make some dinner."

"Mamaw, will you please tell us what happened so we don't worry?"

"We ain't trying to pry," Papaw says, "but . . ."

She draws a long, stuttering breath. "Neither of y'all can do anything foolish."

My heart whirs. Papaw moves slowly back to his rocker and sinks into it. He coughs and wheezes. Stress makes his breathing worse. Mamaw sits in the rocker beside him, but I stay standing.

"It was a busy night and I'm training a new girl, and she messed up the order for Ruthie Cloud's grandson. I don't recall his name right off. Has the gold teeth and braided hair and tattoos."

"Jason?" My heart drums on the wall of my chest like an animal dashing itself against the bars of its cage. *Whatever she's about to tell me, it's my fault. He promised me he would make me sorry if I came between him and Delaney.* My knees tremble. A sourness rises in the back of my throat.

"Jason. So she gets the order wrong. Gives him sausage instead of bacon. Well, Jason starts fussing at her, hollering. Being as ugly as can be. I go to see what's the matter. He tells me. I says, 'Sir, you are our customer. Your satisfaction is our first priority. We'll make you a fresh pie.' But that's not good enough. So I says, 'We'll refund your money too. Keep the pie.' Course *that's* not good enough either. Says he wants a fresh pie, his money back, *and* twenty dollars for his trouble."

"For his *trouble*? Hell." Papaw shakes his head in disgust. *"For his trouble."*

Mamaw continues. "I tell him, 'Sir, I have offered you what I can. I've tried to do right by you. I cannot just give you money from the till. I will lose my job.' Then he opens up his pizza box, and—" Her face crumples. She pulls off her glasses and presses a hand over her eyes. She begins weeping. "He slaps me with a slice, right over the eye. Fresh out of the oven. Pushes it hard in my face." She breaks down sobbing.

Papaw and I cry out simultaneously in wordless outrage. We both stand over her, hands on her back like we're faith healers. Papaw wheezes. He coughs until he's red-faced.

Papaw and I hug her tight from each side for several moments while she cradles her burned face in both hands, one arm of her bifocals clenched precariously between two fingers. I gently take her glasses, go inside, and wash them clean. My belly is an incandescent crucible of molten iron. Papaw is still embracing her to his chest when I come back out.

I give her back her glasses.

"Thank you," she says, voice still quaking. She shakes her head. "This world's come to be so ugly. People didn't always act this way."

"How dare he. He deserves to be shot." Papaw is hoarse. "We ought to call the sheriff on him." He hacks furiously and fights for breath.

Mamaw shakes her head firmly. "I don't believe in calling the law on every little thing." She stands and takes a deep breath, composing herself. "I'll be all right. I just need to take my mind off it. When it happened, I left one of the gals in charge and took off. And truth is, I didn't forget the pizza. I didn't want my boys eating something I'd been slapped across the face with. I'm gonna go inside and cook some real dinner. I'm tired of y'all eating this stuff from a cardboard box."

"You should take a hot bath, rest. You work too hard," I say. "Let us sort dinner."

She summons a wan smile. "I need to do this. There's dignity in serving the people I love, and I could use a dose of dignity."

"I love you." I give her a long hug.

Papaw pecks her on the cheek and embraces her. "Love you, Donna Bird."

She doesn't say anything, but rests her hand on his cheek for a second. Then she goes inside.

Papaw and I retake our seats. He's shaking his head. His face is red and there's a glowering set to his jaw.

Something begins happening to me. My concern for Mamaw of a few moments ago is swept into the rush of a crescendo-ing inside my chest. Something animal and ferocious, bleak and savage. It's growing too big for my body, ready to rip through my skin. A roiling tumult of hatred and fury overcomes me, and a fog of black-and-gray static envelops my brain. I see Jason Cloud's glittering, leering grin mocking me. My head throbs at the base of my skull.

Some beastly voice from the gloom calls me and says, *Stand,* and I do.

It tells me, *Leave the porch,* and I do.

It tells me, *Go to the shed, and pull the axe off the wall—the one you use on October mornings to chop wood for winter.* And I do.

I run my hand down its work-worn smoothness. I weigh the heft of its gleaming, shattered-glass-sharp head. I take good care of it like Papaw taught me.

And the serpentine voice tells me, *Bury it in Jason Cloud's face.* The voice bids me, *Do this.*

And I will.

I toss the axe with a clatter into the bed of my pickup and jerk the door open.

I'm half inside when Papaw breaks through the malignant buzz in my brain. "Where you going with that?"

I look at him. "To kill Jason Cloud."

"No you will not either," Papaw roars. His voice booms with its old authority.

But whatever has me in its grip is too strong. I hesitate for only a moment before I sit behind the wheel.

"You get up here right now if you love me," Papaw shouts, with what must be the last of his strength. In the dim of the porch light, I see his eyes, ardent with furious love. It burns through the darkness in me. It pulls me from the maelstrom and drops me, dripping and shivering on the shore. I trudge back up to the porch, my head bowed. I sit. Every cell in my body pulsates with hatred.

Mamaw opens the front door. "I heard hollering."

Papaw wheezes. "We thought we saw a coyote on up the road and Cash went to go see. I called him back because I didn't know if it had rabies."

I meet Mamaw's eyes for a second, but I quickly avert my gaze.

"Okay," she says uncertainly, and goes back inside. She knows Papaw is lying. But I appreciate his doing it.

Papaw sits beside me and coughs and coughs, as though paying a debt for a moment of his old strength. While he does, I listen to the rain fall and feel the red tide of adrenaline recede from my chest, leaving me queasy and spent. It's a long time before Papaw can summon back his breath. And when he does, he lets the silence grow thin enough to burst.

My voice trembles when I speak, and a searing rage floods back into me. It feels like running hot water over frost-numbed fingers. "I'd kill that son of a bitch for what he did." I'm ashamed of how I sound. I never curse in front of Papaw and Mamaw.

Papaw just listens.

"He humiliated her," I say.

"I know it," Papaw says quietly.

"Someone like him killed my mama. Drug-dealing piece of shit."

Papaw shakes his head and exhales heavily out his nose.

"You said Cloud deserved to be shot," I say.

Papaw looks down, then at me. "That was talk. You think visiting you in jail is how I want to spend the time I got left?"

From nowhere, some new and unfamiliar emotion levels me. I put my face in my hands and begin sobbing. I'm so ashamed.

Papaw rubs my back, his rough hand scratching on my T-shirt. He pulls me gently by the shoulder over to him and hugs me while I cry. "C'mon, now. Hey. Hey, now."

After several minutes I compose myself and sit back in my rocker, my eyes puffy.

"You know one reason I think you ought to go to that school?"

I shake my head.

"This here's a good place to live. Beautiful country. Decent folks. But it's real easy to come up here learning there's only one way to be a man. Live hard. Take blood for blood. You think maybe that's what's going on here?"

I look at the ground and nod.

"I want you to get out in the world and see there's more than one way to be a man. We're having Betsy and Mitzi over for supper in a few days."

"I remember."

"We said it was to celebrate two years sober for Mitzi—" Papaw pauses to cough. "But really it was to get you and Bets in the same room so's she could talk about this school opportunity. You've always listened to her."

"I listen to you and Mamaw."

"The hell you do. In one ear, out the other. We're bringing in reinforcements."

I smile a little with the corner of my mouth.

Papaw reaches over, pinches the top of my ear, and tugs my head down to him, mussing my hair. "I believe I saw a bird nest in your hair. Lemme get it out."

We sit and rock, listening to the rain dwindle to a patter, the sky slowly bleeding.

The buttery aroma of hot homemade biscuits wafts out to us from the cracks around the front door. We're about to get up when Mamaw opens the door and calls us inside to eat. She has a look of contentment underneath her fresh burn, like she's channeled all her indignity into creating something to nourish and comfort herself and the people she loves.

My stomach is still knotted and queasy from earlier, and my mind is protesting that I'm not hungry, but my heart is telling me something else entirely.

"See you don't leave the axe in the pickup," Papaw says as we go in. "Someone'll steal it and swap it for a pill."

Chapter 10

"There were many times, during the toughest days, that I imagined us sitting together at a table, celebrating your sobriety, your coming through the storm into sunshine—" Aunt Betsy looks away, blinking fast, the back of her quaking hand pressed over her lips while she collects herself, her other hand on her daughter's hand. "I thought the day I heard your voice on the phone to try to tell you about Blake would be the last time I ever heard it. God has moved in our lives, and I praise him for it. I thank you for the gift you are, Mitzi."

Tears stream down Mitzi's cheeks, and her eyes are red and puffy, but she looks radiant compared to pictures I'd seen of her from when she was using: pockmarked; scabby, sallow skin; patches of missing hair; scarecrow-thin; a feral, hunted look in her eyes.

Papaw raises his glass of Dr. Enuf. "To two years clean and sober. And many more."

We raise our glasses. *To two years clean and sober. And many more.* We say grace and dig into the spread before us. Aunt Betsy's chicken and dumplings and sweet potato casserole, Mamaw's white beans, skillet cornbread, and greens. Papaw and I teamed up on some mac and cheese. *Just keep adding butter and cheese; won't get no complaints,* Papaw said.

Our old air conditioner can't keep up with the heat we generated with all of the cooking and conversation, so we sit, sweating, around our scarred oak table, which Papaw built. I look around at us.

Here we are, survivors of quiet wars. Like trees that have weathered a brutal storm, but with broken branches and fallen blossoms littering the ground around us.

We finish and lean back in our chairs, bursting.

"Y'all wanna set for a while and digest. We got banana pudding," Aunt Betsy says. "Don't worry about the mess. Cash and I'll get it."

Papaw, Mamaw, and Mitzi get up slowly and retire to the porch. My chest tightens like I'm in trouble, even though I know I'm not.

Aunt Betsy runs hot, sudsy water in the sink. I join her with a handful of greasy dishes.

She takes them from me one by one and lays them to soak. "You get enough to eat?"

I smile. "Could say that."

"I thought about Cassie a lot tonight," she says softly.

"Me too."

"I miss her."

"So do I."

Aunt Betsy scrubs at a spot on a plate. "On a happier note, Pep tells me an amazing opportunity has arisen for you."

I set a half-full casserole dish on the counter and hunt through the cupboards for one of the plastic Country Crock butter containers Mamaw uses to store leftovers. "Yeah."

"He said you're hesitant and not sure whether you should go."

"Also true."

Aunt Betsy shakes soapy water off her hands, rests them on the edge of the sink, and looks at me. "Cash, you are a brilliant, hardworking young man. You can't convince me you shouldn't jump at this chance just because you weren't born with a silver spoon in your mouth."

I swallow hard and turn away, sweeping some crumbs from the counter into my hand. "That's not even the main issue," I say quietly.

"What is?"

I lower my voice and glance at the front door. "Him. If I leave I won't be here for him. He's the only dad I've ever had."

"You're right. I know it. *He* knows it. And you also might be right about not being around here when he goes if you leave for school. And still I think you ought to go."

"Nobody thinks my being here for him is as important as I do."

"Of course we think it's important." Aunt Betsy motions to the table. She pulls out a chair and sits. I join her. "Death is frightening and I know how tempting it is to let fear guide our steps."

"That's not what I'm—"

"Hold on." Aunt Betsy raises her hand. "I took Blake and left my lifelong home to move to Nashville so's he could attend art school there. You know how that turned out."

"I do."

"Would he have gotten into that car accident if we hadn't moved there? No. Would he have had the amazing opportunities he had, the friends he made, if we hadn't moved there? Also no. You knew Blake."

"Yes."

"He and I talked about almost everything. So I know this with great assurance: Blake wouldn't have let death make that decision for him. He wouldn't have traded the wonderful friends he made there, and the life we built, just to put off the inevitable. How concerned is Pep about dying while you're gone?"

"Obviously not much," I say.

Aunt Betsy gets up, goes to the fridge, and retrieves her glass mixing bowl of banana pudding. She gets out five small bowls and spoons. She returns to the table and serves me a generous helping. "I think the real problem is you feel so lucky to have survived what you did, you think you bagged your limit of luck by finishing out your childhood in a safe and loving home."

I stare at the table and toy with my spoon. "I'm serious about worrying over Papaw dying."

Aunt Betsy takes a bite and catches a piece of Nilla Wafer before it can fall. "Losing your mama was a big deal. I know you're afraid to lose what you have left. If you go, you can always come back later. That's what I did."

My throat narrows. "I'm scared."

"I'd be too. I don't guess this is a decision you ever thought you'd have to make."

"Nope."

"You trust me if I make you a promise?"

"Yeah."

"You'll never regret a decision more than the one you make out of fear. Fear tells you to make your life small. Fear tells you to think small. Fear tells you to be small-hearted. Fear seeks to preserve itself, and the bigger you let your life and perspective and heart get, the less air you give fear to survive."

Aunt Betsy and I hold each other's gaze for a long while. She and Papaw have the same eyes. Gentle, but piercing when they need to be. Sometimes both at once, like now.

"You *had* to use an example about not being able to breathe?" I let a little smile tug at the corner of my mouth.

Aunt Betsy snorts through the bite of banana pudding she just took. She covers her mouth, and shakes and chokes with laughter.

I laugh with her. "I'm going to hell for that joke."

"You kidding me? I know my brother. Pep would be so proud."

Our laughter subsides. "I don't want to live a fearful life," I say soberly.

"So don't. The opportunity is there. Take it. You are a *courageous* young man."

Aunt Betsy has this *way*—she reaches you somehow. Papaw was right. I do listen to her. Everyone I most love and respect is telling me the same thing.

I guess maybe it's like this: Sometimes you agonize over something. You war inside yourself trying to defeat uncertainty. Then you look around, and the field of battle is deserted and you've been striking vainly at the air. And there's nothing before you but a path marked Uncertainty. I guess uncertainty isn't always something you can conquer. Sometimes it's a path you have to take.

And I realize something else: Betsy is wrong. I don't have a choice to do this.

I have to do it.

"Guess we should take some of this out to the others before we eat it all," I murmur.

"I guess we ought," Betsy says, looking me square in the eye.

I rise and pick up the bowl of banana pudding, and I can tell she sees me trying to stand a bit taller.

Chapter 11

There's a secret place we go that overlooks the town, its hazy lights unfurling under us in the muggy night. Above us, mirroring them, the summer stars float bright and creamy in a sea of indigo.

We sit on the tailgate of my pickup, our legs gently swinging. I grin at Delaney as she licks banana pudding from the front of her plastic spoon, then the back, then the front again.

"What?" she asks.

"I say something?"

"I feel your judging stare."

"I think you might've missed a molecule there."

"See?"

"I had three massive bowls of Betsy's pudding myself. It just cracks me up how much you love sugar. You work with it all day long; I can still bring you more and know you'll appreciate it."

Delaney shrugs. "Nothing wrong with sugar, other than many scientists think it's literally low-grade poison." She raises the clear plastic container so it's backlit from below, scanning it for lingering traces of banana pudding.

"Don't get your head stuck in it trying to lick it out."

"Stop pudding-shaming me."

"So." I fidget and toy with a twig next to me. "I actually had something I needed to talk to you about."

"So talk."

My heart patters in my ears. "I'm gonna do it."

"What are you talking about?" Delaney sets her container and spoon to the side and eyes me warily.

I let a few seconds pass with my eyebrows raised. Let her guess.

"Do *what*?"

"Middleford. I'm going." I pause for her ecstatic response.

She starts weeping into her hands.

Delaney doesn't always act the way you'd expect, and this is a surprise. I reach out gingerly to touch her shoulder. "Red. Hey. Hey. Delaney. Hey." She allows me to put my arm around her, and she flows into my side like two raindrops meeting on a window. I rock her gently back and forth. This has helped before and it helps now.

"You being serious?" Her voice is frail and tear-sodden.

"I am."

"You're going to school with me in the fall." She says it like she's defying me to deny it.

"If they'll have me still."

She weeps. "I'm not gonna be alone?"

"Nope." I hug her tight to my side. Her tears soak warm into my T-shirt.

"Why the change?" She wipes her eyes with the back of her hand.

"You. Papaw. I had a talk with Aunt Betsy tonight that kinda sealed it."

"You scared to go?"

"Course I am."

"I was terrified. But now much less." She draws a deep, shuddering breath and wipes her eyes again.

"Shit, hang on." I jump off the tailgate and walk to the cab. I rummage under the seat and come up with an unopened box of candy canes. They're her favorite candy—maybe her favorite food. I buy a few extra boxes every Christmas and keep them around in case I ever need to get myself out of hot water. This time, I brought it to celebrate, but tonight it'll pull double duty. I return and hand it to Delaney.

She beams and pokes a hole in the cellophane of the box, sliding her finger underneath and tearing it off.

I stare incredulously. *"Now?* You just ate a huge container of banana pudding and had who-knows-how-much sugar at work."

"You worry about you," she says, stripping the wrapper off a candy cane and sucking on the end.

"They're your teeth and liver."

"The pancreas regulates blood sugar." She offers me the box. "Naw, thanks."

"You've been changing your mind a lot lately. Celebrate with me."

I sigh. "Gimme a damn candy cane. Lord."

She hands me one. I unwrap it and hold it up, with my pinky out, as if it's a champagne flute. "To the future."

"To the future." She giggles and raises her candy cane. "I can't believe it."

"Don't tap it with the end you've been sucking on. I don't need to get sick from the taste *and* your germs."

"Oh please, if we were up here to hook up like any normal high school guy and girl, you wouldn't care."

"No, but that'd be more worth it than getting sick for a candy cane."

The funny thing is, I know I'm right on this. Delaney and I did make out once. Well, we kissed. It was almost exactly a year ago. We were intoxicated on moonlight, and I guess we looked pretty good to each other at that moment. For my part, I'd have been perfectly okay with doing it more. A lot more. But I got the vibe it freaked Delaney out. Made sense. Neither of us had much outside of our friendship, and we came to a mostly unspoken agreement that we weren't going to risk it on a fling. Sawyer was too small for that. Plus, I'd always sort of assumed that Delaney would end up with someone much smarter than me, so why break my heart for nothing?

Still, I'd be lying if I said I didn't think about that kiss sometimes. For someone who'd never, to my knowledge, had a boyfriend, Delaney was a bizarrely good kisser. Somehow her genius extended to that.

I put the end of a candy cane in my mouth. "Mmmmmmmm, hard toothpaste stick."

"Eat shit."

"Already am. Of the peppermint-flavored variety. Feels weird and gross to be eating a candy cane when it's so hot and sticky out."

Delaney shrugs and nibbles off a small section. "It's like having an air conditioner blow directly in your mouth."

"Oh. *That* thing people definitely enjoy. Having AC blow right in their mouth." I manage to suck the end of my candy cane down to a sharp point before I've had all I can stand.

Delaney savors hers like a fine cigar. "Did you know that as of 2020, President John Tyler had two living grandsons?"

I look at her incredulously. "Wasn't he like the fourth president or something?"

"Tenth. From 1841 to 1845. Born in 1790."

I shake my head. "There are two people alive today whose papaw was born in *1790*? How?"

"John Tyler had kids when he was super old. That kid had kids when *he* was super old. Those kids are super old. Think about it. If someone had a kid when they were eighty, and that kid had a kid when they were eighty, and that kid lived to be eighty, you've got a span of two hundred forty years. That's almost the age of the US."

"This is blowing my mind. I think Mamaw and Papaw had my mama when they were like twenty-four. My mama had me when she was seventeen. I'm sixteen."

"It's called a human wormhole when this happens. When people live long enough to create what seems like an impossible link to the past. Here's another. There was a witness to Abraham Lincoln's assassination on a TV game show in 1956. He was in Ford's Theatre as a five-year-old."

"Whoa."

"Supreme Court Justice Oliver Wendell Holmes shook hands with President John Quincy Adams and President John F. Kennedy." Delaney grows contemplative. She unwraps another candy cane and gnaws the end pensively. "I've started to think about my future for the first time."

"Yeah?"

"I never let myself have dreams. Didn't want to be disappointed."

"All those projects you've done, all that reading—"

"It was something to pass time that didn't involve pulling the fentanyl out of a patch and shooting it up or getting pregnant. Just wanted to die with a full brain."

"Now?"

"I want to go to MIT. I'm gonna become an epidemiologist with the CDC."

"Maybe I need to start dreaming a little bigger."

"Wouldn't hurt."

We sit for a while without speaking, taking in the man-made firefly phosphorescence beneath us.

"We should visit New York City," Delaney murmurs. "It's close to Middleford."

"You said you wanted to do that. Go to all of the museums."

"Yeah." She giggles. Then starts full-on laughing. "I can't believe this is really real. This is happening. To *us*." She sighs and hugs me around the middle, from the side.

I put my arm around her shoulders and pull her close to me. We have a physical intimacy that people usually mistake for romantic if they don't know I'm the only source where Delaney gets hugs.

"Who knows where the future will take us," she says through a deep yawn.

I shake my head. *One of these days, life is going to take us down separate paths. Just not yet.*

Within a few minutes, her breathing slows and she goes limp in sleep. This happens to her sometimes when we're together. She saves up vigilance for the times she doesn't feel safe—it's what I used to do—and it all comes crashing down when she's in a secure place, a burden she can no longer bear.

You're her safe harbor. You're where she can rest. I knew, on some level, what it would mean to her if I went with her. But it didn't really sink in until now.

She sat by me at my mama's funeral, holding my hand, a faint violet bruise on her cheekbone, where one of her mama's boyfriends had knocked her around.

We were always meant to be side by side in this world for as long as we could be. Always.

I let her sleep as long as I can before I need to get home. When the time comes, I gently extricate myself from her grip—firm even in slumber, like she's afraid she'll get swept off by flood-waters if she lets go—and carry her bird-bone weight to the cab of my truck, buckling her in. She slumps against her window for the trip back to my house. I drive with extra caution, to not jostle her. When I arrive, I carry her slowly up the front steps, taking pains not to wake up Papaw and Mamaw. I lay her on my bed, pull off her worn flip-flops, and set them on the floor. I tuck her in, and she curls into a fetal position with a faint mewling noise and the grinding of teeth.

For a second I consider checking her thumbs to see how torn up they are. They're a reliable indicator of how she's doing. But I don't, because it bugs her when I do that when she's awake.

Her mama won't care or even notice that she didn't come home. This isn't the first time Delaney's spent the night at my house. If people knew, they'd talk. Let them talk. Mamaw and Papaw won't mind. They know her life.

As I nest on the couch a few yards from where Delaney

sleeps, I ponder, *Why me? Why me to be allowed to know this strange and remarkable girl and all that comes with her?*

I've seen that life is filled with unimaginable horror. But it's also threaded through with unimaginable wonder.

Live through enough of the one, maybe you're due some of the other.

We tell Mamaw and Papaw in the morning when we wake up. Papaw coughs for a solid two minutes in excitement. He and Mamaw take turns hugging the breath from Delaney. Mamaw throws together a quick celebration breakfast—I have to mow lawns. While we're eating, she looks up the school. Turns out I'll need a new wardrobe. The dress code for boys is navy blazers, button-down shirts, ties, khaki pants, and leather dress shoes.

"We'll have to pay a visit to Sawyer Dry Goods when my check comes," Papaw says. "Get you some new duds."

"No," Mamaw says. "He's going to a fancy school. He needs nicer clothes. We're going to Sevierville, to the Old Navy."

Chapter 12

I pass the rest of the summer working as hard as I can and saving furiously. The scholarship covers tuition, board, and meals, and that's about it. Any spending money comes from me. On top of mowing lawns, I get a job working a few nights a week stocking shelves at the Tractor Supply Company.

I don't see much of Jason Cloud. He must have heard Delaney and I were leaving and lost interest in us. It's not like his drug-selling business is hurting. And, as Delaney pointed out, who even needs help to find new and exciting opioids to kill people with when you have Chinese and American pharmaceutical companies innovating for you?

But I run into him once more that summer. We're stopped on opposite sides of an intersection, and when our eyes meet, mine bore into his. For all the time we're stopped, I don't look away. I don't shrink. His eyes are vacant and dim, those of a starving man whose only thought is his hunger. I guess when you love money like he does, you're perpetually starving.

Delaney's mama worsens. Delaney has to Narcan her back from the brink of death at least once, that I know of. Three hours later, her mama was back out looking for a fix. Their electricity gets cut off. Then their water. They start getting eviction notices. By the end of summer, Delaney is essentially living at our house.

Papaw's health deteriorates too. But one shining morning a few weeks before I'm set to leave, he wakes up and he's having one of his good days. He asks me to take him out on the river. I call my lawn-mowing appointments and tell them I can't make it and why. They understand.

He sits in the front of the canoe, like I used to, with his oxygen tank. He doesn't paddle. He's not having *that* good a day. I sit in the back, the way he used to, and paddle for us both.

We stop at the bank for a while to rest, still sitting in the canoe, the water slapping gently at the sides like the sound of a baby clapping.

Papaw looks around, lances of sunlight piercing the clouds, insects flitting across the river's surface. A golden day.

"This is a beautiful world," he murmurs.

"Yeah, it is."

"I'm going to miss it when I'm gone."

I start to say, *It'll miss you too*. But my voice catches.

Fortunately, he doesn't look back. I can't bear eye contact with him in this moment. He keeps gazing outward. "If I make the cut, I hope heaven is this exactly. To hell with your clouds and harps. Give me a fine day on the water with my grandson. It don't get no better'n this."

My throat aches as it dams up sobs.

Papaw turns and looks at me. His eyes are ancient and gray as a February sky weighted with snow. "I hope you bring your children and grandchildren here."

I nod and try to speak, but the bulwark breaks and tears cascade down my face. I can't meet his gaze anymore.

He gives me a slight, sad smile. "Mickey Mouse?" he says softly, and waits until I meet his eyes again. "I love you." He falters as he says it, but not as if doubting what he is saying. Like someone who believes what they're saying so much that saying it doesn't feel like enough. There's only so much weight words can bear.

"I love you too." I hear the same hitch in my voice.

"We best get home."

"Yessir."

As we turn into the boat pullout, I'm certain this is the final time I'll ever be on the river with my papaw.

But then he turns and asks me quietly if I'll scatter his ashes on the river when he's gone, as we did with my mama, and I know that this is the second-to-last time I'll ever be in this hallowed place with him.

Chapter 13

The week before we leave is a tornado of preparation. We go to the Old Navy in Sevierville to get school outfits. Delaney needs new clothes too. Blouses. Skirts. We buy hers also. What little savings she had squirreled away, she spent to pay up the rent on her mama's trailer—a parting gift. She sent the money directly to her mama's creditors so it couldn't be used for drugs.

I ask Delaney what's going to happen to her mama when she's gone. She doesn't say anything but gives me a slight shrug, then looks down and back up at me, like I already know. And I do.

Four days before we go, I drive Delaney to Nashville to get an abscessed tooth pulled. I'd caught her trying to find a YouTube video on how to do it herself. I contacted Dr. Srinavasan, who called in a favor with a Yale classmate who's an oral surgeon at Vanderbilt.

Delaney refuses to accept a prescription for Lortab.

The surgeon says, "You don't have to fill it. But if the pain gets bad enough, you'll be grateful for it."

"I know. I don't want to want it," Delaney says. "Even if the pain is too much. But thanks for pulling that tooth. It hurt like shit." And that's that.

Two days before we go, I take Delaney, still aching, to the Knoxville zoo. We spend all day there, her face alive with wonder in spite of her discomfort. She cries on the drive home and I don't ask why. I know it's not tooth pain.

The day before we go, Mamaw and Aunt Betsy make a huge dinner. Papaw mans the grill until he can't anymore and Aunt Betsy takes over. We invite Delaney, but she says she wants to be alone. It sounds more like she doesn't really want to be alone but needs to be.

Chapter 14

I rise with the sun on the morning we're leaving. I drive to the river. Mist whispers from its surface in the early September dawn. I remove my boots and socks, pull the hems of my jeans up, and wade in. The water feels like the cool side of a pillow on my skin. I stand there for a moment, the current coursing past my bare calves and ankles.

But I'm still hungry for communion, so I wade farther in, filling my lungs with the dew-scented air, and immersing myself completely in baptism.

Carry off my fear like it's sin.

Fill my reservoir of courage.

Cleanse me of doubt.

Make me strong enough to cut myself a path through the world, like you.

Remind me that there are things I love that can last.

Goodbye.

I rise from the water, letting each drop falling off me rejoin the march to the ocean. "If you can see me, Mama, I hope you're proud," I say to the currents that bore away her ashes. Before I go, I fill a glass Dr. Enuf bottle to take with me.

This must be what it's like to die. You look around you and see how much of what you love you leave behind.

Chapter 15

After everything, we didn't have the money for plane tickets to school. Papaw and Mamaw were embarrassed, but I told them I was scared to fly because I've never flown before, which isn't a lie. So we bought Greyhound tickets. Twenty hours on a bus, from Knoxville to Stamford, Connecticut.

Mamaw and Papaw drive us to the bus station. They told Delaney her mama could come. She said her mama couldn't make it. I question whether she passed along the invitation. I doubt even more her mama would have accepted.

Mamaw and Papaw hug Delaney and kiss her on the cheek.

"We're going to have a good *Longmire* party when I come back over Christmas break," Delaney says to Papaw.

"I'll bank on it. You go and figure out how to save the world."

Delaney gives Papaw her crooked smile. "I will." She pauses for a second. "Love you, Pep." She says it with the unsteady lilt of a question.

Papaw beams and doesn't hesitate. "Love you too, Tess. See my grandson don't trip over his shoelaces up there."

She smiles wanly and boards the bus.

Mamaw gives me a bear hug and a kiss on the cheek. "We're so proud of you," she says, on the thin edge of losing composure. "You'll do great things. I know it."

"I'll hug you all right," Papaw says. "But first I'm gonna shake your hand how I'd shake a man's hand. You're a man today." He looks me in the eye and shakes my hand, his grip strong and callused. He starts to cough but tamps it down. I see him fighting for his old strength, pressing his whole weight against the coughs that would fold him in half in a moment when he's trying to stand his tallest, trying not to cry. Then, he pulls me into him, his hand on the back of my head, pressing his cheek on the crown. I feel him trembling and then surrendering. He quakes with muffled weeping.

He puts his damp cheek, lined as a valley of rivers, to mine and whispers hoarsely in my ear, "Go make us proud. I will not leave without telling you goodbye in the flesh. God as my witness, I won't. I love you, Mickey Mouse."

Chapter 16

For the first hours of the journey, we're glued to the window, ticking off every milestone.

First time leaving Tennessee.

First time in Virginia.

First time seeing a bird in Virginia.

First time eating in Virginia.

First time pissing in Virginia.

The bus has Wi-Fi, and outlets at our seats to charge our phones, so we read about Middleford Academy until our eyes burn. We put together possible class schedules, even though they told us counselors would need to help us with that. We google teachers. We google famous alums of the school (there are many). As dusk settles and the ride becomes less scenic, we watch movies on my phone using Papaw and Mamaw's Netflix account, sharing a set of earbuds.

Soon, there's only blackness outside.

A dense, coarse blanket of fatigue drapes itself over me, and without the excitement and elation of the early journey to fight it off, a fog of fear and melancholy begins to creep in, a deep sense of foreboding and regret.

Delaney can feel it radiating off me. Or maybe I'm absorbing light, the way she told me black holes do. She starts talking about near-impossible journeys. What it would be like to send humans to Mars.

"They've thought about sending whole families, to combat loneliness and incompatibility," she tells me.

"Sorta like us right now," I say.

"Sorta."

As it grows later, one by one, each reading light and glow from a tablet or phone disappears. The family across from us succumbs to sleep, huddled together.

Our conversation becomes more yawns than words, and soon, more silence than words or even yawns.

Delaney nestles herself into my side and asks me, "If you could know everyone who's ever loved you, would you want to know?"

I think about my answer for a few moments. *Would I? Would it be better to know that someone you never thought loved you did love you? Or would it be worse to know that someone you always thought loved you didn't?*

It's not a question you can answer, like so many she poses, and I go to tell her so. By the time I do, though, she's sound asleep—soon twitching and jerking as her slumber deepens. Careful not to rouse her, I pull a hoodie out of my backpack and drape it over her. I sit with my ghostly reflection in the finger-smudged window for company, as the new and sprawling American countryside blurs past us in the darkness.

FALL

Chapter 17

We exit the bus, glassy-eyed, the spiky mechanical stink of diesel exhaust singeing our noses. September here feels like October would in Tennessee—summer losing its grip. We're almost to our final destination, but my adrenal glands went dry about twelve hours ago, so I can't muster much excitement. My mouth is parched. I didn't drink much because I didn't like using the bus restroom. It reminded me of the bathroom in my mama's and my trailer. I open a stick of Big Red and pop it in my mouth. I offer one to Delaney.

She takes it, unwraps it, and starts chewing. "Officially that trip was twenty-four hours and five minutes."

"Felt like three days."

We collect our bags. Delaney slept better than I did—or at least longer—but she still has a dazed and shell-shocked energy. A hank of her hair bulges from the side of her head where she nestled against me.

"Come here," I say, smoothing her hair down. "Gotta look presentable."

Delaney's phone starts buzzing. She answers. "Hello? Yeah, hi. This is her. Yep. Yep. He's with me. Got them. Okay. White van? Okay. Got it. Thanks. Okay. Bye."

"Our ride?"

"Yep. We're meeting him on Station Place. Look for a white van with *Middleford Academy* on it."

We orient ourselves and walk out to the street. A white van pulls up. A squat, ruddy middle-aged man wearing a cabbie hat and a navy blazer with too-long sleeves hops out with a grunt. He exudes good cheer. I like him immediately.

"You my two pickups?" He doesn't give us a chance to answer before he's at our side, grabbing our bags from us and tossing them in the back of the van.

"Hope so," Delaney says. "Because it looks like we're coming with you."

He laughs wheezily. "You looked lost. I've picked up enough Middleford kids to know." He extends his hand to her. "Chris DiSalvo."

They shake. "Delaney Doyle."

He extends his hand to me. "Chris DiSalvo."

"Cash Pruitt."

"Pleasure to meet you." He opens the side door for us to get in.

I help Delaney into the van and follow behind. It smells like cherry inside. "You're the first person from Connecticut I've ever met," I say.

Chris laughs as he opens his door. "Aw now, that's a lotta pressure. Meg Ryan. She's from Connecticut. There's a good ambassador."

"Katharine Hepburn too." Delaney buckles her seat belt and continues. "Ethan Allen. Noah Webster. Annie Leibovitz. Charles Goodyear. J. P. Morgan. Suzanne Collins. P. T. Barnum. Samuel Colt. Henry Ward Beecher. Dean Acheson. Christopher Lloyd. Karen Carpenter. Glenn Close. Paul Giamatti."

"All from Connecticut?" Chris puts the van in gear and pulls away from the curb.

"So I read."

"See? They all represent Connecticut better than me. And I don't even know half of them."

"Michael Bolton."

"Okay, maybe not him." He glances back. "You rattling these off from memory?"

"Yep."

He whistles. "Jeez Louise. Been driving Middleford kids around for fifteen years now, and they sure don't let dummies into this school."

Not unless they're friends with a genius.

I like how he talks. He says *sure* like *suah* and *sharp* like *shop*. I've only ever heard a New England accent on TV before.

We drive in silence for a while. I stare out. I've watched so much landscape sweeping past a window over the last twenty-four hours, it's hard to make myself look, but curiosity compels me. Green foliage hugs tight the sides of the four-lane road in a familiar way. It's not as hilly as Tennessee, but otherwise it looks similar. That's something. I haven't yet started to feel the pangs of homesickness, but I know I will.

It's like Chris read my mind. "Now, to listen to you talk, you guys aren't from around here." He gestures back first at me and then at Delaney. "You more than you. But both of you, it's pretty obvious."

"We're from Sawyer, Tennessee," Delaney says. She's also fixed to the window.

"Where's that?"

"Near the Smoky Mountains."

97

Realization dawns on Chris's face. He snaps his fingers. "Hey. They told me about you guys. Said you invented a new medicine?"

"Sorta," Delaney says. "We discovered an antibiotic fungus."

"*She* did," I interject.

"*We* did." Delaney glowers at me.

We'll need to figure out the choreography of this discussion, because it's one I imagine we'll be having a lot in the days to come.

Chris laughs wheezily and raises a hand, cutting us off. "Look, it's more antibiotic than *I've* ever discovered, okay? Anyhow. Now that you're here, we're gonna have to get you some lobster rolls. Some clam pizza. Make Pats fans outta you."

"My papaw would skin me alive if I ever had a favorite football team that wasn't the University of Tennessee," I say.

"Just the lobster rolls and clam pizza, then."

We fall quiet again.

"Long trip?" Chris asks.

"Twenty-four hours," Delaney says.

"Go through New York?"

"We had a stopover there to switch buses," I say.

"Early as you guys got in," Chris says, "you weren't even my first stop of the day. Picked up this young lady from Dubai. Flew in on a private jet. Considered asking her, 'Don't you have a limo for this kinda thing?' But she told me—get this—she preferred to pull up to the school like a normal kid."

Delaney and I glance at each other. *We're going to be meeting a whole new type of person. The sort who actually belongs at a school like this. A sort not like us.* The slow creep of anxiety starts passing through me.

Chris reads our silence and sounds apologetic. "Private jets, Greyhounds. We're just glad you get here safe. You guys are gonna love Middleford. We're only a couple minutes out."

We pass a sign for the school. A couple of minutes later, true to his word, Middleford Academy looms into view. Forested hills surround the school. I breathe faster, whirring with anxious energy. *Please don't be the place where I disappoint Papaw and Mamaw and Delaney.*

Delaney has a sickly pall to her face. She starts to lift her thumb to her mouth. I intercept her gently. She puts her hands under her thighs and starts bouncing her legs like she has to pee.

We slow and turn onto a long drive. At the end is an imposing mechanized gate with a guard shack. Chris turns back to us. "Welcome to your new home."

Queasiness spreads through my lower belly as I look out the window at the ivy-covered buildings. It's exactly as I imagined: a place I could never imagine myself being.

As he drives, Chris points out stuff. "You got your Elm residence hall. Javits residence hall right next door. Name 'em all after trees or big donors. Dining hall over there. Those are classroom buildings. That's the athletic center. You a lifter?"

I'm so busy ogling I miss the question. "Do what?"

"The athletic center's got weights and such. You a lifter? Look like you are."

"Oh . . . no. Just work. Landscaping. Chopping wood."

"Chopping wood? Regular Paul Bunyan here." Chris points off to the left. "Hey, Miss Memory, there's the library. You gotta couple days before school starts to memorize all the books."

Delaney smiles shyly. "Duly noted."

Chris nods right. "There's your auditorium. Three times a week they have an assembly there before class. Back behind it is the lake. Nice little path goes around it."

It's not quite eight a.m. yet and it's the Friday before school starts, but there's still a fair amount of activity. Two girls and two guys stroll toward the athletic center in workout gear. Two girls in hijabs sit on a bench, showing each other things on their phones. There's a mishmash of small U-Hauls and luxury SUVs parked around the residence halls, with parents helping kids lug in boxes.

I feel a sudden, sharp pang of missing Mamaw and Papaw. I snap a few pictures to send them.

"What do you think?" I murmur to Delaney, who looks simultaneously petrified and ecstatic.

"Looks like a school."

"Guess this is really happening." My voice is uncertain, like it's walking on ice.

"Guess so."

We pull up in front of a stately stone building with an Administration sign on the lawn out front. "Ladies and gentlemen . . . we have arrived," Chris says grandly.

We hop out. Chris helps us to the curb with our bags. "They'll get you checked in. This is only farewell for the moment. I'm gonna see you guys plenty over the next year." He extends a hand to Delaney and tips his cap. "Miss Memory, it's been a pleasure. I'd tell you good luck, but I don't think you'll need it." He turns to me. "Paul Bunyan, good luck to you too. Head through those doors. Office is on the right. They'll take good care of you." Chris walks back to the van, gets in, and drives away.

Delaney and I stand there for a second, our bags surrounding us. I sling on my backpack and heft my two suitcases. "Might as well do this, I guess." I start to walk up to the front door.

"Wait," Delaney says, her voice abruptly thorny.

I turn to her.

"Let's get something straight right now, because I don't want this to become a thing. This aw-shucks-I-don't-deserve-to-be-here horseshit. Knock it off."

"They're waiting for us." I head toward the building.

"They can wait. We're talking about this now."

"Jeez. It's how I feel."

"Stick how you feel right up your ass," she says loudly.

I stride back to Delaney. *"Calm down.* This how you wanna arrive? Acting like a couple hillbillies arguing on the front lawn first damn day? Shit. Should I take off my shirt? Get some deputies down here to stand between us?"

"Don't tell me to calm down."

"Talk quieter." I touch her elbow.

She slaps my hand away. "Don't tell me to talk quieter."

"What's your problem?"

Delaney gets in my face. "My problem is, your little act makes us both look stupid. It makes me look like some nepotistic hillbilly mayor who makes her brother-in-law chief of police."

"I don't think—"

"Don't interrupt me. It makes *you* look like someone who's willing to ride my coattails and take something you didn't earn. That what you want?"

"You're tired."

"Condescend to me again."

"We're *both* tired. We were on a bus for twenty-four hours."

"I stuck my neck out for you."

"I know."

"So stop acting like you shouldn't be here."

"I'm sorry. Okay? I didn't think of it like that. I screwed up."

"You're done saying you don't belong here. I can't stop you from thinking it, even though it's dumb and not true. But if you do, keep it to yourself."

"Fine. I promise. Happy?"

Delaney picks up her bags.

"Red?"

She takes a deep breath.

"We good?" I ask.

"Yeah."

"We have to be a team," I say. "We can't afford to be at each other's throats."

"Being at your throat is usually the only thing I *can* afford," Delaney says.

"I'm serious, Red. I know you're gonna be you, but you gotta cut me some slack every now and again."

"Fine. But don't do dumb stuff." This was generally as close as Delaney got to an apology.

"I try not to. Hug it out?"

She nods.

I embrace her. "We're here. In Connecticut. Standing at our new school."

"I know," she says, breaking the hug and pushing me away. "We better stop standing and start walking." She heads toward the administration building, lugging her suitcases. She tries not to let me see, but a smile sneaks onto her face.

Chapter 18

They buzz us into the administration office, and a youngish, stylishly dressed woman greets us. She moves with crisp but warm efficiency.

"Hello, hello! Welcome to Middleford! Delaney and Cash?"

We nod.

"I'm Yolanda Clark, one of the associate directors of admissions here. I'll be getting you settled in. How was the trip? How did you guys come?"

"Greyhound," I say.

Yolanda's face briefly registers surprise. "From . . . Tennessee?"

"Correct," I say.

"*Wow*, you two must be tired."

"Yeah," Delaney says. "We slept some, but I don't think I ever entered REM sleep."

Yolanda seems unfazed by Delaney's scientific precision. "Well, let's do this: Are you hungry?"

Delaney and I nod.

"We'll swing by the dining hall, get you some breakfast, take you to your residence halls, get you squared away, let you sleep for a few hours before you meet with your counselors to put your schedules together. Good?"

"Yes," we say.

Yolanda makes a call on a walkie-talkie, and soon after, a golf cart pulls up. We load our bags on the luggage carrier and climb in. I've never ridden in a golf cart before. I sure don't know when Delaney would have.

On the short ride, Yolanda rattles off facts about Middleford. "This school year we have eight hundred twenty-one students enrolled, representing twenty-one countries, from every continent but Antarctica, and twenty-nine states. This makes for a student-to-faculty ratio of six to one. Classes, which have between twelve and fifteen students, are taught using the Harkness method, in which students and teachers sit in a circle around a table and have a discussion—it's not a teacher standing in front of a room full of kids, lecturing at them while they text and fall asleep."

The driver drops us off at the dining hall. Yolanda instructs him to go on and leave our luggage at the front desks of our respective dorms.

"I understand you two are already pretty close?"

"Best friends," Delaney says.

Yolanda smiles. "That's great. I'm an alum of Middleford. I came from Oakland, California, and I would have *loved* to have come here with a friend. Anyway, Delaney, you're going to be in the Maple dorm, and Cash, you're going to be in the Koch dorm."

"Like the drink?"

"Like the brothers. David Koch's son went here." Yolanda says this as we walk through the doors to the dining hall.

It smells like a real restaurant inside. It triggers memories of going to breakfast at Cracker Barrel with Mamaw and Papaw. The rogue wave of homesickness unbalances me for a second.

It's as though Yolanda can see it. "Now, have you called your parents to let them know you got here safely?"

"Yeah," Delaney says. She's lying. I would know—she hasn't been out of my sight, even to use the restroom, since we arrived.

"Not yet," I say.

"Let's do that as soon as things quiet down," Yolanda says.

We get plates of scrambled eggs, pancakes, and bacon. There are many other choices. Bagels. Breakfast burritos. Roasted potatoes with peppers. I promise myself I'll branch out a little more. But not today. We sit.

Realization dawns on Yolanda's face. "Hang on." She gets up and walks quickly back to the kitchen. She returns a few seconds later, beaming, a small plate in each hand. "Middleford bars. A proud tradition. On the first week of school, we actually mail these to people who graduated the year before to remind them of the fun they had at Middleford."

I didn't realize how hungry I was until now. I feel like I'm sinking into the floor with exhaustion. Small groups of students sit and chat brightly. Nobody is wearing their uniforms, and they seem to be living it up in pajama bottoms and hoodies. Here and there a student sits alone, headphones on, fixated on their phone or laptop.

Delaney scans the room, processing, computing, deducing, downloading information to her memory, looking for patterns and formulas to understand her new environment, some grand theory to predict some grand phenomenon.

Yolanda left the office with a portfolio under her arm. She opens it. Her nails are painted the blue of the night sky after the sun's been below the horizon for an hour. "Would you like an introduction to your roommates?"

Delaney still looks deep in thought but nods absently.

"Yes, please," I say. The reality of the situation hits me. *You're going to be living in a room with a total stranger. Sleeping. Dreaming. Studying.*

"We try to put new students with other new students." Yolanda scans a paper. "So . . . Cash. You'll be rooming with Patrick McGrath III—he goes by Tripp. He's from Phoenix, Arizona. His father was actually just elected to the US House of Representatives."

My newly full stomach roils. *Hope you're a good guy, Tripp. Sounds like you're a rich and powerful one.*

"Now for you, Delaney." Yolanda leafs through her papers. "Here we go. Viviani Xavier. I think I'm saying that right? The *X* is a *sh* sound. She comes to us from Rio de Janeiro, Brazil."

"You better brush up on your Spanish," I tell Delaney.

"They speak Portuguese in Brazil," Delaney says. "It's the language most spoken in South America."

"Viviani speaks excellent English," Yolanda says. "You'll have no trouble communicating."

"Rio de Janeiro is closer to Boston than it is to Houston," Delaney says.

Yolanda looks at Delaney for a second. "Is that true?"

"Yes," I mutter immediately. "Guarantee."

"But Houston is *much* farther south than Boston, and Rio is in South America," Yolanda says.

Delaney shrugs. "Check it."

Yolanda turns over the phone that she had laid facedown on the table. "Okay, I believe you, but I have to see numbers . . . Boston to Rio: 4,845 miles. Houston to Rio: 5,022 miles. Wow."

Delaney smiles slightly. "I need to learn more about Rio. I

wish I'd known in advance who my roommate would be so I could have studied up."

We get to our Middleford bars. They're basically chess pie in bar form. No wonder they're a beloved tradition.

While eating, Yolanda tells us about day-to-day logistics: how our student IDs work as a debit card to buy things on campus and do laundry, how we show them in the dining hall. She gives us a forecast of what our daily and weekly schedules will look like.

As we've been sitting and talking, individual students and small groups have trickled in. Parents accompany some. There's a studied casualness about the other kids that unsettles me.

"How competitive is it here? Between students?" I ask.

Yolanda mulls the question. "It's competitive. You can't put this many overachievers in one place and avoid it. But we strive for a collegial and collaborative atmosphere."

Overachiever. I've never once thought of myself using that term. Its weight rests uneasily on me.

Yolanda senses this. "We don't admit anyone who can't keep up. Your being here means you have what it takes."

Delaney gives me a look defying me to renege on our new agreement. I know better and hold my tongue, but I have to stifle the impulse to confess my unworthiness. I see Yolanda's answer has put Delaney somewhat more at ease too. Delaney assaults people with facts and trivia when she's jittery.

Not that I blame her for being on edge. The more I see of Middleford, the more apprehensive I'm getting, feeling like I'm in over my head.

We finish our breakfasts and sit back from empty plates. Yolanda calls over a couple of mousy rising sophomores and introduces us to them. It's strange to me that she's taking pains to introduce us to sophomores, because we'll be juniors, but I go with it. They seem like they'd rather be doing anything but meeting us. I'm not offended. I could really use a couple of hours to clear my head. Plus, Mamaw and Papaw are going to start worrying if I don't check in soon.

"All right," Yolanda says. "On to your new homes."

Chapter 19

Yolanda tells us the residence halls are close, and we're no longer carrying suitcases, so we walk. We arrive at the front doors of Koch Hall, a large brick building.

"Mr. Pruitt, your new home. I'll take you inside. I can't take you up to your floor, in case there are students walking around in towels."

I turn to Delaney. "Okay. Here goes."

"Hope you don't trip all over yourself meeting your new roommate," Delaney murmurs.

"Because his name is Tripp."

"That's right."

"Don't quit whatever ends up being your day job."

"I won't."

"Good luck, Red."

"Same."

"Don't . . ." I motion as if biting my thumb.

After a quick glance at Yolanda, who's busy on her phone and not looking, Delaney gives me a lopsided smile and flips me the bird.

"You two will be seeing each other again in just a few hours," Yolanda says, "so . . ."

"Right," I say. "Let's see my new home."

"You fine hanging out for a minute?" Yolanda asks Delaney.

Delaney is back to observing. She nods without speaking.

"Hey, Cash," Delaney calls after me as we start to walk away. I turn.

"See you in a little bit." She gives me the sort of beseeching expression that says she doesn't want the last thing I remember her doing before our temporary separation is flipping me off. She looks small and alone standing there.

"Bye, Red," I reply.

We enter the dorm building. It smells clean, but not harsh and antiseptic. More like a fancy hotel. Like a warm breeze blowing across a grove of cedar and orange trees. I'm sad that I'm going to go numb to the smell. Delaney told me about something called olfactory fatigue, which is when you just stop detecting scents that are around you every day.

The dorm is orderly and well maintained, and clearly belongs to a wealthy institution, but everything is simple and functional. It almost seems consciously so, like part of the building's purpose is to teach kids—who have lived in, and will again dwell in, far more lavish arrangements—that you can make do with less.

This is probably the worst place some of my new classmates will have ever lived. I remember my mama's and my trailer. The chaos. The rot. Everything broken and peeling and warped. Humidity-swollen doors that wouldn't close right. Suspicious spongy spots on the uneven floor like oozing sores. Perpetually clogged drains. Stains. Stickiness. The skittering of tiny claws and legs in the walls and ceiling. The putrid animal stench. I guess olfactory fatigue doesn't always set in, because I never escaped the stink of our home. Maybe you never acclimate to odors warning of danger and disease. It's why I spent so much time outside. Whatever challenges await me here, tolerating poor physical living conditions will not be among them.

We pick up my suitcases in the lobby. Yolanda turns to me. "Cash, it's been a pleasure. You're going to take the elevator to the fourth floor, and you're in room four thirteen. Get settled in. Unpack. Take a catnap. Get acquainted with your roommate if he's around. At eleven-thirty I'll have someone take you back to the admin building to meet with your counselor and get you all signed up for classes. Good?"

"Good. Thanks."

Yolanda bustles off.

I ride the elevator to the fourth floor. Growing up, I'd never envisioned myself ever living in a place with elevators. My pulse speeds as the numbers on the doors go up. *410. 411. 412. 413.*

I set down my suitcases and knock.

"Come in," a voice calls.

I gently open the door and peek in. "Anyone naked in here?"

"Naw, dude," Tripp (I'm guessing) says. There's a jockish swagger in his voice.

I push the door open a bit wider, lug my suitcases inside, and look upon my new home. A bank of windows takes up much of the wall I'm facing. To my left is a bare-bones twin-sized bed and a spartan mattress. Nothing worse than what I've slept on before. At the foot of it, an unassuming desk and chair abut the wall. Next to that is a large wardrobe.

The right side of the room is a mirror image of the left side. A laptop, a lamp, and various odds and ends cover the desk. What I guess is a lacrosse stick leans against the chair. Tripp lies on the bed, texting, headphones on, one leg crossed over the other. He's wearing white ankle socks, basketball shorts, and a white tank top. Shaggy platinum-blond hair spills from under his baseball cap. He's resort-tan with eyes the color and warmth of blue bottle glass. He has the kind of perfectly defined arm and leg muscles that obviously come not from work but from a gym. A massive container of Muscle Milk sits on the floor next to the head of his bed. He seems like the sort who trails privilege behind him like a wake. He's what the well-off kids at my old high school tried to be but never quite nailed.

Tripp makes no move to get up, so I set down my suitcases, go to him, and extend a hand. "Hey. Cash Pruitt. Good to meet you."

Tripp slaps my palm, one eye still on his phone. "What up. Glad you speak English."

"Oh. Yeah." I'm not sure how to respond to this statement, which Tripp delivered with a faint smirk and an unmistakably contemptuous tone—one that suggested that if I'd had trouble speaking English, I'd be in for a long school year. Not that I'm especially sure at the moment that I'm *not* in for a long school year.

He continues. "I'm just saying."

I laugh nervously. "Jury's still out on how well I speak it." I hope my dumb joke spins this conversation off into less awkward territory.

"At my old school, my first roommate was Taiwanese. It sucked."

"This is your first year here too?"

"Yep. Old school was shitty."

I wait for him to elaborate. He doesn't. "They said you were from Phoenix," I say.

"North Scottsdale."

"My bad."

"Good golf there." Tripp's phone dings, and his eyes snap to it.

"I'm from East Tennessee. Near the Smokies. Town you probably never heard of called Sawyer."

"Cool."

If Tripp is trying to feign interest in my life, he's doing a terrible job.

"Anyway. I'll leave you alone."

Tripp nods absently. His phone dings again.

My heart sinks. I knew this whole experience wasn't going to be easy, but having a warm and friendly roommate would have made things a little easier.

Meeting Tripp makes me think of the people in my life who *do* give a shit about me. In the bustle of arrival and settling in, I've forgotten to call Papaw and Mamaw. I rummage around for my headphones, but I can't find them.

"Hey, man, cool if I videochat with my grandparents?" I ask.

"Knock yourself out," Tripp says.

"I can't find my headphones and I don't wanna bug you."

He shrugs and stares at his phone with a faint smirk, as if to say, *We'll see.*

I sit on the bed and call.

Papaw answers the phone with a coughing fit. "How you doing there, Mickey Mouse? Make it all right?" He wheezes.

"Hey, Papaw. I did. Just ate, and now I'm unpacking. What are you doing?"

"Watching some programs."

"Mamaw there?"

"Left for work a bit ago."

"You got a sec to videochat?"

"I believe I do."

"Get the tablet and the instructions Delaney wrote and call me like we practiced, okay?"

"I'm like as not to screw it up."

"You won't. Follow the sheet."

"Tess said it was idiotproof. Guess we'll see."

I hang up and wait a few minutes. I'm about to call back and check in on him when my phone lights up with the incoming video call. I answer, and Papaw's face fills my screen. Their internet connection is slow, and his picture is poor quality, his movements herky-jerky. He holds the tablet at an awkward angle that distorts his facial features. The lighting is unflattering in our living room, and his skin has a waxen and sallow cast. Purple-blue rings encircle his eyes like bruises. He looks far sicker onscreen than he does in person. I hate how this way of talking robs him of dignity. He wasn't meant to converse through pixels and wires.

But my spirit lifts when I see his face.

"Breaker breaker one nine," he says, using the slang he told me truckers use on their CB radios. "You reading me?"

"Loud and clear," I say, reclining on my bare mattress, mirroring Tripp's pose.

"Good to see your face, Mickey Mouse. How was the ride up there?"

"Long. Tiring."

"I'd guess. How's it up there?"

"It's good. Weather's nice. Wanna see my room?"

He lets a storm of coughs subside. "I surely do."

I hold up my phone and slowly scan the room. "That's my roommate, Tripp."

"Howdy, Tripp!" Papaw calls, and waves. The effort sends him into another coughing spasm.

Tripp, clearly annoyed, looks vaguely in my phone's direction and nods. "'Sup." He makes no effort to return Papaw's cheerful amiability.

I turn the phone back to myself. "I have a couple hours to settle in, then I'm meeting my counselor to sort my schedule. Apparently it's tricky when you transfer."

"Sign up for stuff that'll make you sweat."

"I will. So. How y'all doing?"

Papaw coughs and wheezes. "Just got done running a marathon."

"You win?"

"Came in second."

"Pick up the pace next time." We smile at each other.

Sometimes a clear day will cloud up without your noticing, until a gust of rain-scented wind nearly steals your balance. That's how the homesickness hits my center of gravity in that moment.

I'm not supposed to be lying on a bare mattress in this little room, in this unfamiliar place, with a standoffish stranger—one I now live with. I should be home with Papaw, sitting beside him and Mamaw, sinking into their old sofa, whiling away the morning watching old episodes of *Law & Order* with Papaw as he talks to the TV.

"I miss you and Mamaw already," I say, leaning into the ache.

"House's too empty without you here."

"Delaney says hi."

"Tell Tess we miss her too."

Tripp sighs loudly. He's not looking at me, but it's clear I've exhausted his small reserve of patience. It's probably best that I try to avoid unnecessary conflict right off the bat with someone I have to live with.

"All right," I say. "I'm gonna unpack and try to take a little nap before I get my schedule made."

"If you can, call later and say hi to your mamaw."

"I will. Love you."

"Love you, Mickey Mouse. Do good up there."

I'll sure try. "I will. Bye."

"Bye, now."

I hang up and stare at my phone for a couple of seconds until it goes dark, and then I look at my reflection in the black glass, feeling hollow. I'm putting myself in a lose-lose situation being here. Back home, there was never any risk of disappointing Papaw and Mamaw. Sawyer High was easy. I was good at mowing lawns. Here, the best-case scenario is I do as well as I did back home—and there doesn't seem to be much chance of that. More likely the last thing Papaw sees me accomplish in this world is a string of C's (if I'm lucky) and D's.

"Ep thar," Tripp says, smirking.

I look at him for a second. "What?"

"Ep thar," he says, as if I'm not getting an obvious joke.

"Not following."

"It's how your gramps says 'up there.'"

No one's ever mocked my grandparents to my face. Something volcanic builds in my chest. It grows so quickly, I know it'll detonate if I don't stop it. It's the same wave that engulfed me when I found out what Jason Cloud did to Mamaw. I imagine Papaw: *You get to school and start acting like a roughneck your first day? Hellfire, Mickey Mouse, I believed in you. Didn't I tell you there was more than one way to be a man?* I imagine Delaney: *You get kicked out of school your first damn morning for punching in your roommate's front teeth and leave me here alone? After all I did to get you in here? You piece of shit.* I don't want to let her down any more than I want to let down my grandparents.

"Hadn't noticed," I say, looking away, breathing down the sizzle of adrenaline.

"It's funny."

"Guess if you aren't from where we're from."

"What's it you called him?"

I don't want to say it. But I do, to keep the peace. "Papaw."

"Papaw?" He snickers.

"It's an East Tennessee thing." *I should have waited until I found my headphones.*

"You must have gotten a fire-ass scholarship."

Because we sound unsophisticated and hillbilly. I want him to stop prying. I don't feel like telling him why I called my grandparents instead of my parents.

Tripp turns, sits at the edge of his bed, and stands, stretching and yawning. He slips on a pair of New Balance running shoes. "Hitting the gym." He picks up a duffel bag at the foot of his bed and starts to leave, sauntering with an easy arrogance. He's almost out the door when he turns back. "By the way, your pop-pop or whatever sounds like shit. He should go to the doctor— like today." There's no concern in Tripp's voice, only the casual contempt of someone annoyed at the inconvenient reminder that our bodies fail us and we die.

"Yeah," I murmur to the door as it closes behind Tripp. "I know."

After Tripp leaves, I make my bed and put away my clothes. It doesn't take long. I hide my bottle of river water under my socks.

The emotional and physical toll of the last twenty-four-plus hours overtakes me, and I try to sleep, the familiar smell of the Arm & Hammer laundry detergent that Mamaw uses perfuming my sheets and salving my homesickness a bit. But every time I'm about to drift off, Tripp's mockery reverberates in my mind, the stab of anger acting like a shot of caffeine. It's always just enough to keep me awake for another ten minutes, wondering if anything about Middleford will be easy, wondering if I'm destined to spend a year being scorned and making my papaw's last memories of me ones of defeat.

Solitary, in my small room, in a building full of boys, is the most lonely and afraid for the future I've felt since I sat trembling on the front porch of my trailer, listening through the jagged wailing in my head to the distant crescendo of sirens as they came to collect what was left of my mama.

Chapter 20

I hear someone approaching in the hall, and I pray it isn't Tripp. I'm relieved when there's a knock, and I check the time—it's right about when someone was supposed to be by to take me to see my counselor.

I answer the door, and a friendly-looking kid with wavy dark hair and glasses, who appears a couple years older than me, stands there.

"You Cash?" he asks.

"Yep."

"I'm Cameron, one of the fourth-floor dorm proctors. Welcome to Middleford." He gives me a firm handshake. He exudes cheerful generosity.

"Hey, man."

"Ms. Clark told me you're from Sawyer, Tennessee."

"Yeah."

"I'm from Nashville."

I brighten. "No way!"

"I know Sawyer. We passed through there on family vacations in Asheville. Beautiful area."

"For sure." *Thank God not everyone here is like Tripp.*

"Just FYI, the dining hall is mostly great, but they never get biscuits quite right. And—trigger warning—you're going to see people putting sugar and maple syrup on grits. Bless their hearts."

I grin. "Thanks for warning me."

"I'm supposed to shepherd you to your counselor. Ready?"

"Let's do it."

As we walk, Cameron gestures toward a small open area with sofas and chairs arranged around a wall-mounted television. "This is the fourth-floor common area. We have movie nights, video-game tournaments, that sorta thing. If you ever feel home-sick, we have a Saturday-night tradition where we watch this funny show called *Midnite Matinee* on New Canaan public access. These two ladies who have no business being on television— which is why it rules—dress up like vampires and do goofy skits and show cheesy old horror movies. They're from Tennessee. Sunday nights, we watch *Bloodfall*."

"Cool."

Cameron points down the hall. "On every other floor, there's a big corner unit where someone from the faculty lives. In this building, they're on floors one and three. So if you have an issue one of the dorm proctors can't handle, pop down to the third floor. Me and my roommate actually live in the corner unit on this floor."

I vaguely remember reading about this, but it didn't register at the time. "Teachers live right *here*? In the building?"

"I mean, they get pranked sometimes, but always very inno-cent, deeply nerdy stuff. A voice instructor, Mrs. Torres, lives on the first floor with her husband, who teaches history. They've lived there for twenty years or something like that. Raised two kids there. Dr. Karpowitz from the English department lives on the third floor with his wife."

We pass a couple of open doors, with students sitting inside rooms, chatting in small groups or arranging things.

"Hey, Cam," someone calls. "You got any duct tape?"

"How many times have I told you it's less painful to shave your balls?"

"But then it grows back twice as thick. Seriously, though."

"Yeah, it's in a tub under my bed. Raheel's probably there, but if not, get up with me in a sec and I'll let you in."

We keep walking. Cam looks at me apologetically. "Sorry, man. Atul and I always roast each other. I should've made sure you were okay with that sort of joking around."

I flash to Delaney flipping me off. "*No* worries."

While we're in the elevator, Cameron asks, "You sign up for laundry service?"

"Not in the budget." It never even entered the conversation with Papaw and Mamaw. It was hundreds of dollars a year extra that my scholarship didn't cover.

"I hear you, dude. So, laundry facilities are in the basement. You work the machines with your student card."

Cameron and I keep chatting as we walk. I'm still feeling low-grade despair at the thought of spending the next year here, rooming with Tripp, but knowing there are at least *some* friendly people here other than Delaney (and even that depends on the day) helps a bit.

As I walk up the steps of the admin building, Cameron says, "All right, man. You know your way back?"

I nod.

"Let me know if you need anything. Duct tape. Whatever."

"I normally just shave," I say.

Cameron grins. "Well played, dude."

"I know it's unwelcome news," my academic counselor, Victoria Kwon, says. "But believe me when I say that you're better off repeating sophomore year here than being a junior at an ordinary school."

I must appear as gut-punched as I feel. "So I'm not a junior this year?" *Another year away from Papaw and Mamaw? Thanks for telling me, Delaney.*

"No. And also because we don't have junior year here. It's called 'fifth form.' Sophomore year would be 'fourth form.' But I know that's little comfort."

"Yeah, no."

"It's common to have to repeat grades when transferring from public school to a private school like this one. You have no reason to feel ashamed," Victoria says while looking again at my transcript.

I rub my forehead and exhale in a low whistle. I'm imagining calling Papaw and Mamaw and telling them their grandson is basically getting held back. *Looks like I get to start disappointing them immediately.*

"I bet you'll end up glad you got the extra year here." She turns back to her computer monitor and scrolls. "Okay . . . okay . . . so all Middleford students are required to have an after-school sport. I don't see that you played any sports at your old school."

"No, ma'am."

"Ever wanted to try any?"

"Hmm." I'd considered going out for football. Thought I'd have done all right, too. Papaw would've loved it. But I mentioned it to Delaney and she freaked out and started lecturing me about concussions and chronic traumatic encephalopathy (she made me repeat the name until I had it memorized) and reciting statistics until I promised her I wouldn't.

"What do you love doing?"

"I like being outside. Canoeing. Let me think—"

Victoria perks up. "How about crew?"

"I'm not even sure what that is."

"Workouts are hard, but you look like you could handle it." She types and motions for me to come around and look at her monitor. She's pulled up a YouTube video showing a long, narrow boat gliding knifelike through the water. The boat's oarsmen row with a hypnotic, machinistic precision. It's strangely beautiful.

I keep watching, mesmerized. It's deeply soothing—something I could use. "Sure."

"Yay!" Victoria gives a little clap of delight. "Almost done. You need an English credit. Any preferences?"

"Not really." I almost say, *Something easy,* but I remember Papaw's admonition.

She taps a pen against her lips for a moment in thought. "A space just opened up in Dr. Britney Rae Adkins's Intro to Poetry class. She's brilliant. Her poetry collection, *Holler,* just came out with Copper Canyon Press, and it's been getting huge awards buzz." Victoria leans in confidentially. "Between us, I'd be surprised if we were able to keep her here. You better take advantage."

I've never in my life thought about taking a poetry class. "I don't know if I'm a big poetry guy."

"It's an intro class. You might not be a big poetry guy. But you might. Based on Dr. Adkins's evaluations, if you are, you'll know it by the end of her class."

I lean back in my chair, my elbows on the armrests, steepling my fingers in front of my mouth. "Sign me up." I try to sound confident and casual. *What are you getting yourself into?*

Victoria cheers and high-fives me. "Well, Cash, looks like we've got your class schedule locked down. The rest of the weekend is yours to get settled in. We'll be having a mixer tonight. A bus is going into New Canaan tomorrow if you need to hit Target or the mall. I can get you the schedule for on-campus worship services, or we have vans that can take you off campus. The athletic center will also be open. Try to fit as much playtime as you can into the next couple of days, because, come Monday, we'll be working hard."

This sends a fresh wave of anxiety through me. I leave Victoria's office. The air is warm and sharp with the familiar green smell of cut foliage as groundskeepers whip campus into shape. More students mill around. I stand on the front steps of the administration building and step aside to let a few people pass. I wait for a lull in foot traffic, close my eyes, and turn my face to the sun, the insides of my eyelids fluorescing red. I envision the metronomic beat of the rowing from the video. I want to be there, letting my hungry muscles burn off my anxiety, one stroke at a time.

I hear in my mind the swish of the boat cutting through the water, a whisper of a thing that returns to perfection the moment we leave it.

I like knowing there are bodies whose scars heal completely right in front of you. I expect I'll need that reminder in the days to come.

Chapter 21

Delaney and I sit with our trays. A basket of chicken tenders for me, a chicken salad wrap for her. Fries for both of us. The dining hall is more crowded than at breakfast. Students fill the space with an animated buzz; mini reunions are happening here and there. I overhear one student ask another how Geneva was over the summer. "Sucked ass. Annika and my dad were smashing every night, and I could hear them. How was Mumbai?" she asks. "Hot as hell," her friend responds. "How was Kuala Lumpur?" All fresh reminders of how out of place I am here.

"Why'd I get a wrap? They're always such a bummer," Delaney says.

"So you knew we'd be repeating sophomore year?" I ask her.

"Fourth form," she says with her mouth full. "And no. I thought there might be a possibility but I wasn't sure."

"Why didn't you tell me?"

Delaney shrugs. "As you'll recall, you took a fair bit of convincing to come here. Why hand you another excuse not to come if I wasn't certain?"

I'm sure I'll be angrier when I've had time to think about it, but I don't have the energy right now. "Whatever. How's the roomie?"

Delaney brightens. "Cool. Smart. Wants to become a video-game developer. How's yours?"

"The opposite."

"I looked him up. Before his dad became a US House rep, he was some big-time private security contractor. Like he provided mercenaries to governments. Some of his guys got prosecuted for killing civilians in Iraq."

"My high school roommate is the heir to a mercenary army?"

"Yep."

"Cool. He mocked Papaw's accent, by the way."

"*What?*"

"Yeah, I was videochatting with Papaw without headphones, and Tripp could hear. And he made fun of how Papaw says 'up there.'"

"Piece of *shit*."

"I wanted to beat his ass, but I also didn't want to get kicked out on my first day."

"I'd have been real mad. But damn."

"He said his old school was shitty. Bet he got kicked out for something and he's pissed about being here."

"I'd hate being here alone," Delaney murmurs. "I'm glad you're here."

I nod and we eat quietly for a moment.

"What you end up doing for your sport?" Delaney asks.

"Rowing team," I say through a bite. "You?"

"Field hockey."

We snort-laugh. But Delaney will probably make a pretty decent field hockey player, especially if scrappiness and the ability to take a hit, dust yourself off, and get back up again make for success in the sport.

We compare schedules. She's on a special STEM track. So no class overlap, which isn't surprising but is disappointing. I'd feel better if there were at least a class or two where Delaney could help with my homework.

"Intro to Poetry?" Delaney giggles. "Gonna buy you a beret. Get you one of those striped French-guy shirts."

"Go on. Laugh. *There once was a man from Nantucket.*"

She suddenly turns gravely serious. "I think it's awesome. Why come here if we just take classes we could've back home?"

"Poetry teacher's supposed to be great." Out of the corner of my eye, I see three bookish-looking girls approaching timidly.

"Hey, sorry to interrupt," one of the girls says.

"No worries," I say.

"Are you—" The girl points at Delaney, who looks up expectantly, waiting for the girl to finish. After it becomes clear that Delaney isn't going to finish her sentence for her, the girl continues. "The one from Tennessee?"

"There's more than one from Tennessee at this table," Delaney says. I know her well enough to know that she's not trying to be prickly—just precise. But her questioner wouldn't know that.

I give Delaney a take-it-easy-we're-new-here look, but she refuses me eye contact.

The girl blushes. "I meant the one in the Middleford newsletter."

"Oh," Delaney says, looking at her tray. "Maybe? Haven't seen it."

"There was a picture that looked like you. You discovered a plant or something?"

"A new strain of penicillin. They named it after me. *Penicillium delanum.*"

One of the girl's friends behind her pipes up. "We have kind of a weird question. Hope it's not offensive or anything."

"Okay," Delaney says apprehensively.

"We heard you guys were, like, married?"

Delaney and I stare at each other for a second, speechless. We burst into laughter.

"No," I say. "We're best friends and we came here together. We are definitely not married."

The three girls laugh nervously. Their curiosity seems genuine and not an attempt to belittle us. This school must be full of socially awkward and curious kids. "We had just heard—Never mind," the first girl says.

"So people are saying we came here together because we're *married?*" Delaney asks.

"Yeah, I don't know. People are weird," the girl says. "Sorry to interrupt." The three begin edging away. "See you guys around?"

"See y'all later," Delaney says.

The girls leave, and Delaney and I share a look.

"This school must be a very small world," Delaney says.

"Who reads their school newsletter?"

"Middleford kids."

We pick at our food for a few more seconds.

"Bet they wouldn't have asked that if we were from LA or Paris," Delaney says quietly.

"We should probably get used to it," I say. My heart sags further.

We've both finished our food, but we stay put. For the first time, it sets in how lonely I would also be right now if I had stayed behind while Delaney went on without me. No winning.

Delaney pushes back her seat and stands.

"Where you going?" I ask.

"Give them something to talk about," she says with a puckish gleam.

"Red."

"You'll like it," she says over her shoulder.

"I'm worried."

"Don't be." She walks to a large silver machine with a spigot, picks up two clear plastic cups, and fills each with a towering ivory spiral of vanilla soft-serve, complete with a little loop on top. They could have been carved from white marble. Her Dairy Queen training on full display.

She swaggers back, a cup in each hand, choosing a route that will take her past the most students. She smiles serenely as behind her, those who bother to notice point discreetly and whisper at her craft. Obviously, none have had a job that required them to learn how to dispense soft-serve in a visually pleasing manner. Someone says, "Nice." Someone else says, "Hell yeah."

She arrives back at our table and sits, sliding my ice cream across the surface like an old-timey bartender. I catch it before it careens off the edge.

"See that? I changed the narrative. Now we're not married anymore. Now I'm the Ice Cream Queen and you're my humble servant." She takes a huge bite and wrinkles her nose. "They need to clean their machine."

I admire her handiwork for a moment. "Almost hate to destroy something so perfect."

Delaney points with her spoon. "That right there? That was an alpha move I just made. Humans are pack animals, like wolves. We honor shows of strength."

We each make it about halfway down our respective towers

before we succumb to ice cream headaches and sugar overload. We lean back in our chairs and sigh, the stress, exhaustion, and excitement of the day finally wrestling us into submission.

I stare at my cup. "You realize you getting a perfect ice cream for me only makes it look *more* like we're married, right?"

She holds up an unadorned left hand. "Better start ring shopping. You look like a cheap bastard."

"You call your mama yet?"

"Speaking of those perpetually in relationships with shitty cheap bastards?"

"You gonna call her?"

"She knows my number."

"All right. You ready?"

"Yep."

We clear our trays and leave the dining hall. We stroll the campus for a while to acquaint ourselves. We walk aimlessly, trying to project verve and mimic the air of belonging our future classmates give off. We comment on the people and buildings we pass, trying to commit landmarks to memory.

"I probably won't ever get married," Delaney says out of nowhere as we stand outside the science center, squinting up at its gleaming, angular modern whiteness in the afternoon sun, shielding our eyes with our hands. "But there'd be worse people in this world to be married to than you."

Delaney could do a lot better than me. She'll end up with some fellow genius someday. But it still feels good to hear.

Chapter 22

Tripp is back in our room, already with two new friends who resemble him in appearance and demeanor. I hear them from the hall, guffawing about something. They quiet down in a hurry when I enter.

This time, I make sure I have my headphones, and I go out to the fourth-floor common room. Mamaw's and Papaw's faces fill my screen. Seeing them together, side by side, crammed into the small glowing frame, runs me through with a keener homesickness than before.

"Long time no see," Papaw wheezes, smiling and coughing.

"Pep tells me you're getting settled in," Mamaw says.

"Yep," I say. "Hey, here's some fun news. I have to repeat sophomore year. I guess my credits don't transfer over completely or something. They explained it."

They chew on the information for a moment.

"The scholarship cover it?" Mamaw asks.

"They said it did," I reply. "Takes me through graduation."

"I s'pose it is what it is," Mamaw says. "And if your scholarship covers it, what's the harm?"

"Bright side: You get more time at the good school," Papaw says.

"It's another year away from y'all," I say.

"College would have been that anyway," Mamaw says.

"I guess," I say. "Hey, Papaw, wanna hear something funny?"

He coughs. "I do."

"I'm taking a poetry class." I wait for Papaw to crack some joke like Delaney did. He doesn't.

"Well, now, I think that's great."

"You don't think it's funny?"

He gives me a reproachful look. "Why would I?"

My smile fades. "I don't know. Poetry. Me."

"What is there about you that you don't belong in a poetry class?"

I fidget. "You know me. I'm not a poetry guy."

"I think of poetry lovers as people who love beautiful things." He stops to catch his breath. "You love the beauty in this world. Ain't a reason I can think of you don't belong in a poetry class. Hold the gizmo, Donna Bird," Papaw says. Mamaw takes hold of the tablet. Papaw raises his scarred and labor-worn hands to the camera. "See these hands? Worked hard with them to give you the things I never had. You taking a poetry class is a thing I never had. By God, I want you to have it."

"I guess it isn't funny, then," I say quietly.

"Pep's not trying to fuss at you," Mamaw says.

"I surely ain't," Papaw says. "Same time, I'm letting you know where I stand."

"All right, Pep, you hold the tablet now. My turn." Mamaw raises her hands to the camera. "See these hands? I've also worked hard with them to give my family a good life. I want you taking classes that let you work with your mind."

"You win," I say. "What are y'all doing tonight?"

"We started a jigsaw puzzle of a lighthouse last night. Likely as not, we'll keep on that," Mamaw says. "How about you?"

"There's supposed to be a get-together tonight for the students. But I'll probably skip it." Delaney and I customarily blew off school functions to hang out together. "Hey, maybe you can set up the tablet and we can chat while you do the puzzle."

"Well, I think you ought to go to the shindig," Papaw says.

"Make some new friends," Mamaw says.

"I'll have plenty of time to meet people. Just tonight let's hang out," I say.

"No, sir," Papaw says. "Booting you out of the nest. Get with Tess and go be kids. You don't need to be hanging out with the old folks on a Friday night."

"Jeez."

"It's best you give this whole experience your all. You can't do that when you got one foot at home. When I was in the service, me and the boys had a big time together. There weren't no such thing as gizmos where you could get on the video camera with the people back home."

"I'll go. Dang, y'all."

I shower off the Greyhound voyage and the last residue of home. My old life, washed down the drain.

I'm sure a lot of kids arrive here and find the lack of doors in the bathrooms unnerving. I might be the only one who finds it a comfort. Then again, they get to be free of the memories that make me appreciate the lack of bathroom doors. So I guess they win there too.

Back in my room, the sun is setting through the window. Tripp is gone, and so I pause to drink in the stillness.

I put on my best, least-wrinkled button-down shirt and nicest jeans. I use a tissue to blot a couple of smudges from my boots. I fix my hair. I got it cut last week, and I marveled at how much summer-bleached smoky-blond hair dappled the floor by the end.

I'd thought about how funny it would be if when you got to heaven, God could give you a printout with all of your life's vital statistics. How much hair you produced. How many colds you defeated. How many times you skinned your knees. How many nightmares you endured. How many pancakes you ate.

Every brave thing you did.

Every heartbreak you overcame.

Everyone you mourned.

Everyone you ever loved.

Everyone who ever loved you.

Chapter 23

The day gave up its heat quickly at sundown, and the early autumn twilight feels like cool water on my face. From somewhere I can smell wood smoke. The moon gleams in the periwinkle sky before the sun is even completely gone.

I stroll with Cameron and his roommate, Raheel, to the gymnasium, where the mixer is being held. Cameron and Raheel had made a sweep looking for stragglers to muscle into going to the mixer, and they'd caught me.

"Okay, back to what we were talking about before," Raheel says as we walk.

"I think this is batshit," Cameron says. "And I both love it and hate it already, but I'm listening."

"Have you seen *Game of Thrones?*" Raheel asks me.

"Never had HBO," I reply. "And it wasn't my grandparents' type of show. My pap—grandpa—used to call shows like that 'wizard grabass.'"

Raheel grins wolfishly and rubs his hands together. "Ahhhh, but now you have your new buddy Raheel, his box set of all eight seasons, his willingness to serve as your tour guide, and his ever-readiness to rewatch the entire series."

"So regale us with your theory," Cameron says. He turns to

me. "Raheel thinks *The Princess Bride* takes place in the universe of *Game of Thrones*."

"I *have* seen *Princess Bride*. My mom loved that movie," I say, reminding myself to keep mention of my mama to a minimum.

Raheel clears his throat grandiosely. "Cameron, nod vigorously in agreement. We begin with Westley. He leaves home, and when we see him again, he's dressed in all black and has been at sea. Clearly he became a man of the Night's Watch and was assigned to Eastwatch-by-the-Sea, where he was kidnapped by pirates."

"This is already a lot to remember," I say.

"Raheel will remind you," Cameron says. "*Trust* me."

"Next, we have Fezzik, Vizzini, and Inigo Montoya. Clearly, Fezzik was rescued from the fighting pits of Meereen. Vizzini? A eunuch from Lys, like Varys. Inigo Montoya? Braavosi dancing master like Syrio Forel . . ."

"I've never heard anything more brilliant and stupid simultaneously," Cameron says when Raheel is finally done.

"It sounded pretty well thought out," I say.

Raheel puts his arm around me and speaks to Cameron. "This guy? I like him. Now I finally know a cool person from Tennessee."

"I'm still waiting to meet a cool person from Las Vegas," Cameron says.

Raheel blows on this thumb like he's inflating a balloon and slowly raises his middle finger.

We arrive at the gym, where small groups of two, three, and four are entering, the faint sound of music bleeding outside as they open the doors.

"Y'all, thanks for walking with me. I'm supposed to meet my friend Delaney and her roommate out front here," I say.

Raheel points at me. "This weekend. *Game of Thrones*. Winter is coming. That'll make sense later."

I give him a thumbs-up, and they enter, the last remnants of their conversation fading from earshot—"Dude, Callie is not gonna be here tonight." "How do you know?" "I'm just managing your expectations so you don't . . ."

I feel awkward standing there alone while people trickle around me. I'm about to text Delaney when I look up to see her approaching with another girl. As they near, I notice something different about Delaney. She's wearing dramatic smoky-pink eye makeup. She looks great.

"Your eyes. Wow," I say.

"Viviani did it."

Viviani stands behind Delaney. She's short, about Delaney's height. Her hazel eyes are ablaze with the same makeup that's on Delaney. Dimples bookend an incandescent smile. Shiny copper-colored hair in tight curls frames her face and crowns her head. It's rose gold at the ends, like she's growing out a dye job. She wears a Captain America T-shirt and black jeans tucked into black boots. She waves. "Hi. I'm Viviani. Vi."

The way she says her name—*Vee-vee-AH-nee*—effervesces on her tongue. It makes the way I say it sound leaden and earthbound. "I'm Cash."

"I recognized you. Delaney said you looked like a young River Phoenix."

"I don't even know who that is," I say.

"*Stand by Me. Sneakers. My Own Private Idaho.* He wasn't in very many movies, because he died young," Delaney says.

"Is that good?"

"Dying young?"

"No. Looking like River Phoenix."

"I wouldn't compare you to an ugly actor, dumbass," Delaney says.

"All right, well, everything else Delaney told you about me is a lie," I say to Vi.

"She said you were cool," Vi says.

"*That* you're also allowed to believe."

"I didn't say that," Delaney says. "I maybe implied it."

"You guys want to . . . ," Vi says.

"Let's do this," Delaney says, sighing.

As I walk side by side with Vi, whatever perfume or lotion she uses wafts over. It's a buoyant, shimmering blend of honeyed pineapple; something lemony and floral, like magnolia blossoms; something verdant, like ivy; and freshly laundered cotton sheets drying in a humid breeze.

"Delaney told me she doesn't like big crowds," Vi says.

"Me neither," I say. "You?"

"I'm from a city of six million, so I have no choice but to be used to crowds."

"Delaney and I are from a town of six thousand, so we get lots of choice."

My pulse accelerates as we enter the dimly lit gym, sidestepping a pair of girls filming themselves. Music blares. There are tables set up with food and drink. Small groups of students huddle in close circles, talking, holding plates and cups. Occasionally one cluster will send an envoy to another. I scan the room, and I don't see Tripp and his new posse, which suggests this isn't the cool place to be. Which is fine. We form a small, tight ring.

"I want to know how you convinced Delaney to let you do her makeup," I say to Vi.

"She told me I had beautiful eyes," Delaney says. "Flattery will get you everywhere with me."

"No, it won't. I've tried it so many times," I say.

"It'll get some people everywhere with me. It'll get *you* to certain limited places."

"It's cool you two came together here," Vi says. "My best friend from Brazil, Fernanda, is at Phillips Exeter. I tried to get her to come here."

I nod at Delaney. "Here's who needs to talk to your friend."

Delaney says to Vi, "I had to twist his arm to get him to come."

Vi is aghast. "This is such a good school!"

I wave it off. "I'm here now."

"I'm getting a Coke. Get y'all anything?" Delaney asks.

"Coke," I say.

"Also," Vi says.

Delaney ventures toward the tables with coolers on them, leaving Vi and me alone.

We smile awkwardly at each other.

"So how did you get the name Cash?" Vi asks. "Like Johnny Cash?"

"My mama loved Johnny Cash. My grandpa used to listen to him a lot with her. So, yep."

"I knew it!"

"You speak incredible English."

"When I was growing up, we lived part of the time in Miami, so I've practiced. Also, I've watched lots of American movies and TV shows and played lots of video games online with Americans."

Delaney stops to chat. Maybe another person asking if she came here with her husband.

"What are your favorite movies and TV shows?" I ask. "I'm guessing *Captain America*."

"Marvel movies. *Star Wars. Lord of the Rings. Game of Thrones. Bloodfall. Supernatural.*"

"I've never seen *Game of Thrones*. As I was coming here, one of the guys in my dorm roped me into watching it with him later."

"I'm jealous of you seeing it for the first time. Can I come?"

"If we're allowed. I'm not sure of all the rules yet."

"You've seen the Marvel movies, though, yeah?"

"Most."

"Who's your favorite character?"

I think it over. "Who's yours? Wait. Lemme guess."

"Go."

I rub my chin and squint at her shirt. "I'm gonna say . . . Captain America."

She laughs. "Good try."

"No?"

"My vovô knows I love Marvel, and he gave me this shirt for Christmas."

I look at her quizzically. "Your . . ."

She blushes. "My grandfather. *Avô* in Portuguese. So, vovô."

"That sounds like what I call my grandpa—Papaw."

"I like that. *Papaw.* Okay, guess again."

"All the girls like Thor."

"Thor is hot. But no."

She sometimes says *th* like *tuh* and *t* at the end of words with a faint *tch*. I like it.

"Okay . . ."

"I think you won't guess."

"Yeah, I give up."

"Shuri from *Black Panther.* She's the one I identify with the most."

"Why's that?"

"I love technology. I want to be a video-game developer."

"Man, that sounds awesome."

"Are you a gamer?"

"Not really."

"We'll have to change that," Vi says. "Your turn. Your favorite Marvel character."

I think for a second.

"This will decide if we stay friends," she says.

"No pressure. Shuri too, then."

"Really?" She laughs.

"I mean, she's awesome, obviously, but—"

"I was kidding about not being your friend if you choose wrong. Brincadeira, we say in Brazil."

"Okay, for real, then? Bucky Barnes."

"Good choice."

"Did I pass?" I ask.

"You passed. Why him?"

"I don't know. He seems like a normal guy." *Bucky, who lives in the shadow of his best friend. Bucky, who knows he'll never be as important as Captain America.* "He doesn't have magical powers or whatever."

"None of the Avengers are *magic.* And he has a bionic arm."

I suddenly remember Delaney and look for her in the crowd. I see her, three cans of Coke in hand—watching, observing—at the periphery of the congregation. I know her expression well. She's gathering. Storing. Processing.

She told me once that she used to spend whole afternoons lying on the floor of her trailer, studying the ants—the one inexhaustible resource she and her mama had. She saw patterns emerge, over hours, from what seemed like chaotic movements. There was an overarching logic and intelligence to their motion, and if you could only figure it out, then you might have a clue to unlocking the secret of the seemingly random interactions of more sophisticated creatures. Like Middleford Academy students.

From there you could make predictions and formulate hypotheses. The sort that help you survive life with an addict by bringing an underlying order to apparent chaos. Ones that'll help you survive a place where people think you're married to your best friend, a place where children of the world's most powerful families will wonder why you never mention your parents.

Vi sees me looking at her. "She's really brilliant, yeah?"

"She's a genius," I murmur.

"She knows more about the history of Rio de Janeiro than I do."

"She learned it in the half hour she had between the time she found out y'all were roommates and the time you met."

"I should get her to help me with my homework."

"One time she helped me with my math homework, and she thought the kind of math I was supposed to do was dumb. So she basically invented her own new kind of math to do it. But I was supposed to show my work, so I got a shitty grade, because Delaney math wasn't what I was supposed to be doing."

"She invented a new kind of math?"

"I mean, that's what it looked like to me, but I'm real bad at math."

"You must have been really good at other stuff to get in here," Vi says.

You bet. Canoeing. Caving. Making the right friends. "I guess." It takes all my effort to keep my earlier promise.

Delaney walks up and hands Vi and me our Cokes. While we crack open our cans and sip, she surveys the crowd once more. "Everyone here is going to be dead in a hundred years," she says—not to us, to the air. "I wonder who the last person here to die will be."

Vi's eyes widen. She looks to me. I give her a shrug that says, *You'll never completely understand Delaney, but at least you'll never be bored.* I want to ask Delaney what inferences and deductions she made, but she'll tell me when she's ready and not a minute sooner.

We huddle in our tight circle, talking in meandering spirals. Delaney's favorite Marvel character (Dr. Strange). That they put corn on pizza in Brazil (I don't tell Vi that my mamaw is a pizza expert). Our class schedules (no overlap). Our sports. Vi makes me guess hers. I guess soccer, and I'm wrong (volleyball, also popular in Brazil).

A pair of teachers force us to mingle awkwardly with a couple of other clumps of new students. We make stilted small talk and peel back away from each other.

I don't know why Vi stays by our side. She's so effervescent and outgoing, she could easily be making many new friends. But she isn't looking over our shoulders for a better opportunity.

Delaney abruptly vanishes into herself. "I have stuff to do."

This isn't a surprise. I knew she would need time to process her new information and surroundings.

The exhaustion of the day and my desire to keep hanging out with Vi are arm-wrestling, and fatigue is winning. "I'm gonna head out too." But there's still one thing on my list before turning in. I need the smell of water. "I'm going to swing by the lake if either of y'all care to join me."

"I'll go," Vi says. "I haven't walked around the lake yet."

The din of the party slowly dies behind us, replaced by the nocturne of crickets, as we exit the gymnasium. The moon is high and nearly full, bathing everything in light the color of candle smoke.

It's cooled down even more. I wish I'd brought a jacket. A familiar tart, haylike smell lingers in the air from all the landscaping to ready the school.

Before Delaney peels off to head to her dorm, we make breakfast plans. Vi tells us that the spirit is willing, but the flesh weak when it comes to waking up on Saturday mornings, so she might join us, but we shouldn't plan on her. We both hug Delaney and continue to the lake.

A hush falls between us as we walk.

I smell the lake before I see it, the aroma of mud and composting marsh grasses, carrying on its shoulders the unripe-watermelon-rind scent of water. It reminds me of my river. *This is where you can find sanctuary when you need it. And you'll need it.*

The lake is compact—a glorified pond. But it's serene and picturesque and it reflects the moonlight like it should. Here and there a frog adds its voice to the cricket orchestra.

A paved path, dotted with benches, rings the lake. We have it to ourselves except for a girl who passes us at a near sprint with a mutter of "On your left," listening to music so loud we hear it through her headphones.

Vi pulls out her phone, snaps a picture of the moon, and examines it. She sighs. "Never good."

"Nothing'll break your heart like trying to take a picture of the moon. It's like, 'Here, look at this picture I took of a coin in a parking lot.' "

Vi giggles, then laughs harder, starting to snort.

"What?"

She takes a second to gather herself. "I was remembering once when I was running on the beach, and the moon was up, and I thought, 'I'll keep running and get closer to the moon so I can get a better picture.' "

We laugh and then subside into quiet. Vi pauses at one of the benches and sits.

I join her. "What will you miss most from home?" I ask.

"The ocean. I love it. I think I'm part mermaid." Her voice is wistful.

"I've never seen the ocean."

"*No?*" She sounds like I just told her I've never tried chocolate.

"Nope."

"I'll show you the ocean someday. I want to see your face when you see it for the first time."

"Deal."

"What will you miss most from your home?"

"The river where I live. My papaw and I used to canoe together."

"We both miss our water." Vi slowly points. "Look," she whispers.

A large orange-white fish—some sort of decorative carp, I'm guessing—has swum into the shallows, where it sits nearly motionless, lazily sculling to stay in place. It seems to luminesce in the silver moonlight. We both sit as still as we can.

"Hello, Moon Fish," Vi murmurs. "Did you come to say hello?"

"I wonder if it's laying eggs. It looks like it's stirring up mud."

"I think this is a good—ah, I can't think of the English word. *Presságio* in Portuguese."

"Like an omen or a sign?"

"Omen! That. I think it means we're going to have a good year here."

"Are you scared to be here?" I ask.

"A little bit. Are you scared?"

"Yes," I say.

"What scares you most?" Vi asks.

I fidget. "I dunno. Letting down my grandparents. Letting down Delaney. Looking stupid. How about you?"

"Same. Disappointing the people I love. Looking stupid."

Curfew is at eleven on Friday and Saturday nights, with lights-out at midnight. I make it into my room at 10:50. Tripp enters at 10:57, dragging the sour whiff of alcohol behind him. All substance use is forbidden at Middleford, an expellable offense. But something tells me that gets ignored a lot, especially by the kids like Tripp who don't need to concern themselves terribly with blowing an opportunity or ten. We grunt greetings to each other and take refuge behind our respective phone screens. We're interrupted a few minutes later by Cameron and Raheel making their curfew check.

I find Vi's Instagram and follow her. I browse through her pictures. Her at the beach, aglow. With a group of classmates, wearing identical khaki pants and white blouses, at a pizza place. In line at the movie theater. Hugging a small fluffy white dog apparently named Pipoca, which I look up and which means "popcorn" in Portuguese. There are photos of her vacationing with what I take to be her family—skiing, standing together in Times Square(?), grinning at Disney World, posing with the Eiffel Tower in the background.

Her father is handsome and fit and has thick gray hair and a CEO air about him. Her mother appears to be much younger than her father and has a former-beauty-queen vibe. Vi looks to have a brother who's significantly older than her—fifteen years or so. I'm not sure which of the photos show her house. Or houses. Or luxury hotels.

Your life sure is different from mine, Vi. Hope that's okay with you.

My phone illuminates with a text from Delaney. **Sounds like you and Vi had fun.**

> **Me: Yeah, we had a big time.**
>
> **Delaney: She seems cool.**
>
> **Me: You never told me you thought I looked like River Phoenix.**
>
> **Delaney: You never asked.**
>
> **Me: I'm supposed to check in randomly and ask hey do I look like any actors????**

Delaney: Yes.

Me: Do I look like any other actors?

Delaney: Nope, just the one. There's a bus going into New Canaan tomorrow. Wanna go?

Me: Sure.

Delaney: I'll see if Vi wants to come.

Me: Cool.

Delaney: You have fun at the thing?

Me: Yeah.

Delaney: You glad you came?

Me: Ask me when they start dropping homework on us.

Delaney: You think we're missing out on anything in Sawyer right now?

Me: Some quality driving in circles. Shooting road signs with shotguns.

Delaney: Hahaha.

Lights-out comes. I lie awake in the dark, thinking about destiny. Thinking about where I'd be right now if I hadn't sat next to Delaney Doyle at that Narateen meeting years ago.

Chapter 24

I awake on Saturday morning to find that Vi has followed me back on Instagram. A shadow of insecurity passes over me at the smallness of my life on display there. A lot of photos of Punkin, my river, me and Papaw and Mamaw, me and Delaney. None of ski trips or beach vacations or fancy hotels. But I figure I might as well get used to my life feeling tiny compared to the other kids here, and I head to the dining hall to meet Delaney for breakfast.

"You sleep good?" I ask as Delaney approaches alone.

"Best I have in years."

We walk into the dining hall. "Vi not coming?" I ask.

"Don't know. She was asleep when I left."

"She was up earlier, because she followed me back on Insta."

"Let me check again and see if I know now. Nope, still don't know."

"Hey, can I take a video of you admitting you don't know something?"

Delaney smiles crookedly. "Eat shit. I say when I don't know stuff."

"Never once."

"Didn't say it happened much."

"Speaking of Vi, will you not mention to her about my

whole family situation? I don't want every new friend knowing that right off."

Delaney fills a bowl with Lucky Charms and milk and grabs a cherry Danish. "Secret's safe with me. On that fun topic, after the thing last night, I tried to call my mama."

"No shit?" I select a couple of foil-wrapped breakfast burritos. Once I start rowing, I'll probably have to eat healthier.

"Didn't get her. She must have been busy perfecting the semiconductor again."

"Do what?"

"I'm joking."

We sit. "You gonna try again?"

She shrugs. "She really doesn't give one shit about me. Hard to get the energy to keep trying." She raises her thumb to gnaw it.

I reach across the table to stop her. "You know they probably have, like, counselors and stuff here, right?" I say.

She sits on her hand. "So?"

"So maybe they could help with you chewing on your thumbs."

"We'll see. Once I settle in."

Vi doesn't join us in the dining hall. But she does show up for the day trip to New Canaan. She's wearing a canary sundress under a jean jacket and greets us with a wide, sunny smile.

We load onto several vans to go into the city. Delaney, Vi, and I grab a row, and I sit next to Vi.

"I wanted to wear my favorite necklace today, but it's all rolled up," Vi says.

"Tangled?" I ask.

"Yes, that one."

"You're in luck," I say. "I'm *really* good at untangling things."

"He is," Delaney confirms.

She reaches in her jacket pocket. "I have it here." She pulls it out and hands it to me, a delicate and intricate network of silver chains. "It's supposed to look like this." She shows me a selfie in which she's wearing it.

I cradle the necklace in my palm. "First: I just hold it for a few seconds and breathe. I remind myself, 'It got tangled on its own. It'll get untangled on its own.'" I move my hand around gently, tipping it and tilting it slightly. "Then I see how it lies. I look for a good place to start. And . . . there," I murmur, picking it up by a corner.

Vi leans in close. She's absolutely still, like I'm defusing a bomb, and I can hear her breathing.

"The trick is, don't pull and yank. That'll get it more tangled. And you might break it. Just let it untangle itself with a little help. Let it come to you." I suspend it and shake it gently, the twisted whorls falling slack. I see my opening and take it. A few moves, and I'm done. I raise the necklace delicately but triumphantly.

"One of your best times," Delaney says.

Vi gasps in delight. "You need to start a business doing this."

"I ran my own business during the summers."

"Yeah?"

"I mowed lawns."

"Mode?"

"Cut people's grass at their houses."

"Ah. My dad started his own business when he was our age, delivering groceries on his bike. Now he has . . . What is it when you have many stores?"

"A chain?"

"A chain of grocery stores in Brazil and Argentina, called

Campos Verde. He opened his first stores in Florida and Texas last year. It's called Green Fields here."

That would explain her lifestyle.

"Speaking of chains." She twists in her seat, gathers her abundant hair, and holds it off her neck. "Here. Put it on me."

"You want me to put it on you?"

"Yes. More easy with help."

"Here, give it to me," Delaney says. "You'll screw it up, Cash."

"I mean, I won't, but here." I hand the necklace to Delaney. She carefully loops the necklace around Vi's neck, avoiding an errant strand of copper-colored hair.

"Yay! I wanted to wear this today."

They take us to Target. Delaney and I trail Vi as she makes a few last-minute school-supply purchases. We don't buy anything.

While Vi is checking out, Delaney turns to me, batting her eyelashes, and says in a breathy voice, *"Put it on me."*

When we're done at Target, they take us downtown, quaint with its brick sidewalks and upscale shops and restaurants. Some of the storefronts are already bedecked in autumn regalia.

Delaney tells us New Canaan is one of the richest cities in the United States. "A lot of people live here and have fancy jobs in New York, I guess," she says.

We stroll aimlessly in the sun and talk and laugh. We sit outdoors at a coffee shop and nurse glasses of water while Vi sips a cappuccino with an ornate feather drawn on the surface in milk and muses on how tranquil and orderly (read: boring) New

Canaan is compared with Rio de Janeiro. I remember learning in Bible study that Canaan was the name of a promised land.

It definitely seems like this is a promised land for Delaney. I already see something changing in her. Her stretches of intro-spection seem more placid than they used to. She's still been at-tacking her thumbs, but without her usual furious urgency. She's freer with laughter and jokes. Some of the edges of her usual prickliness have smoothed.

Our pickup time is in the early evening, and the day passes too quickly. Before I left, Papaw told me that if I'm ever hang-ing out with a group, I should be the one to suggest getting ice cream, because it'll always be a good time and it'll be my doing. So before it's time to leave, I do exactly that, and he's right.

We get back and eat dinner together in the dining hall, then go our separate ways. I'm tired, but it's amusement-park tired, not ditch-digging tired. I videochat with Papaw anyway. This time, I go to the lake, far from Tripp.

"Now, your mamaw ain't here to help work the doodad," Papaw wheezes as he signs on, his image moving jerkily with their slow internet. He coughs long and loud. Just as I think he has it under control, he starts in again. It might be my imagina-tion or the cheap tablet camera, but he's already visibly thinner, and I've been gone for fewer than four days. It occurs to me that after we talk, I'll go watch *Midnite Matinee* with the guys on my floor, but he'll be alone until Mamaw gets home. Delaney told me that a high percentage of people die shortly after a longtime spouse or partner dies. Johnny Cash did. I hope it's not the same deal here, with my leaving.

I tell him about going to the mixer and meeting Vi. I tell him about Tripp. (I don't mention his mocking Papaw's accent.) I ask him if he's improved at all, even though there's no good answer that isn't a lie. This isn't a thing that improves. You don't kick emphysema. You have good days and bad days, but eventually the bad days outnumber the good, until no days outnumber any others. It's like how once I commented in front of Delaney that it was cold that day, so global warming must be improving. Big mistake. She explained the difference between weather on a given day—an isolated snapshot within some trending larger system—and climate, the larger system. Papaw has climate change with some days of good weather.

Papaw starts to answer but slides into a coughing fit. Which is its own answer.

I tell him I hope I don't disappoint him here. He says I could never. I'm not so sure.

We talk for almost an hour. Being outside by the lake makes me feel like we're together on our front porch. As my battery starts to fade, I sign off and text Delaney to see if she wants to say hi. She sprints down, and we call Papaw back. For the first couple minutes, she's as short of breath as he is.

"Hey, Pep!"

"Tess!" Papaw beams. "You look happy."

"I am. Also got a lot of sleep last night compared to what I usually get."

"You and my grandson staying out of trouble?"

"Mostly. We went to a party last night."

"Cash said. Now tell me something I don't know."

She tells Papaw that trees have a sense of time—it's how they know that warm days are spring and not late summer, that they can share nutrients with each other to help ailing fellows, and that they send out chemicals to attract wasps to attack insects that are a threat to them. He asks her if she's working on his cure with her fancy new science lab. She says not yet; she's been too busy and hasn't had a chance. He tells her to stop horsing around and get to it. She says she will. The three of us talk until my phone battery verges on dying.

I invite Delaney to come watch *Midnite Matinee*. She declines. I join the guys on my floor. There are a few girls mixed in, twelve or thirteen people total. Geeky, goofy welcoming types. Raheel and Cameron are there. So is Atul. I get quick introductions to those I don't know.

We crowd onto couches and beanbags and open bags of snacks. The show begins, and everyone sings along with the theme music, with lyrics they've invented. The show is a decidedly low-budget, cheesy affair. The two host ladies dress like vampires and do skits and read viewer mail during breaks in the movie *Dawn of Dracula*. They're no TV professionals, but they seem to be having fun, and so do we.

For one of the interstitials, a tarot reading, the two ladies have a visibly unenthusiastic man, playing someone named Professor Heineken, assist them. During this, I surreptitiously check my phone with my remaining three percent of battery, to see that Vi has tagged me in a couple of photos she took of us in New Canaan. It lifts my heart to see that someone like her thinks I fit somewhere into her glamorous existence. Maybe I'll do all right here after all and my world will grow. Maybe I'm not so different from everyone and I'll have a great year. Maybe this is where my life finally turns a corner.

My spirit floats on this swell of hope until 11:55, when Raheel and Cameron make us turn off the show before the end credits—another tradition—so that we can make a mad dash to brush our teeth and be in our rooms with the lights off by midnight. Tripp and I mutter "'Sup" at each other but say nothing else.

I lie in the moonlight that leaks in through the edges of the blinds and carries me off to sleep.

I hoped to dream of sun-drenched days, laughing in the company of new friends, surrounded by love and opportunity.

But we don't choose our dreams; they choose us. So instead I dream of doors sealed by death and wake up sweating in the mute darkness, my roommate sleeping in blissful oblivion a few feet away and a world apart.

Memory is a tether. Sometimes you get some slack in the line and you can play it out for a while. You forget and think you're free. But you'll always get to the end and realize it's still there, binding you, reminding you of itself, reminding you that you belong to each other.

Chapter 25

Delaney and Vi holed up in their room all day Sunday, taking advantage of one last opportunity for meandering free time before school starts. They texted me goofy stuff occasionally, like they were at a sleepover. It's wild to see Delaney connecting with a new friend.

Raheel, Cameron, and I camped on their floor and watched about eight hours of *Game of Thrones*. It helped alleviate my anxiety over starting class the next day—but only a bit.

Now I'm nervously sweating under my navy blazer, even though the morning is crisp, as Delaney, Vi, and I approach the auditorium for our first Middleford morning assembly—a mandatory full-school meeting occurring every Monday, Wednesday, and Friday before class begins. Aunt Betsy's words echo in my head: *Fear tells you to make your life small. Don't give it the air to survive.* But I'm giving it a lot of air today—I'm basically pumping a bellows on it.

Delaney had hooted with laughter as she saw me approach the dining hall earlier, wearing my uniform: khakis, white dress shirt, haphazardly tied tie, and blazer. I grinned sheepishly and did a little spin, arms outstretched. "Never gonna get used to you done up like that," she said. "Back atcha," I said. It's jarring to see her in her white blouse, navy skirt, and plain black shoes.

Vi's clothes look crisp and expensive and fit her perfectly. But she seems jittery too, and we're quiet except for sporadic small talk.

My already-thrumming pulse revs as we join the other kids flowing into the auditorium and take our seats. I survey the crowd. Groups of seven to eight students sit talking and laughing among themselves. I can taste the ambition and intelligence in the air, smell the wealth. I begin spiraling. *You don't belong here. What are you doing? Who do you think you are? Go back to where you belong. You don't belong with these people.* I remind myself of the time I spent with Cameron and Raheel, and of Vi tagging me in her photos. I remind myself that the shining prospect of Middleford's science program chose me as her best friend. It helps a little.

The animated cacophony in the auditorium quickly tapers off as Middleford's head of school, Dr. Archampong, takes the podium, dressed in an immaculate charcoal three-piece suit. "Good morning, students of Middleford Academy." He speaks in a stately baritone. "To those of you who are returning, I say, 'Welcome home.' To those of you here for the first time, I say, 'Welcome to your new home. You are now part of a long and proud tradition of excellence . . .'"

He talks about his impoverished childhood in Ghana. He exhorts us to cultivate a love of learning and of each other. He has a formal but warm and welcoming air. I wish I could give him the attention he deserves, but anxiety is winning out, gripping me like a snare that tightens the more I strain against it. I scan the sea of heirs and heiresses surrounding me, dressed in crisp khaki, gleaming white cotton, and navy wool. I feel rumpled and wrinkled. My clothes, which are new, still look shoddy and cheap compared to my classmates'. I must look like I'm wearing a rich-kid Halloween costume. *Hillbilly trash,* they'll think. *Who let him in here?*

I glance over at Delaney, who's watching Dr. Archampong with rapt attention, looking equally thrilled and scared shitless. Ditto Vi. I imagine myself five years ago, peering into a crystal ball, seeing future-me sitting here. I would have been astounded.

Dr. Archampong finishes. "And so, new friends and old, let us go forward into another school year. May we walk in the light of love and learning. May we write our names into Middleford's proud history."

Everyone applauds, then stands, and files out, chattering.

Delaney looks at me. "Here we go." All color has departed her face.

"Here we go." I try to keep the quaver from my voice but fail.

My head aches by the time I get to Intro to Poetry. I'm starving just from my brain's expenditure of energy trying to keep up.

My classes are small, and we all sit around a table and have a discussion. There's nowhere to hide. And nobody seems to want to anyway. I'm used to kids racing for seats in the back of the classroom, slumping with hoodies pulled up, stealthily texting or vaping while the teacher tries their damndest (or not) to keep them engaged. Not here. Everyone jumps right in.

I look around at the other students in the poetry class. All of them—eight girls and four guys—look like poetry kids, with a dreamy or haunted air. They look like artists and readers. I feel like a cartoon bear in a trench coat among them. *What am I doing here? Why am I intentionally seeking out failure?*

Dr. Britney Rae Adkins enters and takes a seat at the table. The air changes. I sense immediately that this class is going to be different from the others. Her eyes are the luminous electric gray of lightning through a rain-washed window and contain a piercing intelligence. Her iridescent-blue-tinged black hair falls to her shoulders in tight curls. She has a silver nose ring, and silver rings cover her slender fingers. She's lean and compact. She actually reminds me a lot of Delaney.

She wears a sleeveless black blouse, and covering one pale forearm entirely is a photorealistic black-and-gray tattoo of a wolf's head. Covering the other is a similarly lifelike and grayscale tattoo of a red-tailed hawk. She has black line-drawn symbols inked on her knuckles.

She somehow looks neither old nor young. She's missing a tooth on the right side. It's a jarring sight after how immaculately composed all of the other staff members we've met are. Her voice has some aged and worn quality about it, like leather rubbed to a dark sheen.

She calls roll. She pauses when she gets to my name, as though she recognizes it. She finishes and puts down her pen, eyeing us for a long time before finally speaking. "You can't fix a car with poetry. Poetry won't help you build that new app and make billions. It won't win you an election. There are so many ways that poetry isn't useful in the way we think of things as being useful. And yet . . ." The corners of her mouth turn up in the faintest smile. "We bring poems to read at weddings and funerals. We write them to lovers. When our lives have been burned down around us, we look for that single glowing ember

160

remaining, and that's a poem. Poetry is one of the highest artistic achievements of humankind.

"I told you that there are many things that poetry won't do. But there are many things poetry will do. Poetry makes arguments. It presents cases for better ways of living and seeing the world and those around us. It heals wounds. It opens our eyes to wonder and ugliness and beauty and brutality. Poetry can be the one light that lasts the night. The warmth that survives the winter. The harvest that survives the long drought. The love that survives death. The things poetry *can* do are far more important than the things it can't."

She speaks with the fervor of a true believer. As I listen, spellbound, there's a slight stirring deep in me, the rise of a wind you don't notice until it rattles the leaves around you. I may not belong here, but I wasn't misled on what a great teacher Dr. Adkins is.

She finishes her introduction and explains that we won't be writing poems in this class—that's for Intermediate Poetry—but we'll be analyzing poems to understand how poetic language functions, to understand metaphor and subtext. I have a vision of myself taking apart my Chevy engine with Papaw, but instead of setting out combustion-blackened pistons and connecting rods on a greasy tarp, we'll be laying out words and phrases.

She goes around the circle, and to get to know us, she asks us if we have a favorite poem or poet. I hear a lot of names I don't recognize. Charles Bukowski, Sylvia Plath, Rupi Kaur, Langston Hughes. My heart thuds in my throat. I don't have an answer I'm not embarrassed to share.

When I was younger, I'd get Mamaw's old fake-leather-bound King James Bible with red-edged pages from her nightstand and try to read it like I was supposed to. I never got much past the first chapter of Genesis.

But those first verses of Genesis moved me. My head swam imagining the vast emptiness that preceded the Creation, the void and formless world that God called into being. I loved the sparse, gorgeous sentences detailing the Earth's building. I marveled that so few words could contain all of Creation.

I hurriedly scour my brain for something that won't draw inward snickers. I already feel conspicuous enough. I don't need everyone thinking I attended some snake-handling church down in the holler. I figure surrender is my least embarrassing option. "I don't have one right now." I'm the only one who can't name one. My face burns.

Dr. Adkins says gently, "It's called *Intro* to Poetry for a reason."

Chapter 26

By 3:40, as I'm entering the gym for my first crew prac-tice, I'm too mentally exhausted to even be nervous. At my old school, I consistently felt at *least* on the upper end of average intellect, if not above average. Here? Thoroughly below average. I'm going to have to work every second to keep from disappoint-ing Papaw and Mamaw and Delaney.

To distract myself, I fixate in my mind on the rhythm of the rowing from the video, the whisper of the boat gliding through the water, the smoothness of its motion seemingly unconnected to its human machinery. *Nothing will improve this day like being on the water—in your element.*

Even though it's only been days since I was on the river, it feels like years. I mentally rehearse the movement of water, the two tiny vortices that spiral away from the edges of my paddle on each stroke. Digging in and feeling my heart pump more oxygenated blood to my hungry muscles. Whatever chemical in your body causes stress and exhaustion, it can't survive that.

I arrive at the meeting place—a corner of the gym with sol-dierlike ranks of rowing machines. A tall, thickly muscled man with a shaved head, a stopwatch around his neck, and a clipboard under one arm greets me with a crushing handshake.

"Wes Cartier. Novice and JV crew coach. You're?"

"Pruitt. First name Cash."

He pulls out his clipboard and checks off my name. "Pruitt. Ready to sweat?"

"Yessir."

"What I like to hear. Hang tight; we'll get started in a sec."

I scan the room for any familiar face, seeing none. Here and there, guys stand in little clumps talking. A few stand alone and apart like me.

Coach Cartier claps and sticks his pinkies in his mouth and whistles. "Circle up." He has a military bearing. "Welcome to crew. Racing is one of the purest and oldest forms of human sport. We're born to race. Speed is survival. Not only that: The pack is survival. Teamwork is survival. Here, we work on speed and we work on teamwork. Every movement you make in a racing shell—which is what we call our boats—affects everyone else in the shell. There is no *I* in crew. But there is a *we*."

"Technically an *ew*," some brave smart-ass behind me whispers.

Coach Cartier cups his hand to his ear. "Sorry?"

Everyone shakes their head—*wasn't me, nope*—and stares at the ground.

He continues. "I'd hate to interrupt anyone's cleverness by talking about crew. Did we get it out of our systems?"

More staring at the ground. Slight nods.

"Good. Now, the first rule of speed is strength. So for the next several practices, the only water you'll be getting near is what you use to rehydrate after you've sent weakness packing. We can't work on technique until the conditioning is there."

My flagging spirit stumbles headlong and skins both knees. Being on the water was the one thing I needed today. Maybe at least a good workout and sweat will help.

"And the good news," Coach Cartier says, "is that because we're working on pure strength and conditioning today, rather than finesse, we can jump right in."

He takes a few minutes to explain the workings of the rowing machines, aka ergometers, aka ergs. Then he starts assigning us to machines in alphabetical order. "Alvarez . . . Dunn . . . Haddad . . . Nguyen . . . Olsen . . . Pak . . . Pruitt . . . Schmitt . . ."

And we begin. It's one of those workouts where you think, *Okay, I can survive this for a couple of minutes.* But we don't do it for a couple of minutes. We row in three-minute intervals, highest resistance, all-out, with short breaks. They don't help. My heart feels like it's pumping lava to my muscles and organs. Every breath only reminds my lungs of what oxygen is, only making them hungrier. *This must be what Papaw feels like.*

During one of the intervals, when we're frantically trying to cram as much air back into our blood as we can, I make eye contact with the guy next to me. It's the sort of look I'd imagine exchanged between soldiers pinned down under fire. *Hope we make it out of this. Me too.*

We do somehow. Coach Cartier counts us down and we halt. I trudge a slow circle around the perimeter of the room, fighting nausea. Even this exertion feels dangerous and I stop, with my hands on my knees, bent over, gasping in the sweat-humid air.

I sense someone beside me, mirroring my pose. It's the guy who was on the erg next to me.

"Bro," he says between wheezing breaths. "I was this close to asking you to tell my parents I loved them."

"You're assuming I would have survived."

"I can see it now—someone rolls up at my parents' door: 'At least your son died doing what he loved: transforming his finite number of heartbeats into mechanical energy to spin a fan on a rowing machine while a dude who looks like a Predator drone screams at him.' "

I laugh even though I can't afford the oxygen.

The guy extends a sodden hand. "Alex Pak. Sorry, all sweaty."

I shake his hand. "Cash Pruitt. Sweaty too."

"*Pshhh,*" Alex says. "Man, I'm from Houston. There's *one* weekend in January when you're not soaked. That's it for the year."

"I thought Tennessee was bad."

"You from there?"

"Sawyer, Tennessee."

"We gonna have to throw down about Texas barbecue versus Tennessee?"

I smile. "Maybe."

"Even if Tennessee wins, I'll still rep that Korean barbecue hard."

"Never had it."

Alex looks aghast. "Dude."

"Wanna guess how many Korean restaurants are in Sawyer?"

"Is it zero?"

"Ding ding."

"We're gonna set this right," Alex says. "I'm not going to let you die slumped over a rowing machine without it ever having passed your lips."

"Bring it on, baby."

"Honestly, though, I'm so hungry I could eat California barbecue."

"I've never had that either."

"I don't even know if it exists. But if it does, it sucks. They probably use, like, mashed avocado and mango LaCroix as barbecue sauce."

"Just as I was getting over feeling like puking," I say.

"I should keep it down. I don't know how many of these guys are from Cali."

"You new here?"

"Just transferred in. First day."

"Same!"

"Sweaty high five!"

We high-five. Sweatily.

Coach Cartier claps once. "Gentlemen, hit the showers. We'll pick it up tomorrow. Come ready to work."

"Hey, bro," Alex says. "What're you doing now?"

"Meeting my friends Delaney and Vi in the dining hall for dinner. Wanna join?"

"I was gonna invite myself anyway."

"Cool."

"How do you have friends already?"

"Long story. Tell you on the walk there."

Alex casts a quick rearward glance at Coach Cartier, who's busy on his phone. He turns back to me, and in a low voice says, "Cartier forgot to mention there's both an *ow* and an *ache* in *rowing machine*."

I wait for Alex just outside the gym, my bag at my feet. The rose pink of blood still warms my face despite the ice-cold shower I took to try to simulate the feeling of river spray on my skin. But I do feel better. My muscles devoured a lot of my stress.

Alex comes out, his thick black hair standing in wet spikes. "Tell you what, bro. That felt *good*."

"The shower or the workout?"

"Mostly the shower. But the workout, in retrospect."

We start for the dining hall. "Gorgeous night too," I say.

"I cannot get used to it being under ninety degrees in September."

"What's Houston like?"

"Hot and *huge*. Supposedly the most diverse city in America too. Every kind of food. It's amazing. My parents own a Korean restaurant there."

"For real?"

"Yeah. You ever come to Houston, we'll do you right. Bibimbap. Tteokbokki. Bulgogi. Korean fried chicken."

"Don't forget the barbecue."

"Don't you worry. So, what's Sawyer like?"

"*Not* the most diverse city in America. Small. Quiet. Real green. Like if people stopped cutting back the plant life, it'd turn back into forest in about five years. People there don't have much money. But it's home. I miss it."

"What do you miss most?"

"Besides my grandparents? There's a river that runs through town. My grandpa and I used to canoe on it. Then his health got to where he couldn't, and I'd go with my friend Delaney, who we're meeting."

"Hence crew?"

"Yep. How about you?"

"I've been canoeing one time, with my church youth group. Didn't play any sports in junior high and high school. No time.

After school I'd help at my parents' restaurant and do homework between rushes. So I figured I'd do a sport that most people were gonna be new to. Thought maybe there'd be a chance of getting a college crew scholarship."

We merge into a stream of kids entering the dining hall. "You here on scholarship? Sorry if that's a rude question. I don't know all the etiquette or whatever. I'm on scholarship."

"Oh, for sure, dude. My parents could never afford this place."

"Same. I mean—" I almost say, *Even if my parents were still around.* But as easy as Alex is to talk to, I'm not ready to open up that much. "Yeah."

Inside the dining hall, it's a potpourri of good smells. I survey the room. "I don't see Delaney and Vi yet."

We get in the food line. I tell Alex how Delaney and I came to school together.

"Sherlock Holmes and Dr. Watson up in here, bro." Alex pauses, reads a placard, and points at some foil-wrapped burritos or sandwiches. "Yes!"

"What?"

"Banh mi!"

"Do what?"

"Vietnamese sandwich. They're so good, dude."

"Think I'll like it?"

"Depends on if you like delicious things."

I shrug and grab one. "Bottoms up." I hold it up as if in a toast.

Alex grabs one and tosses it on his tray, grabs two more, and tosses one on my tray and another one on his. "Save you a trip back. You earned it on the erg."

"Ergs are aptly named. *Errrrrrrgh.*" We laugh, grab cardboard sleeves of fries and cups of coleslaw, and find a table with a couple of spare seats for Delaney and Vi.

"So," Alex says, unwrapping his banh mi, "what's your plan?"

"What, like—"

"In life."

"Shit, dude. I'm probably the only person here who hasn't known since preschool their plan for when they grew up. You?"

Alex takes a huge bite of his sandwich and chews for a second. He looks at it appreciatively. "This is better than it has any right to be." He takes another bite. "My plan: Graduate. Princeton undergrad. Then get my law degree and div degree at somewhere that has a joint program. Maybe Yale."

"Div?"

"Divinity. Study of religion."

"Gotcha."

"Start a social justice ministry. Organize in the community. Run for city council. Run for state office. Run for US Congress. House or Senate. Probably House. From there: the second Korean American president of the United States."

He rattles it off with such ease and nonchalance, I study his face for some hint of a joke, but it reveals none.

I laugh anyway. Alex stares back evenly.

"You're serious."

"Yep."

I redden. "Sorry for laughing. It's just if one of the kids I grew up with said that, they'd be joking."

"I'm not saying it's one hundred percent that I'll be president someday."

"No, yeah, I gotcha. Why *second* Korean American president?"

"Because it should have already happened by the time I'm old enough."

I've known Alex for fewer than two hours, and I can already see such a steely, quiet confidence in him. There's not a doubt in my mind he's going to do exactly what he says he will. I'm jealous. He seems like the kind of person who never lets down anyone he loves. I wish I were that.

Alex takes another bite of his banh mi and shakes his head. "Real good. Tell you what, though, man, I do a brisket banh mi." He kisses his fingertips. "You gotta try it someday."

"You cook?"

"Used to help my folks out at their restaurant. Me and my sisters. I'm gonna be the first president to put a Korean-Vietnamese-fusion food truck on the front lawn of the White House."

"My roomie's dad is a US House rep," I say.

"Yeah? Maybe I should talk with him."

"Wouldn't recommend it."

"He suck?"

"He ain't great. How's your roomie?"

"Don't have one."

"Serious?"

"I was supposed to. Then he pulled out at the last minute and went to another school. Wait list came through or something. So I have the room to myself."

"Lucky."

Behind Alex, I see Delaney and Vi enter the dining hall, look around, and spot us. They get their food and join us at our table.

"Delaney, Vi, this is Alex Pak from Houston, Texas," I say.

Alex nods and smiles broadly. "Hey, good to meet you."

"How do y'all know each other?" Delaney asks.

"Crew," I say. "It was like being in war together."

"In World War II, the Russians repaired roads by laying the bodies of German soldiers side by side and spraying them with water to freeze solid," Delaney says.

Alex nods. "Wild."

And with that . . . Alex, meet Delaney. I glance down at my french fries, lying side by side. "Sometimes I wish you knew less stuff."

"So, Delaney, I know where you're from," Alex says. "Vi?"

"Brazil."

"Awesome. Welcome to America."

"I see you already have a good immigration policy, Alex," I say.

Vi looks quizzical.

"Alex is going to be president someday," I say.

Alex shrugs. "Gonna try."

"How was field hockey?" I ask Delaney.

She holds up a skinned knee. It's all the answer I need. I can picture Delaney standing just outside the fracas, looking zoned-out, while she observes the patterns of play and searches for the right formula, ignoring the calls of her coach to get into the action. Then, she strikes. She's smaller than the other girls on her team, but none of them have the scrap and grit she does. None of them have her pain threshold. All of them are more afraid to see their own blood.

Delaney doesn't look exhausted like me. Her cheeks still glow from field hockey, and she has a luster and alertness in her eyes that make her appear energized and eager for more.

"How were classes?" I can predict her response, from her face, before I even ask.

"In physics we were discussing quantum entanglement within like three minutes of taking roll," Delaney says.

"Wow."

"Don't say 'Wow' sarcastically like I haven't told you several times what quantum entanglement is."

"It didn't take."

Delaney shakes her head and rolls her eyes.

I turn to Vi. "How were your classes?"

She rests her chin on her palms with her pinkies at the curved corners of her full lips. An errant streak of sunset falls across her face through one of the tall dining hall windows, illuminating the copper of a lock of her hair.

"Good." She says it with a little contented sigh. "And how was—mmm." Vi pantomimes rowing.

"Crew?"

"Yes! Crew. Sounds like the word for 'raw' in Portuguese: *cru*."

"That works, because I'm feeling pretty raw right now. My arms are hamburger."

Vi reaches across the table and grips my left biceps and squeezes. "Feels okay to me. Maybe we can replace it with a robot arm like Bucky Barnes's."

"Now, hang on, you buy a ticket to the gun show?"

Vi looks at me blankly.

"So, uh. In America sometimes we call biceps 'guns,' like, as a joke. And there are these big shows or conventions or whatever called gun shows. But for real guns, not biceps. Obviously. And you have to buy tickets. To the gun show. And yeah." *Very successful joke.*

"So I just got into the gun show without a ticket?"

"That's right."

"Don't tell the police."

"I won't."

"They'll send me back to Brazil."

"I definitely won't, then. We need you right here in America."

"Right here in Connecticut." She pronounces it *Connetchicut*.

We rejoin the conversation between Delaney and Alex. Delaney is telling Alex that science doesn't know why anesthesia works.

"I think we're officially a crew now," Alex says as we're finally getting up to leave.

"Dude, can you not say 'crew' right now? Too soon," I say.

Alex laughs. "Good point. Squad, then. I officially declare us a squad."

Chapter 27

We leave the dining hall together. Vi and Delaney split off. Alex and I keep strolling. The air smells aquatic, verging on rain.

"Where you live, bro?" Alex asks.

"Koch Hall."

Alex beams and goes up for the high ten. "Koch too, baby."

I high-ten him. "Fourth floor."

"Third."

"You gotta come up to the fourth floor on Saturday night for *Midnite Matinee.*"

"What's that?"

"Oh . . . you'll see. Kinda tough to describe."

"Can't wait."

My phone starts buzzing, and I pull it out. An incoming video call from Papaw and Mamaw. I try to decline it, with the intention of calling them back, but I accidentally answer. "Sorry, dude," I say to Alex. "Accidentally answered this Skype from my grandparents. I better take this."

"I wanna meet your grandparents!"

My insides cinch tight just above my stomach. I flash to Tripp mocking Papaw's accent. But something reassures me that that won't happen with Alex. "Cool."

Papaw's face appears—drawn, sallow, and at the unflattering upward angle at which he tends to hold the tablet. "Hey, Mickey Mouse," he wheezes. "Thought I'd try to catch you before I turned in. Had to see how the first day went."

"Good. I'm beat. Classes were hard but good. Got a ton of homework already. Just got done with crew practice, which completely destroyed me. I'll be lucky to stay awake to study."

He staves off a coughing fit. "Go get yourself a Coke-cola, put some pep in your step. How're the kids there? Nice?"

"Yeah, I made a new friend—"

Alex pops his head into the frame. "Hi!" He grins and waves. "I'm Alex."

Papaw smiles. "Howdy, Alex. Pleasure to meet you. My friends call me Pep, and so do my grandson's friends."

"He just met Delaney," I say.

Papaw chuckles and coughs. "Ain't she something?"

"Indeed," Alex says.

"Now, you from up in Connecticut?"

I hand my phone to Alex. Might as well.

"Houston," Alex says.

"Guess I better call you Tex, then."

"My last name is Pak. Tex Pak has a nice ring to it."

"It surely does. Now, how'd you and Cash meet?"

"Crew practice."

Papaw coughs but quickly recovers. "You ought to come down with him, visit Tennessee sometime. We got a fine river right near."

"I'd like that. Cash told me."

I'm awestruck at Alex's ease in befriending an old man from Tennessee in mere seconds, with pauses for coughs and labored breathing, over a sputtering video call. With this gift for connection, he might just become president after all.

"I'm gonna stuff him full of Korean food and Texas barbecue. Show him the true barbecue."

"Them's fightin' words, Tex! You come down here, I'll throw a pork butt on the smoker, show you what for," Papaw says, grinning.

"Sounds like even if I lose, I win," Alex says. "I'm gonna hand you back to Cash. Good meeting you, Pep."

"Pleasure meeting you, Tex. You make sure my grandson keeps his nose clean, hear?"

"Yessir!" Alex hands my phone back and slaps me on the shoulder. "I'm gonna go on in." He claps and points at me. "Tomorrow, baby. We enter the valley of the shadow of death together again."

"Can't hardly wait."

Alex leaves.

I turn my attention back to Papaw. "Alex is great, huh?"

"This is why I wanted you to go. So's you could meet good people like him."

"It's early to be turning in."

Papaw coughs and wheezes like he'd been saving up during his brief chat with Alex. "Felt tired."

"Mamaw there?"

"Working."

"Shoot."

"Tell me more about your first day."

I sigh. "It was tiring. They move fast here. Everyone's super into school. Kinda makes me feel like the dumbest one in class."

"You ain't."

"Feels like it."

"No, sir, you ain't. I wager many of these kids been in an environment like this all their lives. So they got a leg up. But you got a strong mind, and you know how to work. You'll be fine."

I hope so. I don't want to let you down. I don't want that to be the last you know of me.

Papaw coughs and coughs. Even his coughs sound weak and tired and thin.

"You okay?" I ask.

"Ye—" he starts to say, but more coughing cuts him off. He can't stop.

"Hey, Papaw, I love you. I'm gonna let you go so you can get some rest, okay?"

He waves. "Love you, Mickey Mouse," he manages as best he can, and the screen goes dark.

I do my best to focus on my homework. I'm not used to trying to study with someone sitting indifferently a few feet away, listening to music so loud I can clearly hear it through his headphones.

In addition to that distraction, I'm fighting being bone-weary and thinking of how Papaw has visibly declined in a matter of days. I'm also thinking of the new light in Delaney's eyes compared with what must surely be the dull glaze in mine. I'm petrified for what this means for the future of our friendship. *How long do I have before she finds her real people—the ones she'd have chosen over me if she could have in Sawyer?*

Most of all, I'm struggling to get a grip on the unfamiliarity of this new life, and it's proving very slippery.

All this adds up to a patchwork of undefined emotion. A whole lot of *feeling*, most of it bad, stealing my focus.

Then, one final distraction. A gust of wind lightly rattles the window, followed by a constellation of rain on the glass. Tripp either doesn't notice or doesn't care, and I'm glad to have this bit of minor holiness all to myself. If nothing else, this one thing in my life can be perfect.

Chapter 28

"Dude, I told you not to touch anything," Delaney says, without looking up from her laptop screen. She enters something and moves back to her microscope.

"I'm not." I wouldn't dare. The Middleford Science Center is an intimidating place—everything gleaming new and antiseptic, brushed steel and LED lights. It feels like being on a spaceship.

"I know. But by the time you do, it'll be too late, so I'm reminding you," Delaney murmurs, staring into the microscope. "Anyway, yes, horseshit is a greater degree of lying than bullshit."

"I just disagree. I think they're the same."

"Horseshit is more emphatic."

"Says you."

"You've heard of people referred to as 'bullshitters.'"

"Sure," I say. *She's setting the trap.*

"You ever heard of someone referred to as a 'horseshitter'?"

"No." *And I walked right in.*

"There you go. It's too harsh. Not affectionate."

Of course she's right.

"What are you working on?" she asks.

"My Social Ethics homework."

"How's that treating you?"

"Pretty ethically, I guess. What are you doing?"

"Observing cell growth. We put lung cells in nutrient gel to grow them into the architecture they'd have in the body. Then we can test stuff on them to see how they respond."

"That sounds pretty advanced."

"Hence why I wanted to come here, buddy." Delaney goes back to her laptop, makes another entry, and exhales through pursed lips.

"Aren't you supposed to be wearing a lab coat or something? Like on TV?" I ask.

"Naw. Just gloves and eye protection when you're working with dangerous stuff." She picks up her phone and starts scrolling. "So . . ."

I look up when, after an extended time, she still doesn't finish the sentence. She's fixed on her screen, chewing on the side of her left thumb, her face draining of color.

"Red?" I ask.

She doesn't answer.

"Hey."

"Nothing," she says. She closes her laptop brusquely and jams it in her backpack. "Tell you later," she mumbles, eyeing the other students at work in the lab.

Her legs are shorter than mine, but still I have to hustle to keep up as we leave the science center. "So?"

Delaney looks down and slows her pace. "The other night, I followed one of the girls in Biology Club on Instagram, and one of her pics just popped up in my feed. In it, she's hiking, and she's captioned it, 'Hey guys, just going for a hike in the woods. Maybe I'll find a magic mushroom that cures cancer and they'll name it after me and it gets me a cool scholarship that makes everyone think I'm a genius.' Full-on shit-talking me. And all these people from Biology Club and STEM were liking it and commenting and laughing."

"Wow. Assholes."

"And, like, I'm trying here, you know? Back home, I didn't give a shit who liked me and who didn't. But I've been trying here."

"That's amazingly shitty and immature behavior. The kind of people who sit around and talk trash on other people who have accomplished more than them are the worst."

"I mean, I thought I *might* fit in here? Turns out it's just a different kind of hater than in Sawyer." Delaney sounds despondent.

"I don't know. In Sawyer, the haters hate because you're smarter and more awesome than them. Here, same deal."

Delaney gives me a half smile. *"Very* comforting."

"Petty people are petty wherever you go. No matter where they've gotten in life."

"I guess."

"What do you want me to do about them?"

"I want you to *not* kick the shit out of them like you did with Jaydon Barnett."

"I could take them." I drop into a fighting stance and do some quick shadowboxing.

"Dude, Madeline Scott and Edward Hsu would team up and destroy you. They're small but vicious. Like honey badgers."

"Isn't that why I'm here? To whup ass on your behalf?"

"Ideally, no," Delaney says.

"What can I do? You want me to get Papaw on the phone? So he can give you a—"

"Cash."

"What?"

"Don't do it."

"Do what?"

"What I know you're about to do. I'm warning you."

"So he can give you a . . . *Pep* talk."

"Damn it, Cash. You dad-joking piece of shit." But now Delaney is fully smiling.

"Hey," I say, my voice serious. "Don't let this get to you, okay?"

"Easier said than done."

"That's why I'm saying it. We still have a half hour before dorm check-in. Wanna go to the lake?"

"Yeah," Delaney says. "Let's go skip some rocks."

"Or in your case, throw rocks squarely into the water."

"*Now,* dude? You're gonna crap on my rock-skipping abilities now? While I'm vulnerable?"

I motion her toward me. "Come get you a big old hug."

She comes in for an embrace, and I pick her up and spin her around. She squeals. "Cash! Don't make me drop my shit." But it seems to lift her spirits.

We arrive at the lake and sit side by side on a bench. We're quiet for a while. Finally, I say, "I hate for you that you have to deal with this. I guess being a genius has a downside."

Delaney nods.

"By the way, I was talking about how *my* being a genius comes with the downside of me hating this for you," I murmur.

She backhands me in the thigh. "You are *such* a jackass. Let's skip some rocks."

We skip rocks for a while. Or, more accurately, I skip rocks while Delaney throws rocks in the water.

"Did you know you can't fold a piece of paper in half more than eight times?" Delaney says.

"You serious? That can't be right. What about a super thin piece of paper that's, like, a mile wide."

"Nope. And if there were a way to fold a piece of paper in half one hundred and three times, it would be as big as the universe."

"Is that true?"

"Yep. Exponential growth."

We throw rocks for a while and talk until it's time for us to check in.

"Thanks," Delaney says, hugging me.

"You feel better?" I rest my cheek on top of her head.

"A little. I'm glad you're here."

"I always got your back. You know that, right?"

"I know. See you at breakfast?"

"Yep."

I watch her until she gets into her building safely. I think on the wonder of things expanding to fill the universe, even as they're being folded in half.

Chapter 29

Middleford students have a saying: A day feels like a week and a week feels like a day.

Over the weeks, I settle into an uneasily steady routine. Roll out of bed. Rush to get ready. Go to morning assembly. Go to class. Go to lunch. Go back to class. Go to crew. Go to dinner. Hang out with Delaney, Vi, and Alex. Talk to Mamaw and Papaw. Study. Sleep. Repeat. Repeat. Repeat. In the mornings, my breath mists silver and the air pinches at my skin. All around, the leaves are beginning to turn and drop. The New England autumn is dazzling—I'll give it that. Here I thought nothing could rival an East Tennessee autumn.

I continue my *Game of Thrones* watch with Raheel. I make a few new casual acquaintances. Nobody I'd share any of my big secrets with, though. I deflect, divert, and outright lie when the subject of parents comes up. Everyone knows I'm close with my grandparents, but I've never said *why* I'm so tight with them.

Alex clearly has loving, if demanding and tough, parents. Vi's parents sound busy but doting. Delaney's pretty open with the state of her homelife: "My mom sucks." I'm not totally sure Delaney has talked to her mama even once since she got to Middleford.

On Saturdays, we go into New Canaan or laze around

campus. I've come to prefer the latter because going into town means pressure to spend money I don't have. Neither Alex nor I have the laundry service, so on Saturdays, we do laundry and ironing in Koch Hall's basement. One day after crew practice, Alex eyes me in my rumpled khakis and wrinkled button-down shirt and says, "Man, I'm giving you an ironing lesson." What he says without saying it: *We may be scholarship kids, but we don't have to look like it.* Alex's clothes aren't much nicer than mine, but he looks much sharper. He teaches me the finer points of stain removal, learned on the white tablecloths and napkins of his parents' restaurant.

On Sunday mornings, I go with Alex to a sparsely attended nondenominational Christian worship service on campus. Church is something I can take or leave, but it brings back fond memories of going with Mamaw and Papaw, and I like hanging out with Alex.

Vi's and my friendship grows tighter. We talk a lot, when we can. She's a diligent student, and when she's not studying, she's teaching herself programming and working on one of her video-game projects. I imagine learning to speak Portuguese. I wonder if she's a different person in her native tongue. I want to know that person. I look at photos of Rio and imagine sitting on the beach beside her, talking and listening to the waves breaking on the shore.

In my classes, I struggle to stay afloat. I've never had so much information crammed down my throat at once. At night, I dream about class. It's an improvement from my normal nightmares, at least. The hardest part is the contrast with Delaney. She's not foundering like me. She's flourishing, like I knew she would. No, actually, that's second place. The hardest part is the constant fear of letting down Papaw and Mamaw and revealing how unspecial I am.

If I had to choose, my favorite class is poetry, of all things. Not that I'm much better at it than my other classes. If anything, I'm further behind than in my other classes. But there's something about Dr. Adkins that puts me at ease. And her love for poetry is contagious.

I do a lot of my studying in the lab with Delaney, where she spends most of her free time during the week. She's pretty secretive and vague about what she's working on. I wouldn't understand it anyway. The science program and Biology Club are taking up more and more of her time, even on weekends. I live with an ever-growing, constant buzz of fear of Delaney's ditching me finally for her science friends. She must get more from hanging out with them than I can offer.

Tripp remains aloof. He's constantly surrounded by a cohort who also sweat the smell of money. He only talks to me when he can't find something he misplaced (basically accusing me of taking it) or when he's complaining. Generally these gripes take the form of a teacher or fellow student having ventured to challenge something he said. A couple of times he's made cracks about my being on scholarship, as though his being born into wealth isn't its own sort of luck-based full-ride scholarship to life. I seethe quietly, trying to keep the peace. I have more to lose, and he knows it.

For the first couple weeks of crew, it's one grueling erg workout after another in the sweaty, stuffy gym, while sparkling early-autumn days pass by outside. But on one such perfect afternoon—seventy-four degrees, the sun shining—we hit the water. Coach Cartier shows us around the shells. We hoist an eight-seat shell off the boathouse rack and onto our shoulders, carry it down to the dock, and place it in the water. The coxswain sends half of us to get the oars, while the remaining rowers open the oarlocks and hold the shell in place. Alex and I ask to be assigned to the same shell, and Coach Cartier shrugs and says, "As long as you're good at working together and working hard." We sit in the "engine room"—he's on port in three seat, and I'm sitting on starboard in four seat. After a shaky shove-off at the dock, we embark gingerly onto the Five Mile River.

At first, we're slow to synchronize our movements, despite our coxswain sitting in the stern shouting commands, and we wobble all over the river. It's unnerving how tippy the shell feels—so different from a canoe.

We get splashed a lot with cold water before we learn how to feather and bury the blades cleanly. Pulling an oar is different from using the erg or paddling a canoe. But I learn quickly, as do my teammates, and we fall into a rhythm. *Catch drive release recover catch drive release recover catch drive release recover catch drive release recover.* We're able to maintain a straight(ish) course and pick up a little speed. The prow of the shell shushes through the water. Sunshine filters through the trees on the riverbanks. A clean, aquatic smell surrounds us.

Over the barked orders of the coxswain, I hear Alex murmur, beneath a grunt of exertion, "Finally, bro. This is where it's at."

I nod and smile and quietly say, "Yep."

Catch drive release recover catch drive release recover catch drive release recover. Every muscle in my body a component of a machine. My body a cog in a larger gearwork. I sweat and cycle clean, fresh air through my lungs. By the time we put in, the sun is low in the sky, kissing the treetops. My heart still pounds and my brain is awash in endorphins. When I first saw the video of the crew team, it looked like their arms were doing all the work. But the reality is that your legs do most of it, so my quads feel rubbery afterward. Even though I have calluses on my hands, blisters form on my palms from gripping the wet oar handle. But I feel pure joy for the first time since arriving at Middleford. I don't expect it to last, so I chisel it into my mind to run my fingers over later.

Most nights I videochat with Papaw and Mamaw, at least for a while, if she's not closing at work. Delaney joins in when she can. Our chats have been getting earlier, as Papaw's been running out of steam sooner in the day. He laughs less now. I guess partly because it runs such a risk of sending him into a coughing vortex he can't escape. His eyes are glassy and dim. His voice has taken on a more wheezing quality.

Something I imagine a lot lately is Papaw sitting on the porch alone and counting each dwindling breath as it flares in the yellow porchlight and disappears. I wonder if he sees his final October in the falling leaves.

Chapter 30

Last night Papaw couldn't talk for more than a couple minutes. I talked with Mamaw for a bit, and she said wearily that she expected he'd rally soon. Her purple-rimmed eyes lied. Afterward, I sat quietly with Delaney for a long time by the lake. *He was just having a bad day,* she said. I only nodded.

Now I'm trying to pay attention to Dr. Adkins, but there's a tight knot under my solar plexus and anxiety shortens my breath. *Is it asking too much to have one whole hour when I don't think about the sword hanging over my papaw's neck?*

Outside the window is a stand of flame-hued maple trees, and the sight of it soothes me. It reminds me of the time Delaney, Papaw, Mamaw, Punkin, and I sat on our porch on a biting and gray Saturday morning toward the end of last October. The smells of wood smoke, coffee, frying bacon, and cold dew on grass hung in the air. Mist threaded through the hills like cobwebs. Delaney explained why leaves change in autumn. I don't remember the explanation, just the perfect feeling that my life, encircled as I was at that moment by beauty and people I loved, had become fuller than I'd ever hoped it could be.

And now it's slowly becoming bare again, leaf by falling leaf.

". . . and, Cash, will you read the next stanza, please?" Dr. Adkins says.

It feels like being stung by a bee. I look left, heart galloping, where Holden, one of my classmates, offers the book to me expectantly with a sympathetic look.

I swallow hard. "Sorry. I'm—Where?" My voice cracks. My classmates avert their eyes, justifiably embarrassed for me. So far, I'd somehow managed to avoid too much public shame in this class. No more.

Dr. Adkins rises and comes over to me, brushing a piece of hair from her face. She takes the book from Holden, finds the stanza, and points to it. "Here you go."

"Sorry," I say.

"No worries." Her tone is gentle, which makes it worse somehow.

I read the stanza, my face blazing to match the trees I was just staring at. I stumble over words and lose my place, reading the same line twice. *Why does humiliation always seem to come in six-packs?* By the time I'm done and I pass the book to my right, my heartbeat throbs in my temples. I pray that Dr. Adkins doesn't ask me to offer an interpretation of what I just read, and she doesn't. We finish passing the poem around the circle and start analyzing it when we're done.

I have nothing to add to the conversation, but I will myself to stay engaged (or at least looking like it) as best I can. The refrain of *Why are you here? Papaw is dying while you're gone, and you're not even good at this* plays on a loop in my head.

Class ends and everyone starts filing out, chatting happily. Mini cliques have formed in the class among those with similar tastes in poetry. This has left me—with no particular poetic inclinations—in the cold. I bring up the rear, with Dr. Adkins behind me.

As I'm about to leave, she says, "Cash? Can you hang on for a sec?"

I turn and meet her eyes, a sharper and more insistent apprehension replacing the dull hum of anxiety and embarrassment. "Yeah. Sure." *She's going to ask you why you're here. She's wondering if maybe you wouldn't be more comfortable in more remedial classes.*

I follow her back into the classroom. She sits and crosses one leg over the other. I sit also, staring at the table, fidgeting.

She's wearing all black, like usual. I've never sat this close to her. She smells like a bonfire made of cedarwood soaked in smoky vanilla.

We don't speak for a second while she fixes her gray eyes on me. I quickly crack. "I'm sorry, ma'am. I should've been paying attention. I won't—"

"What were you looking at earlier?" Her tone is calm but insistent. I wish she'd be unambiguously angry or annoyed. I can't read her mood and it's unnerving.

"Nothing." My head is pounding.

"I can tell when someone isn't looking at nothing."

"Um. The trees outside."

"Why?"

I take an extended pause before speaking. I consider inventing a story. But she's already sniffed out my bullshit once. "I was thinking about my pap—my grandpa and—"

"What were you about to call him when you caught yourself?"

"*Papaw,*" I murmur. "It's our word for *grandpa* back home."

"I called my grandpa that," she says softly. "Where's home?"

"Sawyer, Tennessee. You haven't heard of it."

"No?"

"You have?"

"I got my MFA in poetry at Warren Wilson in Swannanoa, North Carolina. My wife used to cater in Nashville, and we'd drive through Sawyer."

"I can't believe you've even heard of it."

Dr. Adkins twists one of her rings with the adjacent finger. "My turn. I'm from Louisa, Kentucky."

I shake my head. "Never heard of it."

"It's about four hours northeast of Knoxville, almost in West Virginia."

As she says the last sentence, I detect a hint of accent for the first time. "So . . ."

"I'm Appalachian too." She pronounces it right. *Apple-atchun.*

"Wouldn'ta guessed," I murmur.

"My name is Britney Rae Adkins. That name sound more like I was born in New York City or in a place like Sawyer?"

I laugh.

"My latest book is called *Holler.*"

I'm brightening as I realize she didn't keep me back to fuss at me. "I heard that. I assumed it meant yelling, as opposed to a place where people live."

"Nope. And my hunch about where you were from was absolutely right."

"What tipped you off?"

"Your name. Your accent. Mostly your looking lost all the time, though—no offense."

"None taken." (But I am embarrassed again.)

We look at each other. Her eyes are the sort that burrow inside you to see hidden and buried things.

She says, "Now. You were going to tell me what you were thinking about while looking at the trees."

I take a deep breath. "I was remembering a morning in October when I was sitting on our porch with my papaw and mamaw and my best friend, Delaney—who's at Middleford too. It was a good morning. And I was thinking about it because now my papaw—" I don't know what made me think I was ready to tell a near stranger about his condition. I haven't even told Vi or Alex. The immediate waver that comes into my voice tells me I'm not prepared.

Dr. Adkins doesn't fill the silence as I look away and back out the window that got me into this. I've come this far, so I finish. "Is dying. He has emphysema and he wasn't doing great even before I left. And now—" I stop before I break down.

"He's doing worse?" Dr. Adkins asks gently.

I nod.

"And you're here, and here is far from him," she says.

I nod and stare at the ground.

"And so you're thinking about him a lot."

I nod. A lone tear escapes and flows down the side of my nose. I quickly brush it away with the ball of my thumb. I lower my head so Dr. Adkins won't see.

She pushes back her chair and stands, then walks purposefully to a bookshelf. She returns with several slim poetry volumes and hands them to me. "New homework assignment: Read at least one poem out of each of these books. Then, *write* a poem."

My heart starts racing again. "About what?"

"Whatever. About your favorite deodorant, for all I care."

"I didn't think we were gonna be—"

"Correct. We're not writing yet. Just reading and listening. But lucky you, going on the advanced track."

"I don't know anything about writing poetry. I don't even have a favorite poet."

"Guess how that changes."

I eye the books in my hands.

Dr. Adkins continues. "I have two intuitions about you. The first is that you've got it in your head that poetry has to be elaborate, and that's what's fueling your hesitancy."

"One for one."

"Number two: that you're someone who pays attention to the world around him."

"I mean . . . if I were good at paying attention, we wouldn't be talking."

She smiles. "Fair point, but nothing I say in this class is as important as watching leaves fall. You pay attention to the right things." She hesitates and then quickly adds, "But don't push your luck with other teachers. They might feel differently."

We laugh.

"Mary Oliver—she's one of the poets in your hand—said something important about writing poetry: 'Just pay attention, then patch a few words together and don't try to make them elaborate.' Do that. Pay attention. Patch a few words together. Don't try to make them elaborate." She looks at me. "You're still skeptical."

"Kinda."

"Ever sit on your porch with your papaw and listen to him tell stories?"

"All the time."

"Appalachian people are storytellers," Dr. Adkins says. "We're lovers of words. Poetry tells stories through words. This runs in your blood. You named after Johnny Cash?"

"Yeah, my mama and my papaw used to listen to him together."

"You even have a poet's name."

I sigh. "Okay. I'll try."

"I pay attention, Cash. You can't be a poet unless you do. And I see in you someone who wants to experience joy and is having a tough time doing that right now. Life often won't freely give you moments of joy. Sometimes you have to wrench them away and cup them in your hands, to protect them from the wind and rain. Art is a pair of cupped hands. Poetry is a pair of cupped hands."

Tears well in my eyes and I try to blink them clear.

"Okay," Dr. Adkins says softly, pretending not to notice my crying. "I've taken up too much of your lunchtime. Go eat. Go read. Go write."

I clear my throat a couple times and hold up the books. "I'm gonna do my best."

I'm almost out the door when Dr. Adkins calls out behind me, "Ever tried the cornbread in the dining hall?"

I turn. "My mamaw makes amazing cornbread."

"Figured. That's why I asked."

"No. Scared of it."

"You're right to be."

I've saved Dr. Adkins's homework for last because I know it'll be the toughest.

I open the Mary Oliver book and skim as my mind wanders. I think about what Papaw's funeral will be like. I wonder if his old friends will show up for him. I wonder—

I force myself back to the page. I promised Dr. Adkins I'd give this my best. I start reading again. Really reading. Letting myself taste the words, each one melting on my tongue.

Something happens. A slow daybreak inside me, the first rays of a new sun peeking over the gray horizon. I don't always understand what I'm reading. Poets use language in ways I've never considered, to describe things I thought defied description.

Dr. Adkins picked poets who write about the world. About rivers and fireflies and formations of geese and deer and rain and wind. Things I love.

By the time I'm done reading at least one poem out of each book (usually more), I'm experiencing a deep calm, like I feel after being on a river, under the sun, in the wind, feeling the spray off my paddle. For those brief moments strolling through the forest of words, everything had disappeared. Papaw wasn't dying while I was far from him at a place where I didn't belong, always on the precipice of disappointing him. I had stolen moments of joy from a hungry world that devours them and protected them for a while in cupped hands.

I sit with the feeling for as long as I can before it fades and loses definition, like a cloud formation.

Then I remember the second part of my assignment. To write a poem. This part makes me more apprehensive. I open my notebook to a blank page. Something about using a pen and paper feels more right. I stare at the white wilderness in front of me. It seems to grow with every second. I sit for almost an hour. I'll write a line. Then I'll think it sounds dumb or trite, and I'll scratch it out and start over. Repeat. Repeat. I get distracted by the sound coming from Tripp's headphones across from me.

Why can't writing be like mowing lawns or chopping wood? You put your back into it; you get sweaty; you get the job done.

Well. She told me poetry doesn't need to be elaborate. I write,

> *Words are stuck in my mind*
> *Like an axe buried in a stump*

I dwell on it for another few minutes. It feels half-assed even for an incomplete poem. As if I were hurting for yet another way to fail here.

I told Dr. Adkins I was no poet. If she pays attention like she claims, she'll see it.

Chapter 31

I sit across from Delaney at dinner. Alex is at either a Young Democrats or a Christian Student Fellowship meeting, and Vi is at Coding Club. So it's just the two of us. This doesn't happen often anymore. I haven't had a great day. I got a C on a paper for my marine biology class—one I'd worked my ass off on.

"Talked to my mama yesterday," Delaney says.

"No shit?"

"None."

"And?"

Delaney gives me a what-do-you-think look.

"She's gotta hit rock bottom," I say. "Isn't that what they say?"

"That does seem to be what they say." Delaney takes a bite of burrito.

We chew quietly for a few minutes.

"I gotta go," Delaney says, standing.

"Already?"

"Got work to do in the lab."

"Just hang out a little longer. The work'll still be there."

"Can't."

"Can't or won't?" I ask.

"Won't because I can't."

"Come on, seriously? We've barely hung out for more than ten minutes over the last two weeks."

Delaney rolls her eyes.

"Don't," I say. "You're never around, which is fine. But when we hang out, you don't even ask me about my day."

"How was your day?" Delaney asks with fake sweetness.

"You really wanna know?"

"Sure."

"Well, shitty, Red, thanks."

"Sorry it was shitty."

"Wanna know what the day before that was like? Shitty too."

"You accusing me of something?"

"You feel accused?"

We don't speak for a few moments. We've certainly fought in our time as friends. But this feels uglier. More fraught. It's scary to fight with someone who doesn't seem to have any need for you anymore.

"You realize this is the first time it's been just us two hanging out for like two weeks?" I ask.

"Been busy," Delaney says.

"No shit. All your new science nerd buddies."

"First off, no; part of it is science program stuff taking up time. Second off, they're nice; don't be a dick."

"Oh yeah. They were real nice a while back when they were shit-talking you."

"I'm not friends with the shit-talkers; I'm friends with the cool ones. And you've been perfectly happy to make friends with Vi and Alex."

I push my tray to the side, my appetite gone. "Not at the cost of our friendship."

"I'm just doing what you're supposed to damn do when you go to a new school."

"Yeah? Maybe I should start doing what I'm supposed to be doing and abandon you back."

"I'm tired of you acting like I'm a bad friend," Delaney says loudly.

"Keep your voice down—you're embarrassing me," I say through gritted teeth. "And stop being a bad friend, and I'll stop acting like you're one."

Delaney stands, draws close, and whispers in my ear. "I hope this isn't too quiet for you to hear me tell you to fuck off and not talk to me anymore."

And with that, she stalks away briskly without a rearward glance.

My stomach feels like it's filled with ice shards. I sit still, my face burning, staring at the table for a long time. I pull my tray back to me and pick at my food for a few minutes.

Delaney and I have always fought this way, on a tightrope, with no net, spiraling out of control before either of us knows what's happening. I don't know why we're like this. Maybe it's because we both assume that loss is life's default setting and we can beat it to the punch by setting fire to our friendship. I couldn't tell you. We've always managed to mend things, but that was back home, when neither of us had much else. Here, Delaney has a new paradise, full of people smarter and more interesting than me. People who'll be able to accompany her on her journey upward.

This isn't the first time Delaney's told me to never talk to her again, but this might be the time it actually sticks.

I have nothing in my life that isn't falling apart.

Chapter 32

As I'm packing up to leave class, Dr. Adkins waves me over. "Stick around for a sec," she says. Everyone files out. She motions for me to sit back at the table and I do. She slides a piece of paper over to me. "Short poem, short comment."

I look at the paper. It's my poem.

> *Words are stuck in my mind*
> *Like an axe buried in a stump*

Underneath, in messy, chaotic handwriting, Dr. Adkins has written, *Bullshit.*

Ever since Delaney and I stopped talking, every day's been even harder and lonelier, and this doesn't help. I'm so tired of looking dumb here. Blood courses to my face. "I wasn't trying to be cute," I say. "That's all that came to me."

"I believe you. And yet: bullshit. What did you mean by 'Words are stuck in my mind'?"

I ponder the question. "I guess . . . that there are words in there. I can hear them like someone is talking on the other side of a wall. But every time I go to write them, they're gone."

"You read from the books I loaned you."

"That's part of the problem. They're all so good. I got nothing compared to them."

"That's exactly the opposite conclusion from what I hoped you'd draw."

"What was I supposed to get out of it?"

"That poetry is observing and speaking truth, and that there are many paths to do that. You have a truth. Speak it."

"Easier said than done."

"You have to give yourself permission to fail."

"So you want me to write more poems?"

"Sure do."

"Seems kinda unfair that I'm the only one having to do extra work in class."

She shrugs. "Don't do the assignments I give the rest of the class. Do this instead." She looks at me for a while. In this light, her eyes look like an overcast sky with the sun shining bright behind the clouds. She hesitates before speaking, toying with one of her rings. "Cash, if I'm overstepping here, tell me."

"Okay," I say apprehensively.

"I sense you've dealt with a lot in life. Not just with your papaw's health."

I pause for what feels like an inordinately long time before I murmur, "You're right."

She points to her missing tooth, the one I'd wondered about. "When I was sixteen, my stepdad left me with this nice gap after he found a love poem I wrote to a senior girl with blue hair and a lip ring. I could've gotten it fixed by now, but that would have felt to me like an acknowledgment that he'd made me *less* somehow. I wear this absence as a monument to living the life

I chose for myself. I know the look of someone holding on to something."

I want to tell her about trying to open that death-sealed bathroom door. About numbly sitting on the porch and listening to distant sirens. But the moment I do, it will all follow me here. I need to hold on to the illusion for a little longer that I can outrun it.

"Is that why the poetry?" I ask.

"Every hurt, every sorrow, every scar has brought you here. Poetry lets us turn pain into fire by which to warm ourselves. Go build a fire."

Chapter 33

Since we quit talking, I haven't checked out Delaney's Instagram. It hurts too much, and I don't want to see evidence that I've been replaced. I'm about to head there anyway, though, when beside me Tripp flips the book he's reading—*Between the World and Me* by Ta-Nehisi Coates—onto the floor.

"Racist. Dude hates white people," he mutters to the air. *"Wahhhh, there was slavery a thousand years ago and now my life sucks and it's everyone's fault but mine,"* he says in a mocking voice, pulling his headphones down around his neck.

The only thing worse than studying wordlessly next to Tripp is trying to study when Tripp has something to hash out. And he only ever does that when he has a grievance of some kind.

"I've never owned a slave," Tripp says. "You ever owned one?"

"No," I say tersely and quietly, setting down my phone and picking my poetry book back up. I don't like the goading in his tone.

"How about your parents? Or grandparents?"

"Why you asking?"

"You're from the South. If anyone would have, you guys would have."

"I think slavery's evil and people who owned slaves were evil."

"How about your neighbors *ep thar* in Tennessee? Any slaves?"

Tripp smirks as he mocks Papaw again, like it's some sort of inside joke we share.

I want to knock his teeth out. My blood rises as I put my book down. "Naw. No neighbors who own slaves. Just neighbors who fly Confederate flags."

"So?"

"People remember stuff for generations. There are folks in Sawyer who hate their neighbors for things their great-great-great-great-grandparents did to each other. And if there are people still flying the flag of ancestors who *owned* slaves, maybe slavery still affects people whose ancestors *were* slaves. All I'm saying."

Tripp snorts and shakes his head. "All the rednecks in Tennessee, and I get the one snowflake for my roommate," he mutters.

"I know plenty of racist-ass people back home you could be roommates with instead."

"You're totally missing the point, but whatever. There's not a racist bone in my body."

I get up with my book under my arm and grab my notebook.

"Going to your safe space?" Tripp asks with a sneer.

"Got shit to do."

Tripp gives me an okay sign. "Go get untriggered."

I don't respond.

As much as I love the lake, I don't normally study by it. The light is dim by study time. I figure, though, if I'm just writing a poem, I don't need a lot of light. And I need a place that inspires me, that takes my mind off Delaney and is far from Tripp.

My mind's full of words from my reading. But they're fruit hanging from a branch that's just out of reach, my fingertips brushing them as I try to grab hold. Dr. Adkins's voice sounds in my head. *You have a truth.*

What is true in me?

I love my home. That's true. I write the first line that comes to me:

Ask me where I'm from.

I sit frozen for a half hour. My fear and frustration start congealing into anger. Intro to Poetry was my one class where I briefly didn't feel like the biggest idiot in the room. Dr. Adkins must have seen it and thought, "Better put an end to that." I sit for another half hour. Nothing.

I feel like I'm pushing on a door someone has died against.

I look at my page.

Ask me where I'm from.

What a stupid line. I'll tell you where you're from. You're from Sawyer, Tennessee. You have no mother or father. You have a roommate who hates you and many other kinds of people. You've maybe lost your genius best friend forever and you're about to lose your papaw, but first you're going to disappoint him and your mamaw by showing them exactly how unspectacular you are at a school where you don't belong and don't deserve to be.

You're sure as hell no poet.

Someday you'll be back in Sawyer, mowing someone's lawn

or painting their house, and you'll stop to mop the sweat off your brow with the faded bandana you keep in your back pocket. And the way the light hits will remind you of walking from the dining hall to class when you were a kid at Middleford Academy. And you'll laugh at the great accident of how you ended up at that school. Maybe you'll have enough distance to forget the humiliation and failure you met there, but probably not. You'll stuff your bandana back in your pocket and return to work.

That's where you're from. Never forget it.

Chapter 34

"Where's Alex?" Vi asks as she sits down with her tray.

"Not sure. I kinda remember him saying he had to crunch on a group project for his Law and Government class." *And you know why Delaney isn't here.*

My mood lifts to see her. It was looking like I'd be spending this Friday night dinner alone. Ever since Delaney and I stopped talking, Delaney hasn't been showing up for dinner.

"Just us?" Vi asks.

"Apparently."

A ribbon of tangerine-colored sunset light falls across Vi's face. I've never noticed before now, with the sun illuminating it, how many shades of red, bronze, copper, and gold thread through her hair. "What are you doing after dinner?" she asks.

"Dunno. Chillin'."

"There's a football game tonight," she says.

"Here?" I look at her for a second, fork suspended over my teriyaki bowl. She returns my look expectantly.

She nods. "We're playing against Deerfield Academy."

"You wanna go?" I ask.

She clasps her hands in front of her chest. "*Yes!* You'll go with me?"

I smile and set my fork in my bowl. I don't have much of an appetite anyway. "Yeah. I'll go."

I stand in front of Vi's (and Delaney's) dorm. Part of me is hoping Vi returns with Delaney in tow. I guess the next best thing would be if Delaney learns we're hanging out and gets jealous. I hope she at least misses spending time with me.

Vi emerges, ebullient, practically skipping, grinning widely. She's wearing a Middleford hoodie and a wool beanie. The day was warm, but a chill fell like a curtain when the sun dipped below the horizon.

"Man, you are *really* pumped for this game." We start strolling in the direction of the stadium.

"I've never been to an American football game before. I hope it's like the show *Friday Night Lights*."

"Who knew you were a big sports fan?"

"In Brazil I would go with my dad and brother to watch my favorite soccer team, Flamengo. They play in the stadium of Maracanã, and it holds seventy-eight thousand people."

"Whoa. When I was younger, my papaw took me once to see the University of Tennessee play football. That's a huge stadium too." I google quickly. "Holds one hundred thousand. Bigger than—"

"Maracanã? It used to hold two hundred thousand."

"Well, well."

"Flamengo was a crew team before they became a soccer team. Like you do."

"Seriously?"

"Delaney told me."

I feel a sharp pang of sadness mingled with regret at the reminder that Delaney's not here and someone else is getting her supply of random factoids tailored to their interests. "Did you see her tonight?"

"Yes. I invited her, but she said she had to study."

Even here Delaney doesn't need to study on a Friday night. "Oh." I don't have the energy to pretend it doesn't ache.

Vi hears it. "Are you two okay?" She asks it like she's walking on a frozen lake.

"We will be." *Hopefully.* "Did Delaney say anything?"

"She never says anything to me about you that isn't good."

Oof. "Can we change the subject? We're hanging out now."

"Okay."

An infectious energy permeates the air as we approach the stadium, a halo of artificial daylight above it from its blazing white lights. Packs of students in Middleford gear chatter animatedly as they file in.

I flash to a memory of going with Papaw to see Sawyer High play. How he'd clap me on the knee when Sawyer would make a good play. I loved seeing how young he seemed when he got excited. It made it feel like he would live forever.

Vi and I find seats. She sits closer to me than I expect. The sides of our legs touch. But I don't scoot over. Her thigh is warm against mine and I like it. She smells like smoky jasmine and spiced vanilla.

I scan the bleachers as the game kicks off. I spot Tripp and his crew. Palmer and Vance, his two minions, sit behind him. He's taking a selfie with Dewey Holmgren, his current fling. Since one of the only reasons he'll talk to me is to boast, I know she spent last summer in Milan, modeling. I suddenly want Tripp to see me, so he knows he's not the only one out with a pretty girl tonight.

Almost as quickly, I realize how long it's been since I was on something resembling a date—which is what this has started to feel like. My romantic life has mostly gone as my life generally: unspectacular. In July between seventh and eighth grade, I kissed Syvana Swindall at an Independence Day church potluck, around the side of the church house, while the ramshackle HVAC unit clattered over the noise of people laughing and playing horseshoes. The preacher's brother's wife almost caught us, and that spooked Syvana enough that it ended things before they started.

In ninth grade, I had a twenty-three-day thing with Jade Sutton—holding hands in the hall, kissing goodbye after school. But then she pronounced an ultimatum: her or Delaney. I tried to explain what Delaney and I were, but Jade was having none of it. And so ended my brief fling with Jade Sutton. As a parting shot, she said, *Just FYI, you're a good-looking guy, but no one'll want to be with you long as you're always with her. Y'all spend as much time together as if you were boyfriend and girlfriend. I literally don't get what you see in her. She's weird and rude.* Delaney thought even less of Jade and wasn't afraid to show it. I didn't regret my choice. I sure hope Delaney and I start talking again so I didn't dump Jade for nothing.

Without Delaney and Alex around, Vi and I trade flirtatious smiles and find excuses for unnecessary touching. Sometimes she flips her hair out of her face, and her scent wafts over to me and makes me woozy. At halftime, I buy her a hot chocolate. We laugh a lot. I love her laugh—a radiant sound as good and pure as the best and purest things: A puppy licking your face. Eating the point of a piece of pie. Remembering it's a three-day weekend on Thursday night. Delaney's and my feud melts away. Papaw's illness melts away. All my struggles with my classes and home-sickness melt away.

The crowd rises as Middleford scores in the final moments of the game, putting us on top. The seconds tick down and we roar. Vi whoops and we embrace in jubilation. The game ends and we join the ecstatic crowd strutting back to the residence halls. It's rare that I feel any sense of belonging at Middleford, but I do right now.

As we walk, I graze her hand with mine. That small contact feels like the thrill of crossing an empty highway at night and pausing in the middle—something forbidden and delicious. It's still early enough that we don't have to be back in our rooms quite yet, so we stroll a few laps around the lake. The stars are endless and sparkling in the black sky. The air is that ideal crisp temperature where you need a jacket and the minute you take it off you're cold, but as long as you have it on, you feel perfect.

"Did you know that a Brazilian invented the airplane?" Vi asks.

I study her face for some hint of a joke but see none.

"I'm serious," she says.

"Delaney tell you that?"

"I learned it in school. The name of the man was Alberto Santos-Dumont."

"Pretty sure it was the Wright brothers."

"They taught us in school that Americans think that. But it was Santos-Dumont."

"Yeah, well, they teach us in American school that Brazilian girls will lie to you and tell you some Brazilian dude invented the airplane."

Vi laughs and pushes me. "Do they also teach you in American school that root beer tastes like medicine?"

"That's it. Now you've gone too far."

We walk and talk for a while more before it's time to head back. I accompany Vi to her residence hall.

"Thanks for inviting me to the game," I say. "I had a really fun time."

"Me too. I like American football, even though it's named wrong."

"I'll take you to a UT game sometime."

Her eyes sparkle and she smiles, showing both of her dimples. "Serious?"

"Yes." *I am now.*

"Are you going on the trip tomorrow?" Vi asks.

"Apple picking? I was thinking about it."

"I'm going. You should."

"Okay. I will."

We smile at each other for a couple of seconds before we each avert our eyes bashfully.

Maybe it's my imagination, or wishful thinking, but there seems to be something here between us. Some electric space of possibility, like the moment when you start to hear a waterfall before you come around the bend and see it.

She hugs me before we part—it lasts slightly longer than it ever has before—and as I get on the elevator, I notice a bit of her perfume lingering on my shirt collar. I sniff at it again and again as I ascend, until I get light-headed, committing it to memory before it disappears.

Chapter 35

"Your *favorite* fruit is apples?" I ask, plucking a particularly nice one and tossing it gently into my basket below.

"Why is that weird?" Vi asks, scanning the branches above her.

"I mean, in Brazil, don't you have, like, fancy fruits?"

She giggles. "Fancy fruits?"

"Mangos. Coconuts. I don't know."

"Those are normal fruits."

"Not to me."

"That's how I feel about apples."

"I guess." I call out, "Alex?"

"Yo," Alex calls back from a few trees over.

"You hear what Vi and I were discussing?"

"Wasn't paying attention. I'm in my apple-picking zone. No distractions, baby. Game face all the way."

"Guess Vi's favorite fruit."

"Uh. Pineapple?"

Vi rolls her eyes.

"Close, dude. Apples."

"*What?*"

"I know. They're for her like mangos and coconuts are for us."

"Eating apples makes me hungrier," Alex says. "I've read it's because they're a negative-calorie food."

"Do what?" I say.

"Your body burns more energy digesting it than it gives you."

"So if you were stuck on a desert island full of apple trees, you'd starve to death?" I ask.

"Guess so," Alex says.

"That doesn't sound right," I say.

Alex shrugs. "Maybe not. I don't care enough to research it more carefully."

"I'm going to ask Delaney if it's true," Vi says.

Alex yawns and stretches. "They're running a great racket here. We provide them with labor and we pay for the pleasure."

It is pleasure, though. Apple picking is exactly the sort of frivolity I shouldn't be spending my money on. But I wasn't going to miss a chance to be outside on a mild October day, with friends, the blushing, heady freshness of sun-warmed apples perfuming the orchard around me. *I could do this forever,* I think. *This could be my job and I would never want more.* But I guess it's hard to get paid to do something people will *pay* to do.

This is the sort of thing I'd write poems about if I could.

Vi comes down her little stepladder and sits cross-legged under her tree. She rummages through her basket for an especially choice apple.

I walk over. "Mind if I join you?"

"Sit," she says.

I do, leaning against the tree, the roughness of the bark a prickle on my back through my T-shirt.

Vi and I look at each other and smile. She hands me the apple she'd picked out for herself. "Here. You need to learn to appreciate apples more."

She rummages in her basket and comes up with another

ruddy, perfect specimen. She twists off the stem and takes a big bite from the top. She sees my quizzical look. "Do you know this way of eating apples?"

"There's a secret method?"

"You eat from the top, and the middle part—"

"The core?"

"The core disappears."

"Seriously?"

"Try it."

I do. True to her word, as I eat from the top down, the core seems to simply vanish. I spit out a couple seeds. "That's wild."

"Pretty cool, yeah?"

"When I was a kid, I'd sit on the porch with my papaw, and he'd get an apple and cut slices of it with his pocketknife and hand them to me."

Vi scoots backward to lean against the tree beside me. "See? You should like apples more."

We sit without talking, the crunch of apples and the wind the only sounds. Then we hear the honking of geese in the distance. It crescendos as they near and fly over us in their triangular rank. They fade from sight and hearing, into the distance.

Vi sighs wistfully. "I wonder where they're going."

"South. Don't know where exactly."

"Where we're from," Vi says.

"That's right."

"How do they know where to go?"

"That's another question for Delaney." *I hope I get to ask her someday soon.*

Vi sighs again, but less wistful and more sad.

"You okay?" I ask.

"I had a big fight with my parents this morning and didn't think about it until now. When you said to ask Delaney that question, it reminded me of how I asked my parents things before I knew how to look online."

"What was the fight over?" I ask.

She picks up a fallen twig and starts breaking off little pieces and flicking them away. "They don't like that I want to develop video games. My father wants me to study business so I can help with his company."

"That sucks."

"I told him, 'I won't be helpful to you if I don't love what I'm doing.'" Vi gets to the end of her twig.

"You deserve to do what you love in life." I pick up another twig and hand it to her.

She gives me a melancholy smile and accepts my offering. "I love my parents, but I think they don't always know who I am very well."

"There anything I can do?"

She snaps off a piece of the twig, reaches over, and gently sets it upright in my hair. "Let me grow apple trees on your head so every time we hang out I can have free apples."

My entire body hums at her closeness and touch. The crackle I felt last night at the game is still present. I sit stone-still. "Anything you want." *I've never meant something more.*

She plants another piece of twig in my hair. "You don't talk about your parents."

I don't answer until I'm sure I can do it with complete nonchalance that won't betray me. "Nah, not really."

"What are they like?" Another section of twig in my hair.

"You know. They're cool. They're just . . . parents. They love me. They want me to do well." Every lie feels like holding a hot pan handle, but I'm too far from anywhere I can easily set it down without making a mess. *Please change the topic.*

Blessedly, Alex calls over. "Anyone catch what kind of apples these are?"

"Pink Lady," I say. "Sounds like a strip club."

"These are a thousand times better than Red Delicious apples," Alex says. "'Red Delicious' is half a lie."

"You gonna call out Red Delicious apples like that?" I say.

"I just did. Red Delicious apples can bring it."

"Damn, son."

The three of us talk for a while. After this we're going to a corn maze. Neither Alex nor Vi have ever been to one. We'll have doughnuts and cider and go on a hayride. We'll get back in time to catch *Midnite Matinee.*

Our conversation subsides, and I look up at the sky and think what a wondrous color it is. Delaney told me once that some scientists think humans only started seeing the color blue about 4,500 years ago. Or maybe they didn't have the vocabulary to describe it. She said that in ancient writings, like Homer's *Odyssey,* the sea is described as being the color of wine. I miss Delaney and her facts.

Vi and I turn to each other. She selects two more apples from her basket and hands me one, keeping the other for herself.

"You'll get sick if you eat too many," I say.

"I'm not afraid." She reaches over and gingerly plucks out the twigs she placed in my hair, one by one.

"Did you change your mind about wanting to grow apple trees on my head?"

"Yeah. We can just come back here for apples."

219

"Works for me."

She scans the orchard, looking at the blaze of sugar maples in the distance. The wind breathes through the orchard's laden branches and dry leaves. "I like autumn in Connecticut," she says softly.

"I do too."

We eat our apples and let the juice dry sticky on our fingers. It's late in the afternoon, and she glows like something holy in the golden, waning light.

I think of her touching my hair, the warmth of her thigh against mine.

I guess apples aren't the only sweetness that can consume you.

Chapter 36

I'm jumpy as we wrap up our analysis of a Marie Howe poem. I hope Dr. Adkins won't think I was being a smart-ass by turning in a poem that's half the length of my already-terse first effort.

"Okay, we're out of time. Tonight's reading is amazing. I know I always say that, but this is not empty hyperbole. Go eat lunch."

I stand to the side of the door while everyone streams out.

"Come, sit," she says, walking to her desk to get my poem. I sit. She returns and sits across from me.

I'm angry with myself for failing a teacher I like so much, who's taken such an interest in me. I try to get out in front of things. "I'm just not a poet. This one sucks more than my first try."

Dr. Adkins crosses her legs, looks down at my "poem," and then back up. "I beg to differ."

She reads. "*Ask me where I'm from.* Wanna know why I think this is an improvement on your last poem?"

"Why?"

"Because your first poem didn't invite dialogue. This one is shorter—and I don't think it's complete—but it invites engagement."

"Uh, yeah, that's *totally* what I was thinking when I wrote that. It *definitely* wasn't that I just got stuck and had to turn in something." We laugh.

"So, Cash Pruitt," Dr. Adkins says, clasping her hands around her knee. "You told me to, so I'm asking. Where are you from?"

"Sawyer, Tennessee."

"What's that?"

"It's a town."

"But it's more, or that line wouldn't have come into your mind. Why did you invite me to ask you where you're from?"

"I guess it's important to me. It's home."

"So?"

"So I think people don't understand why it's beautiful and special to me."

"Would you like to tell them?"

I shrug.

She picks up my paper and holds it in my face, pulling the edges taut as though to tear it in half. *"Yes!* You would! It's right here! What does this place mean to you?"

"Um."

"Think. What do you love?"

"The quiet. The stillness."

"What image represents that quiet and stillness in your mind?"

I ponder for a few beats. "Intersections with no cars. The yellow lights blinking for no one."

Dr. Adkins pushes my paper back to me. "Write that."

I do.

She must be able to see the steam rising off my head as my brain labors. "Disconnect yourself from literalism and concreteness. This sometimes gets you closer to the reality of an idea—the *essence* of an idea—than a more concrete representation."

I keep thinking. I write a few more lines. I gaze at what I've written.

> Ask me where I'm from
> I'll tell you about yellow lights
> blinking at intersections
> like the last heartbeats
> of the drowning
> downtown hardware store

Dr. Adkins stands and beckons me to fellow. "Let's grab lunch and keep working. Good things are happening."

When we get in the dining hall, she gets in line for food while I run over to Vi and Alex to tell them I'm working on a poem with Dr. Adkins.

"Wooooo," Alex says. "Look who's fancy now."

"More like she's putting in the time to help the kid who can't keep up," I say.

"I doubt that," Vi says. "I want to read it when you're done."

And I gleam inside, even though I don't have the slightest intention of letting her do that.

I grab a plate of pad Thai and join Dr. Adkins at a table not far from my friends. It's strange to see her in this setting. It occurs to me for the first time that we'd probably have been friends if we were in high school together. It reminds me of Delaney and it pierces me with regret.

"So," Dr. Adkins says. "We were at 'drowning downtown hardware store.' You could move on or you could comment on the store, use it to develop a theme. Do you have some memory or sentiment attached to the store? What would you buy there?"

We press on like this, exchanging ideas between bites. Vi and Alex drop by our table as they're leaving, and I introduce them to Dr. Adkins. I'm proud for her to see I have cool friends, and I like that they got to see a teacher taking a special interest in me. I wish I could introduce her to Delaney.

We push through my lunchtime and into my free period, working. She prompts me and prods me with questions and suggestions. *What do you think of when . . . ? What do you feel when . . . ? What does it smell like? What does it look like? What do you love about it? Why do you love that? What's a word you can use to describe that? What if you tried saying . . . ? What's something you can compare it to? What does it remind you of?*

I sit back and read what we've written.

"How does it feel to have written this poem?" Dr. Adkins asks.

"I didn't really write it."

"Cash? *You* wrote it. I wouldn't let you quit or convince yourself that you don't have the language to express what's inside you. That's it. How does it feel?"

I look at the page again. "Really good," I murmur, and I'm not just saying it to mollify her. It's the same abiding peace I experience after being on the river. The time we were working slipped past me without my even noticing. For that little while, I didn't hurt. Nothing gnawed at me. Not my distance from Papaw and Mamaw and home. Not my distance from Delaney. My mind was quiet.

"I feel like I know the part of you that's proud of who you are and where you come from much better after reading this poem," Dr. Adkins says.

"Thanks for helping me." I want to tell her how happy it makes me to see her so obviously pleased with me. "So I guess I can go back to the normal homework assignments?"

"Nice try. Let's see if they have Middleford bars today."

They do.

Where I'm From

Ask me where I'm from
I'll tell you about yellow lights
blinking at intersections
like the last heartbeats
of the drowning
downtown hardware store where you buy
bolts to fix another thing
that time devours

afternoons so still, you hear the breath
of wind over your own
breathing and the rush
of a river over your own
blood rushing

leafsmoke autumn days
and train-whistle winter nights

aching backs
and aching hearts
and cracked hands
and rusted bodies
in rusted pickups with
cracked windshields
decaying houses housing
decaying hopes

this is the harvest
of the forgotten
everything dies
but some places live
closer to bone

but also starlings rise
from a spirit-white field, breaking
the silence that rejoiced
in your praise-clasped hands.

Chapter 37

I think about the poem for the rest of the day. It's taken root in my chest and sends out green, flowering shoots as the hours wear on. I keep remembering the calm satisfaction I had after finishing it.

I try to carry that feeling through crew practice. It's not easy. We're back on the ergs because it's too late in the year to be on the water. But I manage. I carry it through dinner with Vi and Alex. And then seeing Vi adds another layer to my high spirits.

I haven't yet summoned the courage to tell her how I feel. I'm not in a rush. I figure I'll know when the time is right. Until I do, there's nothing but possibility, and I'm not ready to give that up. Based on the smiles she gives me, the way she lingers on my eyes a second or two longer than she needs to, how she finds excuses to touch my arm—I think I've got a shot.

After dinner, I sit by the lake and call Mamaw and Papaw.

Papaw answers. "Howdy, Mickey Mouse!"

"Hey, Papaw, I missed you the last couple days."

He hacks and wheezes. "Missed you too. Hit a rough spell, but I'm back now. How're things?"

"Real good. Went to a football game Friday. Went apple picking with my friends on Saturday, went to a corn maze. That was fun." Then, something comes over me, and this spills from my mouth: "Hey, kinda had something to tell you, man to man."

Papaw gives me an amused look. "Well. Go 'head."

"I think I'm starting to fall for one of my friends here."

Papaw's eyes twinkle. "Do tell."

"Remember that new friend of mine I told you about? From Brazil?"

"Vicki?"

"Viviani. Vi."

"Okay. I recall."

"It's her. We've been hanging out a lot lately and . . . I don't know. Something's different between us. There's chemistry there. Or something."

Papaw chuckles a little—it sounds like his heart's not in it—then he goes quiet. "What about Tess?"

I'm taken aback. "What about her?"

"She okay with this?"

"I don't know. Remember how I told you the other day that we were fighting? We still are. And why would she care?"

"Ain't she sweet on you?"

I laugh incredulously. "Papaw—no. What? No."

Papaw coughs. When he catches his breath, he says, "You sure 'bout that, Mickey Mouse?"

"We're just friends." I consider telling him that Delaney and I had already worked out what we were a long time ago, while we were still talking.

"You best make *sure* of that." He stumbles into another hacking fit.

"Geez. You even happy for me?" I can't mask my irritation anymore.

He clears his throat. "Now, listen, bubba. I *might* be saving your damn life here."

"I'm good. I promise."

"Didn't you tell me once this gal is Tess's roommate?"

"Yeah."

Papaw whistles through his teeth. "That makes things double tricky. Like trying to date your best friend's sister."

"You sound like you're talking from experience."

"I'll never tell," he says, grinning. He turns serious again. "Now, you wanna take things slow. Don't charge in."

"I know."

"I really am happy for you, Mickey Mouse. Just wanted to make sure everyone was square on the situation and wasn't nobody about to get hurt."

"I appreciate it. Vi's . . . fun to be around. I don't know. Feels good to be near her. She's smart and beautiful. She smells amazing. She has a pretty laugh. She's sunshine."

"You said you and Tess was fighting."

"Yeah."

"Go make that right before you go chasing after this Vi girl. Apologize even if you think you didn't do nothing wrong. Tess is someone you want in your life."

"Okay. I will."

Pitching around in my head for something to change the subject from Delaney, I make a connection I hadn't made before, for some reason. "Hey, let me ask you something."

"Shoot."

"You know how you did woodworking and chain-saw sculptures?"

"Miss it ever' day."

230

"What made you do it?"

Papaw looks at me for a second and scratches his beard. "Ain't nobody ever asked me that before. I'll have to think on it." He ponders and coughs. His oxygen machine hisses. Finally, he says, "I don't know's I can answer that. All's I can say is I felt driven to do it."

"Okay, how about this: What did it make you feel to do that stuff?"

"It felt real, real good." He pauses to collect his breath before continuing. "I ain't never told anyone, but since you're asking: I used to think about this tree growing out there in the woods, collecting the sun and wind and rain and using all that energy and nutrition to grow up. Then, we'd cut down the tree, and I'd transform that wood into something else with my hands. Kinda like I'm releasing the energy of the sun that that wood soaked up and shaping it into a black bear sculpture or a table for someone. I ain't really got the words for it. But when I was done, I'd feel pretty darn satisfied."

I nod and absorb what he's saying. "Yeah," I murmur. "That sounds familiar."

"What put you in mind of all this?"

"I finished my first poem today."

Papaw beams. "Did you? For your class you was telling me about?"

"Yessir. The teacher picked me out to start writing poetry. Guess she saw something in me. Who knows."

"That don't surprise me. I'd love to read that poem."

"I'll email it to you. Anyway, I felt pretty darn great after finishing it up. Peaceful, you know?"

"I do surely know. Hey, your mamaw wants to chat. I'm gonna sign off."

"Love you, Papaw."

"Love you, Mickey Mouse."

Mamaw appears onscreen, and I see she's walking outside with the tablet. I hear her tell Papaw, "It's a pretty night; I'm going to sit out on the porch while I talk to Cash."

"Hi, sweetie," she says once she gets settled in.

"Hey, Mamaw. How's work?"

"If it isn't one thing going wrong, it's another."

"I know that's right."

"Hey, I needed to talk to you about something." Her voice is suddenly fragile. I feel a hot surge of adrenaline in my solar plexus.

"Okay," I say weakly.

"Your papaw took a bit of a turn this last week, and we ended up spending a couple nights in the hospital."

"What?"

"He bounced back but—"

"Y'all didn't say anything."

"Well, no. Pep thought we ought not worry you with it. Let you focus on your studies."

"Mamaw, I need to know this stuff. What if everything hadn't been okay?"

"And that's what I told him. But you know him. Like a mule."

"I know, but."

"Anyway, the thing I had to talk about—"

"There's *more*?"

"I had to miss a few shifts dealing with all this, and it's put us behind on the bills. So we were thinking we'd just have you come home for Christmas and not Thanksgiving too."

My last Thanksgiving with Papaw. For sure. But I can't bring

232

myself to say it. "I was really looking forward to seeing y'all soon."

"We'll still see you soon at Christmas."

"I have enough for the bus ticket."

"Hang on to it. We both need to be saving up money for a rainy day."

Then I realize what she's saying. *Saving for a trip home for a final goodbye. Saving for a funeral.*

I'm silent for a while, and Mamaw says, "We weren't going to make a to-do of Thanksgiving this year anyway. Pep's not feeling up to big shindigs lately. Just a little get-together with Aunt Betsy and Mitzi."

I sigh. "Still sounds great."

"We'll have a nice Christmas. So things are good there with you?"

"I mean, you know. Fine."

"I overheard you telling Pep you were going to send him the poem you'd written. Mind if I read it too?"

"Course not. How you doing? You getting any time for yourself?"

She smiles wearily. "I get to catch my stories now and then. Like as not I fall asleep while watching, but that's from getting old more than anything."

"I wish I were there to help."

"Don't you worry about that. Focus on your studies. We've got it handled."

"It's pretty up here this time of year."

"I bet."

"It'd be nice if y'all could visit someday."

"We'd love that."

A dense fog of sadness descends on any conversation about something wonderful that will never happen, and it blankets us now.

"They'll have things for you to do for Thanksgiving?" Mamaw asks.

"Surely. A lot of kids stick around for Thanksgiving. I imagine Delaney will. Heck, probably thirty percent of the school is from countries that don't even celebrate Thanksgiving." *Like Vi. That's a bright spot, I guess.*

"All right. Well, sweetie, I best go help Pep get ready for bed. I love you."

"Love you, Mamaw."

"There anything you need?"

Need is the only thing I have plenty of. "No, ma'am. All good."

We sign off. I sit there for a while, unmoving. I'm tired of living on the leading edge of a storm front, being buffeted by the rising winds.

I get out my poetry notebook and pen to seek my new shelter, the only one I know anymore.

Chapter 38

I've come to relish Alex's and my sessions in Koch Hall's basement laundry room. It's always just the two of us, talking and working.

"I really think it could take off," Alex says.

"You think people would watch a YouTube channel called *Laundry Boys*?"

"I guarantee people are YouTubing laundry and ironing tips."

"Probably, but."

"You done with the spray starch?"

I hand Alex the bottle.

"So we give laundry and ironing tips and show techniques and add a funny spin," Alex says, spritzing starch on one of his shirts.

I hold up the white oxford button-down I was ironing, shake it, and put it on a hanger. "Dude. You do *not* have funny things to say about laundry."

"Yeah I do."

"Say something funny about laundry."

"Now?"

"No time like the present."

"Okay." Alex claps and rubs his hands together like he's about to perform a magic trick. "So . . . uh . . . we're doing laundry because Cash here has pooped his pants again."

"There's three seconds of content. Say something else funny."

"I gotta get paid. I'm not just gonna say funny stuff for free. Gotta know your value, bro."

"Now *that* is funny."

"We sell ads. YouTubers make bank, son. Get sponsorships. Get that OxiClean coin, baby. Make enough we could get laundry service like everyone else."

"If we get laundry service, we won't have any content for the channel."

"Good point. See, that's thinking like a Laundry Boy."

"That how you want to begin your political career? Laundry tutorial tycoon?" I start ironing a crease into a pair of khakis.

"It's honest work, man. We've had elected officials who've never done honest work." Alex nods at my detergent bottle. "You should switch to Tide, dude. *Consumer Reports* says it cleans better."

"It's expensive, and the Arm & Hammer reminds me of my mamaw. By the way, I'm not going home for Thanksgiving."

"For real?"

"Found out it won't work for me to go."

"I'm not going home either. We gotta Thanksgiving it up here. I'll cook. Is Delaney going home?"

"Don't know."

"Bro, you guys need to kiss and make up."

"You sound like my papaw."

"Anyway, that's three, probably. And I bet Vi won't bother going home. Which I know you'll like." Alex waggles his eyebrows.

My face grows hot. "Of course, Vi's great," I say casually.

Alex keeps waggling his eyebrows.

I laugh and block his face with my hand. "Dude. Stop."

More waggling.

My face reddens further. "We're friends. That's it."

"I'd keep doing the eyebrow thing, only my eyebrows are the only part of me that doesn't hurt after our last erg session, so I'll spare them. But imagine me doing it."

"I will not."

"Bro, I have eyes. I've seen you two over the past while."

"Dude, *fine*. I'm into her."

"Thank you for finally admitting the extremely obvious."

"Think she's into me?"

"Honestly?" Alex holds up a shirt, scrutinizing it for wrinkles. "Yes."

"Hold nothing back?"

"Just say it."

"I do."

A swell of joy rises in my chest. "You messing with me?"

Alex's dryer buzzes. He opens it, checks on his clothes, and starts pulling them into a basket. "Naw, bro. When you two are hanging out, she gets *the look*. It's as obvious as your own look."

"I love being around her. Everything about her. She makes me happy, man."

Alex vaults up to sit on top of a dryer. "I wish I had a mirror to show you your face right now. It's kinda like—" Alex gives me a blissful, moony expression.

"Come on."

"You gonna tell her how you feel?"

I hop onto the dryer directly opposite from Alex. "Should I?"

"The answer to the question you never ask is always no, right?"

"Look at you dispensing wisdom."

"The big question is: Can you be cool if she shoots you down? Because I like our squad and I don't want weirdness."

"I can handle disappointment." *You say that now.*

"Then go for it. You're a catch, bro. Look at those shoulders and guns. Dang."

"Literally the only upside of the erg torture. I'm gonna do it."

"Sometimes you gotta take the plunge."

"Sometimes you gotta take the plunge," I murmur back.

"While you're taking plunges, do *Laundry Boys*."

"I'm not ever doing *Laundry Boys*."

Chapter 39

I find out from Vi when Delaney's going to be at the lab, and I wait outside in the dark, shivering, while I try to get some homework done. She finally emerges, looking deep in thought. When she spots me, though, her face takes on a grim cast. She looks at the ground and walks faster.

"Red? Red." I hustle to walk beside her. "Hey. Can we talk for a sec?" I touch her elbow, but she flinches away deftly. I see people gawking, but I don't care. *Just another marital spat, everyone.*

"Red, come on."

"Fuck off." She walks faster.

I stop and call after her, "Okay, but I miss you really bad. I'm just gonna follow you, loudly telling you how much I miss you."

She slows. I hurry after her again. Time for my secret weapon. I pull from my jacket pocket a wrapped candy cane I had hoarded away in my get-out-of-trouble supply for just such an occasion. I extend it to her. Without meeting my eyes, she darts her hand out and grabs it, like a snake striking. The offering has been accepted. My heart lifts.

"You don't have to forgive me," I say. "But I'm not gonna let our friendship end without telling you I'm sorry and how important you are to me."

She finally turns her face to mine. "You can be a real piece of shit sometimes."

"I know."

She unwraps the candy cane and starts sucking on the end.

"We've all missed you," I say. "It can't be easy to avoid us all so much. This place is even smaller than Sawyer, and it was hard to dodge people there."

"I'm pretty good about things I set my mind to."

"Oh, no shit?" I open my arms to her.

She sighs, holds the candy cane in her mouth like it's a cigar, and comes in for a hug. Her body fits perfectly against mine. We were built to hug each other. I rest my lips on the crown of her head. Her hair smells like cold wind and dandelions. We embrace for a long time.

"What're you doing for Thanksgiving?" I ask as we start strolling again.

"What are *you* doing?"

"Mamaw said it wouldn't work out for me to come home, so I'm sticking around."

"Me too, I guess. Got no reason to go home."

"Alex is staying."

"So's Vi."

"Yeah?"

Delaney gives me an oh-come-on look. "You telling me you didn't know that already?"

"I didn't."

"Thought you two were getting pretty tight. The way she talks about you, you'd think she'd replaced me as your best friend."

My stomach jumps. But just as quickly, I remind myself to

focus on the most important part of what Delaney said. "Hey."
I touch her arm to signal her to stop. "No one will ever replace
you in my life."

"Better not, jackass. I got you here, remember?"

"I do."

"Seriously, though, what *is* going on with you and Vi? It's
something, so don't say nothing."

Papaw's voice reverberates in my mind. *You best make sure.*
I guess if I told Papaw, I can tell Delaney. She's gonna find out
sooner or later. "I think I'm into her. Kinda. Sorta. Like *into* her."

Delaney's eyes flash with hurt. "You *gotta* be shitting me.
You're *such* an asshole. We don't talk for a couple weeks, and you
go and get a boner for my *roommate?*"

"What do you want me to say?"

"Nothing. You're pathetic."

"Well. Yeah. I am."

"I should go another couple weeks without talking to you."

"I hope you don't. What's wrong with Vi?"

"Nothing," Delaney says sullenly.

I still think Papaw is nuts for thinking Delaney's into me
in that way, but I have to admit I'm seeing why he thinks that.
"Wouldn't you rather me be with her than some random girl?"

Delaney sighs and gives me a look that I can't quite read. It's
a strange mixture of sadness and resignation. Her moods can be
as much of a mystery as the workings of her mind. "I mean, you
have traditionally had pretty shitty taste. She's a huge improvement on Jade Sutton. There's that at least." She looks away.

"Thought you might feel that way."

We don't say anything for a while.

"You miss me while we weren't talking?" I ask.

Delaney rolls her eyes and crunches off the end of her candy cane.

"I hope you did."

"Gee, I wonder if after risking my scholarship offer to get you here with me, I missed you." Delaney furrows her brow and taps her lips with the remnant of her candy cane.

"Just wanted to hear you say it."

"I missed you, jackass."

"Wanna go skip rocks for a while?" I ask. "We have a little time."

"Sure."

We walk to the lake. Delaney bends down, selects a rock, contorts her tiny frame, and hurls it into the water.

"How are you still this bad at this?" I ask. "Don't you know, like, angles?"

"Don't I know, like, angles?" Delaney mimics. "These rocks don't skip right."

"You're calling rock error?" I say.

"I am. We're working with defective materials."

"Pick me one at random."

She hands me one. I hold it theatrically in front of her face between my thumb and forefinger, turning it so she can inspect it. Then, I slowly turn, wind up, and skip it four times across the surface of the lake. I turn back to Delaney.

She folds her arms across her chest. "You're my best friend, so I picked you a prime rock."

"Hell you did. You picked a rock you thought would prove your point."

A sly smile tugs at the corners of her mouth. "Nope."

"You oughtta see your face right now. Guilty as all hell."

She shrugs and picks up another rock. She tosses it into the lake with a plop.

"Hey, question," I say.

"Shoot."

"How do geese know where they're going when they fly south?"

Delaney selects a rock and blows the dust off it. I notice her thumbs. They're torn up.

"That's not going to help," I say.

"You worry about you," she says. "And I'll tell you same as I told Vi, right after I told her that she couldn't turn around and tell you. No one really knows for sure. Some scientists think birds can sense the Earth's magnetic field. It gets stronger as you move toward the poles from the equator. So it's like that hiding-and-finding game where you say 'Hotter' as you get closer." She chucks the rock. No skip.

"You told Vi she wasn't allowed to tell me?"

"Yep."

"What if I'd looked it up myself?"

We both laugh.

"I miss going to our overlook together," Delaney murmurs after a while.

"Yeah. This isn't as good."

"There was never failure involved in going to the overlook."

"So now you admit it's operator error and not rock error."

Delaney flips me off. She checks her phone. "I gotta head back."

We walk to her residence hall.

"One more hug," I say. We embrace again. She has a certain wiry strength and tenacity when hugging. Like each time she's not sure if she'll ever let you go. It makes me feel better.

"I'm glad we're us again," Delaney murmurs from the hollow of my chest. "I missed you."

"Missed you more, Red. Let's don't be apart again."

"Good idea. Night."

"Night."

I watch her to make sure she gets inside safely. We're okay for now and I'm relieved. Still, I'm terrified a day will come when we never hug and make up after a fight. I don't know what I'll do if that happens. I have more experience grieving the dead than the living.

Chapter 40

"That's enough for today. We got some good work done. Think about how to approach that last stanza to tie back to your main theme," Dr. Adkins says.

"Will do," I say.

She stands and gathers her things. "Got fun Thanksgiving plans?"

"I was going to go home, but that didn't work out, so I'm staying."

Dr. Adkins doesn't hesitate. "You're coming over. Desiree's gonna cook. Low Country and Appalachian Thanksgiving."

"You're inviting me?"

"What's the point of having teachers live on campus if we don't take in lost sheep?"

"I wish, but my friends are also going to be around, and I shouldn't ditch them."

"Invite them too. More the merrier."

"Serious?"

"Desiree's background is restaurant kitchens, food trucks, and catering. She doesn't know how to *not* cook for a crowd. Come at eleven. Bring nothing but hearty appetites and good stories."

Campus is tranquil and sleepy on Thanksgiving morning. I awake in a miasma of sadness at not being with Papaw and Mamaw today. But, like a fog yielding to the sun, the doldrums quickly burn off after I join Delaney, Alex, and Vi in the dining hall for breakfast. Heeding Dr. Adkins's call to come bearing large appetites, we eat light. "To put down a base layer," Alex says. "A house needs a foundation."

After breakfast, we laze in the common area of Koch Hall, watching a *MythBusters* marathon until eleven, when we're to be at Dr. Adkins's apartment on the third floor of Elm Hall.

Despite Dr. Adkins's command to come empty-handed, Alex cradles a small mason jar like it's filled with some precious life-saving medicine. He sees me eyeing it. "My mom's kimchi," he says. "I emailed Dr. Adkins and asked if I could whip up some kimchi fried rice as a side, and she was down."

"Nice."

"Here's the thing, though. You can't say anything about it to my mom when you meet her. You can only tell her I made regular fried rice if it comes up at all."

"Why?"

"Korean moms get mad at you if you feed anything but the most accessible Korean food to white people who might not like it."

"Don't your folks literally own a Korean restaurant?"

"Parents. I don't know. I guess they figure anyone who comes in a restaurant knows what they're signing up for? Anyway, she told me I could only do basic fried rice."

"Rebel, dude."

We get to Dr. Adkins's apartment and knock. A stunning, tall woman with high cheekbones and long braids, a dish towel draped over one shoulder, answers the door. A heavenly potpourri of expensive scented candles, old books, incense, and cooking food joins her in greeting us. The air is humid with kitchen steam.

"Welcome!" the woman says warmly. "Breebree," she calls behind her. "Our guests have arrived." She motions us in. "Please, our home is your home. I'm Desiree."

We enter and introduce ourselves. When it's my turn, Desiree says, "Oh, Cash! Bree has talked about you. She says you're a poet."

I flush with competing pride and embarrassment. "Don't know about that." I see Vi's impressed look, though, and pride wins out.

Dr. Adkins enters, wiping her hands. Her hair is up in a messy pile atop her head. She wears skinny black jeans with rips in the knees and a black Dearly T-shirt altered into a V-neck. She has a tattoo on the side of her foot showing the phases of the moon. It's strange to see a teacher in such a relaxed environment.

"Hello!" she says. "Can I take jackets?" She hangs our jackets on a coatrack in the corner.

I scan their living room. It's essentially a larger and nicer version of our dorm rooms, but they've completely transformed and owned the space with both immaculate taste and apparently unfailing thrifting luck.

"Y'all have a beautiful home," I say.

"We do what we can," Dr. Adkins says. "The price is right."

Alex raises the mason jar of kimchi. "You know how Cash is all up in the poetry now? I'm about to drop some poetry of the palate."

Desiree puts her hands on her hips and leans back. "Look at *you*! Bring that swagger into the kitchen. You must be the one who emailed Bree."

Alex struts toward the kitchen. Desiree follows him. She turns back to us as she walks, pointing at Alex's back, and mouthing, *I like him.*

"Y'all, sit," Dr. Adkins says.

They have two rocking chairs and a sofa. Vi and I sit together on the sofa, and Delaney and Dr. Adkins take rocking chairs. I notice the faded quilt draped over the arm of the sofa near me. I touch it. It's soft from years of giving comfort and warmth.

"My mamaw made that," Dr. Adkins says softly.

"It's beautiful," I say.

"She was a folk healer too. She'd forage in the woods for ginseng and yellowroot, Saint-John's-wort, ramps, sassafras, that sorta stuff. She'd help birth babies. I didn't inherit her gift of healing. But I did get the love of foraging. I root around for words."

I laugh and point at Delaney. "That's her. Appalachian healer woman. Foraging for medicines."

A flash of recognition comes over Dr. Adkins's face. She snaps her fingers. "You! You're the one who discovered the—" She snaps her fingers again.

"Penicillin strain. In a cave near Sawyer," Delaney says.

"Yes! That was a big deal. I heard you on NPR."

"I read you were a finalist for the National Book Award this year," Delaney says. "I looked you up."

"I'm still waiting to find out it was a mistake."

"You should ask for a raise. You must be in big demand now."

"I've been meaning to request my own personal tray of Middleford bars."

I suddenly remember my academic counselor telling me that she thought Middleford wouldn't be able to hold on to Dr. Adkins much longer, that someone might swoop in to steal her away. The thought sends me spiraling.

"How did you become a poet?" Vi asks, snapping me out of my spiral.

It's never occurred to me that Dr. Adkins might ever have been anything but a poet.

Dr. Adkins shifts to sit with one leg under the other, and her face takes on an introspective, nostalgic cast. "Well. Poets look for how the world is sewn together so they can unstitch it and piece it back together in a new way. I always did that. I remember feeling this vague, gnawing hunger for beauty my whole life. I was miserable and angry whenever I wasn't being fed, which was almost all the time, before I found poetry.

"When I was in tenth grade, a girl named Daisy Treadway, who I had the biggest crush on, gave me a bunch of photocopied pages of Joe Bolton's poetry. He was from Kentucky, like me. He wrote beautiful poems about beautiful things.

"That did it. Reading poetry satisfied the hunger. I blew through the poetry at my school and town library. We didn't have money for books, which is why now . . ." She motions at the stacks of books and crammed bookshelves that fill her living room. "Then I started writing poetry. And that fed me even more. Went to college, studied poetry, started publishing poems, and here I am."

Sometimes you don't even realize you are ravenous until you

start eating. Dr. Adkins's story has identified that feeling I get when I read and write poetry: satiety. I didn't know to call it a hunger until now. I think about my mama. Maybe the Oxys and fentanyl were her attempted cure for a nagging craving she was never able to identify. All she knew was what killed it for a while.

While we talk, the room fills even more with the sumptuous smell of cooking. Alex's kimchi fried rice adds to the aromatic symphony. We hear Desiree and Alex laughing and talking cheerily in the kitchen. Periodically, one will say something like *Nice touch!* or *Never thought to do that!*

Dr. Adkins sees me gazing longingly toward the kitchen. "Desiree starts getting ready for Thanksgiving about forty-eight hours in advance. It's her magnum opus. She had a restaurant called High/Low in Asheville. She specialized in Appalachian and Low Country cuisine. She was a James Beard Award finalist. There was a monthlong wait for reservations. That's actually how we met."

"Tell us! Go!" Vi says, clapping and leaning forward.

"So, when I was getting my MFA at Warren Wilson, I took myself out to dinner at High/Low to celebrate getting a poem published in the *New Yorker.* I made eight hundred dollars, which was supposed to go to rent and student loans. Instead, I spent about a fourth of it on—"

"I hear you talking about me," Desiree calls.

"All kind things, Rayray," Dr. Adkins calls back.

"Better be, because I'm sending Alex out with some goodies."

Alex enters, a snooty look on his face, a dish towel over one forearm, balancing a large platter on his fingertips at shoulder height.

"Don't drop that, dude," I say.

"I used to wait tables at our restaurant, bro. You think my parents didn't make me literally practice with a tray and full cups of water?" Alex lowers the tray to Dr. Adkins with a theatrical flourish. "Please enjoy a premeal appetizer," he says in a staid British accent. "Deviled eggs with deviled crab and crab cakes. A crabstravaganza, if you will."

We all groan.

"Your use of the portmanteau *crabstravaganza* has spared you from a lecture on *premeal appetizer's* being redundant," Dr. Adkins says, double-fisting a crab cake and a crab deviled egg.

Desiree comes out of the kitchen to take in our dumbstruck expressions.

"Now that Desiree is here, you have to finish the story of how you two met," Vi says.

"Oh right! Okay, I was saying . . . yes. I dropped literally two hundred dollars on the meal." She spends the next several minutes listing the various dishes she ordered.

"There's *more?*" Delaney's expression is pure incredulity as Dr. Adkins goes on.

Desiree chuckles. "Oh, sweetie. I'm honestly shocked she survived."

"That's a heroic feat of memory," Delaney says.

"I'm more impressed with the culinary creativity and artistry she's remembering," Alex says.

"My man." Desiree fist-bumps Alex.

Dr. Adkins continues. "I finish and I'm so inspired, I write a poem on a napkin and send it back to the chef with a one-hundred-dollar tip."

"I think the waitstaff is clowning on me until I read the poem and realize no chance did they do this," Desiree says. "I tell them to take me to this poet. We come to this inked-up, witchy little white lady, and I'm like, 'Oh Lord, she fine.'" We laugh as Desiree embraces Dr. Adkins from behind and kisses her neck.

Dr. Adkins nuzzles Desiree. "Anyway. I rave and rave about the food. Verging on indignity."

"I thought it was appropriate," Desiree says breezily. "I tell her, there's more where that came from if there's more poetry where that poem came from."

"I asked, 'What are you proposing?' Desiree came back with 'Write me five poems—for me and only me—and I'll cook dinner for you.' I said, 'Six.' Desiree's like, 'Deal.'"

"The rest is history," Desiree says as she and Dr. Adkins grin slyly and kiss.

I look at Vi out of the corner of my eye. She's shining and giddy. I like seeing her connect so deeply to a story of lovers brought together by circumstance.

Desiree has special permission to use a turkey fryer in the dormitory courtyard. We all accompany her and Alex outside to keep vigil over the turkey. The afternoon sky is incongruously sorrow gray, and it's chilly enough that we'd notice if we stopped talking and laughing for long enough.

While we wait, I videochat with Mamaw and Papaw. Papaw is having a good day, so I introduce him to the group. He calls Dr. Adkins "Doc" and tells her how much I've gushed about her class. He tells Desiree he wishes he could have taken Mamaw to her restaurant for their anniversary. He renews his barbecue challenge to Alex, calling him Tex. He tells Delaney how much he misses their *Longmire* parties. She promises she's still working on his cure.

And he meets Vi for the first time. I pray for him not to embarrass me, even inadvertently, and he doesn't. He tells her he's heard wonderful things about her from me. He tells her she should come visit Tennessee sometime and let me take her out on the river. She says she'd love that. He dubs her Sunshine.

My heart blooms the whole time they speak, my worlds converging in the best possible way.

I take my phone back from Vi and leave earshot of the group.

Papaw coughs and coughs; he went into deep debt during his conversations with everyone. When he recovers, he says, "Well, Mickey Mouse, I see why you're head over heels for that gal. Couldn't ask for a prettier smile and the personality to boot."

"I think I'm gonna tell her how I feel soon," I say.

"I don't imagine it'll come as any big surprise. I seen how you looked at her."

"I'm scared, though."

"Sometimes you gotta just let them chips fall." Papaw coughs and wheezes.

"Guess so," I say.

"Tess know about how you feel about Miss Sunshine?"

"Told her."

"She's good?"

"Yep. Like I told you she'd be. I miss y'all. Who's there today?"

Papaw tries to yell to summon everyone, but coughing cuts him off. Aunt Betsy and Mitzi are there. I chat for a few minutes with all of them and Mamaw before Papaw gets the tablet back.

"You let me know how it goes with Sunshine."

253

"I will." I see Desiree pulling the turkey from the fryer and examining it with Alex. It's a glistening bronze. Even with two deviled-crab eggs and three crab cakes in my belly, I'm ready for more. "Looks like we're about to eat. Love you, Papaw."

"Love you, Mickey Mouse. Hug Tess for me."

It suddenly occurs to me that I'm about to sign off with Papaw for what could well be his last Thanksgiving. I walk still a few more yards away from the group, in case I can't make it through what I'm about to say without breaking into tears.

"I love you, Papaw. I'm thankful for you and everything you've done for me. Tell everyone I love them."

After we end the call, I keep my distance from the group for a little while longer, pretending to continue my conversation by talking into my dead phone, while I pull myself together.

We sit at Desiree and Dr. Adkins's table. It's larger than two people need and takes up much of their dining area.

One by one, Alex and Desiree bring platters from the kitchen, sliding them onto the table and announcing them like guests at a ball.

Roasted sweet potatoes with sorghum and benne . . .

Green beans with clams and Benton's bacon . . .

Cornbread dressing with oysters and andouille sausage . . .

Heirloom kale salad with candied pumpkin seeds, charred apples, and reduced cider vinaigrette . . .

Bourbon pecan cranberry sauce . . .

Corn pudding with jalapeños and cheddar . . .

Baked mac and cheese—sorry, but the ingredients of this one stay my secret . . .

Rosemary-garlic mashed potatoes with sage-thyme gravy . . .

Kimchi fried rice . . .

Cajun-seasoned fried turkey . . .

My jaw aches at the edges with my mouth's watering. I love Mamaw's and Aunt Betsy's cooking, but this is promising to be a once-in-a-lifetime feast.

Alex offers to say grace, and he does. We dig in. Every bite is perfect. We wash it down with mulled cider and ice-cold bottles of Mexican Coke. I have seconds of everything and thirds of a few things. We clear the table and all start working on a huge jigsaw puzzle with a folk-art scene of a corn maze and pumpkin patch. After we've had an hour or two to digest, Desiree and Alex begin to retrieve desserts from the kitchen, introducing them like the dinner dishes:

Banana pudding with homemade white chocolate Nutella, Nilla Wafers, and heirloom Carolina African runner peanuts . . .

Sweet potato chess pie topped with homemade roasted maple-syrup-infused marshmallows . . .

Apple pecan stack cake with apple butter between the layers and cardamom-spiced reduced apple cider sauce drizzled on top . . .

The last one triggers a vague memory. I have the most meager collection of good memories from when I was little. This is one. A wedding. I was very young. I was there with Papaw and Mamaw and my mama. Mamaw had brought a layer for the couple's stack cake on a large platter, wrapped in plastic. I felt warm and safe and loved. The way I'm feeling now. The most so I've ever felt since coming to Middleford.

Beside me, Vi digs into a thick slice of the apple stack cake and her eyes roll back. She murmurs something in Portuguese. It sounds like rubbing satin between your fingers feels.

"What's everyone doing for the rest of Thanksgiving break?" Dr. Adkins asks as she gets a second piece of chess pie with a little dollop of banana pudding on the side.

We all shrug and say hanging out, catching up on sleep.

"How about you?" I ask.

"Tomorrow we're going to New York City. The Strand—this huge bookstore—is having events all day, and TaKisha Biggs, one of my former students, is doing a poetry reading." She pauses. "Hey! Y'all should come! Rayray, our Hyundai seats seven, right?"

"Remember you wanted a Prius? And I told you I can't fit everything I need to cater an event in no damn Prius?"

"Can we bring them? Pretty please?"

"Baby, you know I'm good with whatever."

"Serious?" I ask.

"I mean," Dr. Adkins says, "you've all signed travel releases. There's an educational component to this trip. We'll go down in the morning and come back the same day, so no overnight."

We all look at each other.

"I love New York!" Vi says. "I spent a month there when I was twelve."

"I'm in!" Alex says. "I've never been to New York."

"Can I go to the Museum of Natural History?" Delaney asks.

"Sure," Dr. Adkins says. "Cash? Wanna go to the most exciting city in the world and hear some poetry that will change your life?"

I'm already euphoric with a vision of Vi and me at the top of the Empire State Building at night, the phosphorescent metropolis lying open before us like pages of a book. As the muted sounds of the city's bustle and chaos below waft up to us, I turn to her, and I tell her that for the past weeks, nothing has brought me more pure joy than thinking about and spending time with her.

And she says she feels the same about me.

"Yeah," I say to Dr. Adkins. "That sounds pretty cool."

It's near curfew by the time we leave. Still, our heavy bellies force us to walk slowly.

A dense gray shroud covers the night sky, and mist rings the orange sodium lights that illuminate our path. The air smells like damp brick and ivy and a coming frost.

"Cash, I'm thankful for your poetry skills," Alex says.

"You won us the best meal I've ever had in my life and a cool trip tomorrow," Delaney says.

"I still want to read your poetry," Vi says. "When are you going to let me?"

"Someday maybe." I'll never let her. I'll never be as good as she hopes. Better to let her keep imagining.

"I don't even care about reading your poetry; keep the side benefits coming," Delaney says.

"Was I offering to let you read it? Huh?" I say. Delaney and I lag behind Vi and Alex.

"It was good talking to Pep. I miss him," Delaney says.

"Same. Today was fun, but. Not the same as being home."

"How's he doing?"

"I mean, you saw him."

"I was hoping he was having one of his bad days."

"That's what his good days look like now."

"Shit. I'm still working on his cure."

"Yeah?"

"Best I can."

I look at her, but she's gazing off at something else. "Thanks," I say sincerely.

"Here you were up my ass about being with all my science friends so much."

We arrive at the point where Alex's and my path diverges from Vi and Delaney's. I give Vi a long hug good night. Our cheekbones touch. She smells like caramel, vanilla, roasted marshmallows, and something floral. I can't imagine what will happen if I ever get to kiss her. My heart will probably just dissolve and run down the walls of my chest. But everyone has to die somehow.

Alex and I get in the elevator. He hits the button.

"I'm gonna go for it, dude," I blurt out. "Tomorrow. I'm telling Vi how I feel."

Alex turns to me, an ecstatic gleam on his face. "For real?"

I nod uncertainly. "Taking the plunge."

Alex whoops and throws his arm around me. He starts poking me in the ribs with his index finger, making me double over in laughter. "Cash is in loooooooove. Oooooooooh, Cash is in loooooooove."

The elevator stops at the second floor and the doors open. We stop our horsing around, snap back to normal, and stare forward, clearing our throats. Some senior whose name I don't know gets on and stands in front of us, facing the door.

Alex starts pointing at me, mouthing, *Cash is in looooove.* I flip him off. We start snorting, trying not to laugh. The guy glances back at us, irritated.

"Inside joke," Alex murmurs. We get to his floor. He gets off the elevator, turns back, and says, "Tomorrow," pointing at me and waggling his eyebrows.

"Stop that eyebrow thing." The doors close, cutting me off.

I arrive at my room, where I hold the day close to me— a warmth that won't soon surrender to the air.

I pull off my shirt and press it to my face in the dark, searching like a sailor, nose to the wind, for some hint of a green shore ahead.

Chapter 41

Sometimes you'll come around a bend in the river to see a blue heron standing quietly in the distant shallows. As you near, he coils up and releases himself to the sky. My heart feels like the moment he's coiled up as the miles to the city melt away beneath our feet.

Desiree drives. Dr. Adkins sits in the front passenger seat, twisted around to talk to us. Vi sits between Alex and me in the second row, and Delaney claims the cramped third row for herself. For most of the hour-and-forty-minute drive, I'm alternating chatting with everyone; staring out the window, reflecting on how the last time I traveled this stretch of road it was too dark to see anything; and planning what I'll say to Vi and where I'll say it. I decide it's probably best to let Vi pick her favorite place in New York.

The city thickens in density and starts growing upward, appearing more like I imagine New York City to look. We drive into Brooklyn and park in front of Dr. Adkins and Desiree's friends' brownstone. "They're in Berlin for the next year," Dr. Adkins explains.

I step out into the whir of the teeming city.

Dr. Adkins sees me scanning around. "Wait'll you see Manhattan."

Vi is giddy. "I love this place. There's nowhere on Earth like here. London, no. São Paulo, no."

"Sawyer, Tennessee, no," I say. Everyone laughs.

We walk in the direction of a nearby subway station. The sky is a festive tinsel silver, and a brisk, stiff wind forces our hands into our pockets and tinges our cheeks pink as it rushes between the buildings like it's late for something.

Delaney looks simultaneously dazed and happy. A lot to observe and process here. So many patterns to analyze.

"Can you believe we're here?" I murmur to her.

"Thanks, *Penicillium delanum*," she says.

Alex is still the only person who knows my plan for today with Vi. I was afraid to tell Delaney because she and Vi live in such close contact to each other. I didn't want Delaney slipping up and blowing it for me.

It takes me five tries to successfully swipe my subway card, but even this is exciting. There are seats available on the train, but I prefer to stand and hang on to the steel poles, like on TV.

"Everybody got their phones?" Dr. Adkins asks. "Full charges? The rules are: Check in with me every two hours. Nobody goes off solo."

We get to our stop and emerge from underground into the ecstatic hum and buzz of the city. I can taste the live-wire energy immediately, metallic on my tongue. It takes about three seconds for my senses to be overwhelmed. Alex and Delaney have awestruck expressions. Of the four of us, only Vi takes it relatively in stride.

Our first stop is the Strand, because Dr. Adkins's student's reading is early in the day. It's a temple of books. I've never seen so many in one place. Delaney immediately disappears, as does Vi.

One of the booksellers recognizes Dr. Adkins. Her book *Holler*, its silver National Book Award Finalist seal gleaming, is on an employee-recommendations shelf, which she shows off proudly.

I suddenly realize I've never read *Holler*. I've only ever read Dr. Adkins's poems online. I take one of the copies from the shelf. I shouldn't be spending much on this trip, but "Here's my souvenir from New York City," I say.

"Cash, I have copies. I'll hook you up," Dr. Adkins says. "Sorry," she says to the bookseller. "Teenagers. Fixed incomes."

"Nope," I say. "I've never gotten to buy the book of someone I know. You have to sign it for me." I buy my copy and Dr. Adkins signs it, smiling.

She's no sooner finished than she looks up. "Kisha!" She runs over to a young woman who just walked in, a battered black journal nestled under one arm. They embrace energetically and for a long time.

"Cash!" Dr. Adkins waves me over. "Come meet TaKisha!"

I walk over and shake hands with her. "I've heard amazing things about you," I say.

"Likewise," TaKisha says. "Bree tells me you've caught the poetry bug."

I blush and break eye contact, absently straightening a stack of books with my left hand. "Oh. Yeah. Wasn't expecting it."

"So what inspired you to take her class?"

"Needed an English credit." Everyone laughs. "I grew up in this little town in East Tennessee no one's heard of, and I didn't read much poetry growing up."

TaKisha eyes Dr. Adkins with playful accusation. "Do I see a pattern here?"

"Maybe," Dr. Adkins says coyly.

"I came to Middleford on scholarship from Sardis, Mississippi," TaKisha says. "I listened to rap and hip-hop nonstop, but I had never just sat down and read a poem before. I take Bree's class and, well . . ." She and Dr. Adkins trade wide smiles.

"And by the way. May I?" TaKisha reaches for my copy of *Holler*, and I give it to her. She holds it up to Dr. Adkins and taps the silver seal on the cover. "Can we just . . ." She hands the book back to me.

Dr. Adkins waves her off.

"Girl. Please," TaKisha says.

"I'd much rather discuss the time I picked up my copy of *Boston Review* to read a dazzling poem by my former student TaKisha Biggs."

We talk about that, about Middleford, about Dr. Adkins's sixth sense for finding kids from the rural South and planting in them the seed of poetry. Then we watch TaKisha read.

Dr. Adkins was right about her. She's a brilliant poet. Her lines are sinewy and muscular. They land with the heat and energy of lightning strikes.

Listening to her read feels like standing in a river—any moment you could be swept away. A few times I hold my breath until I am almost gasping, for fear of missing even a single word.

At one point Dr. Adkins looks over at me and just says, "Yeah?"

"Yeah," I whisper.

We think of language as this tame thing that lives in neat garden beds, bound by rules and fences. Then someone shows it to you growing wild and beautiful, flowering vines consuming cities, erasing pavement and lines. Breaking through any fence that would try to contain it. Reclaiming. Reshaping. Reforming.

In my life, I've never known anything else that felt so full of infinite possibility.

Words make me feel strong. They make me feel powerful and alive.

They make me feel like I can open doors.

We leave the Strand. A tall guy with dreads comes around the corner and approaches us.

Desiree squeals, runs up, and hugs him. "Everyone, this is Malik. We worked together in kitchens all over New York City." We all go around introducing ourselves.

"Rayray and Malik are taking me on a culinary tour of Manhattan," Alex explains.

"You get to call her Rayray?" Dr. Adkins looks at Alex, agog.

He looks to Desiree. "She told me to."

"Alex is my son now," Desiree says. "I am adopting him. You can adopt Cash and they can be brothers."

I laugh but with a sharp twinge, because it's only a joke. It'd be a lucky kid who got to grow up with them as parents. It's a real shitty deal that you get to grow up only once and your parents are your parents and you get one shot at it.

Desiree, Malik, and Alex say goodbye and head out on their eating expedition.

Dr. Adkins, TaKisha, Delaney, Vi, and I grab huge pizza slices around the corner. I notice Delaney getting bored and antsy with all the poetry talk.

"If no one's willing to come to the museum with me, can I still go?" Delaney asks, looking at me accusingly.

"I'll go with you; I've somehow never been to the natural history museum," Dr. Adkins says. "TaKisha? What are you doing after this?"

"I've never been either! I'll go," TaKisha says.

"Cash? Vi? You two want to come, or would you rather go explore together?" Dr. Adkins shoots me a glance that says she knows *exactly* what's up and that she knows which we'll choose.

"Vi? You wanna show me around the Big Apple?" I ask.

She claps. "Yes!"

Delaney shoots me a reproachful glare. I return an apologetic look. *I know we said we'd hang out in NYC together, but.*

Dr. Adkins checks the time. "Okay. Meet back at the Strand at eight-thirty."

Delaney, TaKisha, and Dr. Adkins start off together. "Okay, so tell me the whole story of this stuff you found in the cave," I hear Dr. Adkins say. Delaney throws me one last castigating look over her shoulder as they walk away. I shrug sheepishly. *She'll get over it.*

And it's just Vi and me. And the city.

Chapter 42

Vi's not wearing one of her usual Marvel T-shirts today. She's dressed for the city in black jeans with slashes in the knees. She's bundled against the chill with a scarf and a white leather motorcycle jacket. Her russet curls cascade from underneath a broad-brimmed floppy black hat. She looks like a model. I feel unsophisticated by comparison. I'm carrying Dr. Adkins's book, which I hope makes me look a little smarter and more urbane.

I remind myself to play it cool today and wait for the perfect moment to tell her.

"We have to go to Central Park first, while it's still light out," Vi says, checking her phone and striding purposefully in the subway's direction.

"I can't believe you lived here."

"My dad was making some big deal, and my mom said, 'We're going to New York if we won't see you anyway.' So we lived in a nice hotel for a month."

"Whoa. Was that fun?"

"Sort of. I would have preferred to have my dad around, though. You know?"

"Totally."

"Was your dad around when you were young?"

Not today. Not this conversation. Another time. "Pretty much."

"I miss my dad a lot. Being here is making me miss him. It's reminding me of how I felt then." She looks wistful. "There's a word in Portuguese for the feeling I have. *Saudade.* It doesn't really have a translation."

"What's the closest thing?"

"Mmm. Maybe 'the sadness of missing someone or something.' "

We walk for a while. I keep almost tripping as I look skyward at the tops of buildings.

"Where should we go after the park?" Vi asks.

"It's all cool to me. At some point, I want to go someplace where we can get good views of the city at night."

Vi thinks for a moment. "Okay. After Central Park . . . the Metropolitan Museum of Art is near." She pulls out her phone and scrolls and taps. "There's an indie video-game arcade I wanted to go to. It has lots of games you can only find there. Can we?"

I would joyfully accompany you to an arcade where the only game is sticking your hand into a box of rattlesnakes. "Of course."

"Then we could get dinner—maybe Brazilian food, if we can find it—and go walk on the High Line?"

"Is the High Line a good place to see the city lights?"

"Very."

Then it'll be a good place to tell you what I need to tell you. "Cool. I'm gonna need you to guide us on the subway, though. It's a little confusing."

"I got this." She looks up directions on her phone. She starts off confidently. "This way." I quickly fall behind. She turns back. "Come on, Tennessee Boy. You have to walk faster."

Tennessee Boy. A new nickname. I'm searching every word and action of hers for omens.

We get off the subway near Rockefeller Center and walk around there for a bit. It's a wonderland—the likes of which I've only seen on TV. Funny how everyone in Sawyer thinks places like New York City are so godless but New York City is the one pulling out all the stops for Jesus's birthday.

We watch the ice-skaters for a while. Vi asks if I want to skate. I lie and say I'm scared to because I broke my arm as a kid doing it. I'm embarrassed to tell her I can't afford it, especially after buying Dr. Adkins's book. Not if I want to eat tonight.

We continue on to Central Park, walking with our hands in our pockets, the vapor of our breath wafting upward. Joggers wearing knit caps pass us by. I could imagine everyone I'm seeing in a tuxedo or an evening gown. They even look debonair in workout clothes.

Vi sees me looking around. "What do you think of the Big Apple?"

"You really love everything apple, don't you?"

She laughs. "I would still love New York if it weren't named after the best fruit on Earth."

"It's amazing," I say. "But I don't know if I could live here. I love quiet. It's not quiet here much, is it?"

"Never."

"When you're done with college and everything, where are you going to live?" I ask.

She spins, arms outstretched. "Everywhere!"

"You sound serious."

"I am."

"Sawyer, Tennessee?" I dodge a woman walking a small dog wearing a doggie coat that probably cost more than mine.

"Yes. Will you teach me how to fish and hunt for wolves when I live there?"

"Okay, first off, we don't have wolves in Sawyer. Second off, would you want to hunt them if we did?"

She giggles. The tip of her nose is rosy. "No. But I want to go fishing." She pantomimes casting a line.

"That we can do."

"If I catch a fish and cook it, will you eat it?"

"You a good cook?"

"Terrible."

"Yes, I'll eat it," I say.

I smell her conditioner as a sudden gust blows her hair across her face. I reach over and gently move it out of her eyes for her.

Any excuse. Any.

"So this game is nothing but you're a cat and you're walking across people's nuts?" I ask.

Vi fixates on the screen and doesn't deviate. "It's fun. You try."

"I'm good."

"You're not much of a gamer."

"Not really. I had a PlayStation for a while, but . . ." *My mama sold it.* "It wasn't my thing."

The game ends and she turns to me. "Okay. I'm hungry and you need to see more of the city. You hungry?"

"Definitely."

"Are you ready to try Brazilian food?"

"Sure." I have a sudden stroke of brilliance. "But I want the real experience. No fancy Brazilian food. What a normal Brazilian would eat every day."

She searches on her phone for a minute. "Oh! There's a place right nearby. And it looks not fancy."

I breathe an inward sigh of relief as we walk in the periwinkle dusk.

New York City is incredible. You get your mouth set on Brazilian food, and five minutes' walk later, you're sitting at a cheerily decorated modern, casual Brazilian restaurant called Almoço. It looks like a Brazilian version of Chipotle.

I get rice and beans (arroz com feijão) and cheese bread (pão de queijo). My meal reminds me of cornbread and soup beans. It's filling, delicious, and best of all, cheap.

Vi gets feijoada, which is a couple bucks more. It's a stew of black beans and sausage and pork belly. She tells me the real thing would have pig ears and snouts in it. She clearly thinks I'll be horrified, but I'm from Tennessee, so I'm not at all. In fact, it sounds good.

She tells me about her new game idea. You play with a friend and walk around a huge city like New York, rendered in perfect digital detail, interacting with each other and the environment. You just talk while you walk and see the sights. The game isn't the point—the interaction is.

"Brazilian food makes me want to live in Brazil," I say as we finish.

"Knowing me wasn't enough?"

"Oh, it was." I think of telling her exactly how enough while we eat. But I don't. Not yet. Soon.

We finish our dinner and head back into the windblown night. The low overcast sky reflects back the city lights in a wintry rose-gold glow. It's one of my favorite colors.

The temperature has dipped and I walk so as to shield the wind from her. Once or twice she has to clap her hand on top of her hat to keep it from blowing off.

"High Line time?" she asks.

"Let's do it," I say, a widening anxiety churning in my lower belly.

We're mostly quiet as we head there. I take in the carnival energy of the Manhattan night as we walk down to the High Line.

"This used to be a railroad," Vi says as we ascend the steps. "It was my favorite place to walk when I lived here."

A gust of wind catches the brim of Vi's hat and blows it off. I chase it down and bring it back to her.

We meander. The High Line is well lit and meticulously land-scaped. We have it mostly to ourselves, but we pass the occasional person or couple.

We gawk at the views and speculate on what buildings house. We watch people walking on the streets below. We come around a bend, and there's a stunning vista and a bench to take it in. *This is the place.* My breath quickens.

"Wanna sit?" I ask, hoping she'll interpret the unsteadiness of my voice as a shiver from the frigid bluster.

"Sure."

My blood pounds in my temples. I had a plan for what I was going to say, but it left me the minute I sat.

"I almost forgot," Vi says, rummaging in her pocket. "I have a job for you." She pulls out another tangled necklace.

My body sings relief. This might smooth my path. I remove my glove and hold out my palm. She drops the necklace on it.

"Now you're testing my skills," I say. "The cold reduces dexterity, and the light isn't great."

"We can wait."

"I like the challenge."

I hold the necklace in my palm, moving it around slightly, waiting for it to reveal how it'll give up its tangle. I get an idea. "We're going to teach you."

She edges toward me. The wind blows a strand of her hair across my lips. I make no attempt to move it.

"Okay." I start to pull out one of the tangles, but my hand is trembling and I can't get ahold of it.

"I'll try," Vi says. She removes her glove and delicately takes up a small length of chain.

Both of our hands are right there, together. My finger brushes hers.

And then, somehow, my fingers are interlacing with hers. Her hand is smooth and soft and cold. She drops the chain back into my palm.

And now I'm holding hands with Vi Xavier.

Every cell in me sparkles.

I lower my palm with the necklace and turn to face her.

She looks away with a thin, nervous laugh.

"I . . . don't know how to say this. I have to tell you something." I'm a trembling mess. "I've . . . *liked* you for a really, really long time. As more than a friend. I guess that's the thing I needed to say. I couldn't keep it inside anymore. But. Yeah."

Quite the poet. Dr. Adkins would be so proud.

Vi takes a deep breath, as though gathering herself. She looks at me and then at her feet.

"Cash," she says softly. She pulls her hand from mine so gently it makes me wish she had yanked it.

My pulse starts a drumroll at the base of my head, and even the wind seems to hush to hear what she'll say.

"I can't."

I feel like I've been running in the pitch dark, and suddenly, there's no ground under my feet, and the only question as I fall is how badly I'll be broken when I hit the bottom of whatever chasm I've stumbled into. And still I cling to the tiniest scrap of hope, as if I'll land on a giant feather mattress. Maybe this is her idea of humor.

But she looks at me with great sadness—no, pity.

"Oh," I say weakly. "Oh."

"I think you're really amazing. I love being your friend. We have so much fun together."

"What's . . . wrong with me?" I hate the pleading in my voice.

"*Nothing* is wrong with you. It's why I love being your friend. But—" She catches herself.

"What?"

She shakes her head.

Maybe this is the one doubt I can resolve that will make everything work. "Vi. Please tell me what you were about to say."

She looks at her feet and doesn't speak.

"Please." My voice is brittle.

She raises her head to meet my eyes. "Cash," she says softly. "You're in love with Delaney."

I give a small disbelieving laugh. "Wait. *What?* No. No. Vi. I am *not* in love with Delaney. I mean, yes, we're best friends. But we're not *together.* We've never been."

"I know you're not together," Vi murmurs. "But it's obvious."

The warmth inside me that was protecting me against the cold has been extinguished as surely as pissing on the embers of a campfire. I start shivering violently. The awful prickly chill of impending sickness cascades down my back like a legion of centipedes. "Is there anything I can tell you to convince you I'm not in love with Delaney?"

Vi takes my hand in hers, but with a you'll-get-through-this energy. "You're very important to me. I hope we stay friends. I never wanted to hurt you."

Now I pull away. I clasp my hands in front of me and rest my knees on my elbows. I suddenly feel so tiny and crude and ridiculous. In my cheap clothes with my belly full of cheap Brazilian food. Having met Vi on a scholarship I didn't earn. With my family dying all around me. *Where did I ever get the idea I was in her league? My broken life is no place for her.* I wonder if all my days will be spent pressing vainly against doors forever shut to me.

"Cash?" she says quietly.

"You never asked for this. I know," I say. "I'll be okay." *Maybe.*

"I don't want things to be weird between us."

"I just need time is all." I stand. "We should start heading back."

She stands too and we begin walking.

If only heartbreak were truly what it claims to be, it might not be so bad. But here's the thing—your heart never gets broken quite enough to stop wanting who broke it.

Chapter 43

We return to the Strand, which is still bustling with shoppers. We haven't been waiting long (but it feels like forever) when Alex, Malik, and Desiree roll up, chatting merrily.

"Bro," Alex says. "This New York City place? It's got some food options."

They regale us with their culinary odyssey. They're so exuberant, it eases Vi's and my efforts to act like everything's fine.

Delaney, TaKisha, and Dr. Adkins arrive. They also radiate the aura of having had the time of their lives.

"Well," Dr. Adkins says, "that was my first experience going to the museum with someone smarter than the museum."

"We had more fun than you did," Delaney says, coming over to where I'm standing, slightly apart from the group.

"Yeah."

"Shouldn't have ditched me. After all that talk about hanging out together here someday."

"I know," I say quietly, looking away. I expect Delaney to keep twisting the knife, but she spares me.

She sits beside me on the ride back to Brooklyn to retrieve the car. What a stark difference between this ride and the ride *to* Manhattan. I imagined making this journey in triumph, Vi by my side, our eyes sparkling, everyone giving us congratulatory smiles. Instead, Delaney and Alex sit between me and Vi. I try to hold my head high, but the burden is too much and I slump into myself.

We get to the car, and I immediately call the far back. "Man, this day was tiring. I'm gonna crash on the trip home."

"Same. I'll sit with Cash. Give Vi and Alex room to spread out."

Thank the Lord for Delaney Doyle.

As I'm getting in, Dr. Adkins asks, "Have fun today?"

She knows. So I offer as much of the truth as I can. "Seeing TaKisha was amazing. I'll never forget it."

"That was really something special, wasn't it?"

I rest the side of my forehead against the icy window as the city lights dissolve into the blackness behind us like sugar melting into coffee. I squint at them and remember simpler times—going with Delaney to overlook Sawyer, the equivalent of a few blocks of Manhattan.

"They look like phosphenes," Delaney murmurs, seeing my fixation on the skyline.

"Do what?"

"That's what you call the little lights you see when you close your eyes."

I squeeze my eyes shut and stare at the slow dance of phosphenes on the backs of my eyelids.

Everyone is tired from the day, so the drive is mostly quiet. But after a while Delaney murmurs, "There could have been other intelligent life on Earth before humans. And we might not ever know."

"How?" I ask.

"Hundreds of millions of years ago."

"Yeah, but there'd be pyramids and fossils and stuff."

"Only a tiny fraction of life gets fossilized. Human structures can't last millions of years. Almost everything from millions of years ago is just dust. If there was a civilization of advanced beings that existed for one hundred thousand years sixty million years ago, we'd probably never know."

I look back at the glow in the distance. "All this will be forgotten?"

"Someday."

I think on our passing through the night over the pulverized bones of long-buried loves and memories, and it's an oddly soothing idea—that the world forgets all of our wounds and aches so completely you eventually can't distinguish them from dust.

Delaney slumps into my shoulder. She reaches over and takes my hand. The way she did at my mama's funeral. I feel the roughness of her distressed thumb. *This is the third time you've held hands with a girl tonight, zero of which were how you hoped for.*

She doesn't let my hand go the rest of the drive. This won't help my case that I'm not in love with Delaney, but I don't mind, because without her to hold on to, I would drown in the current of my sadness.

Back on campus, we say our good-nights. Vi and I don't hug like we normally do. I play it as a joke, like I'm afraid of knocking off her hat. But I don't know who I'm performing for anymore.

Alex and I walk slowly back to Koch Hall.

He puts his arm around my shoulders, and we walk for a while without speaking. Finally he says, "You took the plunge."

"From a hundred-foot cliff into four inches of water."

"Man," Alex says.

"Got the old 'I just want to be friends.' " I don't feel like telling Alex about the other part.

"Aw, man. I'm sorry, bro."

"It's all good. I mean, it's not really, but."

"For what it's worth, man, I think she's sincere about that. I can tell you mean a lot to her."

I sigh.

We get on the elevator. Alex drops his arm to hit the button for his floor. As he's about to get off, he turns to me and motions me in. "Come on, bro. Hug it out."

I smile against my will and we hug. It feels good. Alex smells like restaurants—smoke and sizzling oil and spice.

And then I'm alone again. I trudge to my room. I sit in the silence. Tripp is gone for Thanksgiving. I almost wish he were here to provide *some* distraction. Even anger or annoyance would feel better than what I'm experiencing.

I text Delaney.

> **Me:** Sorry again for ditching you in NYC. I regret it.

A few seconds pass.

> **Delaney:** You okay?

> **Me:** I guess you figured out.

> **Delaney:** Yeah.

> **Me:** Did Vi tell you?

Delaney: Your face did. She hasn't said anything. I'm sorry, Cash. I hate to see you hurting.

Me: I feel like an idiot.

Delaney: You don't seem like more of an idiot than normal, if that's a comfort.

Me: Surprisingly it is.

Delaney: You've survived worse. You'll pick yourself back up.

Me: I hope.

Delaney: You still owe me a trip to NYC. Us hanging out like we planned.

Me: Damn right I do.

I try to sleep, and exhausted as I am, it should be easy. But each time I drift off, my brain replays my conversation with Vi and it snaps me back awake, like I'm trying to sleep on a narrow catwalk over a freezing lake, and every time I'm near sleep, my hand falls in the icy water.

It's two a.m. I look at my phone, as though there'll be a text from Vi saying, *Hey, now that I've had some time to think, I wanna be your girlfriend after all.* Of course there's nothing.

I spiral. *Why are you choosing to be so far from everyone who loves you? At a place where you're only going to fail and let everyone down? You could quit school tomorrow and leave all this hurt behind.*

I want to talk with Papaw so bad it makes my teeth ache. I honestly consider, for a second or two, calling him. But I would be pulling him from sleep and I couldn't.

Then I remember Dr. Adkins's book. I haven't even cracked it open to see her dedication to me. I open it and, still under my blanket (I can't bear leaving the warmth to turn on the light), read by the glow of my phone:

> To my fellow poet Cash,
> There is beauty in every wound.
> Find it.
> Your friend,
> Bree Rae Adkins

Fellow poet. I feel about ten percent better immediately. I start thumbing through, reading. It's a garden of aching wonder. She writes about the things, landscapes, and people I know. Her poems massage the hurt from my heart—not by asking me to avoid it, but by asking me to sit with it and to speak with it—to know it.

And I know how to do that. I have a pen on my nightstand. I grab it. I don't even get up to find my notebook. I write in the back of Dr. Adkins's book, the way she once told me she used to do in her favorite poetry books.

It pours from me, unbroken. Seeing my words spilling onto the page dulls the keen edge of my misery. *Beauty in every wound. Dignity in heartbreak. This is what your mama was looking for—just to stop hurting for a while—and it killed her.*

As cures for pain go, poetry is better than most.

A Feast of Apples

You told me apples were your favorite
fruit and you taught me
the secret way of eating
them so their rough
parts vanished.

You told me apples were your favorite
fruit because we desire
most what we can't have.

Did you know you can starve
at a feast of apples?
The more you eat of them
the more they leave you wanting.

You were beautiful
in the dwindling October light.
All around us was the sweet perfume
of apples' sun-flushed skin,
heavy in the burning
season's breath.

I wanted to kiss your lips clean
of the nectar
that anointed them,
I was delirious with want;
there was no amount of you
that would not leave me hungry.

WINTER

Chapter 44

"This is the longest we've talked since Thanksgiving," Delaney says, staring out the Greyhound's window. She had no desire to go home for Christmas break, but I told her she could stay with us, so she acquiesced.

"You're not blaming me, are you?" I ask.

"I'm not *not* blaming you."

"As if you didn't spend ninety percent of December studying for finals," I say. "Same with Alex and Vi."

"As if you didn't spend every free minute you had alone by the lake with your notebook, skipping meals with us. At least when I was doing it, I had the excuse of being mad at you."

My attempts at escape hadn't worked. Every time I'd tried to turn down the volume on my thoughts, they only reverberated louder. "You know why."

"Alex said you promised you wouldn't ditch us if Vi rejected you."

"Why is Alex telling you that?"

"Because we were discussing how much we missed you, piece of shit."

I stare at my hands. "I needed a break from seeing her every day."

"She snores and leaves out used tissues."

"I bet they're beautiful snores. And used tissues."

Delaney rolls her eyes. "Gross. Don't be pathetic."

We don't talk for a while. Then Delaney says, "I mean it, dickhead, I miss you."

"I heard you. I'm working out my shit."

"If we're gonna stay friends at Middleford, we gotta work on it. It's not like in Sawyer, where it was easy because there was no one else. This is like a plant you have to water."

I turn to Delaney. "When we get back, every Friday night we hang out. Just you and me. No Alex, no Vi. Deal?"

"You think I'm committing my Friday nights to you and you alone? Flatter yourself much?"

"What could you possibly have going on Friday nights at Middleford?"

"That's my self-care night."

"We both know the only self-care you believe in is tormenting me."

She smiles a little.

"Thursday dinners," I say. "Just you and me."

"Deal."

"You know this bus ride home was almost the first little bit of peace and happiness I've felt since Thanksgiving?"

Delaney shrugs and cozies against my shoulder, draping her hoodie over herself like a blanket. Soon she's fast asleep. At one point, she stirs and murmurs, "Someday, when you're moping about Vi down by the lake, you should write a poem about how awesome I am to take your mind off your pain."

"I promise you I will," I say. I'm not lying.

Chapter 45

Being home again mends some of the rifts in me.

My first night back, Papaw and I brave the cold to sit on the porch and talk. I'd already told him about crashing and burning with Vi. But I tell him again.

"Sometimes you get your heart broke, Mickey Mouse. Ain't no avoiding it," he says, wheezing.

"What now?"

"You said she wants to be your friend."

"She says."

"Then be her friend. Maybe she'll come around to you. But if she don't, that's all right too. She can still bless your life."

"I'd rather she bless my lips with hers," I say, and Papaw laughs himself into a minute-long coughing fit.

We celebrate a quiet, peaceful Christmas. We sleep late. Delaney and I help Mamaw make buttermilk biscuits and saw-mill gravy with country ham for breakfast.

There aren't many presents to open—it hasn't been that kind of year. I get a couple of shirts and a journal for writing. In the toe of my stocking is a little black bear Papaw carved for me. "You talking about poetry gave me the itch. Took up whittling again since you been gone. This one's about the only thing that turned out," he says, his proud face betraying his attempt at self-effacement.

Except for a few minutes when I drive her to take presents to her half brothers and wait outside in my truck, Delaney spends every minute of Christmas Day with us. She and Papaw start watching *Longmire* just after breakfast and hardly budge throughout the day. Aunt Betsy and Mitzi come by and help us make Christmas dinner. Aunt Betsy says I carry myself differently now, with more confidence. She and Mitzi marvel over how I've bulked up from crew. I don't see either, but I take the compliments.

I spend maybe an hour that day without thinking about Vi once, which is the longest I've gone since Thanksgiving weekend. Sometimes you get used to hurting, the way you acclimate to excessively cold or hot water, and then it's the absence of it you notice.

We sit around the dinner table. Delaney and I tell them about New York. Aunt Betsy says she and Mitzi are planning on going there someday to see musicals. They ask us for recommendations on places to go. Delaney plugs the natural history museum. I tell them the High Line is a beautiful walk. I don't tell them it's also a good place to get your heart turned into roadkill.

Chapter 46

One day, just before we have to go back to school, it dawns a clear, clean fifty-seven-degree day like you sometimes get during the winter here. It's the kind of warm that tells you that by afternoon, the clouds will have rolled in. After sundown, the rain will start and the temperature will drop steadily. You'll awake to a dusting of snow on the ground. But for now, it's pleasant, so Delaney and I go out on the river together. It feels good, like it always did.

"Back where it all started," Delaney says, her paddle resting on her knees while I steer.

"Yeah."

"Gotta admit the last few months haven't been boring."

"No. Not boring."

We're quiet for a while.

"I miss Vi," I say for no particular reason.

"Here we go." Delaney looks back so I'm sure to see and almost tips the canoe with the force of her eye roll.

"Just saying how I feel."

"I know it sucks but you gotta move on, dude."

"Easier said than done."

"Good thing I'm not just saying it, then," Delaney says, trailing her fingertips in the water and flicking away droplets.

"Oh yeah?"

"I'm more familiar with unreturned love than you know, Cash. And I'm telling you that you can survive it. Even though it hurts."

"Anyone who doesn't love you back is an idiot."

"Yeah. They are sometimes."

"Speaking of, you seen your mama yet?"

Delaney scoffs. "You recall me asking you for a ride to her place?"

"No."

She stares downriver. "When you took me to give Noah and Braxton their presents, their dad told me she hooked up with a new dude who works an oil field in North Dakota. So that's where she is." She looks at me with a wistful expression, her amber eyes distant. "You're all I've got now. You. Pep. Your mamaw. Noah and Braxton have already started forgetting about me while I'm gone. Y'all are it."

Delaney faces front again and we drift along for a while in silence. I stare at her back. She's right about Vi. I do need to get over her. Vi and I were never supposed to be more than friends. It really sucks that Delaney and I couldn't get together in Sawyer because I was her only choice and so the stakes were too high, and we'll never get together now that Delaney is out of Sawyer because now she has tons of choices at Middleford—guys way smarter than me. I'd love to have a girlfriend someday who I'm as close with as Delaney. I want someone who knows me like she does—all the ways I'm weak and strong—and still loves me in spite of and also because of it. That would be great.

It's one of those tranquil days when the river reflects the

brisk blue of the December sky and the pale winter sun, and the wind ripples the face of the water like brushstrokes on a painting. You look at it all and you hope maybe there'll come a day when no trouble seems very important anymore and this is all you see when your mind goes still.

Chapter 47

The night before I leave, Papaw and I sit on the porch for one last time. He says it's okay to love someone who doesn't love you back—that's a love story too and he doesn't care what anyone says otherwise. He tells me there's someone in this world for me—maybe someone I know already, maybe not—but someone.

He tells me about his and Mamaw's honeymoon. How they couldn't afford much of one, so they went down the road to Gatlinburg and got a cheap motel. One night they went out dancing until two a.m. and stopped in at an all-night pancake house on their way back.

He said they were so loopy and love-drunk they started drawing faces on their pancakes in ketchup and made each other crack up so hard they got kicked out. The memory makes him chuckle himself into a fit of wheezing and coughing. When he recovers, he says, "Tell you what, Mickey Mouse. You find that right someone, and ever' minute you spend with them is like a Hawaiian vacation. She's out there. You'll figure it out."

He's never been to Hawaii.

It feels like he's bequeathing me an inheritance of the only wealth he possesses—his memories, his quiet joys.

At the bus station to see Delaney and me off, Papaw struggles to walk even a short distance. Mamaw and I help him as best we can.

Mamaw and Papaw take turns hugging Delaney. Papaw says, "Don't you forget that promise you made me, Tess."

"I won't," Delaney says. "Still working on it."

"I believe you," he says.

I hug Mamaw goodbye. "Take care of him," I say. "And yourself. Don't work too hard."

"I can promise to take care of him, but that's all. I love you, darling."

"I love you, Mamaw." We hug. Her slate-colored hair smells like cinnamon rolls and roses. I wonder for a second at what her life would be like if she had what Tripp's or Vi's parents do. If fate weren't an insect-bored tree limb waiting to fall on her at the first stiff wind. If her world grew just a little greener. Would the same lines surround her eyes and mouth? It's hard now to imagine her so young and carefree that faces drawn on pancakes in ketchup could make her giddy with laughter.

Before I board the bus, Papaw and I hug. He smells like eucalyptus, wintergreen, and wood varnish. I can feel the roughness of his breath and his frailty under my hands.

"Keep working hard up there, Mickey Mouse," he says. "We'll miss you."

"I love you, Papaw."

"Love you too, Mickey Mouse."

From my seat, I watch them through the window. They look

small, standing there holding hands in the cold and the stink of diesel, bundled in the coats they've worn for as long as I can remember. I know they won't leave until the bus is gone from view. Papaw waves feebly.

Tears stream down my face as I wonder if it's the last time I'll ever see him standing. Or if I'll ever see him at all.

Delaney reaches over and brushes a tear from my cheek and holds it up to the light of the window like she's appraising a diamond. "Tears have the same salinity as seawater."

"You told me that once when you were crying," I say after I've had a moment to pull myself together.

Chapter 48

"Cash, can we go for a quick walk?" Vi asks as we're finishing dinner.

My heart stutters. She's going to tell me she couldn't stop thinking about me and we're meant to be together. But that's not the timbre of her voice. I'm still interested.

I meet Alex's eyes as I get up from the table. They're outwardly neutral, but I know him well enough to catch the cheerleading in them. Delaney doesn't meet my eyes.

Vi and I leave the dining hall. She carries a bag.

"Can we go to the lake?" she asks.

"Sure."

We get to the lake and sit. I think about coming here the first night we met. And after the football game. The days when there was still possibility.

There's a prolonged awkward silence. It's the first time we've been alone together since New York. We make eye contact and quickly break it.

We both start to talk simultaneously.

"You go," Vi says.

"No, you," I say.

She sets the bag she brought on her lap. Then hands it to me. "Here's your Christmas gift."

I hold the bag without opening it.

Vi nudges me playfully. Like she used to. The way that made it feel like she was looking for excuses to touch me. "Open it."

I don't want to. I prefer to live in this moment of possibility. For all I know, when I open this bag, I'll find a cross-stitch that says, *I changed my mind over Christmas, and now my heart belongs to you, Cash Pruitt*. But I open it. It's a book by Adélia Prado called *The Alphabet in the Park*. I leaf through it quickly. It's poetry. And it's beautiful.

"She's one of the best Brazilian poets," Vi says, beaming.

"I feel bad because I didn't get you anything. I didn't know if it'd be weird or something."

"I'll tell you the only present I want from you."

My stomach tightens. "Sure."

"I want to be friends again."

"We're friends." I say it half-heartedly, knowing I'm busted.

"Not like before. I have saudade for you."

"I didn't mean to make you feel that. It's just . . . hard."

She stands and extends her arms. "I'm tired of no hugs. Me da um abraço, cara."

I stand. "What's that mean?"

"Give me a hug, man."

I do. We embrace for a long time, swaying gently back and forth. I think she's about to break the hug, but she's only repositioning to hold on to me tighter, laying her head on my chest. I rest my cheek on the top of her head and breathe in her warm-sugar-and-vanilla scent until I'm light-headed.

I missed her so much. Even though she was always around.

"You've been acting like Bucky Barnes," she murmurs. "Being very . . . mmm . . . I don't know the word."

"Sad?"

"No."

"Mad?"

"Like you're carrying something heavy in your heart."

"Brooding?"

"Yes! Brooding," she says in a deep, ominous voice.

We laugh, still clinging to each other.

"You cold?" I ask.

"Yes."

"Wanna go back inside?"

"Not yet. A little longer."

When we finally stop hugging and sit back beside each other, she says, "Read me a poem from your new book, since you won't show me any of yours."

I leaf through the book until I see a poem with a line about apples. I read that one to her.

I know this now: My life is better with her in it, even if it's not how I'd wish.

Chapter 49

Alex sits atop a dryer across from me, kicking his legs restlessly, occasionally hitting the dryer with a hollow *bwong*, while I iron. Something is off with him. He usually emanates cheery, unflappable confidence. The kind that makes you believe him when he says he's going to be president someday.

"You been quiet," I say.

"Chillin'," he replies unpersuasively.

"Yeah?"

He scratches at a spot on the thigh of his pants, sniffles, and nods.

I set my iron on end. "You ain't chillin', man."

"Naw," he says quietly. "Not really."

"Is it Alara?"

"Dude, no. I forgot to tell you she slid into my DMs again last night after I commented on her video. I'd left just like a benign comment."

"She's into you." I pause. "But I may not be the most reliable judge of who's into who."

"All good, bro." Another wan smile.

"If it's not a woman, then what?"

Alex inhales deeply and sighs it out. "My parents called last night, super upset—"

"Dude, you got *one* A-minus and the rest straight A's."

"No, they already lit me up for that. Trust. This relates to something other than my abysmal academic performance."

"Then?" I hold up the shirt I've been ironing, inspecting for wrinkles.

"They told me ICE raided a Korean market back home and arrested a bunch of undocumented people from my church."

"Like, Korean people?"

"Yeah. People don't realize there's lots of undocumented Koreans in America."

"Shit."

"Yeah, so like hardworking, churchgoing people who just wanted a life in America getting rounded up. My dad's friend Young-jin. My friend Becca's dad." Alex is not a contemptful or angry person, but contempt and anger permeate his voice.

"Damn, dude. I hate that shit for them."

"Yeah, well," Alex says, head bowed, toying with a piece of lint. "You know the worst part?" He lifts his head to meet my eyes. His are filled with hurt. "I prayed *nonstop* for this to never happen. Every night. Asking God to keep and protect them. Let them build a life. Let them live in joy with their families. Let them walk in light and peace. That's all. I didn't pray for them to get rich or never have trials. I didn't get greedy. Now this." He starts to say something and checks himself. Then he says, "Feels like God isn't listening, you know?"

I nod. "Felt that a lot."

"Thing is, I don't know which I prefer. To think that God is real and ignores me or to think God's not real at all." He takes a deep breath through his nose.

I've never seen Alex look so despondent. "I've heard people

say God sometimes doesn't answer prayers because he has a different plan for someone," I say.

"You believe it?" Alex's dryer buzzes, and he opens it and starts unloading his clothes into a basket.

"I don't know, man." Then an irresistible urge comes over me, out of nowhere. "Can I tell you something that stays between us?"

"I'm like a vault, bro."

There's still time to turn back. "My mama—" I almost say *OD'd*, but I already feel too naked; I can't tell him about the precise circumstances of her death. "Passed away when I was thirteen. My dad wasn't around. That's why I'm so close with my grandparents. They took me in after."

He's quiet for a long time. "Wow, Cash. I'm sorry."

"Not exactly faith-promoting."

"I wouldn't think."

"It still hurts to have lost her. But without the stuff that led to that, I never would have met Delaney. And then you and I wouldn't have ever become friends. So, like, who's to say, you know?"

"I'll keep praying for you, bro."

"You pray for me?"

"Course," Alex says.

"You say that like everyone prays for their friends."

"I do."

"Dang, man. Praying for the people at your church. Praying for me."

"My prayers get pretty long. Guess there are worse ways I could be spending time. Like . . . peeing . . . out windows."

"Peeing out windows?"

Alex shrugs. "I dunno."

"Yeah, that's not really a way people spend time," I say. "You pray for me with my whole Vi situation?"

"I asked that everything would work out for the best," Alex says.

I punch him in the arm playfully. "Couldn't have just straight-up prayed for me to get with her?"

"Haven't we established my praying results in disaster?" Alex says with a rueful laugh.

"Still, man, I'll keep accepting your prayers."

"I even pray for ex-girlfriends."

"Serious?"

"Mostly that they'll never find anyone cooler than me ever again." We bust up.

"Can't get enough of those unanswered prayers, can you?"

Alex, making eye contact with me, grabs a jockstrap from his clean basket, twirls it around his index finger a few times, and pulls it over his head with a flourish, still making eye contact. Then he strikes a pensive, smoldering expression, rubbing his chin and flexing his biceps. He performs a fashion-runway-style strut down the aisle of washing machines and dryers and tries to execute a spin turn, but catches his heel and stumbles into a washer.

We laugh until we're both hiccuping.

"You win, dude," I say. "Your exes will never find someone cooler."

We keep chatting and laughing, the air thick with steam and the sharp metallic tang of hot steel on washed cotton. As we prepare to lug our bags back to our rooms, I say to Alex—and not as a joke—"Hey, dude, not to add to your list, but can you pray for my papaw?"

Alex looks at me and smiles warmly. He claps his hand on my shoulder and squeezes. "Already on it, bro."

Chapter 50

I've spent the last ten minutes gazing at my ghostly reflection in the window glass of the science center, as it seemingly levitates in the January night behind it. It's a poetic image in theory—the pale image of yourself alone in darkness but still floating. But I'm not finding any entry point. The empty page is daring me to throw the first punch. My writing hand is shrinking from the challenge.

When all else fails, there's always procrastination.

"What you working on?" I ask Delaney.

She doesn't answer for a moment as she peers into her microscope.

"Did you—"

"Yeah, I heard," she murmurs. "Observing changes in cancer cells."

"You're wearing gloves. Shouldn't you be wearing a lab coat and, like, goggles too?"

"I'm fine."

"Well, shit. Don't get any on you."

"That's not at *all* how *that* works," she says as she types on her laptop. "You don't catch cancer. What are you doing over there? I can hear gears grinding."

I set my pen down and close my notebook over it to keep my place. "Poem for Dr. Adkins."

"The one about how awesome I am?"

"Exactly, which is why I'm totally stuck."

Delaney points at me with a pipette. "Better watch that sass mouth. I'll put cancer cells in your Coke. Give you some damn cancer. I don't give a shit." She bends over her microscope.

"I'm jealous of what you're doing," I say.

"Why?" she asks, not looking up. She uses her pipette to add something to the dish under the lens and makes another note on her laptop.

"Because science has clear answers. You put that stuff in the dish and look at it, and either it does what you want it to or it doesn't. That's why you hear of writer's block but not scientist's block."

"Aren't you the expert now."

"On writer's block? Damn right I am."

"I bet science and poetry have more in common than you think."

"Now look who's the expert."

"What are you doing when you write poetry?"

I think for a bit. "I guess I'm reaching inside myself for something."

"What?"

"I don't know. Expression."

"Understanding something about the world?"

"Sure."

"There you go, doofus. That's exactly what scientists are doing. We're both reaching for some understanding we're not sure exists."

"Reaching is right. I'm totally stuck on this poem."

"That's another thing. Failed experiments. You ever start writing a poem and it takes you in a completely unexpected direction?"

"Yeah."

"That's exactly science. Does poetry try to get you to think about processes in a new way?"

"Like?"

"Love. Death. Getting old. Processes." Delaney punctuates her words with snaps.

"Yep."

"That's science too."

We look at each other. "If poetry and science are so similar, help me write this poem," I say.

"Pshhh, no way," Delaney says immediately. "Totally different things."

We crack up. I was skeptical of the comparison Delaney was drawing at first, but she's won me over. I'd certainly like to believe that she and I are working in parallel on equally worthy things. It makes me feel closer to her.

We return to our tasks. I end up with two lines I like, after scribbling out about twenty-seven. A normal ratio for me.

As Delaney is putting away her samples and instruments, I ask her, partly in jest, "So, how close are you?"

"To what?"

"To Papaw's cure."

She just smiles sadly and disappears inward, as though she didn't hear me at all.

Chapter 51

I'm immersed in the warm bath of a dream. An artificial noise enters my mind, but it fits into that surreal world, so I sleep on. The sound persists. I awake. My phone is ringing. I fumble for it. I notice the time: 3:07 a.m. The caller: Mamaw. A wave of adrenaline breaches the floodgates of my lethargy like an injection of caffeine to my brain.

"Mamaw?" My speech is dry and somnolent.

Tripp groans theatrically. I ignore him.

"Cash?" Mamaw's voice is tense and brittle.

"What's up?" I sit, rubbing my face, instantly more awake.

Tripp makes an exaggerated show of flopping over to his side facing away from me and pulling his pillow over his ear.

"We're at the ER. Pep couldn't breathe and he's taken a nasty turn. The doctor says it's likely pneumonia. I think . . ."

I have a premonition of what she's about to say. I know it where I try to bury the things I want most to deny.

There's a prolonged and laden pause on Mamaw's end as she tries to scrape together words but fails. Finally, she says, voice faltering, "You ought to come home."

Much of what happens next is an incoherent blur. I jam some clothes into a bag by the light of my phone while Tripp grouses. I go to the end of the hall and wake up Cameron. He helps me arrange my ticket on the first flight home. Soon after, Chris DiSalvo is driving me to the airport well above the speed limit. "Hope everything turns out okay with your grandpop, buddy," he says as he drops me off.

I've never flown. A generous airport employee sees how obviously lost and terrified I am, and ushers me to my gate. I barely make my flight. By six-thirty a.m., as my plane lifts off, I'm clutching my armrests with the force I use to grip my oar when rowing. What a cruel joke that this is how I get to fly for the first time.

Aunt Betsy and Mitzi pick me up at the Knoxville airport in Aunt Betsy's run-down Buick. She forces a brave face, trying to offer some cheer as she asks me how I enjoyed my first flight. But we both know the score, and so the drive is mostly tomb-like silence undergirded by the death rattles of the various failing parts of her car.

"You been to see him?" I ask.

"Not yet," Aunt Betsy says.

My chest feels like a fist clenched around my lungs. "Sounds like he's bad."

She stares at the road ahead. "Pep's a fighter. When Daddy'd come home after tying one on, Pep would get between me and him and take the hits meant for me, and he always got back up after." Aunt Betsy pauses for a while. "I haven't thanked him enough for that," she says quietly, mostly to herself.

Chapter 52

Sawyer is lifeless and dull in the dim, biting February morning. Naked branches on barren trees, derelict storefronts, lawns the color of sighs, with moribund cars decaying on them. A town crawling on its belly through another winter.

It finally occurs to me to text Delaney and tell her what's going on. It had totally slipped my mind in the turmoil of the morning. I ask her to let Vi and Alex know. I lack the energy.

When Aunt Betsy parks, I bolt for the hospital entrance without waiting for her and Mitzi. It's not my first time in Sawyer Hospital. Papaw's been here a few times, and my mama before that. The standoffish, sterile smell that hits me as the sliding glass door opens resurrects all the worst memories. It's not the aseptic smell of cleanliness, but of a barren place, where it's hard for any living thing, even germs, to survive.

I sign in. They tell me where Papaw is, and I hurry back to his room. Mamaw sits by his side and holds his hand as he watches a game show through bleary and listless eyes. He wears an oxygen mask. He's pallid—his skin a drab, leaden yellow—and scraggy. He looks half-devoured from the inside, a husk.

Mamaw stands and hugs me tight before I reach Papaw's side. I can sense her trying to hold herself together.

"Glad you got in safe," she says in a trembling whisper.

I go to Papaw's side and hug him. "How you doing?" I ask, as though the answer is possibly "Great."

He wheezes. "Been better, Mickey Mouse," he manages, voice muffled under his mask. But his face brightens upon seeing me.

Mamaw looks utterly sapped.

"You slept at all?" I ask her.

"Not a wink. And I close tonight."

"There anyone who can help?"

"No. Just had two employees up and quit."

"Wanna go home and nap before work? I'll be here. Aunt Betsy and Mitzi too." They're standing in the doorway.

Mamaw looks to Papaw, who feebly raises a hand and waves her off gently. "It's okay, Donna Bird."

She kisses him and tells him she loves him. She pulls me aside and speaks in a low, urgent tone. "You call me if he takes a turn. I'll quit on the spot and come down." She leaves.

I sit back at Papaw's side. I lay my hand over his. He starts to speak.

"Save your energy for getting better," I say gently.

He nods slightly and closes his eyes. Minutes later, he's out.

I watch him sleep, machines surrounding him like a prayer circle.

I have the sudden and giddy thought that maybe this isn't the beginning of the end, but the difficult start of a new beginning for him.

Maybe he'll wake in the night, hacking violently, as though finally expiring. It'll be terrifying as we look on, helpless. But even in this fit, a strange new strength fills him. He sits up in bed. He yanks away his oxygen mask. His coughing intensifies, but his vigor grows in parallel.

He stands, coming to his full height. Then he doubles over, hands on his knees, the way he used to catch his breath when we'd go hiking, and enters one last coughing maelstrom. With a gagging noise, he expels a large, slick congealed-grease-colored tumor onto the floor with a fleshy *plop*.

This is his disease. It twitches in its death throes, robbed of the host body on which it fed.

Papaw straightens, wipes his mouth with the back of his hand, and draws, for the first time in years, a full measure of air into both lungs. The color instantly returns to his face and lips. The blue recedes from his nail beds.

He roars with triumphant laughter, prisoner no more. He starts peeling off the tubes and wires taped to him and casts them aside.

This hospital gown ain't doing nobody any favors, showing my ass off like a prize hog, he says, and we laugh through ecstatic sobs.

Sorry about the mess, y'all, he says to the doctors and nurses gathered to witness. *Let's go grab a bucket of chicken. I'm starved,* he says to us. And we do. And he's okay. Everything's okay.

Maybe this will happen instead of what I dread.

Maybe.

Chapter 53

Mamaw returns after work. Neither of us leaves Papaw's side all night. He only worsens.

In the early afternoon, Mamaw leaves to shower and run some errands before she has to work, closing again that night. While daytime TV drones in the background, I text with Delaney, Vi, and Alex. Dr. Adkins sends me a message wishing me well. I guess the school told her I wouldn't be in class.

Papaw rouses. "Mickey Mouse," he mumbles.

I take his hand. "Get you something? You thirsty?"

He wheezes under his mask and shakes his head slowly. "New lungs?"

"You can have one of mine." It's not a joke.

"Keep it."

"Want to watch TV?"

He shakes his head again. "Got more poems?"

"Like, mine?"

He nods, shutting his eyes.

Improbably, in my groggy frenzy of stuffing clothes in a bag, I instinctively grabbed my poetry notebook. It must've become more of a security blanket than I'd realized. I open it and read—quietly, because I'm embarrassed to hear my words out loud from my own mouth.

But a blissful look comes over Papaw's face, and after each poem, he pats me on the hand. "Beautiful," he murmurs once. Just as I'm about to run out of poems to read, his breathing slows and he drifts off.

As the hours creep by, I sit at his side, listening to him breathe, trying to build a store of his presence—like an animal hiding away food for a long season of hunger.

Chapter 54

I hear commotion up the hall. First, the sodden slap of wet sneakers running on tile. Then someone calling, "Miss? Miss! Excuse me. You can't—Someone get her. I have to stay at the front. She can't be back there like that."

I get up from Papaw's side to investigate. No sooner do I reach the door than a sprinting figure almost bowls me over. I don't recognize her at first; she's wearing a stocking cap and doesn't acknowledge me.

Delaney's lips are a faint gray violet to match the circles under her eyes, her face the antiseptic white of the hospital floor. Her clothes are soaked, and she reeks of cold mud and wet denim and down. Her shoes slosh and trail water behind her.

Delaney rushes to Papaw's side. I watch numbly as she unslings her backpack and pulls out a mason jar full of a greenish-black substance. She scans around and grabs a cotton swab from a container on the counter. She unscrews the lid of the mason jar and pokes around in it with the swab.

Blood streams from her right thumb. A drop hits Papaw's sheet with a *pat,* and it snaps me out of my stupor. "Red? What are you—" Then I remember. *Her promise to Papaw. She said she'd find a cure.* For one electric second, a wild hope seizes me. *She's got the cure. She's going to save him like she promised.* But that optimism quickly evaporates. I've never seen her like this—so feral and haunted and desperate.

Delaney still doesn't look at me and starts fumbling with Papaw's IV bag with trembling hands, smearing it with blood and water. "How you work this shit? Help me, damn it."

"I don't know if we should—"

Papaw murmurs something in his delirium.

Delaney bends down to him. "It's Tess. I'm here to keep my promise," she whispers hoarsely, tears at the edges of her voice.

I start toward her. As I do, a pair of middle-aged women in scrubs appear in the doorway.

"Miss! You cannot be in here. You didn't sign in. Come on, let's go," one of the women (a nurse?) says to Delaney, motioning her back. "There are no opioids in here. They're locked up and under guard."

"Ain't no junkie," Delaney spits back.

"You're a mess. You're going to compromise this patient," the other nurse (?) says. "And you're *bleeding*? No, young lady. You can't be in here. Come on."

"Tess," Papaw croaks, and reaches.

Delaney takes his hand.

The two nurses enter and brush quickly past me. Delaney turns to face them, her eyes like a cornered animal's. "I'm gonna help him. Y'all keep out my way."

Nurse One tells Nurse Two to get security. Nurse Two hustles off.

"Delaney," I say.

But she disregards me and goes for Papaw's IV bag again. Nurse One intercepts her and grips her forearm. "Don't start messing."

"*Stop.* You make me drop this, and I'll—"

The nurse, twice Delaney's size, starts dragging her out of the room.

"Hang on," I say to the nurse. "Stop. Don't touch her."

The nurse throws her hands up, retreats to the door, and looks up the hall. Delaney glares at her. Then she edges toward Papaw's IV again. He murmurs something. Delaney kisses him on the cheek.

A short, mustachioed armed security guard in an ill-fitting fake-cop uniform enters, followed by Nurse Two and Papaw's doctor. I forget her name, even though we've talked a few times.

"Let's go," the guard says brusquely. "Out."

"No," Delaney says. "I got medicine for him."

He grabs her by both arms and starts dragging her. "Let's go."

She digs in her heels and shakes loose. "Get the fuck off me," she says through gritted teeth.

"You can't be cussing people like that here," the guard says indignantly.

"Sir, leave her alone," I say.

"You want I'll kick you both out?" the guard says. "I'll get the sheriff down here."

I back off, afraid he'll make good on the threat.

The doctor speaks. "Billy? Will you hold off? Miss, let's talk in the hall, okay?"

"He needs my medicine," Delaney says.

"I hear you. Let's talk." The doctor's tone is calm and even, and reaches Delaney, who relents and follows her out. I move to where I can watch.

"What happened to your thumb?" the doctor asks.

"Nothing. Chewed it up," Delaney says.

"Brenda, will you bring me some Band-Aids and hydrogen peroxide?" the doctor asks Nurse One. Nurse One bustles off.

"I'm Khrystal Goins," the doctor says. "Mr. Pruitt's attending physician. You are?"

"Delaney Doyle."

"What's your connection to Mr. Pruitt?"

"Family. And he's called Pep if you really know him."

"Okay. Now, they told me you were trying to administer something to him. May I ask what?"

"*Penicillium delanum*. It kills MRSA. Antibiotic-resistant TB. Everything. It's named after me. I discovered it. They gave me a scholarship to the best STEM program in America and gave one to my friend, that's how bad they wanted me. And now I gotta deal with this dipshit mall cop keeping me from saving his life."

"You got an ugly mouth on you," Billy says.

"*You* got an ugly mouth," Delaney says.

"Billy," Dr. Goins says, "I'll take it from here."

Billy shakes his head and stalks off a few feet, ruddy and fuming.

Dr. Goins turns to Delaney. "I read about you in the news, and I read about *Penicillium delanum* in the *New England Journal of Medicine*."

"Then you know what it does."

"I also know it hasn't been through human trials or received FDA approval and that it occurs naturally in caves, which is where it looks like you very recently got that." She nods at Delaney's jar.

She must have. And she fell in the river while doing it. That's why she's soaked. In this temperature, that could have been the end of her.

"None of your business." Delaney glowers at Dr. Goins defiantly.

"It is actually my business as Mr. Pruitt's doctor. It's my responsibility to keep people from introducing potentially harmful contaminants into his IV. We're using tried-and-true, FDA-approved medical-grade interventions. And we're hoping for the best."

"Fentanyl is some medical-grade FDA-approved shit too. Ever seen anyone die from that?" Delaney says.

"Many times," Dr. Goins says softly.

Nurse One returns with some bandages and hydrogen peroxide and hands them to Dr. Goins.

"He'll die if you don't let me give him this," Delaney says.

"Not if I can help it. And I know you're smart enough to understand that you don't just scrape something off a cave wall and inject it raw into someone's system and expect a good outcome."

"You don't know how smart I am. I'm a *genius.*"

Dr. Goins absorbs Delaney's fury calmly. "I don't doubt that. But I'm right about this."

"*Khrystal Goins.* I can tell from your name you're hillbilly trash from here. Pep needs a real doctor."

"I am from here," Dr. Goins says quietly. "I worked my way through Walters State Community College as a gas station cashier. Then ETSU, where I worked nights at a Waffle House. Then I went to Emory Medical School, which is where I learned—with all due respect—more about medicine than you currently know."

"You must suck at it if you ended up back here."

Dr. Goins's eyes reflect that Delaney's finally gotten to her. "Or I *am* good at it and I came home to lift up a community I love that's hurting and needs my help. Maybe you'll consider doing the same someday."

Delaney snorts. "Oh, livin' the dream, working in this shitty hospital, getting to smell Deputy Dogshit's fish breath every day." She nods at Billy. He sneers back.

"You're welcome to visit Mr. Pruitt without abusing my staff and interfering with his treatment after you've changed into dry clothes and we've treated your thumbs." Dr. Goins holds up the bandages and the bottle of hydrogen peroxide.

"Ask Pep what he wants," Delaney says. "I promised him I'd make him better."

"I've made myself clear."

"He could sign something. A release or whatever. Let's ask Cash. His grandson."

I step into the hall. "Red . . . I don't think . . ."

Delaney hurls me a look that's simultaneously reproachful, enraged, and beseeching.

"Maybe we should let the doctor do her thing," I continue.

Delaney makes a choked sound—half sob and half cry of rage. Her eyes sear into mine, saying, *Traitor.* She makes another break for it. She pushes me aside like she outweighs me by seventy pounds, instead of vice versa. She skids into Papaw's room, sliding on the water she dripped everywhere.

Billy barges past me, followed by the nurses and Dr. Goins. He grabs Delaney from behind, pinning her arms at her sides. He lifts her off the floor. She thrashes frantically, pedaling her feet in the air. "Stop. Don't you fuckin'—*I hate you, piece of shit.* Hands off me! Stop! *No no no no no!*"

He backs out of the room with her. She kicks the edge of Papaw's bed in her frenzy. He's too out of it to notice.

"Let her go, man," I say to Billy. "Come on, just—" But he pays me no heed. I follow them into the hall.

Billy turns and starts hauling Delaney toward the hospital entrance, tilting back to keep her feet off the floor.

"*Nooooooo! Pep, I love you,*" she yells over her shoulder, flailing. "*I tried to keep my promise. I love you. I tried.*" Her voice is torn at the edges. People line the hall to rubberneck and murmur.

Delaney finally connects her heel with Billy's shin and the back of her head with his nose, and he drops her, cursing fervently (I guess *he's* allowed to cuss in the hospital) and cupping his nose. She sprints ahead a few steps as he limps after her. She turns back and flips him two bloodstained middle fingers. Tears streak her face.

"Delaney." I bolt past the limping Billy, who's now holding his head back with his nostrils pinched shut.

She flees from me.

"Red!" I yell after her, giving chase. I catch up with her just outside the sliding hospital doors.

She spins to face me. "He's going to *die*. Do you not see that? This is his only chance and you won't even get my *fucking back?*"

"She's a *doctor*. She's been to med school. She has experience. You can't think it's a good idea to stick cave slime in his IV. He'll die for sure."

Delaney is on the verge of sobs. "You sound like his redneck doctor. Here." She raises on her tiptoes, lifts the mason jar high above her head, and hurls it at my feet.

I jump back, broken glass and muck splattering against my shins.

She turns and walks quickly away. *"Chickenshit,"* she hisses over her shoulder. I watch numbly as she stumbles off, her face buried in her hands. I'm too completely exhausted to feel anything.

I kneel and pick up the shattered glass smeared with green-black goo. I throw each piece in the garbage. I get to the last chunk, part of the bottom of the jar. It still has a healthy dollop of the gunk. *What do you have to lose? Delaney's right—he's going to die without a miracle. Maybe that miracle is that your mama got hooked on Oxys and fentanyl, which led you to Narateen, where you met Delaney Doyle, which led to your becoming friends and showing her all the things you love—including canoeing and exploring caves. Which resulted in her discovering the one thing that would save Papaw when that day arrived, and you're holding that one thing in your hand.*

I stand there for several minutes, shivering and staring at the chunk of broken glass in the failing light.

I throw it away and return inside.

When I get back to Papaw's bedside, he whispers that he dreamed Tess had come to visit him.

I stay with Papaw until Mamaw comes from work. I tell her what happened with Delaney and that I need to go find her.

I call and text her a few times. Not that I expect her to answer, even if she still has a working phone, which her waterlogged condition makes me doubt. I set out, trying every spot she might have gone. My house. Her half brothers' house. Her mama's old trailer. Our old high school. I finally find her in Sawyer's dilapidated downtown park—pale; huddled, hugging her knees;

and near catatonic—on the peeling steps of the bandstand. She squints her bloodshot and tear-swollen eyes against my headlights. She looks too fatigued to even shiver.

I get out. Delaney stands and walks in silent surrender to my truck. She gets in. I turn up the heater, and she warms her hands. Her thumbs are ravaged.

I don't start driving immediately. She still won't speak.

"We should get you into dry clothes," I say after a while, touching the dampness of her shoulder.

She shrinks from me. "Only brought these."

"We'll throw them in the wash, and you can wear my clothes." I pause. "Unless you'd prefer Mamaw's clothes."

Delaney doesn't smile.

"Get you a nice sweatshirt with geese on it."

But I can't really sell a joke in my current state, and Delaney still doesn't smile.

"Geese holding baskets. Wearing hats."

Still no smile. "You should have had my back," Delaney murmurs.

"You think it would have worked?" I ask after a moment.

But she says nothing and stares off into the heavy winter dark.

Chapter 55

Once warm and clean, she falls asleep almost immediately. I leave her on my bed under two quilts, hair still damp from a hot shower, clothed in an old pair of my jeans and a flannel shirt. Punkin curls up at her side. I put her clothes in the wash.

I return to the hospital and sit vigil at Papaw's side. Mamaw asks me if I'm good to stay with him for a bit while she goes home to change clothes and shower and get a few things. I say I am.

I sit, working on a poem to little avail, listening to Papaw's labored respiration, the muted beeps of his monitors, the ambient mechanical speech of the hospital's intercom system.

He stirs.

I grab his hand. "Hey. I'm here."

He licks his lips. I give him a sip of water. He coughs.

"Not doing so hot, Mickey Mouse," he croak-whispers.

"You'll be good as new in a couple days," I say, hoping it isn't obvious how little I believe it.

He beckons me in and strokes my hair. I nestle up to him awkwardly on the few inches of space at the edge of his bed. He smells like antimicrobial chemicals and medicines. Lurking below that is some pungent, animalic smell of decline. All of it alien for him.

Dignity dies as the body does.

He pulls off his oxygen mask, and it makes a rushing sound, like the advance of wind before a storm. "Tell you a story," Papaw says in his pale whisper, barely audible above the noise of his mask, as he visibly summons himself from the gloaming. "You was just born. Your mama's trailer weren't fit for a baby, so we brought you both home from the hospital. Your mama slept in her old room. Your room." He pauses to muster his strength and continues. "Your mamaw was wore out too. It was spring-time, so I took you out on the porch and sat, just you and me, in the rocker. Had you wrapped up so tight you weren't but a head poking out of a blanket." He stops and gathers himself. "Watched you feel the breeze on your face for the first time. Watched you open your little gray eyes and squint out at the trees swaying in the wind. And I says to you, 'That wind you feel on your face is called wind. Them trees you see are called trees.' Holiest thing I ever witnessed—you feeling the wind for the first time. Seeing a tree for the first time. Speaking their names to you. Saw the face of God in you that day. Ever' time you tell a story, it becomes a little more ordinary. So I swore I'd only tell this one the once." He pauses once more, and with what remains of himself, says, "There was a last time I held you in my arms, and I didn't even know it."

He finishes, spent by this effort. He murmurs something else, but I can't make it out. Something *Mickey Mouse.*

I wriggle closer to him and pull his arm over me. *Let this be the last time you hold me in your arms.*

I slip his oxygen mask back on him. He drifts off, and I hold his hand until it goes limp and heavy.

"I love you. I'll always love you," I whisper again and again to his unconscious ear, hoping he absorbs it somehow.

Hoping he takes it with him to whatever unmapped land he's journeying to.

Hoping he returns.

If only once more.

Chapter 56

While I sleep, he passes into the night of nights, drawing his final breath with no more ceremony than a leaf falling.

My heart howls.

I don't know how to live under the sun of a God whose harvest is everyone I love.

I don't know.

Chapter 57

First there was nothing. A vacuum. A great desolation of sound and thought.

My ears refused to pass the information on to my brain because that would make it real.

Then the message broke through of its own accord, but my brain would not accept it, and so I continued to sit there, numb and paralyzed.

Then the truth burned through my stupor and there was the searing, fresh agony of a new and grievous fracture.

I cried until I was empty—not of feeling but of tears.

I can't bear being in the hospital anymore, and I stumble outside, as if maybe all this will turn out to be a huge cruel joke and Papaw will be out there waiting for me.

The sky is the color of wood ash, the light pale. The morning air smells like diesel fuel and frozen stone. The raw wind is a blade on my cheeks. I've been outside for a while when I see a small figure quickly approaching. It's Delaney. As she nears, her pace slows while her eyes search mine pleadingly. I can only shake my head as new tears blur my vision. She halts, dropping her hands to her sides, and her face crumples soundlessly—like a hurt child's does before the wailing begins. She stomps a couple of times and collapses to the pavement, her palms pressed to her temples like she's trying to hold her skull together. Then she sobs with abandon, rocking forward and back.

I make my way to her, and we hold each other and weep together. People walk past us in the parking lot, averting their eyes, embarrassed by the nakedness of our grief.

We continue like that for a while. Each time we think we've collected ourselves, we slip again, as if trying to scale a steep and icy slope.

Finally, we reach the bottom of some chasm and we stare, dazed and bleary-eyed, at the cars passing on the street abutting the hospital.

"Did he hear me tell him I loved him?" Delaney asks.

"Yes," I say, even though I don't know.

Delaney is quiet for a long time and then says, "There was never a better person."

We don't say much else. There's nothing to say.

Chapter 58

We cremate his body and keep his ashes in a simple urn.

He didn't want a funeral. Aunt Betsy has an idea for what to do instead. Something called a Goodbye Day. We spend a day doing all of Papaw's favorite things. The things we would have done with him if he'd been healthy enough to do them on his last day.

Mamaw, Delaney, Aunt Betsy, Mitzi, and I get breakfast at Cracker Barrel, at his favorite spot near the fireplace, and share memories of him. We laugh and cry.

We walk in the woods. I lag behind the group, and Aunt Betsy waits for me. She tells me, "Sometimes God has to take a life apart before he can put it back together." And I think how God's been hard at work taking my life apart for all my life. I'm still waiting for the putting-back-together part.

We go home and watch an episode of *Longmire*. We listen to his favorite Steve Earle album, *Copperhead Road*.

"I draw the line at trying to carve something out of a tree stump with a chain saw," Aunt Betsy says, and we laugh.

Laid out like this, Papaw's existence was quiet and small, but it was a life defined by the love he gave and got.

It was the life he wanted.

The afternoon is cold and overcast and misty. With our dwindling hours of daylight, we go to the river. Aunt Betsy and Mitzi kiss the urn goodbye before we load it into the canoe. Mamaw is afraid to go out on the water, with it being so cold, but she does. Delaney comes too. I paddle us to where I promised Papaw that I would lay him to rest.

We surrender him to the dark water like we're loosing a flight of doves into the dusk. No elegy but our tears.

I wish our love was enough to keep whole the people we love.

Chapter 59

This memory is a ghost.

I was twelve. It was late November. A hard rain had come two days prior and brought the biting cold, low pewter skies, and piercing, insistent wind that whistled through the naked branches and drove the leaves hissing across the ground, rattling plastic bags impaled on barbwire fences. The air smelled like wood smoke, damp soil, and the sweet rot of fallen apples. We drove far from town and hunted all day, talking only a little. Mostly basking silently in each other's company.

The light faded as the day wore on, and the sky darkened from the color of a new quarter to the color of a tarnished one. The crows called out in the twilight. My legs ached and my fingers and toes had long gone stiff and numb with cold, but it was delicious to be in this pure and clean place, temporarily liberated from the chaos and filth of my home and my mama's sickness. While we waited, a six-point buck wandered into the clearing, oblivious to us, pausing to nibble at the ground.

I felt Papaw's fingers on my forearm, signaling me to be still. I was good at it. My mama's crueler boyfriends had taught me this art of invisibility.

"Yours," Papaw said below a whisper.

I lifted my rifle—it was too large for me—awkwardly to my

shoulder and sighted in like he'd taught me. I centered the cross-hairs on the buck's chest. I remembered not to jerk the trigger but to squeeze until it broke. I waited for the space between my breaths. I squeezed until the break. The bullet jumped from the barrel with a crack, and its recoil made the stock punch me in the shoulder. In the movies, when people are shot, they go flying backward. The deer just flinched, as if stung by a wasp, crouched, and then tried to bound away. But his body failed him. He crashed through the underbrush clumsily, catching his crown of antlers on a low branch. He only made it a short distance before he stopped and collapsed on the ground, tried to rise, and fell under his useless legs.

He was still breathing roughly when we caught up to him. I watched him take his last breaths, a fine spray of blood on the ground in front of his mouth, the silver threads of his final exhalations winding upward. Then he died, the life in his eyes dimming to an ember and expiring.

Papaw clapped me on the back. "Heck of a shot."

Such praise should've made my heart dance. But I was filled instead with a gray and somber silence in every reach of myself. The sort that feels like the last leaf clinging to an autumn-stripped branch looks as it flutters in the wind, waiting to fall. There was nothing for me in stealing another creature's breath.

We dragged the fallen deer back to our pickup and loaded him in the bed.

We drove home in silence, passing through the dark hills and hollers, the radio a low mumble. Here and there a house was lit up like a tiny city. I felt like the ink-smudged and starless dusk sky. I wanted to cry.

Midway through the ride home, Papaw put his arm around

me and pulled me to him, nudging my hunter-orange ball cap askew. He smelled like cigarettes; clean, body-warmed flannel; and the memory of cold air verging on snow. He held me close until we got home. He called my mama and said I was beat and was going to sleep over at their house.

At bedtime, he came in to wish me good night. As he was leaving, he paused for a long time in the doorway, burning logs popping in the living room woodstove behind him. I sensed him seeking the right words. Finally: *I just love to spend time with you, Mickey Mouse. Ain't important to me how.* He spoke it like a prayer, tapped the doorframe a couple times, and he left.

Some people can lift your heart up to the light, reading the truth of you written on it.

I was afraid that being a man meant waging war on what's beautiful.

I wanted to love the world without taking anything from it.

He knew all this. This is what you remember of the people you love when they're gone—the ways they knew you that no one else did—even you. In that way, their passing is a death of a piece of yourself.

Chapter 60

Mamaw and I sit on the porch. The empty rocker beside us is a void—a black hole drawing all light and joy into it.

"I don't have to go back tomorrow," I say. "I can stay here with you."

"That's not what he would've wanted," Mamaw says.

"What do *you* want?"

"Same as him."

"You'll be alone."

"Bets and Mitzi'll check in."

"Still."

We rock for a while.

"He was proud of who you're becoming there," Mamaw says.

"I don't feel any different."

"You are. You carry yourself differently. You're becoming the man he hoped you would. Go back. I'm fine here."

"You sure?"

"I'm sure."

Chapter 61

As I board the Greyhound behind Delaney, after hugging Mamaw one last time, she hands me two letters.

"Pep wrote these after he went in the hospital before Thanksgiving. Told me to give them to you and Delaney."

"I love you, Mamaw."

"I love you, Cash."

"I'll come back home to stay if you need."

"I'll be fine. Just missing him. You focus on your studies."

I get on the bus and hand Delaney her letter. Neither of us opens ours yet. Delaney stares out the window. About an hour passes.

"I gotta know. How'd you get that jar of mold?" I ask.

She keeps gazing out the window. "Jumped on the first bus back. Took a taxi to one of the outdoor outfitters. Paid a guy a couple hundred bucks to take me to the cave. Just as we were getting close to putting in, I fell in the water. All my clothes dragged me down. I almost drowned. Coughed up river water and shit."

"You almost *died?*"

"Almost. The dude pulled me out."

"I'm real glad I didn't lose you *and* Papaw in the same twenty-four hours. You must have spent a fortune."

"Everything I still had saved up from DQ."

A few minutes pass.

"You're gonna leave me and go back home, aren't you?" Delaney asks, still looking out the window.

I shake my head. "I'm staying." I've never sounded less convincing.

And she hears it. She rests the side of her head on the window. She sniffles a couple of times and tears begin flowing down her cheeks.

"Even if I left, you'd still have Vi and Alex," I say.

"Not the same." She cries for a long time, and when she's done, she says quietly, "Someday, someone I try to save is going to let me."

We ride wordlessly for most of the rest of the journey.

The cold cast-iron wrecking ball that smashed my life to rubble now hangs in my chest, crowding out my heart, cutting short my breath.

Dear Cash, also called Mickey Mouse,

I never had the gift of words like you. But sometimes words is all you get to leave behind, so here goes nothing.

I wanted you to know how much I loved our talks together and whatever we spent time doing. I loved canoeing the Pigeon and walking the woods with you. You lit up my life every day. Sending you off to school was the hardest thing I ever did. I'm proud as can be that you were brave enough to go. I know you wanted to stay with us, but I'm glad you saw more of the world.

I wish I could be sure of what happens to us after we're gone. But if we have a soul that lives on, then my soul will keep loving you, even if I smoked and cussed too much to get to heaven.

I hope you grow up to be the good man I know you'll be. I'll be watching you by your side as much as I can. Sometimes when you weren't looking I would stare at you and thank God in my heart that I got to be your papaw. Those were the best years of my life. I wish I'd gotten more of them.

Love,
Phillip E. Pruitt

P.S. Take care of your mamaw and see that Tess gets the letter I wrote her. Tess is a special girl. Always treat her good.

Chapter 62

Alex and Vi await us at the bus station, like an honor guard welcoming fallen soldiers home.

Alex hugs me for a long time and says, "I'm here for you, man. Anything you need. I got you. Been praying for you."

Vi follows suit, whispering in my ear, "I'm so sorry, Cash. We love you." When we pull back from each other, there are tears in her eyes.

Chris comes over and shakes my hand. "It's hard, kid. I know. Lost my dad when I was twenty. It gets better, though. I promise."

But I already know from losing my mama that it doesn't get much better. Delaney told me once that when you burn to death, there comes a point when you don't feel anything anymore because your nerves die. I don't know who reported that to someone. But I think that's maybe what happens when people say it gets better—more dying to ease the pain.

By the time we reach the school, the weight in my chest has tripled.

I don't know how I'll do this. I barely managed when I was only cracked. Now I'm broken wide open.

Chapter 63

I see Dr. Adkins eyeing me during class. She keeps losing her place and sounds distracted. After class ends, we stand in front of each other, my head bowed. I'm reminded of the first time we ever talked alone.

"I heard about your papaw. I'm so, so deeply sorry," she says. "Is there anything I can do?"

"No," I murmur, trying to keep it together. "I, um. Miss him. A lot."

"I know what he meant to you."

I nod quickly and my eyes well. I try to laugh it off, but I start crying. I wipe my eyes and turn away.

Dr. Adkins speaks to my back. "It's okay to let yourself feel what you feel. Where we're from, men and boys are told to bury any sign of weakness, and feeling things is sometimes seen as weakness. But I promise you, it's not."

I nod again, still too choked up to speak.

"Now, more than ever, is the time to turn to poetry. It doesn't demand that you fix anything or come to any conclusions. It only asks you to observe and sit with what you feel. And with grief, there are no fixes. No conclusions. We can only sit with it."

"I feel like I'm never going to be happy again," I say, turning back to her.

"You will. While you're healing, along with writing poetry, please talk to someone. The school has professional mental health resources. Use them. That's another one of those things that men where we were raised see as a sign of weakness, but shouldn't. And talk to your friends. They love you." She rests a ring-bedecked hand on my shoulder. She's wearing a lotion that smells like clean hay and roses. "Okay?"

"Okay."

"There's another thing you need to heal." She walks back behind her desk, picks up a brown grocery bag, and hands it to me. "Good food."

I look inside. It's a perfect golden-brown cornbread.

"Desiree made it. She sends her sympathies too."

"Thank Desiree for me."

"I will."

I nod, turn quickly, and leave without saying anything else. I feel rude, but I hope she can see I don't want to cry in front of her anymore.

SPRING

Chapter 64

Instead of getting better, I'm only finding new and subtle shades of experiencing loss. Turns out it's like the people you love are riding a teeter-totter across from you. And when they're gone, you plummet down and have a hard time getting back up. You never reach the heights you used to.

This is a completely different experience from when my mama died. I guess you don't get good at mourning. There are no grieving muscles you can train. You start over each time.

I miss him at the times I'd expect, like when I'm talking to Mamaw. I miss him at the times we would have spoken. I also miss the feeling of knowing he was there, existing, even at the times we wouldn't have ordinarily spoken.

And I miss him at the times I wouldn't expect, like when Vi or Alex mentions their parents. I miss him each time Delaney gets me ice cream using her Dairy Queen skills. I miss him on every occasion I look in the mirror and remember how we'd go get haircuts together.

I'm realizing that every triumph, large and small, that I have from now until the day I die will be diminished, if only a little, by my inability to share it with him.

Now that I think a lot on words, I realize how poorly they represent absence. We should have a language of loss that we keep in a black-velvet-lined box and only get out when we most need it. Instead, we have:

Dead

Deceased

Departed

Disappeared

Done

Ended

Expired

Finished

Gone

Left

Lost

Passed

Not one expresses the completeness of the idea it represents, the way *apple* represents the completeness of an apple and *river* represents the completeness of a river. They all leave something unsaid. They all have some phantom limb that reminds you of their lack.

Don't they know how much I loved him?

Chapter 65

"You gonna eat your fries?" I ask.

Delaney pushes them toward me. She's been quiet tonight.

"Ain't much point to these Thursday night dinners if we don't talk," I say.

"I'm thinking about stuff. You haven't been chatty either."

"No. You're right. What're you thinking about?"

"Pep."

"Me too. See? We could've been talking about that the whole time."

We laugh a little.

"Tell me something I don't know," I say for old times' sake and to break the silence. It was always a good way to make conversation, to think about something bigger than my life and troubles.

"I miss Pep saying that," Delaney says, smiling. Then her smile fades and her face turns contemplative. "Okay," she says quietly. "Last summer, a little while after all the big news broke, I was having a really shitty day. Like *really*. I was stressed-out about all the news interviews. Middleford had contacted me. I wanted to leave, but I didn't want to leave without you. My mama was doing really bad. You were off mowing lawns, and I needed someone, so I called Pep. We could easily have just talked on the phone. But he came and picked me up and took me to lunch at McDonald's. He obviously wasn't feeling great that day. But we sat there for three hours and talked. I knew how to deal with lots of shitty stuff happening, but I didn't know how to deal with good stuff happening at the same time. That was new, and most people don't really wanna hear about that kind of problem. We talked like a papaw and granddaughter. It felt so good. Probably the kind of thing you got to do all the time growing up.

"I decided to pretend I got to do it all the time too. For that three hours, I felt completely normal. It was maybe the best three hours of my life."

"He never mentioned that."

"I asked him not to. I wanted the memory all to myself, the way it would be if he were my papaw."

"He said once that the more times you tell a story, the more ordinary it becomes."

Delaney reaches across the table and grabs one of her fries. She holds it up and looks at it. "Maybe. Maybe not."

"Either way, I'm glad you told it to me."

"Me too."

"I miss him."

"Me too."

I'm glad I at least have her to mourn with. If I didn't, I don't know what I'd do.

Chapter 66

"What do you think happens after we die?" I ask Alex over the churning of our washing machines. I figure if he plans on being a pastor someday, he won't mind getting a head start on offering spiritual counseling.

He looks at me for a moment, his eyes soft. "I believe we keep living somehow."

"Heaven?"

"Hopefully."

"Isn't that what the Bible says?"

"Yeah. But I'm not the biblical literalist a lot of people are. Like, I don't believe in hell really."

"You don't think my papaw's in hell because he wasn't big on church?"

"Hell? No. See what I did there? Bro. You see what I did?"

I half smile. "No. Can you explain it to me?"

"Well, colloquially, sometimes people will respond to a question by saying 'Hell no,' and I'm not generally given to use of profanity, but on this occasion—"

We both laugh. I don't laugh much these days, but Alex still delivers.

"You think my papaw's spirit is still alive out there somewhere?"

"With all my heart, bro."

"Then why can't I feel his presence?"

"I don't know," Alex says quietly.

"You think God's just making me suffer for some reason?"

"I don't know."

"You better firm up on these answers before you get your own congregation."

"All I can tell you is God has a season for everything. Or that's what I believe."

"A season for feeling like shit all the time, apparently."

"See, I've been trying reverse psychology on God, where I pray for you to feel bad and I hope my prayer won't be answered, as seems to mostly be the case for me now."

Chapter 67

Delaney and I walk slowly back toward the residence halls from the gym. Not that I need extra workouts to stay in shape, with crew during the week, but exercise is one of the only things that takes the edge off the grief for even a few minutes.

It's Saturday and freezing, the smell of coming snow on the wind. The air seems to swallow sound. The overcast night sky is a muted charcoal. Cold. Silent. Dark. These are things the New England winter does well. Lucky me to be experiencing the worst grief and depression of my life here.

"The elliptical always feels too easy," Delaney says.

"You gotta set it higher."

"But then it gets too hard. I've never been able to set it perfect."

"Try another machine."

"I like the elliptical."

"That's because it's easy."

"Yeah."

We smile thinly at each other.

"Jellyfish are biologically immortal," Delaney says after a while.

"As in—"

"As in they never die of old age. Sickness, yes. Predators, yes. But not old age. They think lobsters might be too."

"So every time we get lobster rolls in New Canaan, we're eating an immortal creature?"

"Not exactly. They eventually die during molting."

"What if they invented a pill tomorrow and if you took it, you'd live forever. Would you?" I ask.

"You kidding? That'd be horrible."

"Okay, then say you live to be two hundred."

Delaney thinks for a second. "Still nope."

"Why?"

"Because I'm not sure the human brain is designed to exist for two hundred years. Life expectancy used to be in the thirties or forties. We've already more than doubled that. I don't know if our minds have caught up."

"Like Alzheimer's and stuff?"

"Not even that. You can live a real long life and have a healthy brain. I'm talking about just getting tired. Seeing people you love die. Watching people be terrible to each other. The world leaving you behind. Stuff ending. I don't know."

"Yeah."

We walk slower as we approach Delaney's residence hall.

"I coulda done with my papaw living another good thirty years, though," I say.

"Me too," Delaney murmurs.

"The other day I butt-dialed him. And I had this thought that maybe he'd pick up. I gotta delete his number from my phone. But I can't."

"I get it," Delaney says.

We get to the residence hall, and I go to say goodbye. But

instead what comes out of me is this: "I haven't been truly happy even once since he died."

Delaney looks at me with sad eyes. "Not even one time?"

"Nope."

"What about hanging out with us? Me and Vi and Alex."

"I mean, y'all are great, but."

"I'm sorry, Cash." She steps forward and hugs me. It feels good, but the feeling never lasts long after the embrace is over. "This is worse than when your mama died, huh?"

"Much."

"Anything work then?"

I shrug. "Just time, I guess."

"Time'll work here too."

"Maybe."

"How often am I wrong about stuff?" Delaney looks like she's about to say something else. She covers her mouth with her hand like she's trying to stop something from coming out. She snorts like she's holding back a case of the church giggles. Then she lets go and starts laughing.

"What?" I smile in spite of myself. It still makes me happy to see her laugh.

"Nothing." Delaney tries to collect herself. "It's not that funny."

"Tell me."

She pauses. "So, this was a little while after your mama's funeral, and we were at the Dollar General. This guy comes up to us, and he says, 'Hey, are you Cassie Pruitt's kid?' And you go, 'Yeah,' and he's like, 'How is she?' And you go, 'She died.' And he's like, 'Uhhhhhh,' all awkward, trying to think of something to say, and finally he lands on, 'Well, she was hot.' And then you go, 'Yeah, well not anymore because she's dead.' And then he gave you a card for a free class at his karate studio and told you to stay in school. And as he's walking away, he turns back and tells you he'll teach you how to make a pair of nunchucks from stuff at the hardware store. You remember any of this?"

I laugh a little with her. "That whole period was a fog, but yeah, kinda."

"We just sat there for a while, you holding that card for a free karate class. And finally, you go, 'Con: my mama died. Pro: I got a free karate class out of it.' And I remember thinking how strong you were."

"I was faking to impress you."

"What's the difference between faking being strong and being strong?"

I don't have an answer.

"You ever take the karate class?" Delaney asks.

"No."

"Shoulda."

"Wasn't feeling up to it and then I lost the card."

We look at each other for a few moments. A snowflake meanders earthward and alights in Delaney's hair. Then another. And another. The sky relinquishes its grasp, and they fall thicker and faster, swirling all around us. One falls on her eyelashes and melts.

She's slowly leaving me behind in my mourning. Not intentionally, but still. I can't tell you how exactly I know that—I just sense it. We journeyed together through the wasteland for a time and it was a small comfort, but that couldn't last.

Nothing does, really.

And I don't know how I'll manage to stay here alone in this.

Chapter 68

One night, it overwhelms me—the sorrow and loneliness like staring through black glass.

I know she's working, but I call Mamaw anyway.

"Little Caesars," a bored young woman's voice answers after several rings.

"Um. Hi. Is—can I talk to the manager?"

"Something wrong?"

"No. Just needed to tell her something."

"Miss Donna," the voice yells. "Phone. Someone wants to talk to you. Won't say why."

After a few moments, Mamaw picks up. "Good evening, Little Caesars. How may I help you?"

"Mamaw? It's me. I don't want you to get in trouble for taking personal calls at work, so just talk like I'm calling about pizza. I needed to hear your voice."

"Now, you say these are for your grandson's birthday party? He sounds like an incredible young man."

"Mamaw, they'll know I don't have a grandson. I don't want to make problems for you."

"I have a grandson too. He's my pride and joy. Loves pizza."

"I miss Papaw really bad tonight."

"I was thinking about him not five minutes ago."

"Mamaw, don't—"

"Sweetie, I'm the manager. Every one of my employees is texting as we speak. I'll be fine."

"Okay. I love you."

"I love you too, Cash."

"You doing all right?"

"No. You?"

"Not really."

"The other night I came home and I wanted to tell him something so badly. Someone who came in reminded me of someone he and I knew, and he's the only one who would understand. But he's gone and I couldn't."

"I realized the other day, he's never once going to see one of my crew meets. I mean, it's not like he'd have gotten to see many of them anyway. But I thought he'd get to see at least one."

"He wanted so badly to. He talked all the time about going up there to visit you. We both knew it was idle talk, but it was fun. He was so proud of you. He'd always bring up that poem you let him read. Out of nowhere. 'How about that poem of Mickey Mouse's?' he'd say, while we were eating supper or something."

I breathe down tears but my voice cracks anyway. "I'm tired of losing people I love."

"Me too, sweetie."

"I'll be your new jigsaw puzzle buddy when I come back home."

"I can't bring myself to put up the one Pep and I were working on when he passed. You can help me finish."

I start to tell her how much I want to come home now, but I

already know what she'll say. "I better let you get back to work. I'm glad I got to hear your voice. I love you. I miss you." I want to see her so badly it almost levels me.

"I love you and miss you too, Cash."

But we don't hang up immediately. We're quiet for a while, listening to each other breathe. There's relief in hearing someone you love still breathing.

Chapter 69

I hold every memory of him like a match I let burn down to the end, singeing my fingers until it hurts too much to hold.

I try to write my way through it, like Dr. Adkins said to. I sit by the lake, teeth chattering, waiting for some inspiration. Nothing. She does what she can to help me make something of my meager efforts, but there's no beauty in me.

Delaney's mostly back to normal now, it seems. I'm glad she's not hurting too, but now I'm well and truly alone in bereavement.

So, on a Friday night in mid-March, at 5:32 p.m., I decide I'm done with this whole Middleford thing. Time to cut my losses. I know because I check the time—that's how tangibly it occurs to me that I'm finished: 5:32.

I'm sitting with Delaney and Vi and Alex, and we're eating dinner, and I just decide I can't be here alone anymore. I can't be strong anymore. And I don't have to be. Billions of people live and die without going to Middleford Academy at all, much less finishing high school there. I can be one of them.

There's no particular catalyzing event that spurs this decision. No special conversation. There's only the slow trickle of grief eroding me down to nothing. At 5:32 that night, the last of me crumbles.

I watch each of them talk. I study their faces to burn onto my memory. Maybe we'll see each other again after I go home. Maybe not. No doubt I'll miss them so badly that when they visit me in my memory, it'll double me over, knocking the wind out of me.

And yet I'm done. I won't miss Papaw any less when I leave and go home. I just need to acknowledge the surrender of my spirit, the failure of my courage. The grief's won. If I'm going to hurt all the time, I'm going to do it around my river and Mamaw. I'm going to withdraw into myself.

I'm not going to show up for class on Monday morning. Instead, I'll go to the administration building and ask to meet with Dr. Archampong. Then I'll tell him thanks for everything, but it all got to be too much.

I'm not going to tell Alex or Vi, and especially not Delaney. I can't look them in the eyes and admit sorrow's victory over me. I don't want to be talked out of my decision. They're going to show up for dinner on Monday, and I just won't be there. They'll be angry and hurt when they find out, but.

I'm not going to tell Dr. Adkins. Maybe I'll send her one last poem—one I wrote for her. I'll send her a note with it, telling her what a solace poetry has been to me, that it brought Papaw some comfort in his last hours, and that I'll always make it part of my inconsequential life. You don't need to be at Middleford Academy to write poetry.

I'm not going to tell Mamaw. She'll try to persuade me to stay. No, she's going to come home from work, and I'll be sitting on the porch, scratching Punkin behind the ear, ready to help her finish that puzzle. She'll try to talk me into returning, but my sorrow is enough to grind down both our wills.

Maybe I'll complete the school year at Sawyer High. Maybe not. In fact, maybe I won't go back to school at all. No one who's hired me to mow their lawn has ever asked me if I'm a high school graduate. I could work nights at Little Caesars helping Mamaw. If I work enough, I won't have time or energy to feel anything but exhaustion. And I can drown that in sleep. Do it all over again the next day. Repeat until I die.

We finish dinner and we walk slowly back to Delaney and Vi's residence hall, where they're having a *Stranger Things* watch party.

I lag behind the group a bit.

Vi joins me. "You're brooding, Bucky Barnes."

I smile. "Good job remembering *brooding*."

"I have to use new words as much as I can so I remember them."

"Am I brooding, or are you just using the word to hang on to it?"

"Really brooding."

"I'm just thinking about stuff."

"Your papaw?"

"Among other things." At least my pining for Vi has gradually eased with time and been put in its place by the enormity of my grief. I'm strangely grateful to her for shooting me down and making my decision easier.

I watch Delaney and Alex just ahead of us, chatting merrily about something Delaney just said. Without Papaw around, and in the face of my betrayal of my promise to stay, I'll probably never see Delaney again. But that was going to happen sooner or later. She wasn't also going to get me a scholarship to Yale or

MIT or wherever life takes her. Our paths were going to diverge. Might as well rip off the Band-Aid.

I look at them, and for one brief, wild moment, the clouds part and the sun shines again and I think I could stay after all. I could choose that life. I think maybe my love for my friends and Dr. Adkins is enough, with the help of poetry, to lift me up and carry me to some temperate shore, to quell the insistent, grinding ache and let me continue here.

Then the clouds bury the sun again.

Chapter 70

When I get back to my floor, about a half hour before curfew, there's a raucous gathering of lacrosse players congesting the hall. I won't miss this part of the Middleford experience.

I pass Atul. He sees the look on my face. "They beat Phillips Exeter."

"Oh."

"I guess they're huge rivals?"

"Wow, who gives a shit."

"Right?"

I'll miss Atul. He's a good guy.

I elbow through a clump of lacrosse players and their respective entourages to get to my room. "Excuse me," I say, but they ignore me. I have to muscle past them.

I open my door. Tripp, wearing only a pair of shorts, is in bed, on top of a girl wearing only a bra and her skirt pushed up high, exposing her underwear. I avert my eyes in embarrassment. "Uh, y'all?"

Tripp jumps out of bed and strides over to me. "Get out." He tries to turn me around and shove me back through the door. But I resist. I've had it. I'm not taking orders from him.

I sweep his hands off me. "Naw. Y'all go somewhere else.

This is my room too, and I'm tired." *And also I don't care about keeping the peace anymore.*

"Dude, we're in here. Get the fuck out now."

Then I notice two things.

First, I recognize the girl in Tripp's bed from my marine biology class. We only talked briefly a couple of times about class stuff. Her name's Siobhan Byrne. She's pretty, and her family in Ireland, where she's from, is obviously wealthy.

The second thing I notice is that she appears to be completely unconscious. Her eyes are closed and she's not moving, not acknowledging what's happening a few feet away.

"She okay?"

Tripp moves to block my view. "Why? Wanna watch, cuck?"

I ignore Tripp and again parry his attempt to push me out. "Siobhan? You okay?"

"She's fine. She doesn't want your pervy ass watching us and busting in your pants. *Go.*"

"Siobhan?" Nothing. I meet Tripp's eyes. "This ain't right."

"Leave."

"Oh, I will." I turn. My next stop is Cameron and Raheel's room. I go for the door.

But Tripp catches my tone. He grabs me by the shoulder and turns me back to face him. "Dude, you better not be a little pussy-ass snitch and say I have a girl in here."

"That ain't all that's going on here, and you know it." I turn back and start to open the door.

Tripp kicks it shut. "Five hundred dollars to keep your mouth shut."

"I'm not for sale." I go to open the door again, and Tripp pulls me back.

"A thousand dollars."

"Eat shit."

Tripp grabs me again. I push him away, hard, and he stumbles backward a few steps.

I open the door and make it halfway out before Tripp tackles me from behind and takes me to the ground in a headlock. The crowd in front of my door scatters to let us tumble into the hall.

Tripp is on my back, pressing my forehead into the ground. He smells like a mixture of his deodorant, weed, alcohol, and Siobhan's perfume. I struggle, but my position affords no leverage.

"*Palmer! Vance!*" Tripp yells to his two omnipresent minions as I writhe against his grasp.

I hear two sets of footfalls running up.

"Get her out," Tripp hisses to Palmer and Vance.

From my awkward angle, I see them out of the corner of my eye running into my room. I muscle out of the headlock and make it to my feet. "WorldStar!" someone yells. Tripp tries to take me down again, but I throw a punch that catches him on the cheekbone. It sends him stumbling and breaks his momentum for a second. I hear a rush of disapproval from Tripp's lacrosse teammates circling up to gawk.

Palmer and Vance emerge from my room carrying Siobhan— her shirt thrown on her—between them like they're helping her walk, but her shoeless feet aren't touching the floor. They head toward the stairs.

I go toward them. "Siobhan!" I barely finish shouting her name before Tripp hits me from behind and to the side, knocking the breath out of me. I catch my foot on the carpet and pitch sidelong. My forehead slams into the wall, and a bright flash-bulb goes off in my skull, my mouth filling with a soapy, metallic taste. Red-black spots explode in my field of vision, blooming like blood spatter on a handkerchief. The crowd gasps—*ohhhh shit.* I try to stand but my legs won't work and I fall back down, crawling.

"Cameron!" I shout.

"Hey, man," someone says. "Don't try to get up."

"*Cameron! Raheel!*" My voice is weakening. I taste blood. It's streaming from my nose. I'm dizzy and nauseous.

"Move! Lemme through!" I hear a familiar voice yelling. Cameron elbows through the lacrosse players encircling me. He kneels at my side. I see four of him.

"What happened?" he asks.

Tripp, hand to his now-swelling cheekbone, replies, "I was hanging out with my friends when he comes in and tells us all to leave the room. And when we wouldn't, he attacked me."

Cameron looks at me.

"He had Siobhan Byrne in bed. She was passed out or asleep or something," I say groggily, my tongue thick and heavy. "He was messing with her."

"He's fucking lying," Tripp yells.

"I hit my head really hard," I murmur.

"Dude, your nose is bleeding," Cameron says. "Someone go get Dr. Karpowitz and tell him we need the nurse and someone from admin. Cash probably needs to go to the hospital."

My field of vision is narrowing.

"Hey, keep him awake. That's what you do for head injuries," one of the lacrosse players says.

"Anyone got an ice pack for my eye?" Tripp asks. "Can't believe he just attacked me like that. Dude's psycho."

Cameron shakes me gently. "Hey. Cash. Don't go to sleep, man, okay?"

"Okay," I mutter. Everything is blurry around me, but I see Palmer and Vance have returned. "Where did you take her?" I ask thickly.

"Take who?" Vance says. "You're not making sense."

"You hit your head *hard*," Palmer says.

"These guys are witnesses," Tripp says. "Didn't Cash attack me?"

"Yep," Vance says.

"They carried Siobhan out," I say to Cameron. "She couldn't walk. You gotta have someone check on her."

"Dude, that's fucking fake news," Tripp says. "Siobhan was hanging out earlier, but she left a while ago. I don't know where she went."

"Take it easy, man," Cameron says to me. He helps me sit up against the wall. Someone hands him a wet paper towel to clean the blood from my nose and mouth. My head feels shattered.

"He punched me for no reason," Tripp says to Cameron.

"You can tell your side later," Cameron says.

"My parents are gonna sue his ass," Tripp says. "For assaulting me and trying to destroy my reputation."

"I didn't attack him," I mutter. "He had Siobhan."

"Anyone know Siobhan Byrne? Will someone see if they can track her down?" Cameron calls to the crowd.

Some time passes, but it's a fog. Dr. Karpowitz comes and talks to me.

I hear Tripp say, "Someone should call the cops. He attacked me, and now he's lying and saying I was messing with Siobhan."

I hear a familiar voice respond. "Bro, get out of my way now. Literally no chance that's true."

Tripp mutters something, and the voice responds, *"Now,* dude. *Move.* I'm not playing."

Then Alex is beside me.

"Hey, bro, how you doing?" he asks, kneeling, hovering protectively.

"How'd you know?"

"Word travels fast in a building."

"Cracked my head on the wall. I feel sick." I breathe through another wave of nausea.

"A bad friend would say you're lucky it was your head and not something you use. But I'm not a bad friend."

I laugh weakly.

Paramedics arrive and load me on a stretcher.

"I'm coming with," Alex says.

"You family?" the paramedic asks.

"I'm his twin brother," Alex says.

"Let's go," the paramedic says.

En route to the hospital, I try to tell Alex what happened. I'm not sure how much sense I'm making.

First I had my inaugural plane ride, to see Papaw die. Now I'm on my first ambulance ride, going to the hospital with a cracked skull.

What a year.

More time passes at the hospital. A doctor comes to see me. She thinks I have a concussion. Because I'm showing signs of disorientation and confusion (I keep asking the same questions over and over), she's keeping me for the next twenty-four hours for observation.

I have a CT scan, another inauspicious first. It's to rule out an epidural hematoma, so I can sleep, which I want to do more than anything.

But first, Alex helps me videochat with Mamaw. She's already up—the school called her. She's understandably upset to see her grandson in the hospital, talking nonsense following a head injury, six weeks after losing her husband. Alex texts Delaney, but she must be asleep already because she doesn't answer.

Middleford sends an associate dean of students to be at the hospital with me while I'm being examined. I don't remember her name. She tells me she'll be back in the morning. They bring in a cot for Alex to stay the night.

As I'm plunging into the abyss of dreamless sleep, I murmur to Alex, "Least I tagged him once."

Alex grins. "I noticed. I'd hate to be on the receiving end of that right hook. He's gonna feel that."

"Did I do the right thing?"

Alex reaches over and pats my forearm a couple of times, then gives it a little squeeze. "Hell yes, bro."

Chapter 71

I sense the presence of people. I open my eyes groggily, and Vi, Delaney, and Alex come into focus.

"I think he's awake," Vi says to Delaney and Alex. "Cash?"

"Mm-hmm," I say.

"How are you?"

"Um." I pause, taking inventory. "Awesome."

"Liar," Delaney says, and they laugh.

"Alex told us what you did," Vi says softly. She leans over me, her hair falling into my face, and gives me a long kiss on the cheek. Even though my crush on Vi has receded, it still feels great.

As she steps back to let one of the others have a moment with me, I say, drunkenly, "All y'all, pucker up and get in line."

They laugh again.

Delaney steps forward. I can't quite interpret her expression—proud, loving, scared, all at once. And then there's something I haven't seen on her before. "You look like shit," she says.

"Hallmark, hire this woman," I say.

"You have two big black eyes from the blood draining into the tissue surrounding them."

"Thanks, doc. Now shut up and come here," I say, extending my arms.

Delaney wraps me in a hug so tight it hurts my neck. Then

she pulls back and presses her lips to my forehead. "Pep would be proud of you," she whispers.

I haven't been able to feel much in the way of emotion—being more preoccupied with my physical state—but hearing this makes me glow inside.

"Okay, dude," I say to Alex. "Where's my sugar?"

Without hesitation, he comes over, grabs my face, and gives me a loud kiss on each cheek. We bust up.

They all stand there for a second without speaking, giving me such looks of fondness and love, it's almost unbearable.

This is when I realize I'm not alone.

This is when I realize I don't have to leave them. I don't have to walk away from some of the greatest richness my life has ever held.

I can choose them. I can choose to stay.

Then something else occurs to me. Staying might not be my choice anymore. If the school believes Tripp that I attacked him—and they will—they'll boot me. Middleford has a zero-tolerance policy toward violence. I'll be right back to where I was on Friday night, with my hand resting on the doorknob of my room.

You always want what you can't have, don't you?

It's not actually funny, but I start laughing anyway. At some point, the extent to which I can't catch a fucking break almost becomes comedic.

Delaney, Vi, and Alex eye me with justifiable concern. Seeing your friend who recently suffered an ER-worthy head trauma suddenly start busting a gut out of nowhere must be troubling.

Probably the only thing more unsettling would be if that laughing dissolved into sobbing, which is exactly what happens.

Chapter 72

They stay with me all day. We watch TV and talk. The doctor says I seem to be doing well, so they'll release me at eight that night, a few hours before the twenty-four-hour observation period is up.

At around four, they leave to go get burgers. They promise to bring me one. I wonder if it'll be the last time we eat dinner together.

They've only been gone for a few minutes when a nurse enters. "Cash? You have a visitor."

"Okay." I sit up a little straighter. Part of me hopes it's Dr. Adkins, even though we've already texted and she's in New Hampshire, helping Desiree cater an event.

Dr. Archampong enters. I don't think he and I have ever been in the same room aside from morning assembly. He's taller and more imposing in person.

"Sir." I sit up straighter still.

"Mr. Pruitt," he says, pulling up a chair. "They've treated you well, I hope?"

"Yes, sir. Very well." My breath is tight in my chest.

"How are you feeling? I'm told you suffered a severe concussion."

"Yessir." My heart thrums in my still-aching head. "I'm feeling a little better."

"That's good to hear. I have some news that I needed to deliver personally."

"Okay," I say faintly.

I wanted to leave Middleford, yes. But on my own terms. Not by getting kicked out so Tripp and his shitty goons can laugh about me mowing lawns back home, all while still preying on people.

"As I'm sure you are aware, Middleford Academy has a zero-tolerance policy toward violence," Dr. Archampong says.

"I know, sir." My voice cracks.

"However, there is an exception to that policy for acts of self-defense . . ."

And Tripp was merely defending himself against your attack. Which is why you're being expelled and he isn't. My breath leaves me.

"And defense of another," Dr. Archampong continues. "We have convened an emergency session of the Disciplinary Council, and we have determined your altercation with Patrick McGrath to be both an act of self-defense and an act of defense of a fellow student."

"I'm not sure what—"

"It means that Mr. McGrath has been expelled from Middleford Academy, along with Palmer De Vries and Vance Barr."

I wish I could trust my own ears and mental processing. But in my current state, I can't. "Sir, I'm not getting kicked out?"

Dr. Archampong shakes his head. "No. Witnesses at the scene corroborated your account of the events as you related them. We heard Mr. McGrath's, Mr. De Vries's, and Mr. Barr's versions. However, several members of the lacrosse team came forward to report that they had seen Mr. De Vries and Mr. Barr carrying Ms. Byrne from your and Mr. McGrath's room, which corroborated your statements. We viewed security video from the residence hall's internal and external cameras, and saw Mr. De Vries and Mr. Barr carrying Ms. Byrne outside, where we found her lying on a bench, clothed in a manner not commensurate with the weather conditions, and which suggested she had not arrived there of her own accord. Ms. Byrne, unfortunately, has no recollection of the incident. But when confronted with this proof, Mr. De Vries and Mr. Barr confessed that Mr. McGrath had asked them to remove Ms. Byrne from the room.

"So, no, Mr. Pruitt. You are not being dismissed from Middleford, nor are you subject to any disciplinary action. You showed courage and heroism by intervening on your fellow student's behalf. You are a credit to our school. We are honored to have you among our number."

I'm speechless. "I was just trying to do the right thing," I say finally.

"I don't know if you are aware of this, but before you were admitted to Middleford, Delaney Doyle wrote us a letter on your behalf. She recommended you as someone of bravery and substance, who would fight for people who needed a champion. She said that you had overcome many difficult circumstances and survived them with your integrity intact. So, that you were willing to do the right thing at great personal cost to yourself comes as no surprise. Our school needs people like you, Mr. Pruitt. If we teach our students nothing else, let it be to do what is right, even when it is difficult and dangerous." Dr. Archampong pats my knee paternally and stands. "Now, please excuse me. There are many issues demanding my attention. My assistant will be in contact with you to schedule a meeting on Monday. We have a few matters yet to discuss. For now, though, focus on recuperation." He starts to leave.

"Sir? One quick thing." It's humiliating, but I need to mention it while he's here. My face burns, and I stumble over the words. "I don't know if—the hospital? My family doesn't have a lot of money. And the bill. I'm not sure—My grandfather just died and we had to pay for a lot of stuff and I don't know if—"

He gently raises a hand to cut me off. "Middleford has a fund for such contingencies. We will handle everything. Rest and give it no thought."

He leaves and I sit with the stillness. I think about what it'll take to stay at Middleford. Things won't magically be good. I'll still live with the persistent anguish of grief. I'll still have moments when I feel alone and like I don't belong.

I'll still have holes in my life.

But I'm ready to try to patch the holes in my life with courage.

Chapter 73

I'm lying in bed, watching TV, as early evening comes. But I'm only half watching, thinking about the last time I was in a hospital.

Delaney enters my room with a Wendy's bag in hand. I'd smelled her approaching. The fresh hot-oil fragrance reminds me of going to pick her up from work at Dairy Queen, waiting in one of the booths for her to finish her shift.

"You're back," I say.

She sets the bag in my lap. It's warm and it feels good. She sits on the side of my bed. "Hope you like it. It was the only place in walking distance."

"Whatever you got me is better than hospital food. Thanks."

Delaney and I meet each other's eyes and smile.

"Where's Alex and Vi?" I ask.

Delaney hesitates. "They had to take care of something. It's just me. That cool?"

"Of course. Dr. Archampong was here a little while ago, by the way."

Delaney's mind is obviously where mine was, because she pales. "And?"

"And . . . I get to stay at Middleford. Tripp got the boot, along with Palmer and Vance."

Delaney collapses into herself, visibly trembling. She exhales from the deepest reaches of her lungs. "I worried about you getting expelled. Holy shit, I'm glad that didn't happen."

Maybe I won't tell her how close I came to expelling myself before all this went down.

I open the bag, grab a few french fries, and eat them. "Man. These are as good as your DQ's fries."

"Because I asked them to fry them twice, the way I always used to do for you."

"That's not how DQ fries normally are?"

"Nope. Always did it special for you. You get more of the Maillard reaction, named after Louis-Camille Maillard. That's a chemical reaction between glucose and amino acids that happens with heat and causes browning. I knew you liked the Maillard reaction in fries."

"Huge fan," I murmur. "Guess I have a favorite scientist now too."

"Thought I was your favorite scientist."

"Okay, it goes you and then Maillard." I offer Delaney some of my fries.

"I'm good." She smiles, but a melancholy cloud hangs over her.

We're quiet for a while. Finally, I say, "You all right?"

She takes a deep breath and starts to nod but catches herself. She turns her face to the window for several beats. Then she turns back to me. "Yeah, I'm fine. I was—" She stops. There's a catch in her voice. She tries to talk again but dissolves and starts weeping into her hands.

"Hey. Hey, Red. Hey." I pull her to my chest and hold her and whisper into her hair.

She cries for a while and then draws a shuddering breath and wipes her eyes with her ring fingers. "Wow. Very cool."

"What's up?"

"I wasn't ready to see you in a hospital bed, looking all banged up. And to see it after everything with Pep. It made me realize . . ." She pauses. I've seen what it looks like when Delaney is armoring herself, and she does it now.

She draws a deep breath and her words rush out. "I need to tell you something because you never know if it's going to be too late. Like what if you'd had an intracranial hemorrhage and died? I'd have had to just carry this around. So this sucks to have to say, especially right now. And I don't expect or, like, *want* anything from you. But I need you to know that I've been in love with you for basically as long as I've known you. I thought it would pass. But it didn't. It hasn't."

"Red—"

"Don't interrupt. I have to say this. It's why I had to get you to Middleford with me. I couldn't be without you. And I don't want a thing like with Pep, where I didn't know if he heard me tell him I love him. I love you more than I've loved any other person in my whole life. Lots of days it was the only thing that got me out of bed, the only thing I had to hang on to. That time we kissed and we sorta decided we probably shouldn't anymore? I know I went along with it, but I didn't really want to. I loved you. I *love* you. And I wish more than anything that I could only love you in the way I'm allowed to. But—"

"Wait, I thought *you*—"

Delaney puts her hand over my mouth, the raggedness of her thumb scratchy on my lip. "I'm talking. *Shhh.* This is hard enough. I think about you *constantly.* And it *really* fuckin' sucks because then I have to watch you fall in love with Vi and pretend I'm okay, so I—"

Because I have nothing to say, because she wouldn't let me even if I did, I pull her to me and kiss her—it's long, deep, hungry, delirious, and somehow both heavy and light with every hour we've spent together looking at stars or the lights of our town, every moment we've spent drifting quietly downriver together, every time we've gone to sleep knowing the other was there somewhere for us. This is so much more than the first time we kissed. We are so much more.

There are secret fires you wall off because you fear what they'll burn if you loose them. Because you choose caution over possibility. But at the first crack in the wall, you feel their warmth and decide you'll gladly risk the burning.

After we've made up for years of not kissing—at one point I think I heard a nurse come in and back slowly out—we hold each other quietly as dusk falls softly outside. The hum of the hospital around us is lost in the sound of our breathing.

We explore our new lands. I trace my thumb along her eyebrow and to the hollow behind her ear.

She strokes my lips gently with her fingertips. "Always wanted to do that," she murmurs.

"We'd already kissed even before today." I push a lock of hair back from her eyes.

"You can't do *that* just because you've kissed someone," she says, and we laugh. "So, telling you all that turned out better than I thought it would."

"Looks like we're both having more fun than the last time we were in a hospital together."

"True."

"Good thing Vi and Alex didn't come back with you."

"I kinda didn't give them a choice," Delaney says. We laugh again. "I almost told you over Christmas, when we were on the river, but I chickened out."

Several moments pass without our speaking. She rests her head on my chest. She can probably hear my heart pounding as I summon my bravery one more time. With two fingers under her chin, I gently lift her face back up to mine, to meet my bruised eyes. "I love you, Delaney Doyle."

She pauses, but only like she wants to inhabit the moment longer. "I love you too, Cash Pruitt. But I'm not telling you anything you don't know."

Skin

I wish it weren't true
that all our skin cells
regenerate every few weeks,
like you once told me they did.

I don't want a new skin.
I want a skin with a memory
longer than the dust's,
which you said also forgets,
only it takes longer.

I want to live in a skin that remembers
you, a skin you've marked.

Chapter 74

I take it easy on Sunday, mostly enjoying the solitude of my newly Tripp-free room while Delaney studies and works in the lab. When I'm awake, I spend most of my time writing something I've needed to write for a long time. Call it an exorcism.

Delaney comes to fetch me for lunch and again for dinner. We walk, holding hands, to the dining hall.

"This isn't gonna help the perception that we're married," I say, holding our joined hands up.

"Nope," Delaney says.

"Tell you the truth, I don't give much of a shit," I say. "Never did."

Delaney giggles. "Same."

But it seems that the buzz isn't about Delaney's and my maybe being married anymore. At both lunch and dinner, a few people I've never met before come up to shake my hand and high-five me. Middleford is a small world, and word travels fast.

At one point during dinner, Alex and Delaney get up to drop off their trays, leaving Vi and me sitting together alone.

"I *knew* it," Vi says with a sly grin, and we both know what she's referring to.

"You were right. I didn't even know it at the time."

"It was very obvious. Women know these things."

"Looks like."

"I could also see how she felt about you. I'm happy for you two."

"Thanks, Vi."

"Delaney's a lucky girl."

I smile and blush. I don't know how to respond, but it's okay, because before I have to, someone else comes up to give me a high five.

On Monday morning, I meet with Dr. Archampong. The school's lawyer is there, as are detectives from the New Canaan Police Department. They take my statement as part of a criminal investigation into Tripp's actions.

We wrap up, and I'm about to leave for poetry class when Dr. Archampong says, "Mr. Pruitt, there is one more thing. Your housing situation. You have two options. First, you may finish out the year with your room to yourself. We ordinarily encourage sharing of rooms, to teach students compromise and conflict resolution and to forge lifelong friendships. But you have certainly earned the right to a solo room."

That sounds pretty great. "What's the other option?"

"One of your fellow students, who currently resides in a single room, has come forward and asked to be placed as your roommate if you so choose. I believe you know him. Alex Pak. An exceptional young man, from what I gather."

An ecstatic bloom spreads through me. "Yeah, I know Alex. He *is* pretty exceptional. Let's go with that."

Chapter 75

Poetry class has been going for about fifteen minutes when I slip in as quietly as I can. I'm already self-conscious enough, with my two wine-purple raccoon eyes.

Dr. Adkins reads a stanza from a poem, her back to the door. She stops to look behind her. When she sees it's me, she puts the book down, stands, turns to face me, and begins applauding. Everyone in the class rises to join her.

I blush and look at the ground. I want to say something snappy, like *You should see the other guy,* but I'm afraid if I try to talk I'll lose my shit. I smile awkwardly, wave, and take my seat. But the class remains on their feet and clapping.

As the applause finally subsides, I venture one sentence: "Man, I should be late more often." Everyone laughs.

Dr. Adkins waits to talk to me until everyone's gone.

"How's the head?" she asks.

"Still pretty sore. You should see the other guy."

"You've been saving that one."

"Yep."

We both smile.

"I'm so proud of you," she says.

"I just did the right thing."

"This world needs more men who do the right thing."

"Speaking of doing what I'm supposed to, I even managed to finish the assignment." I hand her the poem I spent Sunday writing and revising.

"You were totally off the hook. I thought I made that clear."

"It's okay. It felt . . . necessary. You'll see why when you read it." I start to walk out.

"Cash?" she calls after me.

I turn.

"Being a poet takes bravery. Yes, the courage to bleed on a page. But also to bleed for the world we write poetry about. You have it and I've always seen it."

Weight

I have this dream.
I'm trying to push open
a door closed
by the weight
of my mama's body.

Some dreams are fiction
but not this one.
When I was young,
my mama took
too much of what she used
to numb herself
and died in our single-wide's bathroom
with a television
playing sitcom reruns as her last sunset.

Why is feeling so terrifying
that we try to stop it?
Feeling is a thing that's ours only,
a thing we don't borrow.

In my dream, I yearn
for something to lift
that weight from the door,

To make it as incorporeal
as smoke or light,

so I'm not pushing against the gravity
of my own blood.

In its last hour, the body I left
became the body that would
no longer let me in.

Chapter 76

After crew practice, Alex and I are exhausted, but we move his things up to my room. Neither of us cares to wait.

We study side by side that night. Sometimes one of us will break the silence with a quip or an observation. Alex ribs me about getting together with Delaney. I tease him about his agonizing over an ambiguous text from Alara.

It reminds me of sitting on the porch with Papaw, or videochatting with him. It's not the same. But it's conversation and comfortable silence with someone I love.

As it comes time for lights-out, Alex kneels on his bed to begin his private benedictions.

Before he starts, I say, "Hey, man. Real quick."

He looks over.

"Thanks for praying for me. I think it helped."

Chapter 77

"Look. They have *National Geographic.* You love *National Geographic.* You used to read it all the time at our old school," I say, pointing at the waiting room table.

"Too nervous," Delaney says, bouncing her leg. "Don't feel like reading."

"Dr. Hannan's a therapist. Her job is literally to help you be less anxious," I say.

"I'm worried about what she's gonna find in my head."

"What, like going fishing and you pull up an old boot?"

"Exactly that."

"I don't think that's how therapists work."

"It's not. I studied up. Still. Aren't you nervous?"

"I'm mainly worried she won't find anything at all in my head."

"Valid fear."

"Well, come on. Don't agree with me."

Delaney sighs. "I guess we're both people who get help when we need it. It's how we met." She starts to put her thumb to her mouth.

I catch her hand and lower it back to her thigh. "And I have an idea for how you should start when it's your turn with the therapist."

She sits on her hand. "One of the girls I used to work with texted me and said the Phantom Shitter struck the DQ again today."

"That's . . . amazing?"

"Yeah, I don't know what it is. It's something."

"It's weirdly comforting to know that the world continues on in your absence." I reach over and pluck an eyelash from Delaney's cheek.

"Guess who I talked to the other day."

"Who?"

"Dr. Goins."

I shake my head. "Dr. Goins . . . as in the lady-who-you-insulted-repeatedly-and-so-she-kicked-you-out-of-the-hospital Dr. Goins?"

"Wasn't her. Deputy Dogshit did it on his own. He got fired, by the way. She complained to management about how he treated me."

"How—"

"I called to apologize. I kept feeling bad for how I treated her."

"And?"

"It was cool. We had a nice conversation." She starts fiddling with the ends of her hair, tufting them against her thumb. "You know there used to be parrots in East Tennessee?" she asks, staring off.

"Like in dinosaur times?"

"No. In like the 1800s. The Carolina parakeet. Last seen in the wild in 1910. The final one in captivity died in 1918. It was declared extinct in 1939." She pulls up an Audubon drawing of a green parrot with a yellow neck and red head on her phone.

"Seriously?" I murmur in awe. "You used to be able to look out your window in Sawyer, Tennessee, and see parrots?"

"Yep," Delaney says. "Aren't they pretty? *Weren't* they, I mean."

"Yeah. They were."

We're quiet for a long time.

"I'd love if they were still around," I say after a while. I think about how much I wish the trajectory of the world was toward flowering instead of ruin.

But then, as Delaney starts to raise her thumb to her mouth again, I catch her hand, and this time I clutch it tight, interweaving my fingers with hers.

I guess sometimes the world moves from desolation toward blossom after all.

Chapter 78

There are still many long and loss-haunted days. Times I feel like giving up. Moments when grief strikes suddenly, like a rattlesnake hidden in tall grass.

I see his face every day. His absence is so tangible it has its own body.

But the world is filled with new green, and it reminds me that there are beautiful things that continue on.

Delaney and I keep our back-to-back appointments visiting Dr. Hannan. Delaney's thumbs start to heal, and so do I.

I keep writing through the tempests of pain. That helps a lot too.

Chapter 79

And another thing that helps: being on the water. Right now, though, I'm not doing much processing.

My pulse throbs where my spine meets my skull.

My heart verges on exploding.

I can't get enough air.

Every meter is in the red, every Klaxon sounding.

Catch drive release recover catch drive release recover catch drive release recover. The swish of water. The buoys marking the lanes rushing by. The synchronized clatter of the oarlocks as we feather our oars, eight blades slicing through the air as one. My hands strong on the oar. Catch. Drive. Recover. Catch. Drive.

From what seems like a great distance, the coxswain shouts, "Nice and controlled, very nice. There we go, there we go! Drive! Push! Push! Keep it tight! Port side, high finish! High finish! Starboard side, gimme a little more. We're walking up on La Salle. We've been chasing them all season. Looking good, boys! We got it! We got it!"

I hear Alex, directly behind me, huffing like a train engine.

"Pull! Pull! Keep them off us! Keep them off us! I need a power ten in two. One! Two! Hit the gas! Go! Whoo yeah! Whoo yeah! That's it, gentlemen, nice! Straight ahead, all together. Two boats off our bow, this is it! We're walking on stroke! Seven! Six! Do this shit, Middleford! Keep driving! Home stretch!"

My lungs are searing, my muscles ardent and shrieking. But I don't slow. I'm ready to die for this. For my heart to pump my steaming blood right through my pores. For my team. I won't let them down.

We smash through the finish line and we glide to a stop, collapsing, too tired to even hold water. Our coxswain tells us we got first place. We're going to Philadelphia. We're going to the Stotesbury Cup.

Delaney and Vi are waiting for Alex and me. My whole body quivers; I held nothing in reserve.

Delaney sprints toward me.

"I'm sweaty," I warn her. She jumps on me, undeterred, hugging me with her legs wrapped around my waist like a koala. She's tiny but I still can't support both our weights for how exhausted I am, and we collapse to the ground, laughing.

You pass through enough defeat, it feels like you'll never taste victory's sweetness. But then somehow you do, and for at least that moment, you can't even remember a time when it wasn't on your lips.

Chapter 80

My phone buzzes. I check it. "Hoooooly shit, Delaney," I murmur.

Alex doesn't look up from his physics textbook. "What?"

"She got a perfect score on the SAT."

Alex sets his book down on his pillow to mark his place. "Bro, get out." He comes over and I show him Delaney's text. "Is she joking?"

"She wouldn't joke about this." I jump up and put on my shoes. "Come on." I run out of our room, with Alex at my heels. We don't stop running until we reach Delaney's door. I pound on it.

Vi answers, her hair in a messy bun, wearing pajama pants and a tank top. She smiles widely when she sees me and Alex. She steps aside. "Delaney?"

Delaney reclines on her bed in the shorts and tank top she sleeps in. She looks up from her phone and our eyes meet. She looks happy, as well she should.

"Come here," I say.

"I'm busy," she says with a sly grin.

"You know why we're here."

"You gonna embarrass me?"

"Bet your ass."

She sighs theatrically, gets up, and walks to the door. Alex and I kneel, and she obligingly stands between us. We'd all heard about this Middleford tradition.

"Count of three," I say to Alex. "One, two, three."

We hoist Delaney on our shoulders. She squeals, giggles, and teeters.

Alex steadies her. "We won't let you fall." He pats her thigh. "Can't have that genius brain splattering on the ground."

I look to Alex. "Ready?"

"Let's do this, bro."

We run together up the hall, whooping and hollering, with Delaney held aloft on our shoulders, screaming and laughing. Vi runs behind us, clapping and whistling. Girls open their doors to gawk, and they applaud and high-five Delaney. We get to the end of the hall and run back. Then we repeat. Until the proctors make us stop.

When we drop off Delaney at her door, her cheeks are rosy with laughter.

"I love you," I whisper in her ear. "I'm so proud of you."

Chapter 81

"Bro, cut."

"What?"

"I screwed up."

"Dude, you were doing great. We'll never finish if you keep cutting."

"Once more."

"Think of the *Midnite Matinee* ladies. They're on TV every week, and they're fine with screwing up."

"We're aiming higher than *Midnite Matinee* quality here. Where's your Laundry Boy honor?"

"Laundry Boy honor? That's a thing now?"

"Absolutely. Let's go. In five, four, three, two, one . . . Hey, everyone, welcome to *Blaundry Boys*. Okay, cut."

"Dude."

"I said *Blaundry Boys*. We at *least* have to get the name right."

"*Gotta* get the shitty name right."

"Why would you say that? The name is good, man. It's good. Rolling in five, four, three, two, one . . . Hey, everyone, and welcome to *Laundry Boys*. My name's Alex, and this is . . ."

"Cash."

"And we're here to give you some tips . . ."

"And tricks . . ."

"To up your laundry game."

"The first thing you need to know about doing laundry is—"

"Uh, bro."

"What? That was our best take yet."

"Yeah, so I accidentally didn't hit the record button."

Laundry Boys

You helped me believe
that there is no such thing
as a permanent stain;

No such thing
as a wrinkle
that cannot be made smooth;

Nothing that cannot be made
new again.

Chapter 82

On the second-to-last Saturday before school lets out, Vi and I go to the beach. Alex and Delaney are busy with other stuff.

Vi wants to keep her promise to show me the ocean for the first time. The one she made the night we met. As the van nears, she blindfolds me with one of her scarves.

"No looking," she says.

I feel the van stop.

"Have fun," Chris says from the driver's seat. "I'll be back at five to pick up."

I hear everyone getting out excitedly, their animated voices fading.

"Careful," Vi says, holding my elbow and assisting me out.

"You're in for a treat, Paul Bunyan," Chris says. "The ocean is something you gotta see before you die."

Vi leads me a short ways and we stop. She says, "Listen."

In the faint distance, I hear the motion of the water.

My heartbeat quickens. We walk a bit farther.

I feel the hard pavement turn to soft sand. I take off my flip-flops and carry them in my free hand. "Can I look?"

"Not yet," Vi says. "Soon."

I tread unsteadily through the sand. The sound of waves

breaking on the beach grows louder. I smell salt, seaweed, and churning water.

"Okay . . . now," Vi says, and takes off my blindfold.

I'm looking at the ocean, for the first time. It sprawls in an infinite expanse before us, gray green at the horizon. Dazzling sunlight dapples the surface of the waves as they slowly roll in, one by one, like breaths of an immense sleeping creature.

"Wow," I murmur, enraptured. *"Wow."*

Vi beams. "You like?"

I can hardly breathe for the wonder. "I love. I love."

Seagulls screech around us.

"It never stops," I say.

"Never."

"Billions of years. Waves on the shore. Tides coming in and out. Delaney says all life came from the ocean."

"It definitely makes me feel alive to be near it."

We edge closer, and the cool water rushes up and around my feet, dissolving the sand away beneath them, effervescing into white foam before receding.

"You need to write a poem about the ocean," Vi says. "And let me read it."

I look at her and smile. "Maybe."

"Maybe," she scoffs. "Always maybe."

Like the waves lapping at my ankles, a swell of grief suddenly rises and breaks over me. "I feel saudade for my papaw right now," I say. "Did I say that right?"

"Perfect."

"I wish he could see me here."

"Maybe he can."

I think about how we laid Papaw to rest in a river, and all

rivers eventually funnel to the sea, and all the seas are connected, so maybe he is here with me.

We spread out our towels and sit next to each other on the sand, basking in the warm May sunshine, talking, and listening to the surf. Our silences are easy and so is our laughter. We've arrived at a good place in our friendship.

Then I tell her about my mama. About my broken life. Because this sacred and memoryless place seems a worthy location for unburdening.

She listens without judgment. When I'm finished, she's not angry with me for letting her believe for so long that I came from more than I did. She hugs me hard and deep—the kind of hug when you're trying to get past muscle and bone to hug someone's soul.

I'm glad she's part of my life.

Chapter 83

Dr. Adkins and I stand facing each other after our final class.

"It's been quite a year," she says. "Did you think when you started Intro to Poetry that on the last day of Intermediate Poetry class, you'd be reading a poem you wrote?"

"Never." I try to come up with the perfect words, but as they have so often, they elude me. "Poetry's made my life better. Thank you."

"It'll do that. And you're so very welcome."

"I can't wait to take your classes next year."

Dr. Adkins's face clouds and she looks down.

"You okay?" I ask. Something seems off with her.

The air slows. "Cash? Would you—" She motions for me to sit.

I sit.

She draws a deep breath, exhales with a sigh, and fidgets with one of her rings, crossing and recrossing her legs. "I have bad news and maybe good news, and I've been trying to think of the best way to tell you, but I'm running out of time, so I'll just say it. I won't be here next year. I've accepted another position."

I feel how a shot bird must as it beats its wings for the last times and plummets to earth. I knew my life's upward trajectory couldn't last unbroken.

"Oh," I say quietly, staring at the floor. "Man."

"But," she says, making sure she has my eyes before continuing, "the good news is, the University of Tennessee just got a funding line for a poetry MFA program, and one of my old poetry professors is heading it up. She's asked me to join the faculty."

Realization dawns. "So you'll be in—"

"Knoxville."

"That's forty-five minutes from where I live." A surge of elation passes through me.

"I know." She smiles.

"So I'll still get to see you."

"You and your mamaw are invited to Thanksgiving at our house. You going back home this summer?"

"Someone has to mow Sawyer's lawns."

"Once a month, this summer, we're meeting for coffee, and I plan on reading new work. You're not off the hook just because I don't control your grade anymore."

"Deal." We look at each other and laugh spontaneously for a few moments. "I'll follow you wherever you go," I say softly after our laughter subsides. "I was planning on ETSU, but UT works just as well. I'm going to keep studying with you."

"I hope you do."

We stand.

I still don't know what else to say. "Anyway. I'll miss you next year. Like, a lot."

Her gray eyes—now I know them to be the color of the

ocean on the cusp of summer—see me. "I'll tell you the truest thing I know: You are not a creature of grief. You are not a congregation of wounds. You are not the sum of your losses. Your skin is not your scars. Your life is yours, and it can be new and wondrous. Remember that."

"Always."

"Goodbye for now, Cash."

"Goodbye for now, Dr. Adkins."

"My friends call me Bree."

"Bree?"

She looks at me.

"You said something at Thanksgiving I keep thinking about: that you didn't inherit your mamaw's gift for healing. But you did," I say.

Her eyes well with tears. "Thank you. That means everything."

"I have something for you." I pull a piece of paper from my bag, unfold it, make a quick correction, and hand it to her. Then something else occurs to me. "Also, I need to ask a huge favor. Actually, it's for Delaney and me both."

Genesis ~~(for Dr. Adkins)~~ (for Bree)

In the beginning I thought
my favorite poetry
was the story of God moving
across the void and formless world,
calling breath from stone.

But now I know it was not
the story that was the poetry,
but the calling forth
of breath from stone.

Chapter 84

New York City is much warmer than the last time I was here—both emotionally and temperature-wise. The mild spring night breeze smells like new asphalt, gasoline, and the herbal tang of the greenery surrounding us on the High Line. The sky swirls with stars and the moon. Delaney and I stroll slowly, hand in hand, our legs exhausted from all our walking.

I point up at the moon and the brightest star beneath it. "That's actually Venus."

"I'm literally the one who told you that."

"Um, I'm pretty sure you just learned that right now from me."

"I—" Delaney starts to respond, but I cut her off with a kiss.

"Sorry, what?" I say, cupping my hand to my ear.

She starts to talk again, but I stop her with another kiss. "No response? Guess it's true you learned it from me."

Delaney just smiles. She takes a deep breath as if to say something. And then she says, "Blah blah blah," and I take my cue and kiss her again.

"What time were we meeting back up with Bree and Desiree?" Delaney asks when I finally let her finish a sentence.

"Eight-thirty. But they said if we were a couple minutes late it was okay."

"Confession time."

"Okay."

"I don't get modern art at all."

"Me neither." We both laugh.

"Good thing we spent two hours at a modern art museum today," Delaney says.

"It was your idea," I say.

"Wasn't blaming you. Hang on—I wanna sit for a sec. My legs ache."

We sit on a bench. I do a quick memory check to make sure it's not the exact bench that Vi and I sat on. Bad luck.

Delaney pulls her feet up on the bench and rests her head on my shoulder. We gaze at the city as it hums and pulses, alive with lights. I like it so much better this time around.

"Reminds me of our overlook," Delaney murmurs, nestling into my side.

I'd let myself forget that Delaney and I are about to be apart for longer than we ever have before. I put my arm around her and rest my cheek on top of her head. "Gonna miss you this summer, Red. Real bad," I say softly.

"Confession time again," Delaney murmurs.

"Don't say you won't miss me back."

"Nope. I have to admit to keeping a secret."

"Okay," I say hesitantly, my pulse accelerating and a sick feeling spreading from my stomach. After my last experience on the High Line, I'm very apprehensive about where this is headed.

"You'll only be missing me for part of the summer."

"What's that mean?"

"Means you'll miss me for part. The other part I'll be around."

I take my arm from around her shoulder and face her. "Hang

on, hang on. *What?*" My heartbeat is still picking up speed, but for a different reason now.

"I'm doing the CDC internship first half of summer. Second half I'm working at Sawyer Hospital. I'll technically be a nurse's assistant, but I'll be shadowing Dr. Goins and helping out in the lab."

"Wait . . . what?"

"Remember when I told you how I called and apologized for being rude? We got to talking for a while. We have a lot in common. We've stayed in touch. She said she could get me a job."

I jump up, whooping and laughing, and grab Delaney in a huge hug, lifting her off the bench and spinning her around, giving no heed to passersby. "Looks like I'm sleeping outside in a tent. No way is Mamaw letting us sleep in the same house with our current . . . situation."

"Naw. Dr. Goins has a guest room. I'm staying there for free. Keep your bed."

Delaney sits back on the bench, and I do the same.

"I don't get why you're bailing on half of your CDC internship. Isn't that, like, the best thing you can do as a future epidemiologist?"

Delaney stares for a long time at the twinkling skyline with distant eyes. "Don't know if I want to be an epidemiologist anymore."

"For real?"

"Thinking about going into addiction medicine. Maybe find the switch that tells us to destroy ourselves and switch it off. My mama. Your mama. Even Pep, in a way." She doesn't need to finish the thought.

We're quiet for a few seconds, and she smiles to herself. "This'll make you laugh."

"Tell me."

"After everything—after college, med school—I think I might head back to Sawyer."

But I don't laugh.

She continues. "Seeing Pep in that sad hospital. People like him deserve better." She gestures toward the skyline. "Plus, all this is great, but I think best where it's quiet. I get overloaded here."

"Know what?" I murmur. "I think I'm going back to Sawyer after college too. I want to teach poetry like Bree."

"Where?"

"Sawyer High."

"Sawyer High doesn't have poetry classes."

"Exactly."

"You telling me twenty years from now, we might be sitting on the tailgate of your pickup, overlooking Sawyer, and talking about your students and my patients?" Delaney asks.

"I think that's exactly what I'm telling you."

We look at each other and start laughing. When our laughter subsides, we kiss and kiss again.

Delaney says, "Remember how I told you about the time Pep and I went to McDonald's together? I told him then that I loved you."

"Yeah?"

"He told me to be patient. He said you loved me too and you just needed to figure it out. He said that again in the letter he wrote me before he died."

"He was right."

A veil of silver moonlight covers Delaney's face in the gentle breath of the late spring night. I remember first seeing her across the room at that Narateen meeting. Now we're gazing at the lights of New York City together.

I wonder where I'd be at this moment, the smaller life I would have led if we'd never spoken.

You can feel when your mind's building a palace for a memory. A place it lives, glowing and dancing in marble halls. A place you can visit when you need to feel less of the world's gravity.

I feel my mind building such a palace for Delaney and me.

Sometimes I imagine the two of us at an all-night diner, drawing faces on pancakes with ketchup, drunk on each other, and laughing like nothing beautiful ever dies.

I'll always love her.

Every wound, every hurt that brought us together—I regret none of it.

The Poem I Promised You

You should write a poem
about how awesome I am,
you said once.

I promised I would. So here it is.
The poem about how
awesome you are.

How every mile between us feels
like a parched desert.
How my lips remember you
like water holds the sun's heat.

How my heartbeat measures out
the seconds until we're together again.

How I lie in my bed,
seeking the memory of you
on the mattress.

How I love you.
How I love you.
How I love you.

Speak mysteries to me.

Tell me the names of winds.
How birds navigate.

Why storms move
from west to east.

Tell me that the death of stars
is not the death of light.

Tell me the wonders of this world and others.

When it's my turn,
I'll say your name back to you.

SUMMER

Epilogue

It's only been a few weeks since Vi, Delaney, Alex, and I went our separate ways for the summer, but I miss them. I've been texting Delaney off and on all day. I'll videochat with her later, after Mamaw goes to sleep. I've been texting Alex and Vi too. I'm meeting Bree for coffee in Knoxville next week and helping her and Desiree move into their new house.

I'm working a lot to save for next year at Middleford. I've been mowing lawns a few days a week. The rest of my time I spend working as a seasonal ranger at Panther Creek State Park. I guide hikes and canoe tours. They even let me lead a special program I invented called Read S'more Poetry, which started with a moonlit night hike and ended with a bonfire, s'mores, and everyone reading a favorite poem they brought.

I got home from the park a while ago. I step out on the porch, my hair still damp from the shower. Without Papaw to take me to get haircuts, I've let it grow shaggier than usual. Insects buzz in the sultry June dusk. Fireflies have begun their torchlit conversation. The air is rich with clover and honeysuckle, the smell of earth and grass remembering the sun's heat, the smoke of a cookout.

Mamaw sits in one of the rockers, knitting. She smiles. "Pull up a chair."

I sit beside her. Punkin lazes between us. "What you working on?"

"A baby cap."

"For who?"

"Mitzi's started volunteering at a home for mothers in substance abuse recovery called Gilead House. It's for the babies there."

"*Gilead?*"

"I imagine it's named after balm of Gilead. It's a salve for healing cuts and bruises and aches, made out of poplar buds. My mama and mamaw used to make it. You remember the old hymn? 'There Is a Balm in Gilead'?"

"No."

Mamaw sets her knitting in her lap. Her eyes become dreamy and distant. "Oh, let me see if I can recall it. It's been a while." She thinks for a moment and begins singing. *"There is a balm in Gilead . . . To make the wounded whole . . ."*

"Been a long time since I heard you sing," I say when she finishes.

"That was Pep's favorite hymn," Mamaw says. "He used to say he wanted me to sing it at his funeral before he changed his mind about wanting one."

"He told me how much he loved your singing voice."

"Maybe we can set your poems to music and I'll sing them. Get ourselves hired at Dollywood."

We laugh.

"Did your mama teach you how to make balm of Gilead?" I ask.

Mamaw picks up her knitting again. "She did."

"Can we make it together sometime? Sounds like it'd be good

for muscle aches after crew practices. Also want to take some to Bree. I think she'd appreciate it."

Mamaw smiles at me. "Now, I've slept since I learnt how, so I'd have to think on it, but I'll do my best."

"When it gets dark, you wanna go in and work on that new puzzle I got you?"

"Sure. I have to make a cake for Betsy's birthday first."

"I'll help you."

We quietly listen to the day depart, the creak of our chairs, the clack of Mamaw's knitting needles, and the soft chirring of insects singing down the sun.

The rocker on the other side of me—Papaw's favorite—sits still and silent. A vast and lonesome emptiness. One that will ache as long as I can feel.

But I'm healing.

I once thought of memory as a tether. I still do, in a way. But now I also see memory as the roots from which you grow toward the sun.

The dreams of closed doors still come, but less now.

I sit with my notebook and pen in the wild light of the day's end.

In the place where I learned the names of trees and wind, I write.

In the Wild Light
(Elegy for Phillip Earl Pruitt)

You were there when
my life felt like I was trying to stop
a falling axe with my hands,
every time I dreamed
of rows of doors
like teeth in a death-clenched jaw

You spoke "tree" and "wind"
to me for the first time,
as if whispering God's secret
name in my ear

This world is knives and wolves
but also swans and stars;
you taught me that

Once, in August,
before you had to beg
the air for breath,
I watched a hawk descend
on a field and fly back
into the yawning
blue with talons empty

I marveled at a creature
that could fall
without being fallen

and still rise
clutching such emptiness and hunger

To learn of loss is only to know it
a little and not to become armored
against its fearsome edge

The sun is setting now
as I write this in the first season
of your absence

And I see you
in the wild light;
I hear you whisper
"tree" and "wind" to me
in the wild light

Acknowledgments

Every set of acknowledgments has to begin with my amazing agents, Charlie Olsen, Lyndsey Blessing, and Philippa Milnes-Smith, and my brilliant editorial team of Emily Easton, Lynne Missen, and Claire Nist. Of course, *they* couldn't work their magic without the hard work and dedication of Phoebe Yeh and everyone at Crown Books for Young Readers, Barbara Marcus, Judith Haut, John Adamo, Dominique Cimina, Mary McCue, Melinda Ackell, Natalia Dextre, Ana Deboo, Ray Shappell, Alison Impey, Kelly McGauley, Adrienne Waintraub, Kristin Schulz, Emily DuVal, Erica Stone, Caitlin Whalen, Kate Keating, Elizabeth Ward, Jena DeBois, and Jenn Inzetta.

Kerry Kletter: I've never met a person with keener perceptions into humanity. Your writing reminds me of the possibilities of precise, beautiful language and clear insight. I don't know how I ever wrote without your friendship, brilliance, wisdom, and critical eye. Yes, I cut and pasted that last part from my last two sets of acknowledgments, but what's true is true. Here's to huge pretzels, laughter-until-crying, and solving stupid mysteries.

Brittany Cavallaro: Thank you for your patience with my amateurish poetry. It's easy to see why you're such a beloved teacher in addition to being a beloved and brilliant author and poet.

Emily Henry: Thank you for your nonstop hilarity and

inspiring me with your unbounded creative energy. It is such a pleasure seeing the world discover what I know.

David Arnold: There's no one with whom I'd rather watch Wes Anderson movies in front of a roaring fire. I'm waiting to find out when we were separated at birth.

Rich Pak: I hope readers can figure out which character is based on you. Some people are so cool, a version of them needs to be in a book.

Dr. Jeremy Voros: A lifesaver and a hero in every sense of the word, including in helping me with the medicine in this book. Anything that's unrealistic and dumb is my fault, not yours.

My early readers: Brendan Kiely, Adriana Mather, and Janet McNally. Y'all are amazing.

Grace Gordon: The world's best Connecticut consultant.

Vi Maurey: O melhor consultante do Rio de Janeiro no mundo.

Cam Napier: I couldn't have written this book without your invaluable private school knowledge.

Sean Davies: For your invaluable scientific knowledge.

Leslie Cartier: For your invaluable crew knowledge.

My bosses, Michael Driver, Jenny Howard, and Emily Urban. I get asked all the time how I manage to write with a full-time job. You are how. Thank you.

Ocean Vuong: For showing me the possibility of language.

Jason Reynolds: For your work giving youth a lifeline in books.

Sabaa Tahir: For the music you bring the world in your words, and the literal music you bring me.

Silas House: One of my greatest triumphs as a writer is that it has allowed me to know my idols.

The readers, librarians, educators, booksellers, podcasters, book clubbers, Instagrammers, and bloggers (and every other category of book people) who have been such advocates for my books: I see you and the work you do, and I am so deeply appreciative. You make our country a better place when there are so many forces trying to do the opposite.

Mom and Dad, Brooke, Adam, and Steve: I love you all.

Grandma Z, I miss you. You are part of this book.

The love of my life, my best friend, and my first reader, Sara. There's no one I'd rather be quarantined with. There's no one I'd rather spend my life with. I could not have written this or any other book without your love and support and the happiness you give me.

My precious boy, Tennessee. Being your father is the greatest honor I'll ever know. Thank you for being my son. I love you more than words can say.

ABOUT THE AUTHOR

Jeff Zentner is the author of the *New York Times* Notable Book *The Serpent King, Goodbye Days,* and *Rayne & Delilah's Midnite Matinee.* He has won the William C. Morris Award, the Amelia Elizabeth Walden Award, the International Literacy Association Young Adults' Book Award, and the Westchester Fiction Award. He's a two-time Southern Book Prize finalist, has been long-listed for the Carnegie Medal, and was a finalist for the Indies Choice Award. He was also selected as a *Publishers Weekly* Flying Start and an Indies Introduce pick. His books have been translated into fifteen languages. Before becoming a writer, he was a musician who recorded with Iggy Pop, Nick Cave, and Debbie Harry. He lives in Nashville with his wife and son. You can follow him on Facebook, Twitter, and Instagram, or visit him at jeffzentnerbooks.com.